Native Soil/Native Soul

An Odd Assortment of Short, and Not So Short, Stories

Gary Robinson

ISBN 978-1-7352003-4-7
© 2020 Gary Robinson
Tribal Eye Productions
P.O. Box 1123
Santa Ynez, CA 93460
www.tribaleyeproductions.com
www.garyrobinsonauthor.com

Introduction

<u>Native Soil/Native Soul</u> is an odd assortment of short and long stories featuring Native American characters and themes set in various time frames from the 1680s to the present day and beyond.

The bones of our Native ancestors are buried beneath the soil of this continent from coast to coast, and that fact is one of the reasons Native peoples so tenaciously cling to the lands from which we come, the Native soil. But, to us, our ancestors are not dead and gone, but spiritually alive and connected to us today. And our native roots continue to run deep within this sacred soil that has shaped our cultures, our languages, our minds and our lives even today—a concept that seems to elude the planners and developers who seek to gobble up every square foot of seemingly vacant land in the name of progress.

The seven stories in this collection interweave fictional and non-fictional elements, and by that, I mean that they portray fictional characters who experience things that real American Indian people have experienced or feasibly could experience.

Rebellion on the Rio Grande tells the partially fictionalized true story of the Pueblo Revolt of 1680, which Native peoples consider to be the first Revolutionary War of the Americas, through the eyes of a set of fictional characters, except for the very real Pueblo Indian leader, Popé (Popay), and a few of the very real historical Spanish colonialists.

House Made of Lies provides a detailed view of America's search, discovery, and extraction of uranium ore from Native

American lands as witnessed by Navajo elder Bernice Begay. This longer story takes place from the mid-1940s through the 1990s, an era that witnessed the death of hundreds of Navajo miners and millers due to radiation exposure—the dangers of which were never shared with the Navajo people.

Holy Road introduces readers to a curious collection of contemporary Native American characters struggling to be Native in a country that easily ignores their histories, cultures, sacred spaces or views. We begin to understand their frustrations and triumphs during an unusual road trip to a special place.

Set in and around a rural Indian reservation, *Blood in our Veins* hints at the conditions that led many California tribes to establish gaming operations on their traditional homelands in the last decade of the 20th century. Interwoven with that plot is a tale of racism and murder that unexpectedly brings back together two Native characters who belong together.

The Awakening refers to an eye-opening revelation experienced by a contemporary Native teenager when he almost loses an elder whose traditional view of things should be treasured rather than rejected and relegated to the dust bin of irrelevant history.

When a forty-year-old Blackfeet Indian is released from prison, he returns to his reservation to exact his own sense of *Personal Justice* from the man responsible for the death of a younger, innocent brother. This story is set in recent times.

In *Uncharted*, you'll join a research scientist and his Native

American girlfriend as they begin to explore uncharted non-physical realms while evading a renegade Army colonel who desperately wants to use their scientific discovery for espionage applications. Elements of the story are based on the actual reports of out-of-body explorers.

Enjoy.

-The Author

Contents

Introduction

Historically, the Native American uprising known as the Pueblo Revolt of 1680 was the first successful battle for independence fought against a European colonial power in what was to become the United States, and it was the only victory that American Indian peoples could celebrate in their efforts to thwart Spanish colonial expansion on the continent. It has been called the "first American Revolution," though most Americans have never heard of it.

When the Spaniards arrived in the Southwest in search of rumored riches, they found several thousand peace-loving indigenous people living in 70 villages scattered along the Rio Grande River as it flowed through New Mexico. These independent city-states shared many elements of a culture and lifestyle perfectly attuned to the desert environment and philosophically oriented towards a spiritual interpretation of their existence.

However, beginning with the arrival of the expedition of Don Juan de Oñate in 1598, a systematic campaign was initiated to enslave Pueblo Indians, convert them to Catholicism, prevent them from practicing their own religion and force them to economically support the Spanish colony of New Mexico. Early attempts at rebelling against the oppressors were met with swift and cruel punishment: a hand or foot was cut from all the males of an offending village. For 80 years the indigenous peoples of the region endured this abominable treatment.

When drought and disease began taking their toll on the

Pueblo people late in the 1600s, many Pueblo leaders, in particular the San Juan Pueblo medicine man Popé, believed that both the spiritual and the natural worlds were not functioning properly because the People were not allowed to perform their ceremonial duties as they'd done for centuries. To the native peoples of the Rio Grande Valley, the imposition of Spanish religion, taxation, forced labor and abuse of native women was an abomination of proportion equal to those suffered by the Hebrews as recorded in the Old Testament.

What little that's known about Popé and the Pueblo Revolt comes primarily from the biased writings of Spanish political and religious officials of that time period. Their primary objective was to demonstrate that the Spaniards had done no wrong and the Indians had done no right. Consequently, they cast Popé as an evil sorcerer and heavy-handed despot who, after the Spaniards were expelled, supposedly became as tyrannical as those he'd deposed.

The short story you're about to read tells the tale of the Pueblo Revolt from a Native American point of view, interweaving together fictional and non-fictional characters and elements. It is the story of the environmentally and spiritually-attuned Pueblo Indian people and the dire circumstances which compelled them, under the leadership of one of their most respected holy men, to rise up in grass-roots rebellion to rid their sacred soil of a foreign parasite.

Rebellion on the Rio Grande

With outstretched wings, the golden eagle floated on rising air heated by the morning sun's warming rays. The hungry predator's talons remained neatly tucked beneath his underbelly as sharp eyes scanned the banks of the river below in search of the first meal of the day.

At sunrise, this narrow strip of water, which came to be known to the foreigners as the Rio Grande River , was transformed into a river of gold flowing steadily southward between two lines of willows, piñons and cottonwoods flourishing at the river's edge. Beyond these tree-fringed riverbanks, the nearby floodplain was a green patchwork blanket of cornfields, and row upon row of squash, bean and melon plants.

As the eagle's aerial survey continued, a multi-leveled adobe village located to the east on slightly higher ground came into view. And beyond the lush green lands and the sunbaked village, the craggy, hilly desert floor spread for miles in both directions.

Detecting movement along the riverbank, the eagle swooped down for a better view. Upon closer inspection, the bird discovered that it was only an old Indian man hobbling down a well-worn path that meandered beside the water's edge.

Disinterested, the majestic feathered fowl regained altitude and returned to his airborne search.

Meanwhile, on the ground, the old, weather-beaten American Indian gazed upward in time to catch sight of the revered, winged relative as the bird resumed his flight northward. With his hand-carved willow cane, the elder waved his recognition of and appreciation for this brother-of-the-sky before continuing his own journey along the earthen path.

He struggled to navigate past a fallen tree branch that partially obstructed this often-used route. Rounding a large cottonwood, the cripple finally arrived at his destination, a painstakingly constructed stone shrine standing in a small clearing. In between the shrine's unevenly shaped building blocks were carefully inserted prayer sticks and flags made of colorfully dyed cloth.

He laid his own offering of food and tobacco at the foot of the shrine, and then reverently turned toward a distant peak to speak to an invisible listener.

"Rising Mist, spirit of the sacred mountain, it is I, Dancing Mouse, who turns to you in these troubled times. You know the perils that confront us, brought by the foreign invaders, the Metal People, who disrespect our women, disrupt our lives and punish us for carrying out our sacred duties. Guide us and give us the courage to do what must be done. These are desperate times, and they call for unusual measures. If it pleases you, from among us, lift up a leader who will help us throw off this curse and return us to our sacred ways. Thank you."

Then, as if acting on some unseen cue, a gentle wind stirred up the dust near the shrine. The wind became a swirl, and the swirling gained strength, becoming a playful whirlwind that encircled the old man.

A twinkle came to the elder's eye, and a smile spread across his weathered face as he found meaning in the whirlwind's appearance. Moving to the strains of some ethereal music, he joined in the play, and the strange pair—the crippled man and the swirling dust—entered into a kind of cosmic dance that marked the interplay of natural, human and spiritual forces making up the world of the ancient Pueblo Indian people.

After completing his ceremonial supplication, the aged man hobbled back toward the walls of his adobe village reflecting on the events that led him to make this morning's plea.

The strangers had come among his people unbidden and unwelcome many decades ago. Calling themselves Spaniards, the newcomers had no understanding of the supernatural forces that governed the lives of the People who'd settled in in this sacred location long before time even existed. Their strange foreign religion honored a distant god who apparently hated and despised the spirits and gods the Pueblo people cherished and honored.

An uneasy tension strained relationships between the Spaniards, known as the Metal People for their suits of armor, and the elder's People who knew the earth as their mother. As a result of two generations of colonization, however, many villagers had converted to the foreign faith, either because they saw the futility of resisting or because they saw concrete evidence of the power of the Black Book in the tools, weapons and material goods that the Spaniards possessed.

Others had outwardly adopted the appearance of religious conversion, because to do otherwise could result in death or disfigurement. Dancing Mouse had personally experienced the horror of that reality as a young man in a distant village.

II

Miles away from the old man and his memories, in the Spanish territorial capitol of Santa Fe, throngs of the so-called Metal People gathered for the long-awaited arrival of a wagon train that would bring much-needed supplies from Mexico City. Products made through the sweat of local Indian labor provided the items that would be exported and exchanged in the markets of Spain's New World capitol that made this annual supply train possible.

Marcos del Gado, the colony's civilian supply master, often rode out to meet the caravan a few days ride to the south so he could make a preliminary inventory of the arriving goods. And so the handsome, well-built Spaniard had left his Santa Fe trading post four days ago.

As the wagons now pulled into town with Marcos driving the lead wagon, they passed a line of manacled Native men, mostly elders, who were being marched toward the town's central plaza.

Marcos halted the line of wagons in front of the trading post and climbed down from the lead wagon. He was greeted by his very beautiful Pueblo Indian girlfriend, Chamisa. After a brief embrace, he turned to back to the wagons, telling the drivers they could start unloading their goods.

Before the supply master could take another step, El Capitan Fernando Franco, head of the contingent of soldiers protecting the settlement, summoned Marcos to him.

"Is everything with the shipment in order and accounted for?" the commander inquired brusquely.

"Well, almost everything," the younger man replied casually, without much regard for the commander's status or rank. "One of the looms was damaged when a wagon slipped down a steep embankment, and several chickens escaped when their cage fell off the back."

"Why didn't you catch them and re-secure them in another cage?" Franco demanded.

"Oh, we tried. You should've seen the ruckus we raised chasing those birds all over hell and back." Marcos chuckled. "But, alas, they eluded us," he finished with a smile.

"I find nothing amusing about this, Señor del Gado. Need I remind you that you were banished to this colony as punishment for your crimes against the crown?"

"I was falsely accused, as I've told you many times, Fernando," Marcos replied, dropping his easy-go-lucky attitude.

"Be that as it may, don't forget for one instant that I won't throw you in the stockades for your insubordination."

"All right, El Capitan. I stand reminded of your superior position."

"All right then," the commander said, adjusting the coat of his uniform. "I expect your full report on my desk in the morning. Good day." With that the commander turned and walked away.

"Who are those shackled Pueblo men being taken to the

square?" Marcos asked Chamisa after the somber soldier was no longer in sight. He walked with her towards the plaza.

"They are some of our most revered religious leaders from Pueblos up and down the Rio Grande," the distraught young woman said. "For days now your army has been rounding them up, mistreating them and dragging them here to Santa Fe. Today they are to stand trial for being sorcerers and devil-worshippers. It is outrageous."

Though Marcos thought it best to stay far away from these troubles, he finally agreed to attend the trial with Chamisa, because she was so worried about its outcome. They slipped in a side door to the court room and found an out-of-the-way corner from which they could observe the trial.

Presiding over the proceedings was the colonial governor himself, Antonio de Otermin. The interrogation of the native prisoners, however, was conducted by the colony's Bishop, Father Francisco Pacheco. A couple of Otermin's other advisors, El Capitan Franco and the Secretary of War, Francisco Xavier, were also in attendance.

Otermin read aloud an accusation against each prisoner, and each of the accused was invited to respond to the charges. Regardless of the response, each was pronounced guilty. Three of the men were charged with leading satanic rituals, a crime punishable by death. At each pronouncement of "guilty!" by the governor, a resounding cheer erupted from the collection of primarily Spanish spectators.

As Marcos watched the proceedings with a sense of helplessness, he noticed one prisoner who seemed more intently focused and slightly taller than the other Pueblo men. He asked Chamisa about him.

"He is Popé, a well-respected holy man from my own village, Grinding Stone, the one your people call San Juan. I remember that once when I was very ill as a child, he came and performed a healing ceremony for me, and soon I got well. My father says he is a good man."

After the fake proceedings had run their course, Popé and the others were taken outside to the plaza to receive the first phase of their punishment: a public flogging dealt by the hand of none other than El Capitan Franco. Marcos was now unable to tear himself away from this grotesque miscarriage of justice that he could relate to so personally.

With each stroke of the whip, Popé's eyes burned with renewed purpose and determination, and with each stroke of that same whip, Marcos was reminded of the lashings he himself received at the hands of the same man years ago for crimes he did not commit in Spain. Marcos was among those that day in Santa Fe's plaza who witnessed three of Popé's colleagues being hanged for their supposed crimes against the crown, and something shifted within the supply master's being that very moment.

Chamisa was brought to tears by the sight of the pain, humiliation, and disrespect heaped upon these beloved teachers and healers of her people.

After the hanging, Dancing Mouse watched as the mostly colonial crowd dispersed, and the remaining prisoners were taken back to jail. Unbeknownst to the Metal People, Pueblo Indian runners departed from the four corners of the plaza to take news of the hangings and floggings to all the villages in the region.

III

The three medicine men were left hanging on display in the plaza, and, after no one else was left to see, Dancing Mouse emerged from the shadows to approach the suspended bodies. Picking up a length of rope that had been discarded by the executioners, the elder said aloud to the spirits of his fallen friends, "I think they have chosen the means of their own destruction." As a sign of his intention, he tied a series of knots in the rope as he hobbled away.

In the following days, many people from both the colonial and native communities sensed that change was in the wind, even as they carried on with their previous activities. The colonial priests continued to supervise obviously over-worked Indians in the construction of a yet another church. Spanish soldiers continued to beat and starve Native crews as they plowed their oppressor's fields. Elder Indian women wove cloth on looms under the watchful eyes of Spanish matriarchs. Younger native women were still unwillingly bedded by Spanish soldiers.

Several days after the hangings a delegation of approximately seventy Pueblo Indians who'd converted to Christianity marched boldly into the capitol compound with a message for the Governor. Standing outside the governor's palace, the group's leader read the warning aloud.

"We bring a message to Governor Antonio de Otermin from the leaders of all the Pueblo villages. Unless you release our revered representatives from prison, we, the united Pueblo villages of this region, will attack and kill every Spaniard in the colonies. We expect your answer before sunset."

Until that moment, Spanish colonial political and religious leaders had assumed that converted Natives would side with their fellow Christians if conflict between the colonizers and the colonized arose. They now realized that the native teachings were more powerful and meaningful to the local inhabitants than previously thought, and just because an Indian had accepted Jesus as his Lord and Savior, it did not mean he'd renounced allegiance to his brethren tribesmen.

During their deliberations, the leaders of the Metal People admitted that their people were outnumbered at least four-to-one and they believed the Indians capable of carrying out their threat Not knowing that the Indians did not actually have the means, training or organization at that time to actually make good on their threat. So, after conferring with his three advisors, the governor released the medicine men that same day.

To the Spaniards, this affair was an alarming wake-up call to the fact that they hadn't subdued the "savages" to the level they thought they had. But to Popé, the capitulation of the oppressors was a sign of a weakness, as well as an indication that his own people did have what it took to stand up against the foreign power.

Returning to the village of Grinding Stone, Popé called a meeting of village leaders to see if they were ready to consider taking armed action against the Spaniards. Most agreed that their situation was desperate, but none was willing to do anything more than complain, and that they would only do in the privacy of the kiva, out of the hearing of any Spaniard. Popé had expected more from village leaders and was sadly disappointed in their unwillingness to act.

Soon the Feast Day celebrating the Catholic patron saint of San Juan Pueblo arrived. All the Indians of the village were expected to participate, and an army of priests and soldiers was on hand to make sure of this. Since it was one of the few occasions in which the Indian people were allowed to openly enjoy themselves, a mixed sense of both tension and joy permeated the day's festivities.

As part of the day's activities, a contingent of village holy men, including Popé, were expected to carry the statue of the village saint through the streets for all to honor. Unknown to the Spanish priests, however, the medicine men had embedded small traditional Pueblo ceremonial objects within the figure's hollow center, and it was these unseen objects which many of the Indians were secretly honoring.

And out of sight of the soldiers and priests, Indian children mockingly play-acted out the pompous and pretentious behaviors of the Spaniards. And enjoying this side show, Dancing Mouse was quite comfortable in the company of the children, hoping that these small and passive insurrections would build courage for future greater changes.

Marcos and Chamisa also attended the Feast Day activities so Chamisa might visit her family who lived in that pueblo. Knowing of the impoverished conditions in which Chamisa's family lived, Marcos brought them a few gifts that would never be missed from the trading post's inventory.

Marcos was accepted, more or less, by those of the Grinding Stone community who'd come to know him through Chamisa. They knew she was not his concubine, a station forced upon many young Indian women by Spanish men, but rather his companion. And when he asked Chamisa why her family accepted him, she simply replied, "Because you don't think or act like you're better than us."

While at San Juan that day, Marcos met Popé and his family for the first time, including the leader's daughter, Spring Rain, and her husband Nicolas Bua who had recently converted to Catholicism. Bua had been critical of his father-in-law's previous refusal to adopt both Christian and Spanish ways, but today, Marcos noted, he was clearly pleased to see Popé take an active part in the festivities. Bua was not one of those aware of the hidden contents of the saint's image.

Soon after the Feast Day, Popé sought guidance from the spirits on what to do about the continuing presence of the foreign tyrants. One night, while praying alone in the kiva, he fell asleep and had a vision. The Kachina spirit Rising Mist appeared to him and told him that Earth and Sky were suffering because the native people were unable to carry out their ceremonial duties, unable to keep life in balance as they'd been doing for centuries. Rising Mist said that the time had come to revive the ceremonies and expel the foreigners from the land. It was clear that Popé had been chosen to execute the task.

Popé awoke with the firm belief that the time was ripe for action, but he realized that his people must be organized, led by a trusted, decisive leader, and given a spark of inspired motivation to see it through to victory. However, he knew his first task was to somehow secretly revive the key seasonal Pueblo ceremonies that would restore harmony and balance to their world.

To achieve that goal, he began traveling to neighboring pueblos to meet with certain carefully-chosen village leaders and medicine men to speak of his plan to hold secret ceremonies and to eventually rise up against the Spaniards.

IV

Back in Santa Fe, Governor Otermin and his advisors had heard rumors of Popé's activities and decided it was time to remind the Indians of their place in society before they were able to build any kind of serious resistance movement. The Bishop was ordered to institute stricter controls over the religious life of the Indians, while the Governor decided to appoint a new set of secular village leaders who would answer to directly him. These village governors would act as his eyes and ears in each region, and therefore must be chosen carefully.

In order to elevate the perceived status of these village governors, Otermin decided that each would be given a specially created cane, a gift from the King of Spain, to symbolize their direct ties to the monarchy. He sent El Capitan to the trading post where Marcos worked to put in a special order for the canes, which required a rider to make a special trip to Mexico City. The canes, Marcos' superior boasted, would be part of the bribe that Otermin would use to secure the cooperation of Indian informants in each village.

El Capitan's visit to the trading post also gave him an opportunity to humiliate Marcos and flirt with Chamisa, two actions which he knew intensified the soldier's resentment. Aroused by the sight of Chamisa, the captain, whose insatiable lust had been forcefully satisfied by many native women over the years vowed then and there that he would have her—one way or another. But, because he had another Indian concubine to satisfy him for the time being, he would postpone consummation of his desires until the time was right.

That time came when Marcos had to make one of his occasional trading trips to the Spanish settlements in the northern part of the territory. After Marcos departed, El Capitan made his move, sending two of his men to kidnap Chamisa and bring her to him. Fighting and protesting all the way, she was dragged to his opulent quarters. Seeing that she would not be convinced to cooperate, El Capitan had her tied to the bed, where he raped her.

Upon his return several days later, Marcos was unable to locate his sweetheart. The supply master's assistant reported that soldiers took her away in the night.

Marcos rushed to Franco's quarters, where he discovered Chamisa laying half-dead in the captain's bed. One of the captain's other Native concubines was treating Chamisa's many wounds.

Gently Marcos he picked her up and carried her back to the room they shared behind the trading post. He placed her lovingly on their bed. There he discovered something clutched tightly in her closed fist. She regained consciousness enough to realize that Marcos was with her. She released the paper from her grip and he unfolded it to discover it to be a list of the soon-to-be appointed Pueblo governors.

"Warn Popé," she weakly whispered. Examining the list more closely, he found the name Nicolas Bua as the choice for San Juan Pueblo.

As he cradled Chamisa in his arms, she mustered the strength to open her eyes and make one last request.

"Return me to my people," she asked with her dying breath.

Tears filled his dark eyes as he placed her lifeless body back on the bed. Rising from her side, his grief turned quickly to rage. He stormed off to find the despicable Captain Franco. Knowing just where to locate the Spaniard who was fond of whisky, Marcos headed for the nearest cantina.

Spotting his target through the bar's open door, Marcos made a beeline for the man. Two soldiers blocked his path.

"I swear you will pay for this with your life," Marcos growled as Franco's men restrained him. Laughing, the captain rose to meet Marcos eye-to-eye.

"What's the matter, store-keeper?" the large man asked. "Did something happen to your little Indian whore?"

Marcos lunged for the captain, but a blow from one of the guards knocked him to the floor. A second blow kept him there.

"If he makes any more trouble, kill him," El Captain commanded as he walked away.

Vows of vengeance roaring through his mind, Marcos took Chamisa's body to her village for burial. When he arrived, he told her family what had happened and asked to see Popé.

With an introduction from Chamisa's family, the young Spaniard was received immediately by the Pueblo leader. Popé. listened to what Marcos had to say, though not entirely without suspicion. Once the two men were alone, Marcos pulled the Governor's list from his pocket, handed it to Popé and explained its meaning.

Then, in obvious emotional pain, he said, "Sir, I am at your service. Use me as you will. If you truly are planning a rebellion against these oppressive tyrants, then I will make my stand with you."

Popé gazed into this Spaniard's eyes in search of some hidden agenda or ulterior motive. Finding none, and understanding what it meant to lose a loved one under the armed grip of the Metal People, Popé accepted the offer.

"Years ago my wife died at the hands of your countrymen," Pope confided. "Every person in every village has suffered some pain, torture or indignity, and the time has come to put an end to it."

Then the elder invited Marcos to stay in the village to take part in Chamisa's burial ceremony, to be held before sundown the same day.

After the ceremony, Popé approached Marcos with a plan.

"Return to Santa Fe and continue your duties as supply master, but secretly gather any information that you feel could be useful to us in our cause."

Marcos agreed to do so.

Armed with the new information supplied by this new ally, Popé continued his planning and networking, but with the additional understanding that he could only speak of these matters to trusted ceremonial leaders. He also initiated his plan to purge their ranks of informants.

Soon the canes arrived and were distributed to the village governors. Bua showed off his newly acquired symbol of rank to his wife and others in the village, proud of his new position. He took the opportunity to again explain to his wife, Spring Rain, why he had accepted this position.

"Acceptance of Spanish rule and religion is the only way that Pueblo people will survive," he said emphatically. "And that being true, why not achieve some sort of favored position within their regime? This way, they and their heirs may be spared the hardship of manual labor."

His wife seemed to begin to understand his thinking. But he had chosen not to let his wife know of his secondary duties as informant, because he was fairly certain this information would find its way to his father-in-law. As an ambitious man, Bua was convinced that his unique relationship within Popé's family would make him indispensable to Governor Otermin and, therefore, garner him a higher rank within the colonial government.

In the weeks to come, Popé had secretly succeeded in preparing his people for a renewal of their ceremonies, an activity the spirits had mandated. The Grinding Stone medicine men had made plans to conduct a Deer Dance in the middle of the night in a remote location outside the Pueblo. Aware of the risks, Popé had included his grown children in the plans for the secret ceremony, so they could share in the resulting physical and spiritual benefits.

At the appointed hour, and after her husband had fallen asleep, Spring Rain slipped away to participate in the dance. Unfortunately, Bua awoke as she was leaving and managed to follow her to the secret site. But little did he know he, too, was followed by one of Popé's own spies.

When Popé learned that Bua had witnessed the ceremony, he knew what had to be done.

The following day, Popé was pleased to experience the first significant rainfall in years, a direct result of the ceremony. In the rain, Bua left the village headed to Santa Fe to report the previous night's clandestine dance. In a secluded spot outside the village,

Popé's men captured the informant and took him to the hills where he was executed.

Popé knew that his daughter must hear of her husband's death directly from him. Finding her at work grinding cornmeal under a brush arbor beside her home, he called her away from her task. He invited her to walk with him, and they strolled towards the village kiva.

Her anguished cry filled the village as she learned of her husband's fate. She fell to the ground in her grief. Reaching down to help her stand, Popé also revealed what Bua had been up to behind the scenes. Learning that her own father had ordered her husband's execution, she began to beat on his chest in anger. Grabbing her flailing arms, the elder shook his daughter until she stopped. She pulled away from him and ran to hide.

The following day, Spring Rain appeared outside the kiva and began yelling for her father to come out and face her. He climbed down the ladder that led from the kiva's flat roof and faced his daughter.

Before she could speak, he said, "Come with me." Though puzzled, angry, and hurt, the young woman followed.

Popé led her to a small house at the edge of the village. He knocked on the door, and Dancing Mouse came to see who it was. The ancient man invited them inside.

"What are we doing here?" Spring Rain wanted to know.

"Show her," Popé told the old man.

"As you wish," the elder replied, sitting down and

removing his well-worn right boot. Spring Rain saw that old man had no foot. Where his foot should have been was instead a carved wooden replacement, and, for the first time in her life, she knew why he hobbled around with the aid of his willow cane.

"What's that got to do with anything?" Popé's bewildered daughter asked.

"Tell her," Popé said to the old man.

He told her of a time when he was just a boy in his home at the Pueblo of Acoma, known as Sky City. The village had been built on top of a large, round, flat mesa that rose two hundred feet from the valley floor. It was the first time he'd seen the Metal People, the Spanish soldiers in their armor. They were angrily tearing his village apart, entering each home looking for something, throwing all their possessions into the streets, raping women in their homes, shoving elders to the ground. No one knew what this was about, but the men of the village had to put a stop to it. Rushing the soldiers, a large group of villagers overtook them and forced them to the edge of the mesa, and then over the edge to the rocks below.

The people of Acoma thought they were rid of the Metal People once and for all, but to their horror several weeks later, another group of armed soldiers arrived at their village with two cannons in tow. The cannons began blasting the village, ripping the people and the structures to shreds. Then the soldiers stormed the village, killing as many people as they could. Some jumped to their death off the edge of the mesa. Others were thrown. The remainder were captured and marched here to San Juan, which at that time was the capitol of the Spaniard's colony.

"Once we arrived here, a foot or hand was cut from the body of each man and boy, and the women became the slaves of Spanish families," Dancing Mouse said.

"That was the beginning of the nightmare, some seventy five years ago," Popé remarked at the story's end.

"Dancing Mouse was one of those boys, now the only one left to remember and tell of the horror. He is our link to the way it was before the nightmare began, and he is my reminder of my responsibility to the next generation of our people."

Turning to his daughter, he continued, "I'm sorry your husband had to die, and I'll understand if you cannot forgive me. But his death brings us one step closer to the end of this nightmare, which has meant nothing but the destruction of our people and our way of life."

Spring Rain hugged her father and did the same to old Dancing Mouse. With new understanding, she returned to life as she had known it before marriage.

Word of Bua's death spread, and to evade Spanish retribution, Popé fled north to the Pueblo of Taos to hide out in their kiva at the invitation of their ceremonial leaders. And Bua's death precipitated the beginning of the revolt's rapid development.

From this hiding place at Taos, Popé began plotting the large scale revolt inspired by his original vision. In addition to providing information, Marcos also began instructing Indian warriors in the use of Spanish muskets and swords, to supplement the simple bows, lances and other crude weapons used previously by the Pueblos for defense.

In the summer of 1680, by the white man's reckoning, Popé believed his people were finally ready. The spirits instructed him to call his most trusted followers to the Taos kiva. After days of intense ceremony, three Kachina spirits appeared to those assembled. Much like the Biblical Shadrach, Meshach and Abednego, these awesome figures breathed fire from every extremity of their bodies. Their message: it is time to rid the land of the foreigners who do not respect the spirits of the land. The three spirits commanded Popé to set a date for the revolt and to send each pueblo a rope of made of maguey fibers with a number of knots tied to signify the number of days until the day of rebellion. Thus, the resolve set in motion by Dancing Mouse on the day that Pueblo leaders were hanged in the Santa Fe plaza was confirmed.

News of the mystical kiva appearance spread like wildfire among the villages, inspiring the People with faith and hope. Carefully considering the circumstances and the timing, Popé and his inner circle chose a date for the rebellion: August 10th.

As it turned out, this was the perfect time to carry out their uprising. Due to heavy run-off of melting snow in the mountains, the Rio Grande was above its banks. And, thanks to information supplied by Marcos, Popé learned that the Spaniards' supply train would be stuck on the other side of the river to the south for weeks, waiting for the waters to subside. He realized that the colonists would be short on food, ammunition and other supplies.

This date would also fall on a Spanish feast day in honor of Saint Lorenzo, and so most of the colonists would be preoccupied with preparations for that day's festivities.

Following the Kachina's instructions, Popé sent runners to the villages who'd pledged allegiance to the alliance, carrying knotted cords setting August 10th as the day of the first attack. Knowing that word of the coming rebellion had probably been leaked in spite of their precautions, Popé cleverly sent knotted cords that set August 13th as the date of uprising to those pueblo leaders suspected of being informers.

Just before dawn on the appointed day, warriors attacked several Spanish outposts along the Rio Grande, as well as isolated Spanish ranches. Few foreigners were spared in the purge. A few families who'd shown kindness or sympathy towards the Indians over the years were allowed to live. Previous to the rebellion, their homes had been painted with a symbol that told attackers not to strike. These families, however, were held under house arrest to prevent them from aiding their countrymen elsewhere.

All that day, fear-filled Spaniards came riding into Santa Fe to report mortal attacks all over pueblo territory. The Governor ordered all the nearby colonists to gather within the walls of the Governor's Palace, and by day's end, about a thousand people had taken up refuge there.

By nightfall, about five hundred Native warriors gathered

outside Santa Fe to wait, and over the next three days, they were joined by warriors from other villages.

On August 13th, an army of about five hundred warriors approached the palace garrison. To Otermin's surprise, his former servant, Juan, led the group.

With two armed guards, Juan broke away from the others and entered the palace gates. There he offered the Governor a clear choice: either take his people and leave the territory unharmed, or stay and fight to the death. Otermin refused to take the offer seriously, especially from a heathen servant!

Juan returned to the Indian front line and reported Otermin's refusal to reply. He was told to return to the Governor and make the same offer one more time, and again the Governor refused to respond. Instead, to intimidate the Indians, a column of Spanish soldiers took up a defensive position around the palace, as if ready for battle.

The native force, however, did not take the bait, for they were waiting for more warriors to arrive from the northern villages.

The next day, reinforcements from San Juan and Taos arrived, led by Popé himself. Marcos was with them, hoping for the chance to avenge his beloved's death.

Word of Popé's arrival spread quickly among the warriors. Here, among them, was the man who had orchestrated this entire campaign, the man who spoke directly to the Kachina spirits--the man who was chosen to lead them to freedom.

Emboldened by his presence, more than two thousand Indians charged on Santa Fe, from both the north and the south simultaneously. Fighting was fierce, and after several days of battle, the attackers managed to cut off the garrison's water supply. It wasn't long before cattle, sheep and horses within the garrison began to die and the Metal People sickened.

Mustering all the men, horses and weapons he had left, El Capitan made a surprise attack on the Natives. Charging out of the gates, his horses trampled the closest warriors. Then the Spaniards set fire to some of the nearby wooden buildings which were providing cover for the Indians.

Dozens of warriors were trapped in the blaze, and about fifty were captured. In the final act of this maneuver, several Spaniards carrying buckets gather as much water as possible before returning to the safety of the compound.

Seizing his chance, Marcos led a small contingent of well-armed Indian warriors against El Capitan and his wounded and weakened corps of guards before they could re-enter the compound. These warriors, under the supply master's tutelage, had learned their lessons well, and the weapons they wielded found their marks.

Alone and surrounded by native warriors, El Capitan braced himself for the final onslaught. However, Marcos, sword in hand, stepped into the circle to face his old enemy alone. El Capitan couldn't resist one final insult.

"Del Gado, I'm surprised," he blustered. "All this fuss over a pathetic pile of desert rocks, a few pagan idols and a worthless Indian whore."

With that remark, the trader deftly swung his sword, cutting off the man's right foot. The braggart fell to the ground, writhing in pain. In spite of his dire condition, he managed to hurl yet another insult.

"I understand what you saw in her, del Gado," he spat out. "She was the best piece of brown ass I ever had."

And down came del Gado's sword once again, this time removing the man's right hand. Screaming and cussing, the captain yelled, "Is that the best you can do? Go ahead finish it. Finish It!"

Marcos calmly replied, "No. I want you to live so you can suffer as these people have been made to suffer. Spend the rest of your miserable days hobbling the streets of Madrid or Mexico City, begging for food and remembering."

With that, he and the warriors retreated a safe distance from the compound.

Back inside the garrison, the Governor had all the Indian captives tortured and questioned in his quest for information about the strength of Popé army and their plans. None of the captives gave him useful information, and he had them shot.

That night, the resourceful natives set fire to all the remaining buildings that surrounded the garrison, leaving no structures between themselves and the thirsty, wounded and hungry Spaniards inside. As the fires burned, Otermin called his advisors to him for a meeting. It was a short meeting, for all agreed they should surrender and hope that they wouldn't be slaughtered.

At dawn on August 21st, Otermin sent word to Popé that the Spaniards would vacate the territory, and he told his people to prepare for the long and arduous journey.

The eleven day revolt was over.

Later that morning the bedraggled collection of animals and people, wounded soldiers, and thirsty civilians began filing out of the compound. In fear for their lives, these conquered conquerors were convinced the "savages" would murder them before they reached the edge of their burnt out settlement.

However, the surviving 2,400 colonists, soldiers, missionaries and ruling officials were allowed to simply walk out of the territory. Under the silent, watchful eyes of two thousand warriors, they passed unharmed. If Popé and the Pueblo people had been the blood-thirsty, devil-worshipping savages depicted by the Spaniards, no foreigner would have been spared.

To see their once proud and mighty oppressors brought finally so low in humiliating defeat was enough vengeance for the Pueblo warriors. As the realization of victory sank into their minds, jubilant war cries rose up in their throats, and the spirit of celebration spread among their ranks.

From a high point overlooking the ravaged town, Popé, Marcos and a group of Grinding Stone warriors watched the line of Spaniards disappear to the south. Weary and not finding cause for joyous celebration right then, Popé suggested they head back home.

"Thank you, my friend," Popé said to Marcos. "You are welcome to become one of us, but I must warn you, it won't be easy. In the days ahead we will be ridding ourselves of all reminders of foreign domination so we can return to our ancient ways."

"Even though I am one of them, I cannot go with them," Marcos replied. "Their ways now sicken me."

"Then you shall become one of us," the medicine man said with a smile.

Just then, Dancing Mouse passed by them riding in a horse-drawn cart.

"Keep the horses," he advised Popé. "The horses are a good thing."

This brought a round of laughter to the men as they followed Dancing Mouse's cart northward.

And as they left the ruins of what was once their adversary's capital, a small whirlwind rose from the desert floor, twirling the native soil in a triumphant dance that followed behind them.

Epilogue

Historians have noted that to mark complete victory over Spanish rule, Popé mandated that all elements of Spanish culture and symbols of Spanish domination be destroyed: churches, livestock, plants, tools, everything. The Spanish language was forbidden, and Christian names reverted back to Indian names. Baptized Indians were washed with soap made from the yucca plant to cleanse them of any vestiges of the foreign religion.

Within a year, the Pueblo people had returned to their former lifestyle. But many Indians found it hard to resume a way of life they hadn't known for eighty years. Mostly they missed the tools and practical goods to which they'd grown accustomed.

Also, with the successful expulsion of the Spaniards, many village leaders felt that it was safe to return to their independent city-state form of government, and saw no need to continue the union which had been forged by Popé. Ten years after the rebellion, Popé died, and his Pueblo union collapsed.

Unfortunately for Pueblo people, in 1692, two years after Popé's death, a Spanish army led by Diego de Vargas reclaimed Santa Fe and the New Mexico territory. They met little resistance from the unorganized, defenseless Pueblos as the Metal People reoccupied the territory. Subsequently, eighty Pueblo leaders were hanged for their part in the revolt.

But Popé left a legacy hard to ignore. His original union is echoed in the All Pueblo Indian Council active today. And the revolt itself was a catalyst for lasting change. Learning from their earlier colonial mistakes, de Vargas reduced the power of the church, eliminated the ban on the practice of Indian religion, and abolished the system of forced labor and tributes.

Another result of the revolt was that when the Spaniards retreated in 1680, they left behind many horses in various parts of New Mexico. These horses and their descendants were captured by the Apaches, spread far and wide, and traded to tribes from the plains. The introduction of the horse transformed the lifestyles of many groups of American Indian people all across North America.

And in recent times, Popé has finally been honored, at least in a small way, through the creation and installation of a statue depicting what he may have looked like created by internationally renowned Pueblo sculptor Cliff Fragua. This image now stands in the National Statuary Hall in Washington, D.C. in the company of other great heroes who fought for independence and freedom of speech, thought and religion in the land we call America.

HOUSE MADE OF LIES

A mud-spattered 1977 white Chevy pickup bounced and weaved its way down a rutted muddy road that coursed through an ancient, mystical landscape. The rising sun glistened off the few small bits of the truck's chrome trim that weren't caked with dried mud.

Driving the truck was Carmelita Begay, a Navajo woman in her late twenties, on her way to her grandma's house. It was a special day, for her seventy-year-old grandma, Bernice Begay, was going to fly on an airplane for the first time.

Shafts of morning sunlight cut across the tops of the sandy red cliffs standing guard over the community where Bernice lived, Red Rock, Arizona. This scattered collection of homes, cornfields and sheep corrals, lay at the foot of the Lukachukai Mountains straddling a northern stretch of the Arizona-New Mexico border.

The Dineh people, known to the outside world as Navajos, had lived in this part of the world for untold centuries. This land was given to them by the Creator as their permanent homeland after Monster-Slayer had killed the giants who ruled the region and made it safe for human beings to inhabit. The United States government had seen fit to honor that sacred gift, after much warfare and bloodshed, by conferring reservation status on the area in 1868.

It was now March of 1990, and the melting winter snows had left the high desert clay wet and pliable.

Carmelita spied her grandma's hogan up ahead. A wisp of smoke rose from the stovepipe chimney in the center of the eight-sided wood-and-sod structure. As the truck neared the hogan,

Bernice's sheep announced Carmelita's arrival in their best bleating fashion.

Inside the humble dwelling, Bernice quietly waited and rocked in her old wooden rocker, which sat near the cast iron wood stove in the middle of the room. Weaving a multi-colored yarn belt, her aged and experienced fingers worked methodically to intertwine the colored strands of yarn. Her weathered face bore a striking resemblance to the land that gave her birth, and her dark eyes still burned bright with the fiery spark of determination and life.

Hearing Carmelita's truck pull up outside and honk, Bernice sighed and began putting away her weaving. She rose from her rocker as a knock came on her door.

"Always in a hurry," she said under her breath as she opened the east-facing door to greet Carmelita. Her granddaughter was silhouetted against the morning sunlight.

"Ready to go, Grandma?" the younger woman asked cheerfully.

"As ready as I'll ever be," the elder answered. "Where's Mitchell? I thought he was taking me."

"Last night's wind busted up our corral. Dad had fix it, then go find our sheep." She took a step into the hogan. "Better get going, or we'll be late."

"Okay. Just let me put this fire out and get my things." Bernice turned back toward the stove, picked up a metal poker and spread the remains of the coals around inside the stove.

Carmelita noticed her grandma's old carpetbag sitting neatly by the door and picked it up. The leather handle, which had grown stiff with age, had been repaired with silver duct tape.

Satisfied that the fire would safely die out, Bernice closed the grate and picked up her best turquoise sweater.

"I don't know why I let you kids talk me into this," she said, absent-mindedly fiddling with a small leather medicine pouch that she always wore around her neck.

"Ben will be with you the whole trip," Carmelita said. "Don't worry, Grandma."

"I ain't worried," Bernice replied, a little sharply.

She slipped on her sweater, picked up her cane and looked for her carpetbag. Carmelita held it up for the old woman to see.

"I guess that's it then," the elder said.

She glanced around her small home one last time and sighed. Taking the lead, she walked out the door and headed for the truck. Carmelita closed the hogan door and caught up to her grandma who was half way to the vehicle. She took Bernice's arm to support her.

"Airplanes are nothing to be worried about," the granddaughter said.

"Who said I was worried? And I ain't a helpless old woman either!"

Pulling her arm away, Bernice took the carpetbag from Carmelita and marched toward the truck. The younger woman just shrugged good-naturedly and followed.

When she arrived at the passenger door, Bernice stopped. She realized that she did indeed need some help, after all. Carmelita obligingly opened the door and helped her grandmother climb up into the passenger seat of the truck's elevated cab. As the patient Carmelita went around to the driver's side, Bernice took a long look at her little home.

It wasn't much to see: the old hogan, the sheep corral, the horno oven, the shade arbor and the broken down rusting Ford truck. Despite her protests to the contrary, Bernice <u>was</u> a little worried. Would this be the last time she ever saw this place? Only Creator knew.

The cranking of the truck's starter brought Bernice out of her fretful daydream. Taking a deep breath, she returned to her former stoic self.

An hour later, Carmelita steered the truck into the parking lot of the Gitty-Up Gas & Grocery at the edge of Shiprock. The ever-punctual Ben Benally was there waiting patiently, sipping coffee, as he leaned against the side of his pick-up.

Ben was a short, stocky Navajo in his mid-sixties who'd done every job on the reservation from herding sheep to teaching school to serving on the tribal council. Today he looked like a cowboy in his felt hat, western cut jacket, pointy-toe boots and denim jeans.

As Carmelita's truck shuddered to a stop, he stepped toward the passenger door and opened it.

"Ya-ah-tay!" he said, using the traditional Navajo greeting.

"Ya-ah-tay, back," Carmelita replied.

Bernice let Ben help her down out of the seat.

"Well, this is something, Bernice," he said as she walked towards his truck. "Flying on a plane. Going to Washington, D.C. I thought you'd never leave this reservation."

"It's no big deal, Ben," Bernice protested. "It's—. Oh, never mind."

Carmelita threw Bernice's bag in the back of Ben's truck.

"Okay, Grandma," she said. "Dad or I will pick you up here next Thursday."

"At three," Bernice said.

"At three," Carmelita repeated.

"If the plane's late, I'll call you," Ben assured her.

"Thanks, Ben," Carmelita replied. "Goodbye, Grandma."

The elder hugged her granddaughter and then added an extra squeeze for good measure.

"Don't pay me any mind when I'm cranky," Bernice whispered in Carmelita's ear.

Ben opened the passenger door on his truck, and Bernice climbed in. She watched Carmelita drive away as Ben shut her door. The elder woman was already homesick.

"We'll be there before you know it," Ben said, getting in behind the wheel. Bernice realized that her feelings were showing a little more than she wanted them to and quickly recovered. Ben started to say something else but thought better of it. He started the engine and eased the truck onto the highway.

They rode in silence for a while, allowing the passing Navajo landscape to cast its never-changing magic on their minds. Ben turned on his truck radio, which was tuned to KTNN—Radio Navajo. The 50,000-watt station could be heard all hours of the night and day almost anywhere on the reservation, and its bilingual Navajo/English-speaking DJs gave it that distinctive flavor Ben loved.

Listening to the music, Bernice looked over at her old friend, Ben Benally. She tried to remember just how long she'd known him.

"You know, Ben, I want to thank you," she said finally.

"For what?" he asked.

"For everything you've done," she answered. "Not just for me, but for all of us."

"My Dineh people were hurting. What else could I do?"

"I just want you to know it means something. Whether these people in Washington do anything or not. What you've done means something."

"Well, you know, Creator gives us all a job to do," Ben replied humbly.

"And I'm thanking you for doing yours," Bernice persisted.

"Well—."

He fell silent. They watched the landscape pass by for a few minutes more.

"Anyway," Ben said. "I've been meaning to tell you, there's a reporter from Albuquerque who wants to talk to you."

"About what?"

"You know, the mining... Frank's death... the people who've suffered all those years. Pretty much the same stuff you're going to tell the Congressional committee."

"Everybody's so all-fired interested in this now," Bernice said. "When it could have done some good, nobody wanted to hear a thing about it."

"They do now."

"Anyway, reporters and anthropologists--they never get Indian stuff right."

"This'll be different. This reporter is an Indian."

"He is?"

"She is," Ben corrected.

That revelation surprised and pleased Bernice.

"Well, I guess it wouldn't hurt to just talk to her," the elder replied in a softer tone. "Maybe when I come back."

"She's meeting us at the Albuquerque airport. She's going to fly to Washington on the same plane. So you'll—."

"Be trapped. You sure like to spring things on people, Ben Benally."

Ben, who was a little embarrassed, didn't answer. Bernice looked back out the window and smiled a secret smile.

Soon they pulled into the little airport in Farmington. Ben parked his truck in the long-term parking lot that already held a total of five cars. He escorted Bernice into the tiny terminal just in time to hear a woman announce that their flight to Albuquerque would be boarding in ten minutes. They stopped in at the Mesa Airlines ticket counter where Ben presented their tickets and their luggage.

A few minutes later, the tribal councilman led the way as they stepped out of the terminal and on to the small airport's runway. The pair approached a twin-engine, twelve-seater parked not far from the terminal gate. The props fired up when they were about twenty feet away. Bernice stopped dead in her tracks.

"Don't tell me you expect me to fly all the way to Washington in that dinky little thing!"

"No, Bernice," Ben said calmly. "Only as far as Albuquerque. Then we change to a nice big jet airliner that'll take us non-stop to Washington."

Bernice relaxed, but only a little.

A stewardess helped Bernice up the steps and into the plane. She took a seat and looked around the tiny aircraft, grabbing the little medicine bundle and rubbing it gently in an effort to calm herself. Ben sat in the seat beside her.

"We'll be in Albuquerque in half an hour," Ben said. "I've flown on these planes a dozen times. There's nothing to worry about."

Bernice worried anyway.

As the plane taxied down the bumpy asphalt runway, Ben offered his hand, and she took it.

During the flight, Bernice hardly moved a muscle. She sat face forward with her hands tightly gripped on the arms of her seat, knuckles white with panic. Once she looked out the window at the ground below, seeing only distant miniature New Mexico landmarks. Quickly she closed her eyes, took a deep breath and resumed her rigid forward-facing position.

Only when the plane came to a halt at the Albuquerque airport gate did she relax enough to allow herself to breath normally.

"See," Ben said, "Nothin' to it."

Bernice felt like slapping him in the face.

After they stepped down out of the plane, Ben picked up their luggage, which sat on the runway. Inside the terminal, an attractive young American Indian woman wearing a conservative tan suit and high heels approached them.

"Ben? Mrs. Begay?" she said, hand extended.

"You must be Victoria," Ben replied as he shook her hand.

"Vicky. Call me Vicky."

The three paused in the midst of the hustle and bustle of the busy terminal.

"Bernice, this is Vicky Chino," Ben said hopefully. "The reporter I was telling you about."

Bernice sized the young woman up while Ben bit his lower lip.

"Chino?" Bernice said, finally. "You must be from one the Pueblos."

"Laguna Pueblo, as a matter of fact," she said proudly.

"And you're a reporter?"

"Yep–Albuquerque Journal. I'm one of the few professional native women journalists in the country."

"Well, don't that beat all."

Bernice laughed and shook the reporter's hand.

"You strike me as smart young lady," Bernice added. "I'm just an old woman. Why do you want to talk to me?"

The three began walking toward their ticket counter.

"My people were badly affected by the mining, too," Vicky answered.

"Then why do you need me? You probably already know the whole story."

"But it didn't happen directly to me, and you're the one talking to Congress. People will only understand this story if it comes from someone like you—someone who lived it."

She looked back at Ben who was following the ladies.

"And besides, Ben tells me you're the feistiest Navajo he knows."

Bernice chuckled and said, "Ben talks too much."

A little embarrassed, Ben pulled ahead of the women.

"I'll just go on up and get us checked in," he said.

"We're going get along just fine, Victoria," Bernice whispered to Vicky and smiled.

"Vicky," the young reporter corrected. "You can call me Vicky."

Bernice took Vicky's arm as they followed Ben to the check-in desk.

Once they got on the plane, Bernice and Vicky sat on a row with an empty seat between them. Ben sat in the row behind them.

"Now, Bernice, this flight won't be as noisy or bumpy as the first one," Ben said, leaning forward in his seat.

"I'll be fine, Ben."

"I just wanted you to know, so you won't worry."

"Relax, Ben. Read a magazine. I'll be fine. I have Vicky now."

The elder smiled at her new friend.

The flight attendant stopped and checked Bernice's seat and adjusted it forward to its upright and locked position.

"If you need anything, ma'am, just push the yellow call button," the flight attendant said and then moved on.

In another moment, the captain made the usual "flight attendants, prepare for departure" announcement. The engines revved up. Bernice clutched Vicky's arm with one hand and her medicine pouch with the other.

She began to sing a Navajo prayer under her breath.

"Close your eyes and think of something nice," Vicky suggested.

Bernice closed her eyes in concentration. Slowly a smile emerged on her face as an image formed in her mind. She saw a happy day more than thirty years ago when her husband, Frank, was in the sheep corral near their hogan. Frank was in his late thirties then, tall and quiet. In that moment, he was riding herd on their kids who were trying to round up the sheep and head them towards the corral. He laughed at his children's comical efforts. Bernice's smiled broadened.

"Well, we're up."

Vicky's words dissolved the image. Bernice opened her eyes and realized that they had taken off. She looked out the window then quickly turned away. Her hand instinctively reached out for her medicine bag.

"Why don't we get started so you can take your mind off the flight," Vicky offered, taking out her tape recorder and notebook computer. As she set things up, Bernice hailed a passing steward and requested a drink of water.

"My throat's kind of dry," the elder said nervously.

"Where shall we start?" Vicky asked.

"I don't know. Where should we start?"

"Anywhere is fine," Vicky replied. "Just to get you started talking. What was the beginning of it all?"

"Honey, never ask a Navajo to start at the beginning. Tribal tradition says I'd have to start with our creation stories, and that could take hours to tell."

She paused.

"My memory's not what it used to be, but I guess I could begin with the birth of my first son. That's easy for me to talk about."

"All right," Vicky said. She turned on her tape recorder and placed it near Bernice. The elderly woman closed her eyes and summoned up the memories of that day some fifty years earlier.

"He was born at sunrise on the first day of summer," Bernice recalled. Frank and I decided on the Navajo name 'Dawn Boy.' His English name was to be Mitchell. In the Dineh tradition, a few days after a child is born, the parents bury the dried umbilical cord in a special place near their home."

Bernice's story flowed from her mind to her lips and onto the tape.

Four days after Dawn Boy's birth, Bernice stepped out of their hogan carrying the newborn in her arms. At age 20, Bernice was a strikingly beautiful woman. Her husband, Frank, walked just behind her carrying an old shovel. Behind him was Bernice's grandfather, Joseph, a full blood Navajo of unknown age. He was there in his role as medicine man, to help the new parents properly bury Mitchell's umbilical cord. They walked toward a hill near their little homestead.

When they arrived at the hilltop overlooking the hogan, Joseph stood near the lone pinion tree that grew there. Wearing a purple bandanna around his head, a sign of his holy office, the medicine man surveyed the surroundings.

"Is this the place you have chosen to bury my great grandson's cord?" he asked.

"Yes, Grandfather," Bernice answered. "This is it."

"Good. Let's begin."

Joseph took a small leather pouch out of his shirt pocket. Bernice handed the baby to him as he handed her the pouch. The old man began to sing a Navajo prayer song for the baby. From

Bernice's own dress pocket, she took a cloth that had been wrapped around the shriveled umbilical cord.

Frank took a blue turquoise stone from his pocket and handed it to Bernice. Then he dug a small hole in the dirt at the base of the tree. Bernice put the umbilical cord and the turquoise stone inside the pouch and pulled the draw-string tight. Grandfather ended the song.

"We bury this child's cord in the ground today," he said in the Navajo language, "To strengthen his tie to the earth, our mother, and so that he may never forget this place, his home. May he always return to it and protect it."

Frank and Bernice knelt down near the hole while Bernice put the little pouch in the earth. As instructed by Joseph, Frank took a few pieces of tobacco from his pocket and put them in on top of the pouch as an offering.

Then, with their bare hands, Frank and Bernice pushed the dirt back into the hole until it was filled in. When they were done, Joseph put Mitchell back into his mother's arms, placed his hand on the baby's forehead and said another prayer.

"We ask a blessing from the Holy Ones on this child who represents the first born of the next generation of our people. May we choose wisely for him, and when the time comes, may he choose wisely for us."

Then Joseph smiled.

"Now let's go have some breakfast," he said. "I'm hungry."

They all laughed, and the two men headed down the hill. Bernice stayed back watching them, soaking up the moment, and admiring her son. She couldn't have foreseen how much their lives, and the lives of all Navajos, would change in the years to come.

When World War II broke out, many Navajos wanted to do their part to aid the war effort. Hundreds of young Navajo men joined the military and went off to fight against the great enemy across the seas. Many signed up to become code talkers for the Marines in the fight against Japan in the Pacific.

At home, many Indian people of all tribes collected scrap metal and bought war bonds when they could afford it to do their share. Native women even worked in little factories making medals and insignias and other items for the military.

One day, government men showed up at the Post Office and General Store in Farmington, New Mexico, a small town just off the reservation. One of Bernice's nephews, Lydell, was there and reported to the family what happened.

A dusty black Ford sedan pulled up in front of the store, and two men got out. Both men were wearing dark suits, which made them sweat in the hot sun.

They went into the store. Lydell couldn't go in because of the sign in the window that said NO DOGS OR INDIANS ALLOWED. That was a common sight in those days around the reservation—in fact, around many reservations.

Word had already spread that some bilagaanas—white men—were looking for a certain kind of yellow rock on Indian land. These two men came back out of the store drinking Coca Colas. They saw Lydell standing a few yards away with his dog. Further down the road was the sign marking the entrance to the Navajo Reservation.

"Hey kid!" one of the men yelled. "Do you speak English?"

"Yeah, sure," Lydell replied. "Do you speak Navajo?"

"Can you direct us to Lucky-Chooka?" the second man answered, ignoring the boy's remark.

"You mean Lukachukai, don't you?" pronouncing the word correctly.

"Whatever," the first man said. He looked at his partner. "The kid's a comedian."

"He should be on the radio," the other one said. Back to Lydell, he asked, "Where is this Lookychooky?"

"Follow the road to Shiprock and turn south. You can't miss it."

"Thanks, kid," the first man said. "Get yourself a Coke." He flipped a nickel to the boy, and the two men got into the car. Lydell looked down at the coin in his hand. It was a buffalo nickel, the kind with an Indian head on one side and a buffalo on the other.

As the two men drove off towards the reservation, Lydell thought about his chances of getting a Coke from the general store. He knew they weren't good, so he started walking back towards the trading post just across the reservation border line.

It had been Bernice's own uncle, Jake Begay, that showed the government men where to find a sample of the ore. It didn't take much to get Jake interested. A few dollar bills were flashed in his face, and he was convinced they were all going to be millionaires.

Jake was in his thirties then. He led those two men across the desert floor to a cave where he knew you could find the "yellow rock." Those men, it turned out, were geologists, and they immediately sent word of their find back to Washington.

Of course, the yellow rock wasn't really anything new. It had been known by Navajos for centuries and had been considered special medicine. It was only to be used in certain ways, for special things. The first time Bernice ever heard it called uranium was that day when Uncle Jake came to their home.

They all sat under the arbor in front of their hogan. Bernice, her brother Willy Begay, her husband Frank and a neighbor, Jim, listened to Jake. Baby Mitchell played in the dirt at their feet. Bernice had never seen Jake so excited as he sat there holding that little piece of yellow rock.

"They say there'll be plenty of jobs for all of us mining this uranium," Jake said. "And milling it, breaking it down so the military can use it."

Willy listened carefully.

"What for?" Willy asked.

"What do you mean, what for?" Jake responded.

"What are they going to use it for?"

"I don't know," Jake said. "The point is we'll all have good jobs with good wages, and we'll get a share of the profits with what they call royalties. Those geologists told me that Washington wants to get its hands on as much of this stuff as they can."

"What does Grandpa Joseph have to say about this, Jake?" Bernice asked. It all sounded a little *too* good to her.

"You know Joseph," Jake said. "He's suspicious of anything new. He didn't even want me showing them geologists where to find the stuff. He's always talking about the old ways. But this is now. We have something the white man wants and will pay for."

"It don't seem right somehow," Willy protested. "Grandpa Joseph's a wise man. Maybe the white man is trying to trick us again, telling us more of his lies."

"Look," Jake said, standing up. "I say we Indians either learn to live in the present or we'll all die trying to live in the past."

Bernice watched her husband take it all in. Up until then he hadn't said much of anything one way or the other. He walked away from the others a few steps and looked up at the mountains. Everyone fell silent, waiting for his input. In a moment, Frank turned back to the group.

"Maybe Jake's right," Frank said at last. Jake smiled at these words. "Maybe this is our chance to catch up with the times."

"That's right," Jake said, egging him on.

"You know, maybe we can really become more like other Americans," Frank went on.

Jim, an older man, leaned in to speak.

"But our ancestors fought against the white man's army," he said.

"And lost," Frank reminded him. "Now we are fighting with the white man's army against Hitler and the Japanese."

"As part of Indian treaty agreements," Jake chimed in. "Times are different now for the Indian."

"So, if the government in Washington needs this uranium," Frank said.

"They're drooling for it," Jake interrupted.

"And they're willing to pay us to dig it out, then I say why not?"

"As a woman in those days, it wasn't my place to speak out," the elder Bernice told Vicky, who was enthralled by what she heard. "I just listened, but I certainly didn't like the sound of what I heard. I felt that what was being decided by the men under our arbor that evening would change our lives forever. I just didn't know how much."

Bernice continued her story.

"Well, the government and the mining company moved in, and by the early 1950s, uranium mining had become a fact of life on the Navajo reservation. A company called Kurt-Mackie had built one of their mines across the mountains from our place, and what had been a peaceful valley became a noisy, dusty eyesore."

Frank got a job in that mine, of course. Every day, miners with wheelbarrows would go in and out of a large hole that had been blasted in the side of the mountain. Mining carts loaded with rock would come out of the mine and head downhill to trucks that waited at the bottom.

Whole families of non-Indian mine employees moved into little trailers that had been erected by the mining companies so that engineers, managers and bureaucrats could oversee the operations.

Sometimes Frank heard them talking to one another about their situation. One day he passed a couple of them as they were just about to inspect the mine.

"I can't take much more of this desert life," the one called Cal said.

"But if we keep up this level of production, we'll be a cinch for promotion," his co-worker, Bill, replied.

"I don't care about promotions, any more," Cal protested. "Living out here in the middle of nowhere, eating dust all day… It's not what I had in mind when I signed on with the company. And you should hear my wife."

Bill tried to remain positive.

"Believe me, the company's happy, and they're going to take care of us," he countered.

"I'm just glad we don't have to go into the mines like those dumb Indians do. Poor bastards."

"Dumb Indians. That's what Frank heard him say," Bernice told Vicky. "Frank worked in those mines for twenty years—without protection, without any warning of the danger."

As a matter of fact, he worked side-by-side with other Navajo men, chipping out the yellow rock, day in and day out, using antiquated equipment. The dust inside the mines was thick and choking at times. The miners had to cover their faces with neckerchiefs. It was their only safety gear. They loaded the rock into carts, which brought the ore out of the mountain. Then they loaded it onto big trucks that took the rock to milling operations a few miles away.

At five o'clock every day, the whistle blew, and Frank trudged out of the mine, a weary and bent man. One of the men who lived near Frank had a pickup truck, and he would take several of the Navajos to and from the mine each day.

At the end of every workday, the men, their clothes and their boots were covered with yellow dust. It was a strange sort of dust and no matter how much brushing you did, it just wouldn't get off of you.

Most nights Frank got home after sunset. While the engineers and white-collar workers walked a few feet to their neat little pre-fabricated homes, to their neat little suburban wives, the Indian men, bone tired and hungry, were riding miles and miles through the dark to reach their families.

Bernice believed that what was going on must have bothered at least some of those mining company men. They weren't stupid. They couldn't all have believed the government propaganda. Some of the official literature that Kurt-Makie published about the mining said that America was in a race against Communism. It said that everyone who worked for the company was proud to do their part to defeat the Red Menace.

No mention was ever made about health risks to the miners. No mention was ever made that the Indian miners were considered expendable. All that came out later—much later.

So, Frank would get out of the back of his friend's truck in front of their house every work night and stumble toward the door. The kids always dropped whatever they were doing and ran to greet him as he entered the house. And Frank, dusty and tired though he was, would laugh with them as the children all talked at once. He would hang up his jacket on a hook near the door, and they would hug him and hang on him.

The yellow dust from Frank's clothes would get on their hands, clothes and bodies. The baby would play with his father's dusty boots after he took them off. By this time, Mitchell was thirteen and always busy doing his homework at the kitchen table. Night after night, she remembered, the kids went off to clean up and get ready for supper to give Frank some breathing room.

"I swear, Frank, you look older and tireder every day," Bernice would say. "You need to take some time off from that mine."

"And do what?" he would answer. "If I took any time off, I'd never get back on with them. You know that. There's men out there waiting in line for these jobs."

"But you're so exhausted. And—"

"And what?"

"And nothing. It's your decision."

"It's my job, Bernice. It's how I keep this family going."

"I just worry—about your health."

"Well, that's your problem, isn't it?"

"It's gonna be my problem if you get hurt or killed. Then how am I supposed to take care of these kids?"

"Don't worry, Bernice," Frank would say softly. "Everything's going to be all right."

Conversations always went that way, always ended the same way. Bernice didn't want to be a nag.

But one night, Frank gave her some disturbing news.

"Speaking of jobs, I hear your brother Willy got on at the processing mill over in Shiprock," Frank said.

"At the Kurt-Mackie plant?"

"Yep. I bet he's happy. All those kids he's got to feed."

Bernice wasn't happy, though, not at all. But once again, she kept it to herself, deciding it was time to speak seriously to her Grandfather.

A few days later, she went to see Grandfather Joseph who lived in Canyon de Chelly. They walked together for a long time along the river that ran down the length of the canyon floor. Even though he was well over sixty years old then, he was still full of the spirit of the old ways.

"Willy is a grown man," Joseph said. "He must take care of himself and his family the best way he can."

"But he's working for the company, Grandpa," Bernice protested, "with uranium at the mill over in Shiprock."

"So you said," Joseph replied.

"I'm worried about taking the yellow rock out of the earth this way."

"So am I."

"Washington and the mining company say there's no danger, but I don't think they're telling us everything. Sometimes we Navajos are so gullible."

"Well, Bernice—," Joseph tried to answer.

"I mean," she interrupted. "They offer us a few jobs, and we grab at it without thinking. And what about the yellow rock? It's always had special meaning to our people."

"That's true. We've used the yellow rock in small quantities for jewelry and ceremony for as long as anyone can remember. Its glow is powerful, but dangerous."

Joseph stopped walking and looked at his granddaughter.

"You know many of our ways are kept secret, particularly from the white man," he said. "He has a way of twisting things. He uses knowledge in the wrong way sometimes. The medicine men have been meeting, and we know now that we must speak out to share some of our sacred knowledge."

"What do you mean, Grandpa?"

"An ancient warning has been passed down to medicine men for generations. It tells of a sleeping giant, a monster that lies deep within the mountain. We have been told that the monster is never to be awakened or it will rise up and strike us with its poisonous tongue. We believe this monster is the yellow rock, the uranium."

Bernice was quiet for a moment.

"How can we warn our people? You know they won't listen. They want these jobs. People need the money. Your own son won't listen."

"It's true, our warnings do fall on deaf ears. Our younger generation has been seduced by the bilagáana's money. I fear that Father Sky and Mother Earth will stop protecting our people if we go on this way."

"That's beyond my understanding, but I'm worried about Frank and Willy and the rest of my family."

"I know," Joseph said. "I'm holding a Native American Church meeting during the 4th of July weekend. Come to the ceremony and bring Frank and Willy. We'll pray for them. Maybe they will see a vision that will lead them."

"Okay, I'll try, but you know they probably won't come. They've turned their backs on all Native ways, and Frank's suspicious about the peyote medicine."

"Many Navajos have left our ancient traditions to embrace the white man's doctors and religion. Others have replaced them only with alcohol, to numb the pain."

"They only harm themselves and their children," Bernice said.

"I can't blame them too much, really," Joseph replied. "The white man has succeeded in making us feel like second-class citizens. And sometimes our medicine just can't fight against his problems and diseases. But you wait patiently, Granddaughter, they'll come back. One day our people will be suffering and they'll come back. I know it."

At that moment, as if to validate Joseph's words, a hawk screeched from overhead. Bernice looked up to see him circling above them near the canyon's rim. Eagles and hawks were the messengers of the People, connecting them to Creator. Bernice hoped her grandfather was right, for the sake of their people.

"Now, long before I had ever met Ben Benally, he was involved in the struggle to halt the mining," the elder Bernice said to Vicky as they soared high above the ground. "As a tribal councilman, Ben tried to get the tribal council to take a stand against it. But others on the council were either in favor of the mining or indifferent to the issue."

She continued her story by telling of Roy Gorman, a successful Navajo businessman who had introduced a council resolution in *support* of the mining.

"We have all the evidence we need to pass this resolution," Gorman told his fellow councilmen.

"The government is using our people as guinea pigs," Ben, who served on the council at that time, replied. "To them, we're expendable—just a bunch of worthless Indians. If anything, we should be passing a resolution banning uranium mining on the reservation, not supporting it."

"I have here a copy of a letter from the United States Geological Survey, dated March 11, 1949, to the Office of Indian Affairs," Gorman countered. "It states, and I quote– 'With regard to the dangers of radioactivity, it is the consensus of opinion that there is practically none under the conditions existing in any of the mines on the Indian Reservation.'"

"That statement is nothing but speculation," Ben protested. "They haven't even done any tests or carried out medical exams on uranium miners."

"Mr. Chairman," Gorman said, turning toward the front podium. "This debate has wasted too much time already. I move that we put the resolution supporting uranium mining to a vote."

"We're being railroaded here!" Ben exclaimed. "We need facts."

"If Councilman Benally can't accept the word of the United States Government—"

"Councilman Gorman," the tribal council chairman interrupted. "I think Councilman Benally has a good point. One unsubstantiated letter from a geologist to the Indian Office is not enough to go on. I'm going to postpone any vote until more detailed information is available."

The Chairman smacked the table with his gavel over Gorman's protests, and moved on. They didn't endorse the mining, but neither did they do anything to stop it. Gutless wonders, all of them, to Bernice's way of thinking.

But one day, something unusual happened at the mine where Frank worked. As he showed up for work that morning, Frank saw a big mobile van parked at the mine's entrance. The mine foreman approached Frank and pulled him aside.

"Frank, the health department is doing some tests on uranium miners," the Foreman said. "Just a formality really, more government red tape."

Frank just listened, waiting for the rest of it.

"You're one of the miners they picked to be tested," the foreman continued. Frank didn't like the sound of it at all, and his face showed it.

"It's really no big deal," the foreman said, trying to be convincing. "It'll only take a few minutes." He motioned toward the mobile lab.

After hesitating a moment, Frank went inside where he found several people in lab coats surrounded by a lot of unfamiliar medical equipment.

"They said you wanted to make some tests on me," Frank told a woman standing nearby.

"Yes," she said thrusting a clipboard at him. "You'll need to fill these forms out first."

Frank tried to say something, but the woman continued.

"It's just a routine medical exam, you understand. For the government's records. Sit over there."

She pointed to a waiting area where a few other miners are already sitting, mostly staring at their forms.

Frank went and sat with the others. He stared at his form, unable to read a word of English. Eventually the woman figured out the miners' dilemma. None of them could read English. So, one-by-one, she asked the questions on the form and filled them out on the miner's behalf.

It was on the 4th of July that Bernice heard about the tests from Frank. The Begays had joined several other Navajo families for a holiday picnic. The girls played with cornhusk dolls under a big shade tree in the park while the women set food out on the tables for everyone to share. The men and boys played baseball nearby. When everything was ready, Bernice called the men to come eat.

"I wish Mitchell was here," she said to the other women there. "I sure do miss that boy. He just got grown up good, and Uncle Sam whisked him off to fight in Korea."

"My son Billy is coming back next month for a little leave," her friend, Winnie, said. "Says he'll be able to stay home for a few days before reporting to his final tour of duty. I wish they'd transfer him to a post here in the States."

"Will you have a Blessing Way for him while he's here?" Alma Jean, another of the women, asked.

"If his father can get some time off from the mine," Winnie replied. "It seems like he's working longer and longer hours these days. And he comes home more tired and sick feeling than I've ever seen him."

"The same with Frank," Bernice said. "He's been coming home coughing and complaining of chest pains. I'm trying to get him and Willy to go to my grandpa's Native American Church meeting tonight to get help."

Frank, Willy and the other men arrived at the table in time to overhear Bernice's remark.

"What, and sit around a tipi all night, singing some old songs and eating that bitter tasting root?" Frank complained. "I'd rather drink turpentine."

"It's for your own good," Bernice, told him, probably for the tenth time. "It would help you heal the damage the mine's been doing to your body."

"I told you if there was any danger, the company would do something about it."

"The company? What does the company care about you? You're just another spare part to them."

"No. I'm a valuable asset to them. They said so. Why, they had me take some tests just the other day, to make sure I was okay."

"Tests? What kind of tests? You never said anything about any tests."

Bernice's internal warning signal was flashing loud and clear in her mind.

"It was just a physical exam," Frank replied, trying to downplay its importance. "You know, government employees looking for something to do. They said it was routine."

"Frank, why would they be testing you or examining you if they didn't think something might be wrong? It costs money to run tests."

Frank just looked at his wife disapprovingly and began serving himself a plate of food.

"That's what that Atomic Energy Commission is for," Winnie's husband, Chester, said. "To watch out for the miners and the millers. And to make sure the companies are operating properly. I think it's best to leave these things up to people who know something about it, don't you?"

"I just don't see any reason to trust the mining companies or the government," Bernice snapped. "Men are getting sick in those mines, and no one is doing anything about it."

"C'mon, Bernice," Frank said finally. "Don't spoil our holiday. Let's just have a good time, okay?"

He smiled at her, and she calmed down.

"All right. I do get wound up, don't I?"

For the kid's sake, she shook it off.

"Okay, who wants fry bread and mutton stew?"

As the family began to dig in to the feast, Bernice gave Frank a concerned, reprimanding look. He smiled a smile of reconciliation back at her.

That night, Grandpa Joseph held his Native American Church ceremony. As everyone prepared, Bernice watched to see if Frank and Willy would come. Joseph gave the signal and the two dozen Navajos who'd gathered for the meeting filed into the ceremonial tipi that stood next to his hogan. Bernice held back and watched the others.

Lit by golden colored firelight from within, the tipi appeared ghostly. Bernice could see the silhouettes of the people moving around the fire looking for places to sit. The flames made their shadows dance on the tipi's canvas walls.

In a moment, the first song, the welcoming song of the ceremony, began. Bernice scanned the horizon once more looking for signs of her husband or brother. Seeing neither, she gave up and took her place in the circle.

Just as Joseph was about to close the tipi flap, Willy slipped in. He sat down quietly by the entrance and waved to his sister. Her heart leapt within her and she smiled at him. His presence gave her the faintest glimmer of hope.

"But nothing really changed," Bernice remembered, taking a drink of the water the stewardess had brought. "Ten years went by and nothing changed. Navajo men continued to work in the mines and the mills, and Navajo men continued to get sicker and sicker."

Looking out at the passing billowy clouds, Bernice thought back to the early 1960s. Vicky added her own comments.

"I've done some research into the hearings that began in 1963," she said. "That year, some attention began to be paid to the problem of uranium mining in several parts of the country. Congress began to hear rumors and accusations that all was not right in the mines. Finally, the Senate convened a hearing to investigate the overall safety of uranium mining.

"A man named Frederick Wurtz first brought the Senate's attention to the unreported dangers of uranium mining. He presented a medical report that had been hidden for ten years. which revealed the levels of radiation that exist in the mines and the hazards these levels represent to uranium miners. This report also made suggestions on ways to decrease the levels of radiation exposure.

"When the Senate committee members asked why they hadn't seen that evidence before, Wurtz told them, 'Because the Atomic Energy Commission and the uranium mining companies didn't want you to hear about it.'

"That's a serious accusation, Mr. Wurtz. Just what do these medical studies reveal?"

Bernice had found out much later that Washington had run tests, held hearings, and done studies until they were blue in the face, but none of it ever amounted to much. They never told the Indian miners anything about it, and meanwhile, the mining companies and the federal government kept getting what they wanted: cheap labor and cheap uranium."

Bernice continued her story.

"So, the miners kept digging, and the miners began dying," she said.

It was that same year that death first struck close to home, and two new allies came into Bernice's life.

Frank's cousin, Yas, was the first to be taken from the Begay family by the mine, leaving a widow and five kids behind without any means of support.

It was at the funeral that Yas's widow, Sarah, began to realize the reality of her situation. The Navajo preacher who officiated the ceremony closed his bible and offered his final condolences. The few relatives and friends in attendance filed past Sarah hugging her or shaking her hand. Frank and Bernice lingered behind with her at the gravesite.

As the gravediggers began shoveling the dirt in on top of the cheap casket, she burst into tears.

"He was a good man," she sobbed. "I don't know why this had to happen to him."

Frank put his arm around her shoulder and led her away from the sorrowful scene and towards their truck.

"He never hurt nobody," she continued. "All he did was work hard and try to make a good life for us."

"We'll all miss him, Sarah," Frank said.

"How am I going to feed and clothe five kids?"

"You know, whatever you and the kids need, Frank and I…" Bernice offered.

"You have your own. I couldn't."

"Of course you can, Sarah," Frank assured her. "Yas was my cousin. That's what families are for."

"I can help you cook or do the laundry, if you want," Bernice told her.

Just as they reached the truck, two men approached, one an Indian, the other, a blond-haired white man in his thirties.

The Indian said, "Mrs. Begay, I'm Ben Benally, tribal council representative for--"

"I recognize you from all those campaign posters you put up," Sarah interrupted.

"I want to tell you how sorry I am for your loss," Benally said.

"I didn't vote for you," Sarah informed him.

"That doesn't matter. I was elected to represent everybody in this district, no matter who they voted for. Right now I'm trying to get a new tribal program started that would help the widows of Navajo miners like yourself."

He turned to the white man who was with him.

"And this is Doctor Mark Stewart. He works for the Indian Health Service. He's trying to put together a medical report on mining hazards to show to the tribal council. But we need your help."

"I don't see how I could help," Sarah said.

"What's in this for you, Mr. Benally?" Bernice butted in. "That's the real question. All I've ever seen you tribal politicians do is get yourselves elected so you can draw a salary from the tribal treasury and help yourself to special favors from the tribal president."

Frank winced at his wife's bold statement. "You'll have to excuse my wife," he said. "She sometimes doesn't think before speaking her mind."

"I understand how you feel," Dr. Stewart assured her. "I've seen more than my share of corruption in Indian affairs. But, really, Ben and I just want to help."

"I took an oath to serve my people," Ben said as Sarah, overcome with grief, rushed away in tears. She climbed into Frank's truck. Bernice gave the men one last nasty look and followed Sarah to comfort her.

"Mr. Benally, we don't want to do anything that would jeopardize our jobs," Frank said. "This really isn't a good time to be talking about the mines. Now I doubt that Sarah's going to be interested, but why don't you give it a little time and then come around to talk to her. She'll be in a much better frame of mind in a couple of weeks."

"Sure, sure, that'll be best," Ben said as Frank walked towards his truck.

As they drove away from the cemetery, Bernice watched the tribal councilman and the doctor return to their car. There was something about those two that stuck in her mind.

Unfortunately, it wasn't long before Bernice's worst fears began to be realized within her own household, and events out of her control steered her back to Dr. Stewart.

It was a Sunday afternoon. Frank had been coughing and complaining of chest pains for a couple of weeks. As Bernice was putting away the dishes from Sunday dinner, Frank staggered into the kitchen holding a blood-spattered rag in his hands. Bernice screamed as a ceramic plate fell from her hands, shattering into jagged fragments.

Instructing Mitchell to watch the other children, Bernice stuffed Frank into the passenger seat of their pickup, and they sped off towards Shiprock and the nearest hospital. Frank continued to cough little spots of blood into a fresh rag all the way there.

An hour later, she brought the truck to a screeching halt in front of the emergency entrance of the Shiprock Indian Hospital. Bernice jumped out of the truck, ran around to the passenger side and helped Frank out. Almost dragging him, Bernice got Frank into the hospital.

Once inside, Bernice pulled her husband towards the nurse's station. Frank continued to cough, and now leaned on Bernice for support. Hospital personnel moved rapidly back and forth focused on their own immediate tasks, like bees in a hive. Frantically, Bernice tried to get someone's attention.

"My husband is coughing up blood," she said aloud to no one in particular. "He needs to see a doctor fast."

"You'll have to wait your turn, dear," an Anglo nurse behind the check-in desk said. "There's quite a few emergencies ahead of you."

She motioned toward the waiting room, which Bernice saw was full of Indians waiting to be helped.

"This can't wait," Bernice replied insistently, dragging Frank closer to the desk. "He could die if someone doesn't--. Is a Dr. Mark Stewart here?"

"Dr. Stewart is a very busy man and can't--"

Just then Dr. Stewart entered the waiting room. He saw Bernice, then Frank holding the bloody rag.

"Nurse, we've got to get this man into ICU, stat!" he snapped.

"But, doctor--" the nurse protested.

"Move it now!" he demanded.

Several nurses and other attendants jumped to help. They lifted Frank up on to a gurney and raced him to a vacant emergency room. One of the nurses closed the curtain around them forcing Bernice to wait outside as they begin to work on Frank.

Meanwhile another nurse approached Bernice and asked her for her Indian ID card. She pulled the little pink card out of her pocket and handed it over. The nurse thrust a clipboard into Bernice's hands.

"Fill this out while I make a copy of your ID card," she said, and abruptly left the waiting area. Bernice sat down to fill out the usual government hospital paperwork.

Half an hour later, Dr. Stewart approached Bernice. He pulled up a seat next to her.

"Mrs. Begay, your husband is going to be all right."

A sigh of relief escaped from Bernice.

"He's resting now," the doctor continued. "The medication I gave him will make him sleep for awhile."

"You don't know how worried I was," Bernice admitted, a quiver in her voice.

"Your husband's a uranium miner, isn't he, like his cousin Yas was?"

"That's right," Bernice replied. "You were at his funeral. Tell me again why you were there."

"I've been sort of tracking the health of the miners," he replied. "And I've been seeing it a lot men coughing up blood lately. An alarming number of uranium miners, and a few of the millers, have come in with the same symptoms."

"I knew it," Bernice said, gazing out the waiting room window. "It's the yellow rock."

"Excuse me?"

"I knew this uranium business was bad for us," she said, turning back to the doctor. "Its the monster in the mountain."

"I really don't follow," said the confused doctor.

"That's what my father called it—the monster in the mountain."

She paused to think.

"You and Ben Benally are trying to do something about this, aren't you?"

"Well, it's nothing official, you understand, but we've got to start somewhere."

"What can I do?" Bernice asked immediately. "I'll do whatever needs to be done. I don't want to lose my husband."

"Well, the first thing you can do is help me with a study I'm conducting about the negative effects that the mining is having on the workers' health. Just answer a few questions about Frank's work and his health."

"I'll answer your questions, doctor, but what can I really do to help?" Bernice asked sharply.

"You can come to a meeting at the Red Rock Chapter House that Councilman Benally and I are holding. He's trying to get the Navajo tribal council to do something about this problem, but he's just one man, and he's up against some powerful interests."

"Frank doesn't like me to meddle in affairs outside the home," Bernice said almost in a whisper. "You know how some of these Indian men are."

"Mrs. Begay, if you don't get your husband out of the mine, it'll probably kill him—sooner or later."

"All right, I'll be there. Maybe I can get some of the other wives to come and listen. It can't hurt to listen."

"Good," the doctor said as he stood.

"And if Frank doesn't like it," Bernice mused to herself, "well, we'll cross that bridge when we come to it."

Two weeks later, the Red Rock Chapter House was buzzing with activity and chatter. Bernice arrived at the one-story, weathered frame building just as the meeting was beginning. The audience was made up primarily of Navajo women who sat in a collection of mismatched folding chairs. The few men in attendance hung around in the back of the room. Bernice took a seat near the front.

She noticed Dr. Stewart and Councilman Benally sitting at the front to one side waiting for their turn to speak. The chapter president, a heavyset Navajo man in his fifties, made a few announcements from a podium in front of the room. Bernice thought the man would never finish, as he went on and on about fixing up the chapter house and next month's board meeting.

Finally, he got to the important business at hand.

"Well, now I'll bring up our two guests tonight who want to talk to you about the situation with the uranium miners and millers," he said at last. "Tribal Councilman Ben Benally and Dr. Mark Stewart of the Indian Health Service."

As the president sat down, the councilman and the doctor rose from their seats and went to the podium.

"Most of you know who I am," Ben began. "But you may not know Dr. Mark Stewart from the Indian Health Service. He's fairly new to Navajo country, but if you go to the Shiprock hospital, you've probably seen him there. Anyhow, we've come here tonight to ask for your help. I'll let the doc explain."

He turned to Dr. Stewart who moved to the podium.

"There's a terrible sickness striking down the men who work in the uranium mines," the doctor said. "And it's beginning to show up in the mill workers, too. I know many of you have already seen it in your own homes. Your men are coughing up blood and complaining of pains in their chests."

A general buzz of Navajo chatter began in the room as the women talked among themselves, agreeing that they'd seen this happen.

"What's causing it is hard to translate into Navajo," Dr. Stewart continued, "but the nearest thing that Ben could come up with is something that means "dangerous smoke that you breathe in." He looked at Ben.

Ben repeated the phrase in Navajo for everyone to hear.

"It comes from uranium dust," the doctor resumed. "Yellow dust that contains radiation, which can cause cancer of the lungs if you breathe it."

One woman from the audience spoke out. "If you know this is happening, why doesn't the tribal council or the Indian Health Service do something about it?"

"That's a fair question," Ben replied. "I've presented this problem to the full council, but they dismissed it. They say there is no official, published medical study that shows that uranium causes heath problems, and I can't argue that. They say it's the federal government's responsibility to look into it, but I disagree. All I know is that our Navajo people have been getting sick, and now they're starting to die from it. So, I'm willing to do whatever it takes to make it right."

More chatter arose in the room.

"And the I.H.S. won't take any action either without some sort of medical proof," Dr. Stewart added. "You know from your own experience of waiting endlessly in clinic waiting rooms that they're under-funded and under staffed. Something has to be done outside official channels, at least in the beginning."

"Why are you telling us this?" Bernice stood to ask. "We are powerless to do anything. The tribal council won't listen to us. The federal government won't listen to us. Even most of our own husbands won't listen to us."

Other women in the room voiced their agreement.

"We're going to have to build a case, with hard facts, statistics, medical reports, and work records, to prove that there's a link between the mines and the deaths," Ben answered. "Nobody's going to do it for us, not the tribal council, not the federal government. To get started on this, I'll be visiting the mines and documenting the working conditions. What you ladies can do is collect information about when your husbands began working in the mines and at what locations."

The doctor took a sip of water before he continued the explanation.

"If there are any medical records at the Indian Hospital on your husbands or brothers, get them. You have a right to see them and have copies of them. It'll be a long process, but nothing's going to happen if we don't get started now."

Just then the chapter president abruptly stood up.

"I'm sorry to interrupt, but I'm afraid we're out of time," he said. "There are refreshments in the back of the room. If any of you want to talk more to these gentlemen, make it quick because we'll be closing the building in about half an hour."

The meeting broke up and small groups of people began standing around talking. Bernice stood with a small circle of women talking to Ben. She noticed that a white man she'd never seen before was making notes in a notepad in the back of the room. In a few minutes, he put the notepad in his coat pocket, got up and left.

"One of the things we'll need is a place to operate out of," Ben said to the circle of women. "My office has too many ears."

"I don't know if this'll help," one of the women in the group said, "but I've got an empty trailer house over by the trading post that you're welcome to use for awhile. My brother was living there, but he went down to Gallup to go to work."

"Sounds perfect," Ben replied enthusiastically, and plans for the project began to take shape that very night.

It wasn't long before the small group of volunteer workers transformed the trailer into their headquarters. Ben was able to get some old tribal office furniture and equipment donated for their use, though he had been vague when asked to explain what the project was. And Dr. Stewart was able to get surplus I.H.S. materials, originally destined for a government warehouse, delivered to the site.

But the going was slow. The group worked out of that trailer for an agonizing five years before they had enough evidence to make anyone take notice. During that time, Bernice learned a lot about uranium and radioactivity. They took pictures of the mines and the sick workers. They interviewed miners and reviewed medical records. Dr. Stewart collected medical journals and the results from other uranium-related studies around the world. They met with state and federal officials, as well as any mining company executives who would give them the time.

All the while, someone was monitoring their progress. Two men in an old black Buick seemed to show up on the fringes of their activities regularly. From time to time, they could be seen parked a short distance from the trailer. Bernice noticed them. Others in the group noticed them. But no one wanted to mention it, as though to speak of them might bring on an unwanted confrontation. So, everyone just kept working and hoping and praying.

It was during this period, in the winter of the year, that Bernice lost her grandfather. He had been her link to the old ways, her guidepost in the storm of modern life. For awhile after his passing, she felt like she'd been set out in the desert on a cloudy, moonless night with no visible landmarks to provide bearings.

It was Yas's widow, Sarah, who had reminded Bernice of her own inner guidance, which had been prompting her for years. Bernice began to take time to look within herself, and, to her amazement, she found the spirit of Joseph waiting there, along with other of her ancestors, ready to lead her into the uncertain future.

But the work dragged on. Bernice was convinced that the politicians in Washington didn't seem to think the problems of a few Navajo miners was worth much of their time. But Ben never gave up. He kept going to Washington year after year, trying to find a sympathetic ear. He would talk to anyone who would listen.

By 1973, the documents and records of what came to be known as the "Yellow Rock" uranium project had become a stack of papers six inches thick. The little group of volunteers had begun putting copies of the documents inside yellow file folders to emphasize their cause. Most of the time, they referred to the documents simply as the "Uranium Files."

That year Ben presented an updated set of the Uranium Files to Arizona Congressman Henry Baca in his Washington, D.C. office.

"Well, I can say one thing for you, Ben, you sure are persistent," Congressman Baca said during one visit. "What is this, the fifth trip you've made up here in as many years?"

"And you're the third congressman who has tried to help us get this bill passed," Ben reminded him. "But hey, who's counting? I can't quit until we get results. There are too many people back on the rez depending on me."

"I am impressed with your group's presentation and your documentation. These personal interviews with miners and widows are irrefutable evidence. I'll have a staffer get these into the background packets and ready for the full committee. I'm sure we can get this bill passed in Congress this time. We owe it to these people to compensate them in some way for their sacrifices and their suffering."

But, as always, Bernice was skeptical. In spite of all their hard work, nothing substantial had ever been done by any outside agency, and she expected that nothing ever would.

While Ben was in Washington, Bernice got word that her brother, Willy, was in an accident at the Shiprock milling plant. It turned out that the old ore truck the company had provided for him to drive on the job had no emergency brake.

Willy's job was to drive an old, beat-up dump truck up a hill to a large pile of rocks at the edge of the plant several times a day. He would stop the truck and quickly jump out of the cab holding two big blocks of wood. He then had to run around to the front of the truck and stuffed one block in front of one of the truck's tires, the other, behind the tire.

He'd step back into the cab and pull a lever that began dumping the truck's load. The day of the accident, the load had shifted unexpectedly, causing the truck to lurch forward. Willy jumped down out of the cab and raced to the front of the truck trying to secure the wooden block. As he reached the front of the truck, he tripped, falling right in the truck's path as it rolled down the hill. He screamed in agony.

By the time Bernice found out about the accident, Willy was already in the hospital, bandaged up and heavily sedated. Dr. Stewart had been the one to work on him.

After a few minutes at Willy's bedside, Bernice stepped out in the hall to speak to the doctor.

"His ribs are crushed and one of his legs is paralyzed," he said quietly. "I'm sorry, but I'm afraid he'll never be able to work, or possibly walk, again."

That news caused something to break inside Bernice. She stormed out of the hospital and marched across the parking lot. Dr. Stewart followed, trying to keep up with her. She didn't stop until she'd reached her truck. Then she turned to face the doctor.

"We've got to do something, and we've got to do it now," Bernice proclaimed, almost in tears. "My brother's laying in there all crippled up. My husband's life is being drained away, and now my oldest boy, Mitchell, is trying to get a job at the mine. I can't wait until Ben gets some law passed in Washington. We've got to do something here in Navajo country, now."

She turned away to conceal her tears.

"Bernice, what's going on in that head of yours?" he asked, resisting the temptation to put his arms around her to comfort her. He knew that no self-respecting, married Navajo woman would allow that. She wiped her eyes.

"This reminds me of an important story my grandfather used to tell of a dark time in our history. He said that a hundred years ago the army sent Kit Carson and his men to hunt us Navajos down, round us up and move us off our lands. We resisted, so he burned our cornfields. We hid out in Canyon de Chelly where we almost starved to death. Finally, he and his army succeeded. They rounded us up and marched us off on the Longest Walk to a concentration camp in the desert of eastern New Mexico. There, his men beat us and starved us some more."

Bernice removed her truck keys from her pocket before continuing.

"That's the way it's always been between Washington and us Indians," she continued. "They ignore us until they want something from us--our land, our water, our minerals. Then they lie, cheat and steal to get it. That's why some of our people call the capitol in Washington the House Made of Lies."

Bernice opened her truck door but paused before getting in.

"And now this, this yellow rock. They pound us down until they get what they want. They wanted our uranium and they took it. But they had to be sneaky about it because the American public might not like it. But what the public don't know won't hurt 'em, right? Well this is one Indian that ain't gonna roll over and play dead."

She climbed into the truck, closed the door and started the engine.

"All right, if you think you're ready for this, we'll go public," the doctor said. "I've got a contact at the Albuquerque newspaper. I'll get a copy of our uranium files to him. We'll start there and build up. It'll bring some heat, and maybe some trouble for you, but what the hell. Right?"

Bernice put the truck in gear and studied the doctor for a moment. He could see that something had set in her mind once and for all.

"I've been quiet and I've been a good Navajo wife, but now its time to take a stand, and make some noise," she said without smiling. "But the worst that can happen to me is that I'll be ostracized from my community for speaking out. You--, you could lose your job. The question, Dr. Mark Stewart, is are *you* ready for this?"

Without waiting for a reply, Bernice let out the truck's clutch and drove away. Dr. Stewart watched after her as she sped out of the parking lot and off down the road. He knew she had asked the right question of him. Was he ready? He knew it was one of those times in life where you were tested, a moment for which everything that had gone before was but a preparation.

He nodded his head. "Yes," he said to himself, "I am ready."

It wasn't long before Frank finally had to retire from the mine. The good doctor said he had lung cancer--untreatable, lung cancer. Frank's condition was deteriorating rapidly, and soon he was spending most of his time in bed. Bernice gave him medicine three times a day.

"It's hard for me to admit it, Bernice, but you were right," Frank said unexpectedly one night after taking his medication."

"Don't talk now," she replied tenderly. "Save your strength."

"No, I have to say it. I was wrong. We all were wrong, and look at the damage it has done. Do you think it'll ever be right again?"

"If I have anything to do with it, it will. But you rest. We'll talk about it tomorrow."

She pulled the covers up over him and turned out the light.

"If I have anything to do with it, it will be right again," she repeated in the dark.

On August 17, 1973, the story broke. The front-page headline of the Albuquerque Tribune announced: NAVAJOS WHO MINED URANIUM DYING FROM CANCER.

It created quite a stir in high places, one of which was the Southwest regional headquarters of uranium mining giant Kurt-Mackie.

In fact, the newspaper article set off a chain reaction within the "good ol' boy" network that linked politicians to vested business interests.

A phone in the Albuquerque Kurt-Mackie was picked up and dialed. On the other end, the publisher of the Albuquerque Tribune answered the call.

"Curtis, how have you been?" the voice from Kurt-Mackie said. "This is John Deacons."

He paused, waiting for a signal of recognition.

"John," the publisher replied, recognizing the head of the Kurt-Mackie plant and one of the newspaper's strongest supporters. "It's been a long time."

"It has, hasn't it," Deacons replied. "That's why I called. I was just thinking, why don't we do lunch next week? We can catch up on personal business."

"That sounds marvelous," the publisher answered.

"Great," Deacons said as he picked up the newspaper with the uranium mining headline.

"Listen, while I've got you on the phone," he said. "The reporter who did the story on the Navajo miners--you know he didn't come to us to verify any of those facts or statistics."

"Oh, really," Curtis replied.

"That story is filled with mostly unsubstantiated claims," Deacons continued. "I think your man acted a little irresponsibly. I don't have to tell you how much trouble your paper could get into for not telling both sides of the story."

"I talked with the reporter myself, John, and he's confident in the story's facts."

"Curtis, there is no universally accepted evidence linking cancer to uranium mining. Did anyone ever check to see how many cigarettes those miners smoked?"

"John, Tyler is one of our most respect reporters. He won a Pulitzer Prize, for God's sake. I don't think he--"

"Look, we don't want to drag your newspaper into any kind of long drawn out lawsuit, or anything. I'm sure we can set everything straight if you'll just tell me who gave that information to your reporter."

"That's confidential information."

"Do you realize how disruptive an investigation by the FBI can be, John? It can bring an operation like yours to complete standstill."

There was a moment of silence on the other end of the line.

"I'll have a name for you by tomorrow morning," the publisher said.

"Good. I thought we could take care of this quietly," Deacons said smugly. "I'll have my secretary call your secretary to set up lunch." He hung up and smiled.

Later that same day on the Navajo reservation, Dr. Richard Farley, Head of the Shiprock Indian Hospital, marched into Dr. Stewart's office carrying the same front-page headline.

"You wouldn't know anything about this would you, Dr. Stewart?" he demanded, flinging the paper on Stewart's desk.

"I only know what I read in the papers, Dr. Farley."

"I've heard that you've taken a special interest in these miners and their families," Farley barked. "Now, we can't be playing favorites, can we, Dr. Stewart? I mean, we're paid public servants, paid to serve the health needs of all our Indian patients, within the limited time and resources available to us, of course."

"Of course. And it's a real tragedy, isn't it, that a multi-million dollar agency like the Indian Health Service can't do anything effective for the people we are supposed to serve," Dr. Stewart replied, rising from his chair. "All we do is put band aids on brain tumors, prescribe aspirin for amputees, and pass it off as health care."

"That's not the issue here, and you know it. I think you're taking your work a little too seriously."

He started to leave Stewart's office, then turned back.

"I'm going to recommend that you get some time off, Mark, or better yet, maybe a transfer to another post to finish off your commission."

Dr. Farley stomped out the door and down the hall.

"I'd like to see you try it!" Stewart called out after him. "I can't wait to pass along the information I have about the number of miners who are coming down with cancers, and how little this hospital is doing to help them. It'll make for more good reading in the newspapers!"

Dr. Stewart closed his office door and went to his filing cabinet. Reaching way in the back of the bottom drawer, he pulled out a thick stack of yellow files. They were labeled "Yellow Rock" just like the set that Ben had taken to Washington. He slipped the files into his briefcase, locked it and left the office with the briefcase tightly gripped in his hand.

Moments later, he stepped into the surgical doctors' locker room. Checking to see that no one was watching, he opened his locker and placed the briefcase inside. Making sure that he had not been seen, he slipped out of the room and back into his own office.

After dark, he retrieved the briefcase and headed for his car parked in the hospital personnel's lot. As he put his car key into the door to unlock it, he noticed that it wasn't locked. He peeked inside the car and saw that the glove box was open.

Opening the door, he reached into the glove box and pulled out a flashlight. Then he walked around to the trunk of the car and closely examined the trunk lock. It had scratches all around it. He opened the trunk to find that a box of his papers had been scattered all over the place.

"Damn!" he exclaimed.

He was then startled by a man who seemed to appear out of nowhere. The doctor shined the flashlight in the man's face, a middle-aged Anglo with a scar across his chin.

"Where are they, Dr. Stewart?" the man asked. "We've already been to your house, and we know they aren't there."

"Where are what? I don't know what you're talking about. Who are you, anyway?"

The man opened his jacket to reveal a shoulder-holstered pistol.

"Let's just say I'm working in the national interest and let it go at that," he said coldly. "Now why don't we take a peek in that briefcase? I'll bet we find those pesky old files in there."

Both men were suddenly startled by a third man's voice.

"Is everything okay, Dr. Stewart?"

He turned to find a very large and armed Aemrican Indian security guard named Eddie walking toward them. Eddie's flashlight caught the unknown man's face.

"Yes, Eddie," Stewart lied. "Everything's fine. But this gentleman needs help. He's not from around here, and he's gotten himself lost. Could you give him directions? I just don't have the time."

"Why, sure," Eddie replied, stepping between Dr. Stewart and the thug. "Anything for my favorite doc."

"Thanks," Stewart said. "I'll see you tomorrow, Eddie."

With that, he got in his car and started the engine. As he drove away, he watched in the rearview mirror as Eddie escorted the man to his car.

In a few minutes, the doctor arrived home. It was as he had expected. Everything in sight had been turned upside down. The contents of his cabinets and drawers were strewn all over the floor. He found the phone and dialed.

"They're closing in," Dr. Stewart said to the man on the other end of the line. "Someone tore my place up, and a rather unpleasant fellow threatened me as I left the hospital. Are things okay at your end?"

"Yeah, but it sounds like we acted just in time. I'm sure the files will be safe here for awhile."

"Thanks," Stewart replied. "I owe you one."

"That's all right," the man said. "Just get me a date with that pretty Navajo nurse of yours."

Dr. Stewart chuckled. "No guarantee, but I'll try."

The man hung up, and before Dr. Stewart could do the same, he heard a series of clicks on the line. He put the receiver back to his ear in time to hear a buzzing noise and three more clicks before the dial tone returned. He hung up the phone knowing that his line had been tapped.

It rained the day they buried Frank Begay. His dying had been a long, slow process, attended every step of the way by Bernice. The funeral ceremony was an eerie repeat of his cousin's funeral.

A distant cousin of Bernice's, a medicine man, had opened the proceedings with a few words in the Navajo way. But he was no replacement for Joseph. How Bernice missed him.

A Navajo preacher had also been invited to say a few words. Bernice, Mitchell and her other kids, Dr. Stewart, Sarah and a few other miner families stood in the rain as the preacher spoke. When he'd finished, he closed his Bible and shook Bernice's hand. Unable to do more, he turned away as the gravediggers began shoveling the dirt in over Frank's casket.

Ben had been in Washington when word had come of Frank's death. Ben wrapped up everything as quickly as he could and raced back. Bad weather had grounded planes in St. Louis, forcing him to miss the funeral.

He pulled up in front of the Begay house in his muddy truck late that afternoon. On the seat next to him was a bouquet of flowers and a neatly folded American Indian shawl. Stepping out into the light drizzle, he stuffed the flowers and the shawl under his raincoat and walked to the house.

Inside he found Bernice sitting on her worn couch surrounded by her children.

"Bernice, you've got to know how sorry I am that I missed the funeral," Ben said. "It happened so fast." He handed her the flowers and the shawl.

"We'll all miss Frank," he added. "He was a good man."

"Thanks, Ben," Bernice replied with little energy. "I know you would've been here if you could."

Addressing Mitchell, she said, "Son, would you take Ben's wet things?"

Mitchell took Ben's coat and hat and laid them in the bedroom. Bernice watched her son lovingly, and then her face hardened, her eyes cooled.

"It's so good to have my kids here, Ben, but I'm so mad I could spit. Frank didn't have to die like this, before his time, in so much pain. It didn't have to happen."

Ben tried to be supportive.

"But you did everything you could and more than most women in your position."

"But it wasn't enough, was it?" Bernice said bitterly. Then softening, she added, "At least I'm grateful that none of my kids had to go into those mines."

Just then, Dr. Stewart came in from the kitchen drinking a cup of coffee.

"Ben, you're back," he said, surprised. "Want a cup of coffee? I'm sort of experimenting with other lines of work, seeing as how I'm probably going to get fired from the hospital. Maybe I'll become a fry-cook."

Bernice welcomed the lightness Dr. Stewart brought to the dreariness of the day.

"Sure, Mark, I need a good stiff drink," Ben replied jokingly.

"One stiff cup of coffee comin' up." The doctor smiled slightly and went back into the kitchen.

"It does my heart good to see a man puttering around in the kitchen," Bernice said. "The only time Frank ever set foot in one was when it was time to eat."

A moment later, the sound of pots and pans falling to the floor reverberated from the kitchen, followed by a loud "Oops."

"On second thought," Bernice said loudly, for the doctor's benefit, "you'd better come on back in here before you destroy the place. And forget looking for a job as a cook."

Mark sheepishly returned to the living room. "Everyone laughed, and grief's hold on the household was released, at least for the time being.

Bernice admitted to Vicky that anger almost consumed her after Frank died, anger at Frank because he hadn't listened to her; anger at the mining company for what they'd done to her land and her people; anger at Washington for pretending nothing was wrong; anger at the Navajo tribal council for standing by and letting it all happen.

Surprisingly, it was Sarah Begay who provided the guidance that put Bernice on a better path. Sarah convinced her to let the Navajo cultural spirit character Spider Woman, the mother of Navajo art of weaving, help soothe and heal her. Sarah was the one who had found the unused upright loom and had it delivered to Bernice's door. It was Sarah who had helped her drag it inside and set it up right where she had to look at it every day.

Sarah even came over and stayed with Bernice for a while to help her get adjusted to life without Frank. Since she had lost her husband all those years ago, Sarah knew first hand what Bernice was going through.

So Bernice began to weave. She remembered that it was what gave a Navajo woman peace of mind. It wasn't long after she began the weaving that the miners unexpectedly appeared and asked for Bernice's help.

One day she was out in her yard hanging up laundry on the clothesline. The sun was shining, and the beautiful red rock cliffs were visible in the distance. A pickup truck carrying about a half dozen Navajo men pulled in the front gate. The men got out and approached Bernice.

Puzzled, she put down her laundry and walked toward them, recognizing some of the men as miners who'd worked with Frank. A man she knew only as Dixon stepped forward from the group.

"Bernice, have you got a minute?" he asked. "We need to talk to you."

"Sure, Dixon, what can I do for you?"

"Well, it's like this. Me and the boys have all been let go from Kurt-Mackie. We know that we weren't much help when you and Ben and the Doc were trying to collect your evidence and build your case, but we want to help now."

"Well, I'm glad to hear it," the widow said with quiet resignation. "What changed your minds?"

"We didn't help because we were afraid we'd lose our jobs," one of the others admitted. "But we lost 'em anyway."

"You see, what got us fired was the meetings we've been holding on our own," Dixon added. "Just talking to one another about the headaches, the vomiting, the blood we've been spitting up. A Kurt-Mackie foreman got wind of it and had us all fired."

"I'm glad you came to see me. I don't know exactly what we can do, but we'll do something. I can't bring Frank back, but I sure can try to help those of us who are left."

Bernice thought for a moment.

"Come back on Saturday and bring your wives. I'll have Ben and Dr. Stewart here so we can think up ourselves a plan."

The men smiled gratefully. Dixon shook her hand, and they all climbed back into the truck. Bernice watched them leave and returned to her laundry.

A few minutes later, out of the corner of her eye, she caught the glint of chrome from the bumper of a dark Buick coming through her front gate. The car looked familiar, but she couldn't place it right off.

The woman continued her work at the clothesline while watching, out of the corner of her eye, as the car stopped in front of the house. Two white men, dressed in slacks and short sleeve white shirts, got out. She didn't know that the driver was the man who had confronted Dr. Stewart in the IHS parking lot.

Bernice paused in her work but didn't move from her spot. These men looked like common bullies to her. The driver walked toward her. The other one moved toward the house.

"Bernice Begay, if you know what's good for you, and your family, you'll keep your nose out of the uranium business," the man approaching her said. "Know what I mean?"

Just then, Sarah came out of Bernice's front door. Sight of the strangers alarmed her and she gasped.

"Sarah, go back inside. Now!" Bernice commanded. Before she could move, however, the other man grabbed Sarah's arm and bent it behind her back. Sarah screamed, and the man covered her mouth.

Bernice started towards Sarah, but the other goon grabbed her arm and spun her around. He pulled her to him and held her from behind. Bernice was terrified, but defiant, struggling against his grip. Then he whispered in her ear.

"We got to Willy, and we can get to you, or whoever we want. So watch your step, squaw, or else. Nobody's going to notice one less Injun around, are they?"

He pushed Bernice to the ground and nodded to his partner who then pushed Sarah back into the house. When Bernice fell, she hit the hand-crank water pump near the clothesline and cut her shoulder.

As the two hired guns got into their car and drove away, Sarah ran back out of the house. She saw that Bernice was on the ground. Crying hysterically, Sarah ran to Bernice, whose shoulder was bleeding.

But Bernice's anger and determination blotted out all perception of the pain. "Injuns," Bernice said. "That's what he called us, Sarah. And squaws."

Bernice looked into Sarah's eyes. "Them's fighting words," Bernice said as she got up and walked to the house.

On the following Saturday, a small group gathered at Ben's home: Dr. Stewart, Bernice, Sarah, the miners and their wives. Bernice's left shoulder and arm were in a sling, a reminder of the visit from the goon squad. Everyone helped themselves to coffee and donuts that Ben had provided.

Dixon was the last one to arrive. He entered, quietly shook everyone's hand seated around the room and took a seat.

"Yesterday I got a call from our Congressman in Washington," Ben said somberly. "The Uranium Miner's Compensation Bill we've been fighting for was killed in committee once again--for the fifth time."

No one responded.

"He said we'd better try another avenue to get results, maybe the courts," he continued. "And, of course, you know Bernice's life was threatened."

Everyone in the room looked at Bernice sympathetically.

"These men mean business," Bernice said, "which must also mean that the mining company is afraid of us. So we've got to keep moving forward."

"Bernice is right," Dr. Stewart said. "So far, twenty-five Navajo miners from this valley alone have died of lung cancer.

And there must be a couple of hundred more that are too sick to do much for.”

“It looks like our next step is a law suit against the U.S. government,” Ben suggested.

“Can we do that?” Dixon asked.

“It’s already being done,” Ben replied. “A New Mexico lawyer by the name of Jesse Woodall is already suing the Department of Energy for some people in Utah called “down winders” who were contaminated by radioactive fallout from experimental atomic explosions. I think he’ll do the same for us. Bernice, you want to go with me to see him next week?”

“Why wait until next week?” Bernice asked. “Let’s go tomorrow.”

“What's the big rush?”

“If something worse than this happens to me or someone else, I want to know that the wheels are already in motion,” she declared, holding her arm up for everyone to see.

“I’ve got a tribal council meeting in Window Rock all this week,” Ben said. “I can’t go until next week.”

“I can go,” Dr. Stewart offered. “I’m taking a little well-deserved time off from the hospital, you know, to think about my options and to look around for alternative employment possibilities in the area. I’ll take you, Bernice, and we’ll set those wheels in motion.”

“Are you sure that’s what you want to do?” Bernice asked.

"Look, there are too many indications that the mining company and the Atomic Energy Commission want to keep this all quiet for as long as possible," Stewart replied. "And you know the good old BIA and the IHS will bend whichever way the wind is blowing the strongest. It's just a matter of time before they try to transfer me to another reservation, probably South Dakota. Nobody in HIS wants to work up there. So tomorrow, I'll check out the possibilities in Gallup--maybe look for office space."

"All right, then, you two," Ben said. "Tomorrow it is. Let's meet again in a week to get a report back from this meeting with the lawyer." At that, everyone got up to leave.

"And everybody, keep an eye open for those two goons that hurt Bernice," Ben added.

"Don't you worry one bit, Ben," Dixon said confidently. "Me and the boys here know how to handle unwanted bilagáanas who poke their noses in to Navajo business."

The other men chuckled and nodded their agreement.

At noon the next day, Bernice and the doctor were speeding south down the Triple 6 Highway towards Gallup. By mid afternoon, they had found Jesse Woodall's law office on Main Street and gone inside. The receptionist told them that Mr. Woodall had been unexpectedly called to court for the afternoon and asked if they could return in the morning.

Standing on the sidewalk in front of the office, Dr. Stewart said, "I guess our first order of business is to get accommodations for the night."

"Something cheap," Bernice requested.

"I know just the place," the doctor said. They got in his car and in a few minutes pulled up in the parking lot of the El Rancho Motel. Built in the 1920s by the brother of a famous movie director to house film crews who shot westerns there frequently, the rooms were all named after famous movie stars. Bernice got the Mae West room and Dr. Stewart was put in the W.C. Fields room two doors away.

Bernice freshened up in her room and lay down on the bed to watch TV. In a few minutes a knock came on her door. Opening it, she found Dr. Stewart waiting outside.

"Could a gentleman offer a lady some supper?" he asked.

"Why, I thought you'd never ask," she replied. "Do you suppose they've got a Sizzlin' Sirloin here? I'd love a good steak dinner."

"Let us go forth then, in search of steak," Dr. Stewart quipped. He offered his arm, which Bernice took, and they headed down the stairs and through the motel's gaudy western lobby.

Dr. Stewart had discovered that there was a Sizzlin' Sirloin, as requested, a mere two blocks from the motel. They went inside, found a table, and before too long, steak, potatoes and salad were brought to their table, along with a steaming pot of coffee. Finally, they had time to talk.

"We've been at this for over a decade, you know, and it's not over yet," Dr. Stewart said. "What keeps you going, Bernice?"

"The coming generations," she replied without hesitation. "My grandkids and their grandkids and on and on. I realized that I have a responsibility to leave a world fit for them to live in. And, partly, thanks to you all those years ago, I came to accept that responsibility."

She looked at the doctor for a long moment.

"And what about you, Dr. Stewart? What keeps you here with us fighting this battle? It's not your fight. You could leave anytime you want to."

"My grandma," he said, also without hesitation. "She lived her life in a small rural Oklahoma town with a funny name. Weleetka, it was called. I remember when I was little, we'd go up from Texas every now then to visit her. She was all alone and partially crippled. But there was this Native American family that lived nearby, and everyday they stopped in to see how she was doing. They were closer to her and did more for her than her own flesh and blood ever did."

Bernice nodded with understanding.

"After she passed away," he continued, "I went by to see her old place on the way to my first doctor job." He pulled up the image of the house in his mind.

"It was a vacant, dilapidated white frame house. The grass was all grown up and a few windows were broken out. An elderly woman from next door saw me in the yard and came over to the fence.

"She asked if I was Mark. Boy, was I startled. 'Yes, I am,' I said. She told me she was a friend of my grandma's. She said, 'Before your grandma passed away, she gave me something to give to you if you ever showed up.' I waited by the fence while she went inside her house. In a minute, she came back out carrying a small wooden box. I opened it and looked inside. There was a small prayer book inside covered with a soft piece of leather."

Sitting at the table in the steak house, Mark reached inside his coat pocket, produced the prayer book and handed it to Bernice.

"Sewn into the leather cover was the most beautiful Indian beadwork pattern I've ever seen. Grandma had written a note to me and folded it up inside."

He motioned for Bernice to open the little book. She did and found the note. Unfolding it, she read it aloud.

"Mark, I want you to have this prayer book to remember me by, and to remember the Indian family that gave it to me. They were the kindest, most generous people I ever met. I wasn't really able to repay that kindness, but maybe someday you can."

Bernice studied the note for a moment, and then neatly folded it back up.

"It sounds like your grandmother was touched by someone truly special, because, you know, we Indians are just the same as everybody else," Bernice said. "Some good, some bad, all human."

She returned the prayer book to him.

"You don't have to tell me," the doctor said. "I see it first hand at the clinic every day. But, you know, what I'm doing feels right, and I do have a sense that I'm passing along a kindness that was done to her. Also, I think she's in it somehow."

"That's more than most people can say about anything they do their whole lives. I'm glad for you." She thought for a moment. "I didn't know where it came from, but I always felt like you were here among us for the right reason."

Having finished their meal, they sat and drank their coffee for a little while in peaceful silence. Bernice felt relaxed in this man's company.

They strolled quietly back to their motel through the peaceful night. Standing at the door to her room, Bernice said, "Thank you for a wonderful evening, Dr. Stewart."

"How long you known me, Bernice? Ten years?"

"Yeah, I guess so."

"Don't you think it's about time you begin calling me by my first name?"

Bernice blushed. "All right--Mark. How's that?"

"That's a good start. Now, why don't we work on changing our relationship from friends to something more serious? You must know that I think you are an attractive wom--."

Before he could finish the word, she shushed him with her finger on his lips.

"I don't know how to do that, Mark. Frank will always be my husband. If it means anything, I think you're very attractive, as well, and... I enjoy your company, and... I love you for who you are and what you do."

He started to say something else, but she stopped him with her eyes. She looked deeply into his soul for a moment, and then without saying another word, slipped into her hotel room and closed the door.

Mark remained in the hall outside her room for a long moment, pondering this woman and her ways. Then he went to his room, knowing that the words and feelings expressed this night would never be mentioned again.

Jesse Woodall saw them first thing the next morning. He half listened to their story and scanned the yellow file folder they'd brought him with one eye.

"This is a good beginning, but there's a lot more work to be done if we take this case," he warned. "I'll have one of my staff members look this over and let you know if we think we have a chance of winning."

He picked up his phone and prepared to dial.

"Now, you two go on back to the rez and let us take care of this. We'll call you when we know something."

Bernice knew when she was being dismissed out of hand. She stood.

"Mr. Woodall, kindly do me the favor of not patronizing me," she said sharply. "I'm well aware of the work involved. We've been at this for over ten years. Just tell us what needs to be done and we'll follow through. But don't blow smoke in my face."

Woodall put down the phone.

"All right, Mrs. Begay. I'll thoroughly study these files personally. You and Dr. Stewart go back to Red Rock, and I'll contact you as soon as I can, as soon as I've had a chance to discuss this situation with my colleagues. If we think we truly have a strong case, then, and only then, will we take it on. Deal?"

"Deal," Bernice said, satisfied.

"Deal," Mark said as he stood and shook Woodall's hand.

Mission accomplished, the pair headed back to Navajoland. They let Navajo Radio fill the silence for several miles. Then, turning the radio down, Bernice looked at Mark.

"What are you really going to do if they want to transfer you?" she asked, taking Mark by surprise.

"Open a private practice in Gallup or Farmington or someplace near the rez. There's a shortage of doctors all over this region. That way I'll be close enough to still be involved with the case. They can't get rid of me that easily."

Bernice nodded, saying nothing.

"Navajo Fair's in just a few days," he said to change the subject. "Are you going?"

"I don't think so. I'm not really in a fair-going mood, and I want to put in a few hours at the loom."

"Come on, let's both go," Mark said encouragingly. "Ride some rides; watch the rodeo. It'll do us some good."

"Why don't you go, then come back and tell me all about it," Bernice replied, with a sarcastic edge in her voice.

"Well, we still have a few days until the fair. If I keep working on you, I know I can wear you down until you give up and go just to shut me up."

Bernice smiled, turned the radio back on and looked out at the passing scenery.

A few evenings later, Mark was sitting at his kitchen table reading when the phone rang. He picked up the receiver to find Jess Woodall on the line.

"I've got good news," Woodall said. "Can you talk?"

"Not now. I'll call you back in about fifteen minutes."

Mark hung up the phone and went out the back door. In a few minutes he pulled into a Shiprock gas station and parked near the pay phone. He fished in his pocket for a coin as he approached the phone booth.

Before entering, he looked around to make sure he hadn't been followed. He dialed Woodall's office.

"Mr. Woodall, this is Mark Stewart. Sorry for the intrigue, but I'm pretty sure my phone is tapped, and well, you can't be too careful. Anyway, you were saying there was good news."

"My partners and I have decided to take on the case."

"All Right! That _is_ good news. Bernice is going to love this."

"But it's going to be a lot more work," Woodall reminded him.

"What do we do first?" Mark asked enthusiastically.

"We need to do some more in-depth interviews with the same people you've already talked to, and also interview those miners who got fired. We'll make up the questions, if you guys can do the field work."

"Can do," Mark replied happily.

"Then we need to go directly to Kurt-Mackie and ask for any official documents they may have pertaining to the hazards of radiation exposure--sort of give them a chance to 'fess up or deny it all, whatever, they're going to do. How does that sound?"

"Risky," Mark said flatly. "We told you about the gruesome twosome that's been harassing us. We're pretty sure they work for the mining company."

"What you need is an opportunity to chat with those fellows," the lawyer advised. "Make it mighty uncomfortable for them to hang around Navajo country."

"Right," Mark replied, pondering the idea. "I know just the right group of guys for that job."

"How about you coming up and bringing that list of questions we're supposed to ask? Navajo Fair is this weekend."

"Sounds good. Tell you what. I'll come up Saturday and hang out at the fair, get the lay of the land. Then Sunday we'll buckle down and get our strategy going."

"Great. Meet me in Window Rock in front of the Navajo Fair entrance. It's right on the highway. We'll knock around the fair grounds for a couple of hours before we meet with Ben and Bernice. I'll call if there are any changes."

"Meanwhile," Woodall said, "I'll try to think of a way to use your wiretap to aid our cause."

On Friday, at a pre-arranged time, Woodall's main phone line rang. His secretary answered and buzzed Woodall on the intercom. "It's that call you've been expecting," she said. "Line two." He picked up his phone.

"Hello. Jesse Woodall here."

He listened for a moment.

"All right, Dr. Stewart," he said. "Yes, I've got it. Under the Navajo Fair rodeo bleachers at eight p.m. on Saturday. You'll have a set of the files? Good. I'll be there."

Woodall hung up and smiled. The wheels were in motion.

Navajo Fair was a big annual event. There was the all-Indian rodeo, the pow-wow, food and craft booths, the carnival rides, and a number of other activities, including big name country and western acts. Something for everyone. Navajos from all over the rez came to enjoy it.

Woodall arrived in Window Rock at 5 p.m., and the fair was in full swing. He strolled through the crafts booths, eating a Navajo Taco and carrying a cold drink. From out of the crowd, Mark walked up beside him and they kept pace for a moment or two.

"I think you'll be pleased with the little show that we have planned for tonight," Mark said finally.

"Any hints?" Woodall asked.

"That would spoil the surprise. Just enjoy the fair for now."

By 8 p.m., the carnival rides were all lit up, and the place was packed. Navajos of all ages roamed the fairgrounds, laughing, joking and generally having a good time.

Near the entrance to the pow-wow arena, Bernice, Ben, Mark and Jesse Woodall converged.

"I told the good lawyer here that we had a surprise for him tonight," Mark said. "I don't want to disappoint him. Is everything ready?"

"Yes," Ben said, "but are you sure they'll come?"

"That phony telephone conversation we had yesterday should bring 'em out into the open," Mark replied. "If they think there's an opportunity to get their hands on the uranium files, I'm pretty sure they'll go for it."

"You okay, Bernice?" Ben asked.

"I feel like fish bait," she replied nervously.

"All traps need bait," Mark said with a smile. "It'll be all right, Bernice. When they find out how tough and stringy you are, they'll throw you back."

Ben laughed but quit when he saw the worried look on Bernice's face.

"Very funny," she said. "I guess it's easy to laugh when you're not the bait."

Okay, just so we're in sync, let's go over it," Mark said seriously. "Bernice?"

"At 8 o'clock, I go over and stand under the rodeo bleachers with the fake file folders," Bernice recited. "The bad guys think I'm meeting the lawyer to turn the files over to him. Then Mark, you come up to me, disguised to look like the lawyer, and take the files from me. We hope that the bad guys make their move and that's when Dixon takes over.

"That's it," Mark confirmed. "Okay, let's move out."

"Who died and made you chief?" Bernice asked.

Ben and Jesse laughed. Mark joined in, and Bernice even smiled. Ready to begin their little drama, they each headed in a different direction.

A few minutes later, Bernice was standing nervously in the shadows behind the rodeo bleachers holding a thick yellow file folder. The rodeo was in full swing. In front of her was a dimly lit dirt parking lot filled with rows and rows of cars. Every shout from the audience in the bleachers startled her. Any movement in the parking lot shadows scared her. Why did she ever agree to do this, she wondered. Finally, Mark showed up.

"What took you so long?" Bernice barked angrily.

"Relax," Mark replied calmly. "We wanted to make sure they were here."

Bernice's eyes darted around, quickly searching the shadows. "Well, are they?"

"You bet," Mark said with a smile. "Now you go into the arena and take a seat in the bleachers. We'll do the rest."

Bernice handed him the folder and started for the bleachers. Mark headed off through the dark parking lot, and moments later, two other figures stepped out of the shadows and followed him.

In a few minutes, Mark passed a pickup truck with an open camper shell that was parked in the lot. He discreetly gave a signal to Dixon who was waiting inside. The two men tailing him passed by the same spot a few moments later and Dixon said, "Now!" in a loud whisper.

Five Navajo men, seemingly out of nowhere, converged on the pair. There was a brief scuffle, the sound of a couple of blows, followed by two thuds as the goons hit the ground, and it was over. Dixon pulled a flashlight from his pocket and shined it on the unconscious twosome.

"Good work, gentlemen," Mark said looking at the two lying in the dirt. "Now let's move this meeting to some place less public."

Dixon's men grabbed the goons by the arms and threw them in the back of the truck where the pair was bound, gagged and blindfolded.

Dixon drove his cargo, guarded by two of the miners, across town to a pre-arranged office location. Mark and Woodall, who had watched the ambush from the safety of Mark's car, had already arrived.

The two captives were unceremoniously dragged from the truck and dumped on the floor of the dark office. A single bright flashlight pierced the darkness, revealing a group of men who formed a circle around the two.

"You fellows better tell Kurt-Mackie that your usefulness to the company is about over," someone from the circle said. Pairs of hands reach down and ripped the gags and blindfolds off the captives. They blinked at the brightness of the light that shone in their eyes. Fear radiated from their sweaty faces.

Suddenly, a camera flash went off several times, and the goons blinked even more. Then the blindfolds were re-applied and the captives were hoisted into standing positions and shoved back out the door into the night.

Moments later, Dixon's truck pulled up in front of the entrance to the Navajo Fair Grounds. The two goons, with hands and feet tied, were shoved out of the back, once again hitting the ground with a thud.

As they struggled to stand up, they presented quite a spectacle to the dozens of Navajo fair-goers that walked by and gawked at the two white men.

The following day, Ben took a copy of the Sunday edition of the Navajo Tribal News off the top of the stack and opened it. Scanning the front page, he let out a little hoot. On the lower right corner of the page was a photograph of the two goons looking like deer caught in headlights.

Ben read the caption out loud to Woodall, Mark, Bernice and the others who had all gathered to begin their work. They were in the offices of the Navajo Tribal News that had been loaned to them for this meeting. The paper's editor, an old friend of Ben's had been glad to let them use it both for the 'photo session' and the day's meeting.

"These two men have been seen lately around the Navajo Nation," Ben read from the newspaper. "They are running a scam on Navajo elders, swindling them out of their social security and welfare checks. If you see them, do not approach them. They are very dangerous. Call the Navajo police and report their whereabouts immediately."

Ben beamed from ear to ear at their triumph.

"This is great. I hate to see what's going to happen to those two when they come up on the first bunch of Navajos who've seen this." He laughed.

"Everybody 'round here knows they aren't going to be calling the police," the newspaper's editor said. "Indian justice can be swift, direct and hard."

"Speaking of justice," Mark said. "It's almost ten o'clock--time to let our attorney tell us what we have to do next."

Leaving them to their task, the editor left the conference room. Dixon and the miners joined Mark, Bernice and Woodall at the large conference table in the center of the room.

And thus began what turned out to be another five year stint of interviewing, researching, typing, filing--trying to fight the white man's system on his own terms.

All through the late nineteen-seventies they worked to build what Woodall thought would be an airtight case.

In the meantime, things changed, lives moved on. Among other things, Mark began his private practice in Gallup. When he opened for business, he even put a sign in his front window announcing "Indians and Dogs Welcome."

But it appeared that during that time, Washington finally got all the uranium it wanted. The mines began closing, and the mills stopped operating.

But even that didn't stop the yellow rock from harming Navajo people. Ben and Mark finally interested the University of New Mexico researchers in the problem, and what they found was as disturbing as the original cover-up.

The first documented evidence of the presence of harmful radiation on the rez came when Mark convinced Jacob Fieldman of the University's Radiation Information Center to make a trip to the reservation. Mark personally drove to Albuquerque to pick up Fieldman and escort him to the rez.

Navajo resident Harrison Bitsooey had agreed to let Fieldman check his home for radiation.

Mark and Fieldman arrived at the Bitsooey home late that afternoon. They found Ben and Mr. Bitsooey standing outside the house waiting. Fieldman, Geiger counter in hand, was introduced all around.

"Yah-a-tay," Bitsooey said.

"Mr. Bitsooey," Mark said. "This is Jacob Fieldman. He's from the University of New Mexico science department.

"Now, just tell them what you told me," Ben instructed. Bitsooey cleared his throat nervously.

"Like I said, when the mine closed down, they left behind this huge pile of crushed rock. So, several of us in the area used this stuff to build ourselves new homes. The men from the mine said it would be okay. We weren't doin' nothin' wrong."

Fieldman was alarmed.

"Mr. Bitsooey, would you mind if I stepped inside your home with the Geiger counter for a minute to take some readings?" Fieldman asked. Bitsooey looked to Ben to see if it was all right. Ben nodded his approval. Bitsooey did likewise.

Fieldman turned on the Geiger counter and it immediately started a steady ticking. He moved closer to the house and the ticking increased. As he stepped into the house, the Geiger counter went nuts. Fieldman tried to conceal his horror.

Fieldman moved from room to room, and the counter continued its frenetic noise. Then the scientist quickly moved out of the house and towards the car. He motioned for Ben and Mark to follow.

"There are more than 100 rems of radioactivity in there," Fieldman revealed, almost in a panic. "That house is more radioactive than any of the mines could ever be. How long have they lived in it?"

"Three, four years," Ben said.

"We'd better check all the homes in this area," Fieldman said.

Mark thought of something. "Wait a minute," he said, approaching Bitsooey.

"Mr. Bitsooey, can you show us where the rock you used to build your house came from?"

"Sure," Bistsooey answered. He headed off toward a hill behind his house. The others followed.

As the men came up over the hill, they saw a large pile of finely crushed yellowish rock. Next to the pile was a large flattened field of the same material. Three Navajo kids were playing tag in the field. Fieldman turned on the Geiger counter and it began to click immediately, faster and faster.

Mark and Fieldman exchanged a look of frightened disbelief.

"Ben, you'd better get these kids out of here," Mark said.

Ben went over to the kids who had stopped playing and said a few words. Fieldman removed a small plastic bag from his pocket and spooned in some of the material from the ground into it. Meanwhile, the kids ran off, and Ben began speaking to Bitsooey.

Mark joined Fieldman who held up the plastic bag for Mark to see.

"It's processed yellowcake all right," Fieldman said. "We need to get a fence put up around this. Put up warning signs."

"How bad is it?" Mark asked.

"Bad as I've seen. We'd better check out all the homes around here so we know how extensive the problem is."

They spent the rest of the day going from house to house. Sadly, they found almost the same results in each home.

At sundown, the men gathered in Mark's car to discuss the day's findings.

"Twenty-two homes in all, with radioactive levels 10 times the officially published level of safety," Fieldman said. "I can't believe it."

"We've got to get those people out of there as soon as possible," Mark said.

"But where are we going to put them?" Ben asked.

"I don't know, but the tribal council had better damn well do something about this," Mark said angrily. "They've sat on their collective butts for all these years and let their own people die horrible deaths. Ben, you've got to get them to listen this time."

Ben and Bernice got on the agenda and attended the next Tribal Council meeting where they made a very effective presentation on behalf of the affected families. And surprisingly, the council members listened and took action this time. Times had changed, and it had become politically correct for the tribal council to act. Funds were eventually allocated to build new homes for all twenty families.

In 1979, Jesse Woodall finally had his airtight case put together, and he filed suit against the federal government on behalf of thirty-two Navajo miners, in the amount of $500,000 for each case.

The same year, oddly enough, several Congressmen and Senators from Arizona, New Mexico and Utah began holding public hearings into the long-term health hazards of the uranium mines. It seems that white folks had begun complaining about it, so the politicians thought they'd better start listening.

It was during one such public hearing, held on a summer night in the high school gymnasium of Grants, New Mexico, that another change in Bernice's life came. Senator Peter Dominique of New Mexico had scheduled the public hearing to collect input and hear the opinions of area residents.

The Senator sat at a table in the front of the room, along with a court reporter and a couple of other staffers. Bernice and Ben took a seat in the front row of the audience and waited for their turn to present testimony. Bernice was surprised to hear a very familiar sounding story from a non-Indian woman who had also lost her husband to uranium.

"I beg to differ with you, Senator," the woman said from a podium that stood in front of the audience facing the Senator. "Those mining companies knew exactly what they were doing. After my husband died, I had to get a court order to force the clinic to release my husband's x-rays and medical files to me. And do you know what they revealed?"

"No ma'am," the Senator replied. "That's what I came here to find out."

"They revealed that my husband, Bill, had been developing cancer of the lungs for several years," the woman said. "Several years! Did they once mention it to him? No, they did not!"

The audience erupted with wide spread chattering. The Senator banged his gavel on the table.

"Ladies and gentlemen, please," he said, trying to regain control. The audience quieted. "Ma'am, thank you for your testimony," he continued. "It will be entered into the record. Will the next person on the list please take the floor?"

The woman reluctantly took her seat, not quite sure that she was finished. At his seat, Ben collected his papers, making ready to give his presentation. Bernice patted him on the arm and motioned for him to keep his seat. She stood and walked to the podium as Ben watched.

"State your name, occupation, and place of residence," the hearing reporter recited flatly.

"I am Bernice Begay, widow of uranium miner, Frank Begay. I am Dineh, what you call Navajo. I live in the community of Red Rock, right on the border between New Mexico and Arizona, on the Navajo Reservation."

"Thank you, ma'am," the Senator said. "And what testimony do you have to present today?"

"Senator, just like this woman, I lost my husband to uranium," Bernice began. "Since way back in 1943, I have been concerned about the health hazards of the uranium mines on the Navajo Reservation. Since 1963, my friend here, Councilman Ben Benally, myself and others, have interviewed over 500 Navajo mining families, and have collected two filing cabinets full of documents proving that radiation from the mines causes cancer."

She reached over and retrieved a file full of photographs from Ben's hand. She opened the file and held up a series of photographs that illustrated her testimony. The first picture depicted several large, unsightly holes in the side of a beautiful mountain ridge.

"Over one thousand, two hundred mines of different sizes were dug in the lands of the Navajo people over a twenty-year period. For us who believe that the earth is our sacred home, it is like tearing holes in your own mother."

Then Bernice held up a picture of a large bulldozer filling in a large gaping hole in the ground.

"Just last year," she continued. "The Navajo Abandoned Mine Reclamation program began the work of filling in these holes. Because of the large number of abandoned mines on the reservation, their work will take at least another twenty-five years."

She displayed the next picture showing the sick, emaciated and nearly dead body of a Navajo man lying in bed in his home.

"Miners inhaled and swallowed the yellow dust from these mines until it made them radioactive from the inside out. More than two hundred Navajo miners have died from it, and more are too sick to be treated effectively."

"I think we get the point, ma'am," the Senator said. "But with unemployment so high on the reservation, these mining jobs must have been worth their weight in gold to your people."

"Senator, most Navajo families have at least four children to raise, feed and clothe, and yes, jobs have been scarce here. But while the mines were in full operation on the reservation, the average annual income of a Navajo miner was $5,200. Their wages amounted to about a dollar and a quarter per hour."

The audience reacted once more.

"These miners must've known that radiation exposure was dangerous," the Senator protested. "When they began getting sick, why did they keep on working?"

"Because we had no information that linked their symptoms to the handling of uranium. Because the federal government and the mining companies kept this information from us on purpose. And because many of us believed that Washington would never do anything that would harm us. What fools we were. In my opinion, it's a national disgrace."

The audience applauded. Ben stood, clapping the loudest. The other people in the audience began to stand up, their applause continuing. The Senator, seeing the mood of the audience, stood and applauded Bernice with them. After a while, the Senator held up his hands to quiet the audience.

"Mrs. Begay--Bernice, I want to thank you for your testimony today and your powerful words," the Senator said with political sincerity. "I promise you and all the people in this room that action will be taken. When I finish my probe into these matters, there will be a full Senate investigation, followed by swift action, to remedy the appalling situation created by the negligence and malfeasance of these agencies."

The Senator droned on for awhile, and Bernice thought he made a pretty good speech that day, considering he was flying by the seat of his pants. She and Ben left about half way through his self-congratulatory final remarks.

They were just a few steps outside the gym when Mark found them.

"I knew I'd find you two here," he said. "Giving them hell, as always?"

"She gives 'em hell," Ben replied, smiling. "I'm just along for the ride."

"We haven't seen enough of you lately, Doctor," Bernice said. "What brings you back up this way?"

"I came to tell you that I'm leaving."

There was sadness in his voice. The words hit Bernice like hammers.

"My medical practice in Gallup hasn't been doing too well, so, I've taken a job in Washington, D.C., with the Public Health Service."

Bernice tried not to show how devastated the news made her feel.

"Congratulations," Ben said. "What's the new job?"

"Chief Medical Officer, Southwest Region, Indian Health Service." He feigned an air of pomposity.

"After all they put you through, why would you want to work for them?" Bernice asked.

"Things have changed. They fired some of the good old boys who used to run Indian Health, and they're looking for new blood with new ideas. I think I can make a difference."

"You always make a difference, Mark, wherever you go," Bernice said sincerely. "I wish you good luck in Washington."

She turned and started walking away from the two men so they wouldn't see the tear she was unsuccessfully trying to hold back. Mark followed after her. When he caught up to her, he saw the tears that had formed in the corners of her eyes. Bernice pulled a hanky out of her purse to dry them.

"Bernice, I brought you a present," he said tenderly. "Something to remember me by." He pulled a small, neatly wrapped gift from the side pocket of his jacket. She took it and slowly peeled the wrapping paper away, revealing his Grandmother's prayer book with the beaded cover.

"Mark, I can't take this," she said. "It's your grandmother's. She gave it to you to remember <u>her</u> by."

"My grandmother's spirit is in my heart," Mark assured her. "I keep her memory with me always. Just as your spirit is in my heart, and I keep your memory with me always."

For once, Bernice was speechless. They looked searchingly into one another's eyes for a moment. Never having physically expressed their love or admiration for one another, words came awkwardly now at the time of parting.

"I am going to miss you," she finally said, giving him a tender hug. Hugging her back, he said, "I'll miss you, too."

After a moment, he pulled away and looked into her eyes one last time.

"I have to go, now. Gotta catch a plane to D.C. Take care."

He backed away from her, turned and headed towards the parking lot.

"I'll write when I get a new address," he called back, and then trotted off to his car.

Bernice waved back with a slow lingering wave that Mark didn't see. She turned, and as she walked, the tears came down full force. It was then and there that her will to continue on with the struggle began to fade.

After that, time began to blur in Bernice's mind. The years that followed brought more work on the case, more waiting and more disappointments. She managed to keep her flagging spirits up as Woodall slugged it out with the judicial powers that be--until one wintery January day.

When Woodall called Bernice, a thick blanket of snow covered the ground outside her home.

"I'm sorry to have to tell you this, he said. "We lost the case."

And that was all.

Bernice's smile died that day, and she just sort of checked out of everything except her weaving. In fact, the weaving took over her life. Day after day she stared out the window and ran the shuttle back and forth between the vertical threads of yarn on her loom. Her hands did the work, disconnected from her mind. And her well-known spark faded out. Her skin color paled as she became a shell of her former self.

At night she began dreaming about the weaving. In her dream body, she'd get up out of bed, go to the loom and weave. Day and night were indistinguishable. Sarah, and occasionally Ben and the children, were her only real visitors.

It was about a year after Woodall's phone call that the spirits begin coming to her.

For the most part, certain subjects are taboo for Navajos. They don't talk about disease for fear of bringing it on. They don't talk about the dead for fear that their ghosts will come back to haunt and maybe harm them.

But, in spite of these fears and taboos, the spirits of Navajo miners who had died came to visit Bernice in her dreams. As time went by, more and more spirits came. They would watch her while she was weaving. They stood around the loom, and threads of gold and silver energy would come out of their fingertips and flow onto the loom. And Bernice would weave those threads into her dream rugs.

And somehow their energy flowed into her, too, restoring her health, her strength and her will, her will to live and her will to focus.

Then one night in 1989, they were gone. They just disappeared. It was the night before Thanksgiving, and Bernice awoke with a curious feeling of peaceful confidence.

On Thanksgiving Day, Ben arrived with news for her.

Her family was holding their Thanksgiving celebration at Mitchell's house in Shiprock. All of Bernice's grown children, and her many grandchildren, including Carmelita, were there.

Everyone was in a holiday mood, having gathered to share turkey, mutton and fry bread.

Bernice was enjoying the company of her grandchildren in the living room when the front door opened, and Ben entered carrying a covered dish.

"Ben Benally, you old coot," Bernice said. "How have you been doing lately?"

"A new Senate investigating committee has been formed to address the issue of compensation for uranium miners and their survivors," he said, ignoring her question.

No hello, no I'm fine, how are you?

"Is that so?" Bernice replied. She looked towards the kitchen and her family. "Just look at them, Ben," she said. "The coming generations of our people. When I see them, I am hopeful. I know we will survive." She paused. "Now what was it you were saying?"

"I said there's a new Senate investigating committee formed to address the issue of compensation for uranium miners and their survivors."

"Oh, that's what I thought you said," she replied. "I'm really not interested."

"They want you to testify," he announced.

"They what?"

"They want you to go to Washington to testify."

"Really?" she asked.

"Really," he answered. "They're convening next week. What do you say?"

"I say I'd better pack my bag." Color flooded her face. A sparkle gleamed in her eyes. "I'm going to Washington, to tell the truth in the House Made of Lies."

Just then the pilot's voice crackled over the plane's intercom.

"Ladies and Gentlemen, we are approaching Dulles International Airport. Thanks for flying with us today. Have a safe stay in the Washington area, or wherever your final destination might be."

"That's pretty much the whole story," Bernice said to Vicky as the reporter finished jotting down her final notes. She turned off the tape recorder.

"At least that's what I can remember of it," Bernice added.

"You have an amazing memory, Bernice," Vicky said. "Just amazing."

It was sunset, and Bernice watched out the window as the jet touched down on the runway. Her fear of flying had disappeared.

Outside the baggage claim area, they were met by a waiting limousine, much to Bernice's delighted surprise. On the way to their hotel, the driver used a round-about route that took them passed a few of Washington's landmarks: the Lincoln Memorial, the Washington Monument, the old Smithsonian building, the White House and the Capitol building.

Finally, the limo pulled up in front of a big hotel. Bernice was surprised to read the words "Honor the Elders Pow-Wow" displayed on the hotel's marquee.

"Pow-Wow?" Bernice remarked. "They have pow-wows in Washington, DC?"

"Yep," said Ben, "and that's where we're going just as soon as we check in and freshen up."

As they stepped out of the limo, a bellboy appeared and removed their luggage from the trunk. He was about to carry Bernice's carpetbag inside, but she wrestled it away from him. Ben and Vicky broke out laughing as the bellboy relinquished the bag. Finally realizing that he was only trying to help, Bernice joined in the laughter, and gave it back to him.

The lobby of the upscale hotel was something to behold with its marble and glass decor, massive chandeliers and lush indoor plants. Bernice had never seen anything like it. After a brief discussion at the front desk, it was decided that Vicky and Bernice would share a suite. Especially since Bernice refused to stay in a room by herself.

Vicky escorted Bernice into their suite where the elderly woman discovered a huge bed, the largest she'd ever seen. Putting her little carpetbag down on the edge of the bed, she reached for the small chocolate mint that rested on the pillow. She unwrapped it, popped it in her mouth, and let it melt. Wonderful, she thought.

After a little primping, the two ladies were ready to go out into the night. Ben joined them at the elevator, and they rode down to the ballroom level.

When the elevator doors opened on the mezzanine, they were greeted by the sounds of the pow-wow that was already in full swing. They entered the main hall and saw the large banner hanging over the podium in the back of the room that read: Welcome to the 10th Annual Honor the Elders Pow-wow.

The singers, seated around the large drum in the middle of the ballroom, belted out a song at full volume. They were surrounded by an array of tribal dancers of all types circling the drum. There were Fancy Dancers, Traditional Dancers, Ladies Buckskin and Women's Fancy Shawl of all ages, just to name a few.

Bernice took it all in. She never imagined in all her life that she would be standing in the ballroom of a luxurious hotel in Washington, D.C., in the midst of a powwow.

Ben and Vicky whispered a few private words to one another, and then escorted Bernice further into the room. As they walked, several people approached and shook hands with Ben who had made many trips to the nation's capital over the years. When they reached the seats that had been saved for them, Ben excused himself as the two ladies sat down.

Bernice began to get the sneaking suspicion that something was going on that she knew nothing about, but she couldn't quite figure out what it was.

Ben approached the Master of Ceremonies who was just finishing a discussion with the powwow arena director. The MC was a large Native man wearing beautifully beaded vest and a turquoise and silver bolo tie.

Bernice saw Ben point towards her, and the MC looked her way. He nodded his head, and then Ben came back to his seat as the MC crossed to the microphone, making signals to the drum group. In a few beats, the song ended and the M.C. turned his microphone on. It squealed loudly with feedback, causing several people to laugh.

"Thank you, singers, for that wonderful song, and thank you, dancers, for that beautiful dancing. A-ho!"

"I think we got here just in time," Vicky said. "They're going to announce who's this year's honored elder." She patted Bernice's knee.

"The time has arrived," the MC began. "Time to name this year's selected elder. This is a native person we honor for his or her wisdom, courage, leadership, and sacrifice for our indigenous people."

The room fell silent with anticipation. Vicky took out her camera, turned on the flash and checked her settings. Bernice noticed that Ben was grinning from ear to ear. The MC continued.

"The woman we honor tonight has worked tirelessly her whole adult life on behalf of the people of her community. She has given of herself completely in a battle with a much larger force, seeking no reward, expecting no thanks, and giving no quarter to the enemy."

"Who's he talking about anyway, Pocahontas?" Bernice said sarcastically.

"She has done battle with mining companies and agencies of the federal government for over forty years. She has fought for the rights of the Navajo uranium miners and their widows in the belief that the wrong that had been done would be righted. Let's hear it for this year's selected elder--Bernice Begay of Navajo Nation!"

The crowd erupted with applause and cheering. Bernice was, of course, shocked beyond belief. She looked at Ben and then at Vicky. Was this right? She saw from their expressions that they both knew all along! She couldn't stop the tears from welling up in her eyes.

"C'mon Bernice!" the MC said. "Come on up here!" Ben and Vicky helped her get started towards the stage. She slowly walked to the front of the room as the applause continued and everyone stood.

"Here she comes, folks," the MC announced. "Bernice Begay, a Navajo from the community of Red Rock in the Navajo Nation."

She reached the stage and was helped up on to the platform by a young Indian woman. Then the woman picked up a shawl, which had been draped over a chair, and showed it to the audience. The words "Elder of the Year" were embroidered across it, along with the image of an eagle with outstretched wings superimposed over a medicine wheel. The young woman placed the shawl around Bernice's shoulders.

The elder, who was surprised by all this, and thrilled at the same time, held the shawl close to herself.

"How about a few words, Bernice?" the MC asked.

Embarrassed, Bernice shook her head no, but the crowd begged for her to say something. She laughed and stepped up to the microphone. The crowd went wild. The singers showed their approval with a few beats on the drum.

"I don't know what to say," Bernice said tentatively. "You know, this is my first time in Washington, D.C. Back home on the rez, this is a far away place we only hear about. It isn't real. Now that I've seen it, I'm glad I came. I suppose while I'm here I'll have to paint the town--red, of course."

She smiled as the audience laughed and cheered. Bernice began to walk away from the microphone, and then stopped. She returned to the mic, and the crowd quieted.

"Ben Benally, sitting over there, is the one who should be up here getting the honors," she said.

Ben turned two or three other shades of red.

"He got me started in this work," she continued. He coached me all the way. So, to you who honor me, I say that I honor my friend, Ben Benally."

That did it. The crowd stood and cheered again. Ben smiled sheepishly as people near him shook his hand and patted him on the back.

"Just giving Ben a little bit of his own medicine," Bernice said, and the audience laughed as they sat back down.

"I'm a little bit nervous about talking to the United States Senate tomorrow," Bernice continued. "Talking about my personal life and about all the pain and suffering that went on back home. But they've got to know the truth, don't they?"

The crowd was silent.

"Well, that's just what I'm going to tell them. The truth. I'm just one old Indian woman, but I have a voice, and I pray that Creator will help me, give me the strength to say what needs to be said. Back home, we call this Washington place the House Made of Lies. We all know that this country was built on a blanket of lies spread over the bones of Indian people. I pray that those U.S. Senators have their heads screwed on right, and they finally listen to the truth--then act on it."

Everyone in the room stood and applauded reverently. Lulus and war whoops echoed across the cavernous space.

"That's all I have to say," Bernice concluded. She looked toward Ben. "Now I'm going to go give Ben Benally a good thump with my cane for not telling me about all this. You all have a good time."

The crowd let out one more round of cheers and applause. As Bernice moved away from the mic, the singers gave the drum a few good beats, and then began their Honor Song.

Bernice stepped off the platform and into the crowd which began gathering. They came to shake her hand and offer their congratulations. The MC led Bernice into the front of the crowd to begin their wide circle around the drum as the Honor Song rang out. With the shawl around her shoulders, and flanked by several dancers in full regalia, she began her journey circling the room.

After a few steps around the arena, a man stepped forward from the fringes of the crowd and offered his arm to Bernice. She looked up to see an elderly Mark Stewart.

"Could a gentleman offer a lady his arm?" he asked.

With a huge grin, Bernice reached out and took his arm. She kissed him on the cheek as he took a place beside her. Ben moved in on her other side, and the three of them began to move in rhythm shoulder-to-shoulder.

Other people dropped in behind them as they slowly circled the center drum. Soon everyone in the room was dancing behind these three aging warriors in a large slow-moving honor circle. Vicky moved ahead of them taking pictures of the celebration.

Later that night, Bernice fell exhausted into her big hotel bed with a deeply satisfied feeling as the sound of the drum, the singers and the cheers echoed in her mind. Thinking back over the long day, she was glad that Vicky had wanted to interview her. It had given her a chance to practice what she would say in the House Made of Lies. And with the honor she had received tonight, Bernice knew that her Indian people were behind her. She relaxed, knowing that tomorrow was in Creator's hands. She knew that her one voice would be heard.

She fell fast into a deep sleep, and the colorful pattern of Indian dancers spiraled in and out of her dreams all night.

Epilogue

On October 15, 1990, Congress did in fact pass the Radiation Exposure Compensation Act, which stated, in part:

"The Congress finds that radiation released in underground uranium mines... exposed miners to large doses of radiation... the Congress recognizes that the lives and health of uranium miners... were involuntarily subjected to increased risk of injury and disease to serve the national security interest of the United States... that the United States should recognize and assume responsibility for the harm done to these individuals, and ...the Congress apologizes on behalf of the nation to the individuals and their families for the hardship they have endured."

In real life, many of the Navajo people affected by uranium mining waited too long for justice to be served. Bogged down by government red tape and shackled by insurmountable regulations imposed by the legislation, some of the financial compensation due to miners, their families and their survivors never reached them. And for those it did reach, it was often too little, too late.

Today, may we Americans make a sacred promise to our fellow citizens to remain ever vigilant over the corporate and government interests that seek to sacrifice the good of a few for the so-called good of the many.

HOLY ROAD

It was 6 p.m. Friday as Valerie Whitedeer pulled up in front of her one-story West Los Angeles bungalow. It had been another challenging week of working office-temp jobs as she tried to make ends meet while waiting for some signs of life to appear, signaling that her writing career wasn't completely dead.

She gathered the long locks of her raven hair into a knot at the back of her head and pinned it in place with a chop stick she always kept handy for the job. Gazing into her own dark brown eyes in the rearview mirror, she felt much older than the thirty-five-year-old Apache woman who stared back at her.

On her way into the house, she checked the front porch mailbox. Along with two credit card statements and an overdue book notice from the library, she found a long-awaited envelope from Popejoy Publishing. Dropping everything else on the living room coffee table, Valerie tore open the letter.

As she read the words "regret to inform you" for the umpteenth time from the umpteenth publisher, her face and her spirits fell. She had been sure it would be different this time around. Before the letter had dropped to the floor, Valerie was already in her bedroom throwing things in to a suitcase. As she packed, she dialed her best friend.

"Penny, I can't handle the rejection any more," she said, her anger and frustration spilling into the phone. "Its been one slamming door after another."

"Val, What are you talking about?" her friend asked.

"I got another rejection on my latest novel," Val responded. "My agent assured me this publisher really wanted it. I've got five years of my life wrapped up in that manuscript and not a damn thing to show for it."

Holding back tears, she slammed the suitcase closed.

"And I can't take one more temporary office assistant job."

"You sound pretty angry and upset," Penny empathized.

"Yeah, so listen, I've decided to get out of town," Valerie continued. "But I don't really want to go alone. You and Michael feel like a road trip?"

"I don't know," Penny replied. "When are you leaving?"

"Right now, if possible. Tomorrow morning at sun-up, if not."

"Well, we are both between acting gigs and art projects, but I'll have to talk to Michael. He's out in the jewelry studio."

"Tell you what," Valerie said impatiently. "I'll come by there in the morning on my way out of town. If you two want to go, have your bags packed when I get there. We'll be gone for a few days."

"Where are you going, anyway?" Penny asked.

"Some place I've been needing to go to for a long time," Val replied. "I'll tell you all about it when I pick you up. Hope to see you in the morning."

She hung up the phone and jumped in the shower for a hot cleansing purge.

First thing the next morning, she grabbed her suitcase, guitar, blue jean jacket with the Mother Earth patch and her Lakota ceremonial pipe and headed out the door.

Powwow Songs by the Black Lodge Singers blared from her CD player as she drove across town in her aging black Chevy van. The large mural on the side, depicting an American Indian drum group wailing out a powwow song, seemed to synchronize with the CD. A bumper sticker on the van's back bumper declared "Indian Affairs Are the Best." It was truly an urban Indian rez car if there ever was one.

Valerie had been born on the High Mountain Apache Indian Reservation in southern New Mexico, but her parents moved to Albuquerque when she was ten years old, and then to Los Angeles when she was fifteen. There she had lived most of her life.

Ever the fighter, she'd been fighting against injustices her people had suffered, fighting against small-mindedness anywhere she found it, and fighting against those who tried to take away her dreams. As a writer, she had hoped to fight against American Indian stereotypes in the media, movies, history books and everywhere else. But it had been a hard road, mostly made up of unsympathetic executives cloistered away in their corporate skyscrapers focused on stock market value.

Michael and Penny were just coming out into the front yard carrying bedrolls, duffle bags and an assortment of travel gear when Valerie drove up.

"Where are we going?" Michael asked with his usual big smile.

"To a place I used to go with my grandmother when I was a little girl," she answered. "It was our special spot on the reservation, and I haven't been there in years. White people named it Mount Thomas, but my grandma always called it Sacred Mountain. She said it was where the Apache Mountain Spirits came from. She would go up there when she needed to ask Creator for something really important to her. Magic always happened there, and I sure could use some now."

"Far out," Michael, ever the retro Indian said as he and Penny loaded their stuff in the van. Michael, who thought of himself as the coolest Native in LA, often said "cool" or "far out" and not much else in response to whatever conversation or situation he was involved in.

"Bring your drum, your rattles and your harmonica," Valerie suggested, "We might want to make some music on the way." After a quick return to the house to grab their musical instruments, the three Natives headed east toward the rising sun with a high sense of hope and adventure.

Soon they left behind the tangled web of LA freeways, headed east on Interstate 10, north on I-15, and then east again on I-40 across the desert. They made good time as the palm trees gave way to scrubby sagebrush.

Both approaching forty years of age, Michael and Penny were a Native American couple who'd been together for many years, struggling with the ups and downs of acting careers and an art business, and struggling with the ups and downs of just being a couple.

There in the van together they made quite a threesome: Indian artisans fighting an uphill battle in what seemed like a foreign country: modern American society. The trick was to keep your balance and your identity intact when all that anyone else wanted was for you to help them perpetuate their myths.

You know the myths: The Circle-the-Wagons myth, The Noble Savage myth, the Drunken Indian myth, the Medicine Man myth, the Indians-are-never-on-time-for-anything myth. There are a few others.

On the California-Arizona border, they stopped to get gas and snacks at one of those roadside convenience stores with the huge obnoxious red and yellow signs announcing "Real Indian Souvenirs." The funny thing was that none of the Anglo customers knew that the threesome were some real Indians.

After loading up on junk food and sodas, the van headed back toward the highway on-ramp. Walking alongside the ramp was a Native guy loaded down with a backpack and a bedroll. He held a sign that said only "Indian Country." Valerie pulled over.

"Where exactly in Indian Country are you going?" Michael yelled out the window.

"Someplace with soul," came the reply. "I'll know it when I get there."

Michael looked at Valerie. "What-a-ya think?" he asked. "Could be interesting."

Valerie nodded in agreement. Michael opened the door and waved to the hitchhiker who ran to the van, opened the back door and climbed in. Off they roared. One more for the road.

He said his name was Larry. He was in low spirits and had decided to search for the Native Promised Land, wherever that was. It seems that his girlfriend had left him, his truck had broken down, and his Indian ventriloquist stage act wasn't getting many bookings. It all sounded like a sad Indian Country song.

"We're all just pilgrims headed to Sacred Mountain for a little spiritual R & R," Valerie said.

"Then I'm in the right place," Larry replied, and he settled in for the ride.

After brief introductions all around, Larry retrieved his Native dummy Wind-In-His-Shorts from his backpack and gave them a sample of his act.

They could see why his act wasn't getting too many bookings. It wasn't that Larry wasn't funny. He just had lousy timing. And his lips moved when his dummy talked.

"Timing's the thing," Larry said, "and I just haven't got it-- yet. But it'll come to me some day, I just know it." Everyone else in the van doubted it but didn't say so.

Driving across country gives a person time to think, time to reflect on life's challenges and that sort of thing. For some reason that long expanse of road in front of you can cause your mind to split into two parts. One part works with your body to keep your car between the white lines, and the other part begins to present you with new possibilities for old problems. Sometimes miles can whiz by while you're in this whole other state of consciousness. That's what usually happened to Valerie on the road.

But that wasn't happening on this trip.

Everyone wanted to talk, all at once, about how fed up they were with their work, their relationships, conditions in their tribal communities, politics on the reservations, politics in the entertainment business, and particularly politics among Indian artists.

And if that wasn't enough, Michael and Larry got into a marathon Joke-Off trying to out-do one another with their Indian jokes. Their journey was a veritable portable gabfest.

The travelers continued eastward down Interstate 40, passed the concrete tipis, the fifty-foot Indian chief, the cardboard buffaloes and the rubber tomahawks: America's cartoon versions of indigenous people packaged for quick sale at rock bottom prices.

That night they pulled into a roadside rest area and spread out their bedrolls next to the van. The crisp, clear air provided a stunning view of the star-studded night sky. Larry sang a Lakota prayer song as they drifted off to sleep.

The next day, the foursome pulled into a restaurant in Gallup, New Mexico, for a bite of "authentic Native American food." The Turquoise Café, about which the highway billboard had bragged of Indian tacos, buffalo burgers, fry-bread and Indian jewelry, was open 24 hours a day.

Inside, a some-what robust Native American waitress came to the table to take their orders. Her nametag read: Elaine. Michael, in his usual way, began joking with Elaine, trying to make her smile, but without much luck. Larry gave it a try, as well.

"What did the old Indian say the first time he saw pizza?" he asked.

"Who threw up on my fry bread?" came the waitresses matter-of-fact answer.

"You heard that one, huh?" Larry said.

"I heard 'em all," Elaine replied.

A pen in one hand and her order tablet in the other, she dropped both arms to her side.

"I appreciate what you guys are trying to do, but don't bother," Elaine told them. "I'm beyond being cheered up."

She took their food orders, and when she returned with their drinks, asked where they were headed.

"Over to Apache country where I'm from," Valerie said. "There's a special place there, a mountain I used to go to when I was a kid, and I haven't been back in a long time."

After a thoughtful moment, a grin slowly spread across Elaine's face.

"I bet I know that place," she said. "I heard about it from my uncle. He used to take special pilgrimages there every four years. It was a very holy spot to my people, the Zuni, and other tribes in this area, but I've never been there."

The four travelers were impressed with Elaine's knowledge of the place.

"You know there's a powwow this weekend," she continued, "not too far from the mountain. I was kind of wanting to go. Would you guys mind having another passenger for at least part of your journey?"

Of course, no one minded.

"I just live across the street," Elaine said excitedly. "I'll get my things together while you're eating and be ready to go by the time you're done."

They watched with amazement as Elaine walked back to the counter, turned in their order to the kitchen, removed her apron, threw it in her boss's face and marched out of the restaurant.

After lunch, the mobile conversation moved on, with new input from Elaine. She told them her parents' story of relocation to Denver when she was young, so they could get job-training and hopefully work. She added her own aspirations and frustrations to the rich mixture of discussion: frustrations with the local Indian art scene, the poor quality of health care on the reservation, and the botched cases of tribal law enforcement caused by the bureaucrats of the BIA All the while, guitars, harmonicas and drums provided a sound track to the deliberations.

As the day progressed, everyone noticed that Elaine was definitely attracted to Larry, and she tried to sit as close to him as she could. Larry, in turn, welcomed the attention, inching closer to

Elaine whenever possible. Love was in the air, or maybe it was just that Indian taco Larry had for lunch.

They arrived at the powwow grounds just before sunset, and everyone in the van agreed that they should stay at least for the night. After setting up camp, they scrounged some firewood and put a pot of coffee on the fire.

They had arrived in time for the evening's grand entry, the signal that another round of dancing was to begin, so they all went to the arena to watch. During the first Intertribal Round Dance, when audience members are invited into the arena, the pilgrims joined in. The beat of the drum was irresistible. The blood in their veins pulsed in synchronous harmony.

The powwow MC recognized Valerie across the arena as she was dancing and, after the song was over, he announced her presence on the loud speaker.

"We have a celebrity of sorts with us," he said. "The woman who wrote <u>My Heroes Have Always Been Indians</u> a few years ago is sitting with friends on the east side of the arena. Let's give a big hand, everybody, for Valerie Whitedeer, one of our own, making good in the big time."

The crowd applauded enthusiastically as Valerie took a step into the arena, smiled and waved real big for everyone.

"The big time," she whispered to Penny. "What a joke. If they only knew the truth."

A few minutes later a voice that was familiar to Valerie rang out from across the arena. "Val! Valerie!" the man yelled.

Valerie looked around the crowd and found the face of a man she hadn't seen in a long, long time. Sonny Two Bulls, an old drinking buddy from Valerie's early, alcohol-drenched days in LA, was coming towards her. The two always seemed to run into one another every once in a while somewhere along life's path.

"Hey, girl, you're sure lookin' good for a reformed drunk," Sonny joked.

"I guess all that fire-water helped preserve my fine complexion," Valerie replied, striking a pin-up pose and sporting a grin.

"How's the Indian law business these days? Are we winning or loosing?" Valerie asked him.

"Well, up to now it's been about even: cowboys ten, Indians ten," Sonny said. "But somebody keeps changing the rules of the game, and the other side seems to own the football. It's all just about to eat my lunch. It's a long, sad story. That's why I came out here, to drown my sorrows in the sounds of the powwow. And what's your excuse for being so far from home base?"

"That, my friend, is a short, sad story," Valerie moaned. "Come over to the camp with us and we can swap lies, okay?"

The whole group headed to the camp to drink coffee and eat freshly made fry-bread. They talked late into the night about things both profound and profane, about the days of old and the not-so-good old days.

In the background, the powwow songs and drums echoed through the valley, summoning a racial memory of times when the open sky, the grassy plains and the towering mountains ruled the lives of their ancestors.

As the conversation and the fire died down, everyone began to settle in for the night. Michael and Penny spread out their bedrolls near the fire. Larry spread his out beside the van, careful to tuck in Wind-In-His-Shorts beside him. Elaine put up a little two-man pup tent nearby and then quietly invited Larry inside. Larry shyly crawled in with Elaine, leaving his dummy outside in the cold.

Valerie was straightening things up inside the van and spreading out her bedding when Sonny approached her.

"Mind if I camp out here with you tonight?" he asked. "I promise I'll behave myself."

Valerie searched around inside the van for a minute and came up with a spare sleeping bag.

"No, I don't mind, Sonny," she said as she tossed him the bag. "But you'll have to sleep outside with the others. I need my space in here."

"I understand," he said with a frown, and walked dejectedly over to the fire.

Valerie climbed into the van and closed the doors behind her.

She dreamt a puzzling dream that night. She was floating above the ground looking down at her group of friends. They were sitting around the campfire passing her sacred pipe from one person to the next. Michael was singing a pipe song as they smoked. Then Valerie's deceased grandmother came up to them and said, "The road to Sacred Mountain has been moved. You have to go a different way."

Valerie woke up immediately and searched her mind so she could capture every moment and tried to understand the meaning of the message.

"Grandma, was that really you?" she quietly whispered as she sat up in the van. "What do you mean?"

No reply was heard.

Next morning, the pilgrims packed up the camp and loaded their things in the van. Elaine had a sheepish grin on her face. Larry had an embarrassed grin on his. Elaine decided to travel on with the pilgrims. Everyone but Sonny piled into the van.

"I wish I was going with you," Sonny said, "but I have some unfinished business to tend to here."

As Sonny was saying his goodbyes to the troupe, a woman's loud voice rang through the camp.

"Sonny! Sonny Two Bulls," an attractive, angry white woman yelled as she marched through the camp. She spotted Sonny next to the van.

"There you are," she said, marching directly towards him. "You're going to be Sonny No-Balls when I get through with you," she threatened as she drew closer. "Where did you spend the night?"

"I told you we were finished, Liz," Sonny shot back. "Now go back to your camp and stop following me around."

"Well, I'm not through with you until I finish giving you a piece of my mind."

Valerie waved to Sonny as she got into the van. He winked back at her.

"You haven't changed, have you, Sonny?" Valerie commented as she closed the van door. "Who is she, your latest one-night-stand?"

"No, she's my wife," he said as the van pulled away.

"Know any good divorce attorneys?" he yelled as the pilgrims hit the road again.

As they drove, Valerie told the travelers of her dream.

"What do you think your grandma meant?" Penny asked. "Was she fond of practical jokes?"

"Yes, she was," Valerie answered. "She was always joking around and playing little tricks on the people she loved. But she wasn't kidding last night. Well, I guess she was, in a way. She had that little gleam in her eye, like she used to get when she knew something you didn't know, and she was trying to make you guess what it was. She was trying to tell me something, but I'm not sure what."

They drove on toward their destination, which was only one more day's drive away at this point.

Late in the day, they turned off the highway on to the road that Valerie knew led to Sacred Mountain. They noticed a sign that read: HIGH MOUNTAIN SKI RESORT--10 miles.

"That's new," Valerie remarked. "I wonder where this resort is."

As the van wound its way up the mountain road, scores of cars passed them going the other way. Finally, Valerie pulled into the ski resort parking lot and got out of the van, taking a few steps across the asphalt. She looked up in disbelief at the luxurious resort lodge perched part way up the mountain. Even though it was summer, people were riding the ski lifts and hiking around the mountain.

Michael left the van and joined Valerie on the lot.

"What's wrong?" he asked. "Why did we stop here?"

"Because this is Sacred Mountain," Valerie replied, an edge of distress clearly noticeable in her voice. "Or at least it used to be. I've been out of touch with my tribe's business lately, but I can't believe that something like this could've happened."

Everyone else got out of the van and joined the puzzled pair. They all stared up at the resort lodge in disbelief. The sun was setting behind another nearby peak, and the sky was filling with hues of brilliant orange and dark magenta.

The pilgrims, on the other hand, were filled with hues of disappointment. Michael drove them back down the mountain because Valerie was just too paralyzed to function. Back in the low lands, they headed for the nearest campground for the night.

As night fell, a fog formed in the low-lying areas, so their going was slow and unsure. They drove along a little dirt road for a while looking for some place to park the van for the night. Since nothing seemed familiar, and no campsite presented itself, they pulled off into a clearing and killed the engine. Fatigue had settled in, so everyone fell asleep where they were.

Around midnight, Valerie was roused from sleep by the sound of someone moaning somewhere out in the fog. She reached over and shook Michael until he woke up, too.

"Listen," Valerie whispered. "There's someone out there."

Michael got to his knees and peeked out one of the van's windows. He heard more noises, sounding like several people stumbling through the woods, breathing heavily and moaning.

Valerie and Michael woke up the rest of the group. Quietly, they got out and walked toward the sounds. To their astonishment, they found a small band of American Indians dressed in buckskin, breechcloths and moccasins. Among them was what appeared to be a grandmother and grandfather, a middle-aged man and woman, and a boy and girl. They were all dirty, tired and hungry.

Seeing Valerie's group, the man spoke.

"We have walked many miles. We have no food or water. Can you help us?"

Michael ran over to the van and gathered up what food and water he could.

"What happened to you?" Valerie asked. "Where are you going?"

Michael passed out the food as the middle-aged woman answered.

"We were removed from our homes in the middle of the night by the Bluecoats," she said. "They told us they would kill us if we did not leave. They said that our lands were no longer ours, and there was a place they called a reservation that was to be our new home. We ran in fear. Our brothers to the north had already been put on one of these reservations, given rotten meat to eat, blankets filled with sickness to warm themselves, and left to wither and die."

As the refugee woman spoke, the pilgrims listened in confusion and disbelief. What they were hearing did not make sense to their tweny-first century minds. These were words and actions would be part of the 19th century tragedies among their people.

"How is this happening?" Valerie asked of no one in particular. "What are we supposed to do?"

"We must keep moving," the refugee man said. "The Bluecoats can't be far behind. If they catch us, they'll kill us."

Feeling the refugees' sense of urgency, and trying to ignore their own sense of bewilderment, the pilgrims helped the refugees into the van. The refugees were as confused about the van as the pilgrims were confused about the presence of these refugees from a bygone era. But, together, they drove off down the dark and foggy dirt road.

In a little while, they came upon another clearing with a single grass hut standing in the middle, illuminated from within by a small cooking fire. A few horses were tied up near the lodge.

They stopped at the edge of the clearing and got out of the van.

"This looks like the lodge of my cousin," the middle age male refugee said. "He hid his family away at the first sign of trouble with the white soldiers."

Slowly and quietly they crept up to the door of the lodge, following the lead of the Native man. Halfway across the clearing, the horses stirred and a buckskin-clad Native man came out of the hut to see what was happening. He saw the shadowy figures moving through the fog and went for a weapon.

The refugee man called out to him in his Native tongue. The two recognized each other and came together for a brief reunion. After a few minutes of talking together, the refugee man returned to where the group was waiting.

"We are all welcome in my cousin's lodge," he said. "He has food and warmth for us all for the night."

The curious, mixed group of pilgrims and refugees entered the glow of the hut and made themselves at home. With the refugee man acting as a translator, they talked on into the night. The man who lived in the hut told them he had extensively explored the immediate area, and he had found a wonderful place up on the mountain where the ancestor spirits came to speak with him. They told him where to find the best game and how to use the herbs that grew nearby for healing.

"They also told me that you were coming," he said to Valerie in perfect English. "And they asked me to give you a message."

A silence fell over the pilgrims as they listened.

"They said to tell you that Sacred Mountain is not one single place that you journey to find. Sacred Mountain is all around you. Every place is a sacred place and every mountain is a sacred mountain. Indeed, you carry the sacredness with you wherever you go. Men who are disconnected from themselves and their roots may defile a mountain for their own purposes, but only you can defile the holy mountain in your heart."

He fell silent as the message pounded in the pilgrims' minds and echoed in their hearts.

Speaking to the whole group, the man continued.

"To be sure, there is a time to stand and fight for your family, your life and your land. But you must learn when to fight and when to save the fight for another day. When it is time to fight, you must use the best weapons for each particular battle. Sometimes it is the bow and the lance. Other times it may be words and patience. Both require wisdom and courage. Think on it tonight," he finished.

The pilgrims all fell asleep enraptured with the spirit of the evening and the magic of the moment. They were wrapped in a deep, dense sleep that lasted throughout the night.

In the morning, Valerie awoke slowly and with great effort to find herself, not in the hut, but in the van. Her fellow pilgrims were all there too, fast asleep. She peeked out the van's front window and looked around. They were in the very clearing that, the night before, had held a grass lodge, horses and other people. Yet, now there was no lodge, no horses and no people.

Instead, there was a large plywood display sign in the clearing at the edge of the dirt road. The sign had a little roof over it to protect it from rain and snow.

Valerie stumbled out of the van with her blanket still wrapped around her. Slowly she approached the display to get a better look at it. Near the top it read: "Future site of the National American Indian Sacred Lands Memorial--Dedicated to generations of Indian people who have been displaced from their homelands. Sponsored by the Sacred Mountain Institute, an American Indian non-profit organization."

Under the sign was a little container holding several brochures. As Valerie reached for one, the rest of the sleepy-eyed, dazed pilgrims arrived beside her.

Rubbing his eyes, Michael asked, "What's going on now? Where did the lodge and the people go?"

"I don't know," Valerie replied as she handed out copies of the brochure. "They somehow brought us here and made sure we found this project, though. Read the brochure."

The brochure outlined a campaign being launched by the Sacred Mountain Institute to get the holy land where the ski resort stood returned to the tribe from which it had been taken. Each one looked at the other with a blank, bewildered stare.

"I don't know about the rest of you guys," Larry said, "but I know where I'm going to be and what I'm going to be doing for the next few years."

"What I want to know is where I've been and what I've been doing for the last few days," Penny blurted.

"I think we've been traveling in some sort of Indian Time Warp," Larry said, and then, adopting his best Rod Serling impression, continued, "Consider if you will, five modern day Indians, traveling the American Southwest, confused as hell, crossing over into... The Fry Bread Zone."

Valerie looked at her friends and laughed a sort of spirit-freeing laugh.

"This is the best trip I've ever been on," she proclaimed. "But now I'm starving. Let's go find some breakfast and talk over this battle for Sacred Mountain. I think I have an idea for my next book."

All Michael said was "far out" as they walked back toward the van, and the moveable conversation took on new life in search of breakfast.

THE BLOOD IN OUR VEINS

Ten-year-old Tony Mirada proudly worked beside his father, Renaldo, as they cleaned out Mr. Kincaid's horse stables, shoveling the mixture of hay and manure into a wheelbarrow. They were to finish the job by the end of the day. It was hard work, but the boy didn't mind because it was "man's work."

The Kincaid Ranch covered several hundred acres of the hilly grasslands dotted with Oak trees that characterized the Santa Juanita Valley. The Kincaids were one of several Anglo-American families that had moved to the area a few generations back. Many had purchased land there, and with determination and hard work, had carved out decent lives for themselves.

Mr. Kincaid must be a nice man, Tony thought. His father had worked for him on the Valley Oaks Ranch for six months and made enough money for the family to buy food and clothing--at least for now.

Work was scarce for Tony's family and all the families who lived on the Chamala Indian Reservation at the center of the valley. The boy had never really wondered until recently why the Indians in the Santa Juanita Valley were so poor. That's just the way it had always been, as far as he knew.

"Papa, why are our people so poor?" Tony asked as he shoveled another load into the wheelbarrow. "Mr. Kincaid has a nice big ranch with electric lights, indoor toilets and many fine horses, but none of our people have any of these things."

He stopped and looked out at the surrounding countryside.

"That's a hard question to answer, son," his father replied. "Keep working. We'll talk about it later."

Tony continued to gaze out at the beautiful rolling hills dotted with large oaks and Mr. Kincaid's lazily grazing Arabian horses. In the distance, he saw Mount Condor, the mysterious peak he'd heard tribal elders talk about when they thought he wasn't listening.

Then a red-tail hawk came into view, circling above the barn, calling to its mate across the valley. The scene was peaceful, almost dream-like.

Renaldo grew impatient.

"Back to work, I said."

Snapping back to the here-and-now, Tony resumed his labors.

At noon, the boy and his father sat down in the shade of a nearby oak to eat the sack lunch they'd brought with them. It consisted of two baloney sandwiches, two tamales and two grape sodas.

As they quietly ate, the ranch's owner approached.

"How's the boy doing?" Kincaid asked, forming his words very distinctly. "Is he slowing you down any?"

Tony noticed that Mr. Kincaid talked to his father as if _he_ were the ten-year-old. That bothered the boy.

"No, Mr. Kincaid," Renaldo replied. "He ain't slowing me down. Tony is a hard worker. He's been doing manual labor with his brother on the reservation for years."

"Good, I'm glad to hear it. There will be a couple of extra dollars in your pay at the end of the day to cover the boy's hours, but I can't have you bringing him along whenever you feel like it."

"But, sir, his mother works, and his grandmother is very ill, so she can't watch after him."

"So you told me. I'm sorry, Renaldo, but this is no place for the boy. He can finish out the day, but you'll have to leave him with somebody tomorrow. Understand?"

Renaldo nodded.

"Now when you've finished eating, I need you to go help Frank and the boys unload the hay truck that just came in. Then you can come back and finish up here."

After the rancher had walked away, Tony asked, "Why does he talk to you like you're just a kid or you don't understand English or something?"

"Enough with the questions already," Renaldo replied. "That's just the way some valley folks talk to us. They get us confused with the Mexican laborers, I guess. Now finish your lunch so we can get back to the job."

Tony finished his lunch in silence. He had a lot of questions these days that his father seemed unable or unwilling to answer. Sometime the ten-year-old just couldn't make sense of the world he saw around him.

For his part, Renaldo knew his son was waking up more to the world around him and was filled with many questions about their lives and their living conditions. He must be better prepared to answer them when and if he asked.

After finishing lunch, the two Indians walked over to the big barn where the hay truck was parked. Three Anglo ranch hands had started unloading the hay and stacking it in the barn.

"It's about time you showed up, chief," one of the ranch hands snapped as he off-loaded a bale. Ignoring the remark, Renaldo began working. Tony watched, not sure how he could help.

"Just go sit down over there until I'm finished," Renaldo told him. Tony sat down in the shade near the barn.

Within a few minutes, Tony noticed that all three ranch hands had taken a break and were drinking water from a ten-gallon cooler strapped to one of the ranch trucks. His father was working alone.

"Come on, Tonto, put your back into it," one of the hands yelled. "We haven't got all day." The others laughed, but, noticing that Kincaid was approaching, immediately got back to work, hoping he hadn't seen them slacking off.

Eventually, father and son went back to their original stable-cleaning task. Tony was definitely tiring, and he thought of the hard labor his mother engaged in three days a week, doing the only work she knew how to do. She cleaned the house and washed the clothes of another ranching family not too far from the reservation.

Tony was glad when they finally finished their smelly job and went to Mr. Kincaid to collect their pay for the day. The boy was delighted when his father handed him a five dollar bill, more money than the boy had ever possessed.

"Stuff that in your pocket so you don't lose it," Renaldo said. You can start thinking about how you want to spend on our way home.

Then, dog-tired, Tony and his father set out on foot toward the reservation two miles away.

"I don't know all the answers to your questions," Renaldo said as they walked beside a paved rural road. "I didn't make it far in school, and your grandparents never talked much about their lives when they were young. I think it was just too hard to talk about."

Tony looked at his father as the weathered, brown-skinned man spoke. The scar along his right jaw was the most noticeable feature on his face. It had been left by the horn of an angry bull Renaldo had tried to rope on a previous ranch job. That had laid him up for weeks, unable to work, unable to feed his family. That's when his mother had started working to help make ends meet.

"Life will be different for you--better," his father continued. "They say next year a new bus will be taking kids from the reservation over to the school in Springville, so you'll get an education."

Tony was about to say something when a green and white pickup truck zipped by them going much too fast. It stopped abruptly a few yards ahead and backed up until it was even with the two Natives. It paused in the middle of the road. Inside the truck's cab were two of the young hands from the Kincaid Ranch. The passenger, slightly drunk, got out and did his version of a Hollywood Indian war-whoop.

"Well, look Floyd. It's Tonto and Tonto, Junior," the inebriated man said to the equally drunk driver. "What do you suppose they're doing off the reservation--huntin' for scalps?"

Both men laughed.

"We're just walking home," Renaldo said calmly. "We ain't looking for trouble."

"Trouble certainly found you, though," the ranch hand quipped menacingly. "When are you redskins gonna learn to stay on the reservation where you belong?"

The ranch hand hit Renaldo hard on the cheek, knocking him to the ground. Tony ran to his father's side.

The drunk Anglo grabbed Tony by the shirt, but the sound of an approaching car startled him. Hastily, he retreated to the truck and jumped in.

"You dumb, dirty Indians--we shoulda killed all of you when we had the chance," the ranch hand yelled out the window as the truck sped away.

Tony watched as the truck disappeared over the hill. He turned and helped his father up.

"He'd better be glad that car came by," Tony declared. "I was just about to let him have it."

"Son, it's a good thing you didn't try," Renaldo admonished. "Standing up for yourself is always the right thing to do, but you've got to use your head, too."

"What do you mean?" the boy asked.

"I mean you've got to size up your attacker--know your enemy--before you act. That fella had a rifle in his gun rack and was probably drunk enough to use it if we'd fought back."

"Oh, I didn't see that."

"Your grandpa always said a man's got to know when to stand and fight and when to walk away. You've got to learn that lesson, too."

Renaldo reached out and touched the boy's shoulder.

"Let's go to the house," he said as he patted Tony on the back.

They continued their journey in silence.

It was almost dark when the pair reached the Chamala Indian Reservation, an unremarkable piece of land straddling a creek near the center of the Santa Juanita Valley. The familiar dirt road delivered them to their two-room shack, which stood near an ancient oak tree.

A dim light spilled out through a glassless window onto the scraggly family dog that greeted them cheerily out front.

Tony pushed open the warped wooden front door to enter their very humble abode. Renaldo crossed the worn plank floor and turned up the wick on the kerosene lantern that illumined the front room with its sparse collection of Goodwill-reject furniture.

"Renaldo? Tony? Is that you?"

The weak voice of Tony's grandmother was barely a

whisper from the back of the shack.

"Yeah, grandma, it's us," Tony replied.

He and his father entered the back bedroom where his grandmother, Adelia, was propped up in bed.

Tony's mother, Grace, was seated beside the bed. Rising from her chair, she approached Renaldo with something urgent on her mind.

"Mother said the County Health Department was here today," Grace reported. "They found out why half of us are sick."

Tony sat down next to his grandmother, listening.

"Evening, Adelia," Renaldo offered calmly to his wife's mother. Turning to his wife, he asked, "When did you get home from work, Grace?"

Grace didn't seem to have time for such pleasantries.

"Just now," she replied impatiently. "Listen, they say it's the water from the creek that's making us sick. It's contaminated. Sewage from town is seeping into the ground. We shouldn't be drinking it."

"Then where are we supposed to get water from? That river has been our only source as long as our people have lived here--before there even was a town."

Grace noticed the cut on Renaldo's face.

"What happened to you?" she asked.

"It's nothing," he said dismissively. "Some drunks decided to get a little rough after work, that's all."

Grace looked to her son for confirmation, but his face

couldn't be read. She calmed herself.

"Tony, stay here and keep your grandmother company. I'll go fix us some supper." She motioned for Renaldo to follow her.

In the kitchen, Grace began preparing a simple meal. Renaldo stood near the window.

"The health department said we have to come up with five thousand dollars to pay for water lines that would allow us to get clean water from the Santa Juanita water district," she explained.

Renaldo laughed mockingly.

"Where are we gonna come up with that kind of money? They might as well ask for a million." He stared out the window into the darkness. "Nobody in this valley cares whether we live or die."

"That's not true," Grace protested. "The church cares. The Mission has been very good to us. Father Murphy helps us whenever he can."

"You put too much faith in that damn Mission." Renaldo turned back to see the shock on her face. "My father always said it was the Mission that separated us from everything that made us Indian."

"Watch your words, Renaldo Mirada. You could go to hell for that."

"I'm already in hell," he proclaimed as he turned back to look out the window. "You think God don't know what the Mission did to us?"

Tony stood near the door to his grandmother's bedroom

listening to his parents' angry conversation.

"That cowboy that hit me today was right," his father's voice continued. "They should've killed us all when they had the chance, generations ago."

Tony's ten-year-old mind couldn't grasp why his father had said such hurtful words. He couldn't mean it. The boy turned and, as his father had done, gazed out a nearby window. Searching the darkness, his eyes found the distant mountain peak they sought, Mount Condor. Illuminated by the full moon, that mountain kept its ever-vigilant watch over the valley.

Tony whispered a prayer to the spirit of that mountain, a prayer he'd heard his grandpa utter when he was still alive, "Father Mountain, help us, your children, in our time of need."

30 Years Later

One-by-one, aging cars and mud-streaked pickup trucks pulled into the parking lot of the Chamala tribal bingo hall, a fairly new pre-fab metal structure that sat across from the older and smaller tribal headquarters office building.

Tribal members of various ages entered the bingo hall to attend the regular monthly council meeting. They were warmly greeted by Ted Castillo, a friendly, elderly Chamala man they had all known most of their lives. His uniform looked particularly crisp tonight.

Forty-year-old Tribal Chairman Tony Mirada surveyed the crowd as they settled in. These were his people, the Chamala

Nation, whom he'd sworn to serve, whose quality of life he'd promised to improve.

By the time the meeting began, about 75 people were seated in rows of chairs situated behind tables regularly used for bingo games. Late arrivals sat in the back.

The five duly-elected Chamala Tribal Council members were seated in a row at a head table in front of the room. Taking his usual place at the center stage podium, Tony conducted the meeting as he'd done for the past two years.

An elderly man rose from his folding chair and addressed the Tribal Chairman.

"I want to know what you're going to do to bring more jobs for our people," the tribal member said. "Can't we get a loan to start some kind of business that will do more than this bingo hall and the trailer park we've got now? They just don't make enough money to do us much good."

Several people in the crowd echoed the man's opinion, loudly agreeing with him as he sat down.

Tony motioned for them to quiet down.

"I remember what it was like on this reservation not too many years ago," he said. "Dirt roads, no electricity, no running water, no health care, no nothing. We were a deserted and forgotten people. And no one in this valley cared whether we lived or died."

Responsive chatter arose from the crowd.

"But things have slowly changed for the better," the

Chairman continued. "Most of us have decent homes now. Our roads are paved, and we have a health clinic and a lot of the services that a community our size needs."

Another tribal member stood to speak.

"We don't disagree with that," the older man observed. "Things are a lot better. But we're still economically weak, still looking to the federal government to keep us afloat, and those funds are drying up. We have no tax base, no means of generating income to operate a real tribal government."

A third tribal member stood up before the man had finished.

"That's what we elected you to do as tribal chairman–to lead us into a better future, a brighter future–isn't that what your campaign slogan promised us?"

"And that's what I and this entire Tribal Council are working for," Tony replied in a calming voice. "A better future for us and our children. But it takes time, folks. You've got to give it some time. I repeat my vow to you that we will devise a way to make things better for the Chamala people."

Later, after the formal meeting had ended, tribal members enjoyed refreshments and talked informally in small groups. One of the earlier speakers stood with Tony near the punch bowl.

"We have to be cautious and not jump into something too quickly," Tony advised. "That's why we're investigating several business ideas, and when we've narrowed it down to the best ones, we'll present them to the tribe for a vote."

"All right," the man said. "I'll give you the benefit of the doubt--for now. But I expect some action, not just talk."

Just then, Tony's wife, Gloria, stepped up. An attractive Pomo Indian woman in her mid-thirties, she was, as usual, over-dressed for this tribal function.

Tony had married Gloria after experiencing a series of unsuccessful and disappointing relationships since leaving college. At first, Gloria had been the breath for fresh air he had been looking for, but as the years passed, she seemed to gravitate towards the "shallow end of the pool," as one of Tony's friends had put it. It seemed that shopping and fashion had become her top priorities.

"Tony, it's time to go," Gloria said curtly.

"I'm almost done," Tony replied gently, calmly.

"We've got to pick up little Tony from your cousin's house," she reminded him, almost whining. "I promised we wouldn't be out late. You know she goes to bed early."

"All right, I'm coming."

He gulped down his drink and turned back to the man he'd been talking to. Gloria dragged their son away as she headed for the exit.

"Whatever we end up doing," Tony finished saying. "We don't want a repeat of the problems we had with the BIA. Every one of their economic development projects failed. Now if you'll excuse me, I've got to go."

Tony smiled, put down his punch glass and strolled towards

the door to catch up to his wife.

At home, Tony carried his sleeping son, six-year-old Tony Junior, to his bedroom and tucked him in. After giving the boy a goodnight kiss on the cheek and turning out the light, Tony Senior entered the living room.

He stopped at a framed black and white photo that hung on the wall long enough to straighten it--and remember. Staring back at him from the picture were the stony faces of his parents, Renaldo and Grace, standing together, looking as they had some thirty years ago, with himself at ten years of age, between them. That photo was his reminder of what his leadership of the tribe was all about.

His remembrance was interrupted as his wife entered from the kitchen sipping on a mixed drink.

"I don't know how much more of your self-centered attitude I can take," Tony remarked. "Why do you care so little about what's going on here at this reservation?"

"Why do you care so much?" she fired back, sitting down on the couch. "Nobody here appreciates you or the things you try to do. All they do is criticize--point fingers and criticize."

Tony sat down on the other end of the couch.

"It goes with the job of being tribal chairman. The way I look at it, our people have had almost no voice in their own affairs for nearly 200 years. So now they're making up for lost time."

Gloria stood up.

"Oh, please," she said, walking back to the kitchen. "When

are you going grow up? What goes on here on this tiny little speck of a reservation doesn't amount to a hill of beans in the outside world."

This isn't a new argument between them, but it still gets Tony fired up. He has new ideas he wants to share with somebody, anybody. He follows her to the kitchen.

"I know you just don't get it, but that's one of the things I'm trying to change. For decades, people have held our Indian-ness against us. Now I want to make our Indian-ness work in our favor."

"And how do plan to accomplish that?"

He paces, thinking. This has been on his mind.

"I don't know yet," he confides, "but there are a lot of possibilities, and I know one of them is going to be right for this tribe."

"Well, whatever you do, you'd better watch your back," she concluded. "The half of the tribe that voted you into office is getting impatient for results. The other half who didn't vote for you is just waiting for you to screw up so they can vote you out."

Tony smiled knowingly.

"Ain't tribal politics grand?" he said.

A few miles away and a few days later, the citizens of Springville were in high spirits as their annual Pioneer Day Celebration got under way. It was a Saturday and local folks dressed in pioneer garb sampled the wares of the vendors and food booths that lined Main Street while country music filled the air.

Somewhere buried in the back of everyone's mind was the unconscious knowledge that what they were really celebrating was the survival of their immigrant bloodlines and cultures in the rugged west.

"Welcome to Springville's one hundreth Annual Pioneer Days Celebration," blared a loudspeaker. "This morning's parade is brought to you by the good folks at Happy Trails Café, home of the Cowboy Cappuccino, and all of us here at KSJV Radio, voice of the Santa Juanita Valley. Stand by for our live parade coverage."

Just moments later, the parade, made up of an odd assortment of fire trucks, tractors, cowboys on horseback, old time cars and school marching bands, began it's slow journey down the street with great bravado.

Soon, a police car, lights flashing and siren wailing, came into view, followed by a flatbed truck. Police Chief Dwight Whitfield, a muscular blonde man in his 50s, waved to the crowds from the truck bed. A banner on the side of the truck announced "SPRINGVILLE POLICE DEPARTMENT: PROTECTING OUR WAY OF LIFE."

This float was followed by a string of three hotrod pick-up trucks, each towing a horse trailer decorated with flame decals. Draped on each trailer was a banner: RUFF RYDERS RODEO CLUB. In the driver's seat of the lead truck was the Police Chief's chip-off-the-old-block son, Travis, a twenty-something macho blonde. He gunned his engine and waved to the crowds.

Next in line were two beautiful, halter-top clad cowgirls on foot carrying yet another banner: NOW APPEARING – TV STAR ROY EVANS RIDING HIS FAITHFUL HORSE REDSTAR.

Wearing a flamboyant, fringed western outfit and looking every bit as dapper as the legendary Gene Autry, retired cowboy actor Roy Evans followed the young ladies, riding his world-famous stunt horse. Redstar, an aging grey with a roan star-burst on his forehead, dipped and bowed to the delight of the crowd as his rider, ever the showman, tipped his cowboy hat to the ladies.

Behind that spectacle followed another flatbed truck, this time carrying Tony Mirada and several members of the Chamala Tribal Council. Their banner proclaimed: THE CHAMALA PEOPLE: FIRST INHABITANTS OF THE SANTA JUANITA VALLEY.

A weak smattering of applause greeted them.

Bringing up the rear was the final pick-up truck carrying four Indian men seated around a drum. They pounded out a powerful powwow song while two Chamala Indian Dancers performed on a four-wheeled platform being towed by the truck.

Their singing and dancing brought respectful applause from the bystanders who lined the street. And then the parade was over. Onlookers turned their attention back to the vendors.

By early afternoon most people were congregating in the Springville city park or on the courthouse lawn across the street where a speaker's stand and P.A. system had been set up. Tony and a couple of the Tribal Council Members were among those enjoying the spring afternoon in the park.

At precisely 2 p.m., as had previously been announced, Springville's Mayor J.J. Cummings stepped up to the podium to address the assembled crowd.

"Our forefathers fought hard to secure a foothold in this beautiful rural land," the robust man of 50 began. "And it is up to us as their descendants to remember the sacrifices they made, and insure that their sacrifices were not made in vain."

Tony had heard this speech before, or one just like it, at every other Pioneer Day celebration he'd attended. It wasn't anything really new, but it apparently resonated with a small group of supporters standing in front of the podium who showed their appreciation with vigorous applause.

Tony noticed that most of the people within earshot of the mayor weren't quite so enthusiastic and only half-heartedly listened as if it was part of their citizenly duty.

The mayor continued.

"And so, I don't have to tell you how important it is that we celebrate our values and traditions today, and pass those values and traditions on down the line to our kids, so this way of life we love so much will continue."

Tony scanned the crowd to see who was on hand. There was Police Chief Dwight Whitfield, known locally as merely Chief Dwight, with two of his officers standing guard near the podium. They were also scanning the crowd, probably looking for drunks or troublemakers.

Off to the side of the podium, local newspaper editor Ralph Bailey operated in his usual mode, taking notes and shooting pictures for the valley's only newspaper, the <u>Hitchin'</u> <u>Post</u>.

On the fringe of the crowd was Chief Dwight's son, Travis, who leaned against his hot rod pickup with a couple of his Ruff Ryder buddies. They all appeared to be cut from the same cloth as they laughed and joked about the proceedings.

The mayor finally wrapped up his comments.

"With all that in mind, I want to encourage you to come to our town council meeting tonight to witness the unveiling of our Santa Juanita Valley Blueprint for Controlled Growth. I think you'll all be proud of the work that's gone into the creation of this plan. Thank you, and be sure to visit as many vendors as you can here at our Pioneer Day celebration."

The supportive front-row crowd gave the mayor a rousing applause as he wiped the sweat from his forehead with a handkerchief and stepped down from the podium.

Tony consulted with his fellow tribal council members who all agreed that they should attend tonight's public meeting to find out what "controlled growth" meant.

By 6:30 that evening, local town folk began pouring into the Springville Community Building just off Main Street. A hand-painted sign that read SJ VALLEY BLUEPRINT PRESENTED TONIGHT was tacked to a front porch post of this ranch-style structure. Mayor Cummings stood near the entrance with Chief Dwight, watching as people enter.

Tony and two Tribal Council members approached the entrance.

"What are they doing here?" Chief Dwight whispered to the mayor.

"Don't know," Cummings replied. "Guess we'll find out."

Tony detoured to pay a political visit to Cummings.

"Chairman Mirada, how are you this fine evening?" Cummings asked, mustering up all the politeness his position as mayor required. He extended his hand.

"Can't complain, Mayor Cummings."

Tony shook the mayor's hand, mustering the same political politeness his position as Tribal Chairman demanded.

"What brings you to our humble gathering?" Cummings asked.

"We're looking into business opportunities for the reservation," Tony admitted. "So we want to see what's in store for the future of our valley. I'm looking forward to an informative evening." He smiled.

"Well, that's just fine." The mayor smiled back. "Be sure to pick up a copy of the printed plan just inside the door."

"Thanks. We will."

Then Tony acknowledged Chief Dwight.

"Dwight," he said tersely and with a slight nod.

"Tony," Chief Dwight responded with a similar terse acknowledgement.

Tony joined the other Tribal Council members, and they

proceeded inside to collect copies of the Blueprint Plan and to find seats near the back.

A large map of the Santa Juanita Valley covered one wall of the meeting room, showing the Valley's communities and Springville's proximity to the Chamala Indian Reservation. The valley's main artery, a two-lane highway running east-west through the valley, was highlighted. The map indicated that there was one parcel of land sitting along the highway that separated it from the reservation.

Cummings and his Blueprint Committee, who turned out to be among his supporters at his afternoon speech, were seated at a head table. The Blueprint Plan was presented as the work of the entire committee, but Cummings did most of the talking.

"Here's the bottom line, ladies and gentlemen," Cummings stated, as he wrapped up the presentation. "Over the next twenty years, we plan to allow only slow, controlled growth in the valley--no high-density housing developments, in fact no large-scale developments of any kind–to preserve the rural, agricultural lifestyle we've all come to love here."

Polite applause rippled through the audience. Roy Evans, no longer wearing the western outfit seen earlier in the parade, rose from his seat in the audience.

"Isn't it true that you and the other members of this planning committee own some of the largest businesses and real estate parcels in the valley?" he asked.

"That may well be," the mayor offered, "but I don't see

what--"

"So, what you're saying is, now that you've moved in here and established your dude ranch, restaurant and golf course, you want to close the door behind you to prevent anyone else from coming in and doing the same. Is that it?"

A wave of mild chatter spread through the room. In the corner, Ralph Bailey furiously took notes as Chief Dwight watched the proceedings from the door.

"No, that's not it at all," Cummings protested.

"Isn't this whole plan just an attempt to prevent competition in the marketplace?" Evans asked accusingly.

"You're one to talk, Roy Evans." Cummings jumped up from his seat and hurried to the valley map on the wall.

"We all know that you now own plenty of real estate yourself since you retired here to the valley."

He pointed to several pieces of land.

"You bought the old Mission Winery, and you've also opened a bed & breakfast, a coffee shop and a saloon," Cummings pointed out.

"And they were all good investments," Evans conceded.

"But what some people don't know is that you're sitting on a prime piece of real estate right here along the highway you're just itching to develop."

Cummings again pointed out this property on the map.

More chatter spread through the room. Tony was paying close attention now.

"It's not really a secret," Evans countered.

"And we also know the County Board of Supervisors has repeatedly turned down your plans and applications to develop that property for commercial purposes," Cummings continued.

"So what's your point?" Evans was losing patience.

"My point is--"

The mayor's polite layer peeled away slightly.

"Don't pretend that you oppose this plan for altruistic reasons. You claim we have a vested interest in seeing this plan pass. Well, the way I see it, you have a vested interest in seeing it fail, because when this Blueprint gets approved by the County, you'll have a hell of a time getting any of your large-scale development plans approved."

At that moment, a light went on in Tony's mind, and he jotted down a few words on the note pad he'd been holding. A conversation with Roy about his plans would be very useful, he thought.

Later, after the meeting ended, Chief Dwight watched people as they left the community center. He thought it curious that Tribal Chairman Tony Mirada and retired actor, now property owner Roy Evans were quietly talking about something near the parking lot.

Simultaneously, Roy noticed Whitfield's interest in this conversation with Tony and decided that it was time to break it off. He shook the tribal chairman's hand and promised to continue the conversation in the next few days.

Tony, however, had to attend to some other important tribal business first. The following Monday, a faded yellow school bus pulled into the Santa Juanita Mission parking lot and stopped. Almost immediately, about fifty enthusiastic Native American kids poured out of it, followed by a couple of tribal elders, a handful of parents, and finally, Tony.

Standing near the Mission entrance to greet them was Father McDougal, a balding, middle-aged Catholic priest.

"Welcome, children, to the Santa Juanita Mission," the padre said with a smile. "It's such a joy to receive you this morning for your annual mission field trip."

Tony and tribal elder Irene Magdalena approached the priest.

"Thanks, Father," Tony said. "We've got a few more than usual this year." Motioning toward Irene, he continued, "Father, you remember the tribe's cultural advisor, Irene Magdalena?

"Of course," he replied cooling, shaking her hand. "Our paths have crossed several times."

"She wanted to come along this year to help add, well - balance to your presentation of Spanish Mission history."

Tony let that sink in for a moment as they watched the parents attempt to round up the kids and get them settled down.

"Balance?" the priest said. "Whatever do you mean?"

"I guess you could call it an alternate view of history," Irene answered. "It counteracts the propaganda the church has been feeding our youth for generations."

"Uh, Padre, can you give me a hand with the grocery bags?" Tony asked in an attempt to diffuse the situation before a heated exchange developed. "We've got lunch supplies to unload."

Grateful for the change in subject, the priest followed Tony to the rear of the bus and helped unload the food.

Later, the kids were divided into small groups so they could tour the Mission. Tony and Irene accompanied one group as they reached a hilltop at the edge of the Mission grounds to take in a spectacular view of the Santa Juanita Valley. Plowed fields, rolling hills and the riverbed spread out before them.

"All the land of this valley once belonged to the Chamala people," Tony remarked. "It had been our home for thousands of years before the Spaniards came."

Is it true that our people would've starved to death if it weren't for food and shelter provided by the Mission?" one of the boys asked. "That's what Father McDougal said."

"The priest has his version of what happened," Tony answered, following a brief hesitation. "It's the version the church has been telling for 200 years. Irene, how would you answer that question?"

"Are you sure you're ready for this?" Irene looked him in the eye.

"That's what you came for, isn't it?" he replied calmly.

"Most of these kids were baptized by this priest, and contradicting him might have serious consequences from their parents," she explained.

"We've got to start somewhere, sometime. I'll take the heat if there are any complaints. It'll be all right."

"Okay, here we go." She turned to the kids.

"Our people were just fine, and would've continued to be just fine without the Spaniards or the Missions," she stated, picking up a nearby stone from the ground.

"We knew and respected every rock, every plant and every animal in this area. We hunted, fished and gathered all sorts of plant foods that the earth had to offer, and thanked the Creator in our own ways for his blessings."

"Didn't our people learn a better way of life here in the Mission?" a girl asked innocently.

"Not exactly," Irene's replied. "What they don't tell you is that our people, and all the native peoples of this state, were used as slave labor to build the Missions and to do work for the priests and soldiers who lived here. And, in this Mission, we were exposed to the white man's diseases, which killed hundreds of us."

She pointed with her lips towards a field beside the Mission.

"See that field over there just outside the cemetery walls?"

The kids almost simultaneously turned to look in that direction.

"Almost a thousand of our people are buried there in unmarked graves."

"You mean there's bodies under there?" another boy asked, obviously creeped out by the idea.

"Your ancestors' bodies," Irene replied, heightening the drama. "Their spirits are restless. How do you think they like it when people walk all over them?"

The kids responded with an almost unanimous "E-uwww."

"Why don't they have tomb stones like the priests and white people buried in the cemetery?" the first boy asked.

"That's a very good question," Irene said as an idea was forming in her mind.

Just then the bell in the church tower rang. Everyone looked up to see Father McDougal in the tower.

"Time for lunch!" he called down to them.

The kids immediately forgot what they'd been talking about, jumped up and ran toward the church.

"We'll have a story by the fountain after you eat!" Irene yelled to them, not sure they heard her as they ran off.

"I know you enjoy being with the kids and all, but what's the real reason you came out here today?" Tony asked Irene. She was surprised by his insightfulness.

"What makes you think there's another reason?" she asked coyly.

"Your mind's working so hard and so loud it's deafening."

"Okay, I hoped I'd have a chance to talk to you," Irene admitted.

"So talk. I'm listening." Tony stood up, then helped Irene to her feet. They walked through the Mission grounds.

"As the tribe's cultural and spiritual advisor, as I'm called, I'm frustrated. For too long our people have politely sat by and watched others take what they've wanted–our land, our language, our culture, and our means of making a living."

"I know. The Chamala are sometimes slow to act, reluctant to assert themselves."

"That's another thing you can thank the Mission for," Irene interjected. "But, here's what I want to talk to you about."

She paused for a moment.

"I see something big coming for our people," she finally said as they passed through the mission garden. "It's like right here almost in front of us."

"That sounds exciting," Tony replied. "What is it?"

"I don't know exactly."

Irene sighed as she gazed across the valley.

"It's just one of those feelings I get, you know, every now and then. But I wanted to let you know about it so when it comes, and you'll know it when you see it, you won't hesitate to seize it and lead our people into that brighter future you're always talking about."

She looked toward the mountains in the distance.

"When's the last time you've been up to the spring at Mount Condor to pray for our people, to ask for guidance?" She kept her gaze fixed on one particular peak.

"Quite a while, I'm afraid." Tony looked away. "You know how it is. I get busy dealing with the day-to-day problems, and-"

"And what?"

"And for some time now it has seemed that I don't get answers. I don't feel a connection. I don't feel… anything."

"Well, whatever you feel or don't feel, I think you need to take a trip up there to talk with your ancestors and get reconnected."

Tony didn't say anything. He wasn't at all sure he agreed with Irene's prescription.

"I know what I'm talking about," Irene added, as if she read his mind. "An opportunity will come your way soon. You'll see."

She gave him a moment to ponder her words, and then said, "I'm hungry. Let's go eat."

She smiled as she headed for the Mission, leaving Tony standing alone.

"I'll be there in a minute," he called after her, turning back to gaze at Mount Condor. The majestic peak stood as it had for all of Tony's life, but now seemed to stare back at him almost disapprovingly. Maybe Irene was right, he thought--about a lot of things.

The following morning, Tony pulled into the tribal hall's gravel parking lot and parked his truck close to the building behind the bingo hall. Carrying his well-worn brown leather brief case, he headed toward the building's entrance.

The sound of rubber on gravel caught his attention just as he opened the door to go inside. He turned to see a sleek black Escalade pull in and park next to his truck. Tony recognized the Native American driver as he emerged from the car and approached.

"Jackson Pico, what brings you down from the lofty heights of Sacramento to our humble reservation?"

Tony noticed that this old friend from one of the northern California reservations was carrying a shiny black leather brief case with gold hardware and trim.

"Big news in the tribal gaming business. Have you got time to talk?"

"I'll make time."

Shaking hands, they entered the building together. Pico followed Tony to the tribal chairman's simple office, strewn with blueprints, folders and aerial photos. Tony's assistant, Rose Marie, soon came in bearing cups of coffee for both of the men. After brief introductions, she exited, closing the door behind her.

Jackson opened his luxurious case and pulled out a thick document that he handed to Tony. The tribal chairman sat down behind his desk studying the document while his visitor pulled up a weathered wooden chair cross from him.

In a few minutes, Tony looked at Jackson.

"So if I understand what this implies," Tony asked, "We could switch from class two bingo to class three casino g aming, as these other tribes have done, without notifying the state government or waiting until we negotiate an agreement with the state?"

"So far, the state has refused to negotiate compacts with the tribes as the Indian Gaming Regulatory Act compels them to do, so we have to force their hand. It's a fair exercise of your rights as a native nation, and as I always say, when it comes to sovereignty, if you don't use it, you lose it. Remember, the state's always ready to interfere in tribal affairs, even in the face of federal opposition."

"In the meantime, won't the state try to shut us down?"

"They might," Jackson admitted, "but they'd risk losing another battle in the Supreme Court and bad P.R. with the citizens of California who've already shown their support for Indian gaming."

Tony rose from his seat and turned to the window behind him. As he gazed at the oak-lined creek he'd known all his life, an idea came to him. Turning to a counter near his desk, he shuffled through some papers until he came up with what he was looking for: an aerial photo of the Santa Juanita Valley. He examined it closely.

"To really make this work, we'd need a more accessible location, say along the highway, wouldn't we?" Tony was smiling.

"Yes, it would greatly improve your chances of being successful."

Tony laid the large photo out on his desk, and Jackson walked over to take a look at it. The black and white image showed the Chamala Reservation with Roy Evans's land sitting next door, adjacent to the highway. A hand-drawn, red line marked the borders of the Reservation while a yellow line marked the Evans property.

"Roy Evans' land, located adjacent to our current reservation and facing the highway, was also once part of this reservation long ago," Tony explained.

"Really? I didn't know that."

"In the late 1890s, the Roman Catholic Archdiocese for this area, brought a suit in state court against the tribe in order to have the land turned over to the church. We didn't have any funds to mount a proper court battle, and we certainly didn't have good legal counsel."

"And the Indians got screwed once again," Pico said with a chuckle.

"Several decades later the Archdiocese sold that land to bolster the church's coffers," Tony added. "I think they used some of those funds to rebuild the mission that was crumbling due to neglect."

"You'd have to have that property placed in trust with the federal government, which can take a while," Pico observed.

"I know. That's why we've got to start moving on this sooner rather than later," Tony said. "I'm pretty sure the feds would be sympathetic to our cause since we'd only be re-acquiring property that legitimately once was ours."

"Sounds about right," Pico said.

"So, can you come back next week for our tribal meeting? I need you tell them what you just told me."

"I'd be happy to."

"I can present this as a total package to the tribe. This could be big." Thinking out loud, Tony muttered, "You weren't kidding, were you, Irene?"

Inside the tribal hall a week later, Tony and the tribal council were once again in front of an assembly of tribal members. With them on the stage were Roy Evans and Jackson Pico, along with an easel displaying the aerial land survey.

Tony took center stage.

"You told me you wanted action," he announced. "You told me you didn't want a repeat of the failures we had with the BIA business ventures. So we're here tonight to unfold a plan for the next chapter in this tribe's history: a full-blown Vegas-style casino right out there on the highway."

An especially loud roar of chatter immediately spread through the room. Several tribal members jumped to their feet-- hands raised--wanting to speak.

Ignoring the raised hands, Tony continued. "We have two guests here tonight who can help us make this happen, and I want you to hear them out before you start objecting. After they've finished talking and answering our questions, we'll take a vote to see if we proceed.

People in the audience sat back down.

"We'll start with Jackson Pico, Executive Director of the California Tribal Gaming Association."

Pico, Evans and Mirada went on into the night laying out the plan to the tribe.

The next morning, Tony sipped his first cup of coffee as he picked up that day's copy of the <u>Hitchin'</u> <u>Post</u>. He almost choked, then spit, as he read the headline: TRIBE PLANS CASINO: SOME FEAR NEGATIVE SOCIAL IMPACT.

Tony couldn't remember the last time he'd seen such a large headline in the local rag. Reading on, he saw that the story repeated much of what had been discussed at the tribal meeting, along with comments taken from a national anti-gambling organization who opposed gaming on moral grounds.

Moments later, Tony burst through the front door of the newspaper office, a copy of the newspaper in hand. He shot past the front receptionist, barging into Ralph Bailey's office.

Throwing the paper on Ralph's desk, Tony demanded, "Where did you get this information?"

"I can't reveal my sources," Ralph replied, clearly startled, but trying to appear calm.

"Last night's meeting was only preliminary, to see if the tribe even wanted to pursue the idea. We aren't ready for a public announcement, and no one from the tribal council authorized this story."

"It's my job to print the news as soon as I hear about it, and this is news!"

Tony picked up the paper, pointing to a paragraph he'd circled.

"You've got a lot of nerve printing these unfounded allegations against gaming."

"People have a right to know both sides of the story," Ralph countered.

"You and the rest of the people in this valley never paid any attention to us before. Why start now?"

"Indian gaming is starting to make headlines all over the state."

Tony paced. "Our people have been dirt poor and trying to climb out of the hole your greedy, land-grabbing ancestors put us in. Why haven't you done stories on that? That's not newsy enough for you?"

"Okay, okay," Ralph confessed. "I understand where you're coming from."

`He rose from his chair.

"Look, I'm sorry I blind-sided you with this story," he said. " It was late when I got the information."

"Yeah, whatever," Tony replied more calmly. "Next time, at least come to me for a comment before you print something about the reservation. It's what you'd do for anybody else in this valley."

Tony stormed out of the office, and Ralph knew the tribal

chairman was right.

At about the same time, a determined group of town residents marched toward the Happy Trails Coffee Shop located on Springville's main street. The group's leader carried a copy of the same newspaper.

A hand-written blackboard sign in front of the café read "Today's Coffee Special: The Lasso Latte."

The troop stomped past the sign and marched inside. Chief Dwight and his son were eating at a table near the front, and Monica, a robust American Indian waitress, poured coffee into Dwight's cup. Café Manager Jim Grover was busy behind the cash register.

The angry group of citizens spotted Mayor Cummings at his usual table reading the newspaper, and they made a beeline for him. They were really revved up.

"What are we going to do about this casino deal, J.J.?" the lead citizen asked.

"Good morning to you too, Phil," the mayor replied calmly, letting the paper fall to the table. "I was just as surprised as everybody else to read about it. Neither Evans nor the Indians revealed any of this when we were putting the Valley Blueprint together."

"It's an outrage," a second citizen asserted. "How can they just come in here and put in a casino without our permission?"

"I heard those Indians consider themselves to be above the law," a third resident chimed in. "They seem to think they can do anything they damn well please on that reservation."

"Look, I don't know very much about these issues, so I put a couple of calls in to the state capitol to see if I could find out what our options are here."

"And?"

"They're going to get back to me in a couple of days," J.J. replied.

"What are we supposed to do in the meantime, just sit by and do nothing?" a fourth voice in the group asked.

"One thing they did tell me was that we can form a Citizen Action Committee, and begin writing letters and expressing our objections in the press. And there's a group in Sacramento called "Speak Out, California" helping folks organize opposition to the growing number of tribal casinos."

"I can't believe you people," Café manager Jim Grover interrupted, stepping from behind the cash register. "You sound like the outraged town-folk preparing to storm Dr. Frankenstein's castle to kill the monster," he continued.

"But we have rights," the group leader protested.

"Of course you do. So do they. These Native Americans have been robbed of their lands, shoved aside, ignored and relegated to the bottom of the food chain. So I think they have the right to do whatever they need to on their reservation for the good of their people."

Chief Dwight stepped forward. "We're all very aware of your liberal views, Grover, but you should leave these matters to us locals."

"I have a right to express my opinion," Grover said, standing his ground. "I live in this valley just like you do."

"You're a newcomer and a renter, not a land-holder," Dwight pointed out. "Your opinion is about as worthless as a wooden nickel."

He turned to J.J..

"You can go off and start your little citizen action group and write all the letters you want to, but this situation calls for real action!"

He slammed his fist on the table, startling everyone. They remained silent as Dwight returned to his table.

"Come on, son," he said to Travis. "We've got to go." Travis picked up his cowboy hat and prepared to leave.

"You'd better think long and hard about whose side you're on, Grover," Dwight remarked, as he and his son headed for the door.

"I didn't know there were sides. When did that happen?"

Stopping at the front door, Dwight replied, "When it comes to those Indians and that reservation, there have always been sides. Most folks have just forgotten it."

He and Travis exited the café.

"That's got to be the most backward man I've ever met," Jim said to himself, walking toward the kitchen. He noticed that J.J. and the irate residents quietly sat down to begin formulating a plan.

News of the tribe's casino plans spread quickly through the valley, and no one could've predicted what was to happen next. That very night a pick-up truck, traveling with its lights off, sped toward the Chamala Bingo Hall. Two men rode inside the cab of the truck while two others rode in the pickup bed.

The truck stopped in the Bingo Hall parking lot, and all four men got out, each carrying a brick with a note attached. The moonless night concealed the identity of the truck and the men. Each man picked a window and threw his brick through it. The crashing glass echoed in the darkness.

Aging tribal security guard Ted Castillo came running as best he could from the inside of the building. He arrived in time only to see the truck speeding away into the night.

Next morning, Ted led Tony and other tribal council members into the building. They surveyed the damage, which was mainly broken glass scattered around. Ted showed them the notes attached to each of the four bricks.

Tony read one of the messages. "NO CASINO – OR ELSE" was written in red block letters. He passed the note to one of the other council members.

"I'm sorry I couldn't stop them," Ted offered. "It happened so fast."

"Don't worry about it, Ted," Tony replied. "There's nothing you could've done. I'm just glad it wasn't any worse."

Ted and the council members scattered to see if there was any more serious damage in the building, but found nothing. Tony could only wonder if this might just be the beginning of more serious troubles.

Nestled in the foothills at the edge of the Santa Juanita Valley lay the Buckaroo Dude Ranch, owned by none other than Mayor J.J. Cummings. This cluster of ranch-style buildings provided the perfect setting for tourists to live out their cowboy fantasies.

It was to this location that Tony drove now. Stepping out of his truck, he marched toward the main building. He carried one of the bricks used in the previous night's vandalism.

He found Cummings talking to a group of visitors. Barging in and interrupting the cowboy-turned-mayor, Tony held up the brick.

"Do you know anything about this, Mayor Cummings?"

"I'm kind of in the middle of something right now, Chairman Mirada," Cummings replied with an faked politeness.

"Do you know anything about this?" Tony was insistent.

Cummings stepped away from his guests to examine the brick and note.

"No I don't. What is it?"

"A message delivered through the window of our bingo hall in the middle of the night. We heard you're organizing opposition to our economic development plans."

"I'll make no secret of my opposition to your casino, but I wouldn't do such a thing, I assure you. While we're on the subject, I don't appreciate you keeping your casino plans a secret when our

Valley Blueprint was being developed."

"We didn't know about it then ourselves. This is brand new and, besides, it's not really any of your business anyway."

"You can't operate outside the law."

"We don't have any intention of operating outside the law," Tony assured him. "If you're smart, you'll study up on the subject of Tribal Sovereignty before you go running around getting people stirred up."

"I might just do that. Now if you'll excuse me, I have guests to tend to."

Tony took the brick and left.

In the coming days and weeks, he devoted most of his time and energy to the casino development process, first devising a plan to temporarily convert the tribe's existing bingo hall to small Vegas-style casino. He presented this idea to the full tribal council, complete with architectural renderings showing design changes to the existing building.

Once the council had been convinced, then a referendum on the plan was put to the tribal members. Much to Tony's delight, the tribe passed the proposal in a landslide decision.

Contracts were quickly signed, and the transformation began. Bingo equipment was dismantled and hauled away; slot machines were delivered and set up; the old Chamala Bingo sign came down, and a brand new INDIAN SPRINGS CASINO sign was erected in its place.

In a surprisingly short time, the Chamala had their

temporary "trial" casino ready to go.

On grand opening day, a podium and P.A. system were set up in front of the entrance to the new gambling establishment. A large red ribbon stretched across the doorway. An array of local people gathered for the event including Tony, the Tribal Council, Tony's wife, Irene, several tribal members, Roy Evans, Ralph from the newspaper, and a reporter from the local radio station. Tony stepped to the podium.

"A new chapter in our tribe's story begins today, bringing with it the promise of a better future for us, our children and our children's children," he proclaimed. "Our spiritual leader, Irene Magdalena has already blessed the building, so as we dedicate this new enterprise, let us hope our ancestors, who struggled mightily for our continued existence as a tribe, are looking down upon us with pride."

A Tribal Council member handed Tony a large pair of prop scissors and he cut the red ribbon. As the cut was made, Ralph's camera flashed.

That image appeared on the front page of the next day's <u>Hitchin' Post</u> accompanied by a headline that declared: TEMPORARY CHAMALA CASINO OPENS FOR BUSINESS PENDING FEDERAL APPROVAL OF LAND DEAL.

In front of the Happy Trails Café that morning, Chief Dwight inserted a coin in the newspaper vending machine and extracted the top paper. He read the casino headline and frowned. He set his jaw and squinted as he looked off down the street.

Folding the newspaper, he headed for his police car.

That very night at about 2 a.m., a pickup truck pulled up to the new tribal casino. The neon "Indian Springs Casino" sign lit up the parking lot to reveal five men riding in the truck – two in the cab, three in back. This time they wore ski masks.

The group's leader, Masked Man #1, remained in the truck cab as a look-out. Masked Men #2, 3 and 4, got out of the truck, carrying Molotov cocktails and cans of lighter fluid. Masked Man #5 carried only a spray paint can.

They split up to carry out their assigned tasks. The painter sprayed a message on the outside of the building. The other three lit the rags in their Molotov cocktails. One squirted lighter fluid on the front of the building. He was about to set fire to it when a light inside the building came on and the front door opened. A new security guard, a young Indian man named Don Cordero, stepped out.

"Who's out there?" Don called.

Three masked figures threw their burning bottles through windows of the hall and flames immediately erupted.

"Hey, what are you doing?" Don yelled. "There's an old man inside! He'll get hurt! Ted, Ted, get out!"

Quickly, unexpectedly, Masked Man #3 doused Don with the fluid and set him on fire. Don screamed in agony and fear and began running.

"No! No! No one was supposed to get hurt!" Masked Man #5 yelled. He ran to Don and threw him on the ground trying to put out the fire. The other Masked Men headed back to the truck.

Light from the fire reflected off a pendant hanging from Masked Man #5's neck. Don struggled to reach up and grab it. He pulled as hard as he could and the chain snapped.

Masked Man #1 ran back to Masked Man #5, pulling him off of Don, but not before Masked Man #5 has managed to put out the fire on the burning security guard.

"Get in the car," Masked Man #1 commanded. "You've disobeyed a direct order. I'll have you punished when we get back."

He dragged Masked Man #5 to the truck, threw him in, and they sped off. Don was lying on the ground charred, but managed to radio for help on his walkie-talkie before passing out.

The next morning at 4 a.m. Tony surveyed the scene as he rubbed the sleep from his eyes. He'd received the call from the Sheriff's office only minutes earlier alerting him to series of events that had unfolded. What he now saw made him sick to his stomach–the smoldering casino building; Sheriff McKenzie and his men combing the site; the body bag being loaded into the county coroner's wagon; the spray painted message that read: YOU WERE WARNED!

Nearby, two EMT's were loading Don Cordero's partially burned body into the back of an ambulance.

"We'll do everything we can for him," the lead EMT assured Tony. "He's burned badly, but I think he'll pull through."

"Thanks," Tony replied rather numbly.

Tony and Sheriff McKenzie walked to the sheriff's car.

"Even though the reservation is within the county's normal jurisdiction, I think we need to call in the feds on this," Tony told the sheriff. "This is definitely a federal case."

"If that's what you want, Tony, I understand completely," McKenzie replied. "It's a clear case of arson, and with the death of Mr. Castillo, they <u>should</u> take the case. I could make a couple of calls to see which agency should handle it."

"No, I'll take care of it. The Office of Tribal Justice would be the ones to handle this, and I know exactly who to call there."

"Well, I'm available at any time, if you need help." The sheriff shook Tony's hand and got into his car. After the sheriff and his men left, the tribal chairman walked back to the building and surveyed the damage again.

"Who would do this?" he asked no one in particular.

At nine a.m. Tony placed a call to Sacramento. On the other end of the line, the phone rang in a federal government office building located not too far from the state capitol building.

An attractive, athletically built American Indian woman in her late thirties sprinted across the room to answer it. She wore a badge and gun.

"Office of Tribal Justice, Cassandra Del Rio speaking," she said into the phone.

"Cassie?" the voice on the other end asked.

She froze, holding her breath. "I haven't been called that in years. Who is this?"

"It <u>has</u> been a long time, I know," Tony replied. "How are you?"

"Can't complain," Cassie smiled, now recognizing the caller. "How 'bout you, Tony? I hear you're a big time tribal chairman now."

"You heard about that, huh? Well, I heard you were a hot-shot field marshal for the OTJ," he said jokingly.

"I guess the moccasin grapevine is still in operation."

"Yeah, I suppose it is." Changing his tone, he said, "Listen, I could use your help with something down here. It's pretty serious."

"I saw the report just a few minutes ago. You had an arson fire that killed a tribal elder and burnt another tribal employee pretty badly."

"People on the rez are mighty worried."

Cassie studied her desk calendar for a moment.

"Let me shuffle my case-load a little," she said. "I could be down there, say, day after tomorrow."

"Thanks. It'll be good to see you."

"You, too," she said. After hanging up the phone, she stared at it for a moment, as if the device itself was responsible for the surprising call.

Meanwhile back at Springville's city hall, Cathleen Radcliff approached the mayor's receptionist. The mid-thirties blonde had just driven down from Sacramento herself at the mayor's request.

"I'm Cathleen Radcliff with "Speak Out, California." I have an appointment with Mayor Cummings."

"Oh yes, Ms. Radcliff," the grey-haired receptionist responded. "You're the one who's going to help us with our Indian problem, aren't you? The mayor's expecting you. Go right in."

Cathleen nodded and entered the door next to the receptionist's desk.

As the door to his office opened, J.J. rose from the seat behind his desk. Cathleen crossed to the mayor, hand extended.

"Mayor Cummings, the cavalry has arrived," Cathleen quipped with a broad smile.

"I certainly hope so, Ms. Radcliff," the mayor replied graciously. "Our citizens are very alarmed."

They were all smiles as they shook hands. J.J. led her to a conference table in the corner of the room where they took seats next to each other.

"I brought with me a boiler-plate strategy of opposition tactics that are already being applied in other communities with Indian Casinos," she said.

She placed her portfolio on the table and opened it. Pushing it in the mayor's direction, she said, "I think you'll like our approach."

The top page contained the heading "INDIAN GAMING OPPOSITION - PLAN OF ATTACK." Below it was a list of actions: Letter-writing campaign to tribal chairman, newspapers, elected officials; Protest Rally with Media Coverage; and Boycott of Products produced by supporters.

The mayor almost drooled with excitement.

"This is excellent, Ms. Radcliff, excellent," he declared.

"Call me Cathleen." she smiled.

"All right, Cathleen. What do we need to do first?"

"Call your core group together, the ones you can really count on to show up and follow through - you know what I mean?"

"Sure I do," J.J. nodded. "I know exactly who to call on."

"We'll customize this template to fit your situation and delegate members of this group to spearhead different parts of the campaign."

"Got it. When can we get started?"

"Just as soon as I receive the first payment for my consulting fee. Then I'll signal my PR firm and the lobbyists to start working on your behalf."

"Of course - first things first," J.J. quickly agreed. "If you'll accompany me to accounting, they should have your check ready."

They rose, and J.J. escorted Cathleen out the door.

Meanwhile, Cassie sped south along the highway toward the Santa Juanita Valley in her white, government-issued, Office of Tribal Justice sedan. The radio speakers blasted out old rock 'n' roll ballads from the playlist on her MP3 player.

A couple of hours from her destination, she pulled into a drive-in for a quick bite. While waiting for her order, she reached into a tote bag that sat in the passenger seat and fished out a small, yellowed photo album. Lingering a moment over some of the photos, she flipped through the pages until she found what she was looking for: a somewhat faded image of her and Tony on a college campus arm-in-arm, smiling. Those two young people sure looked happy, she thought, and clueless about the realities of life.

"Now there's a relic from a by-gone era," she said out loud, speaking of the photo.

After studying the picture for a while, she pulled it out of the album and stuck it under a clip on her sun visor. Smiling and remembering, she turned up the volume and let the music take her back to very pleasant private moments.

Around 2 p.m., she pulled into the parking lot of the Chamala Tribal Office. She got out, looked around at the tribe's set-up, then entered the building.

Inside, she made her way to the desk of Tony's assistant, Rose Marie.

"Can I help you?" Rose Marie asked in her best professional tone.

"I'm here to see Tony Mirada."

"Is he expecting you?"

"Yes, I am." Tony replied.

Both Cassie and Rose Marie looked up to see that Tony had stepped out of his nearby office.

"Rose Marie, I'd like you to meet Marshal Cassandra Del Rio from the Office of Tribal Justice."

"Pleased to meet you," Rose Marie said with a smile. The very perceptive receptionist couldn't help but notice signs of something lurking in the eyes of these two, something that resembled old flames.

"Marshal Del Rio is going to help us find out who set fire to the casino," Tony remarked, trying to make his voice as flat and unemotional as possible. Turning to Cassie, he said, "Marshal Del Rio, won't you step into my office?"

Cassie stepped past Tony and into his office.

"Please hold all my calls," Tony told Rose Marie as he stepped into his office and closed the door.

Instantly Rose Marie sprang into action. There were people to call and juicy new tidbits to share as she carried out her unofficial job as the reservation's central agent of gossip.

As Cassie sat down in the chairman's office, she noticed a photo of Tony and his family on the desk. She picked it.

"Is this your family?" she asked.

"Yeah. That's my wife, Gloria, and my son, Tony junior."

"Congratulations, he looks just like you," Cassie smiled. "Planning to have more little Tonys in the future?"

"No, not really. Right now Gloria and I are going through what they call a rough patch. What about you? Ever tie the knot?"

"I was married for about a nanosecond to a Miwok man who, it turned out, was personally trying to re-populate his entire tribe with any female target he could nail."

She put down the photo. "Look, Tony, maybe I shouldn't have come. There are other marshals that can handle this investigation."

"I called you because I want someone working on this who gives a damn. As I remember, you do."

She smiled.

"Okay, then let's get down to business."

"Great," he said and handed her a file folder. "The sheriff told me to give you this preliminary file, and he said he'd have more for you in a day or two. His phone number and address are inside."

"All right," she said, thumbing through the file. "I'll contact him after I check into the motel."

Tony accompanied her to the office door. "Ted's funeral service is tomorrow morning, and if you're there I can introduce you around."

"What about the burn victim? Has anybody been able to talk to him yet?"

"No, he's been in I.C.U. and heavily sedated."

"Okay, I'll read the file, get up to speed and see you at the funeral."

She opened the door, starting to exit.

"Cassie," Tony said softly. "Thanks for coming."

"I just hope we find whoever's responsible," Cassie replied in a businesslike tone.

"I'd like to assist you with the investigation. Is that

possible?"

Cassie smiled and softened. "I think that can be arranged. I usually work alone, but with your criminal investigation studies in college and your military experience, your help could speed things up."

"Good," he said. "See you tomorrow." As she walked out of his office, his eyes stayed on her. He hadn't known that seeing her again would cause him to have the reaction he was having.

Cassie spent some time driving around the area to get a feel for the place before checking in to the Wine Country Inn. After a delicious steak dinner at the Oak Barrel Restaurant, she picked up a copy of the <u>Hitchin'</u> <u>Post</u> and headed back to her motel room where she curled up with the case file for a bit of reading.

When Cassie entered the mission chapel the following morning, Father McDougal was leading the congregation in the hymn "Peace in the Valley." She spotted Tony sitting with his wife and son near the front of the congregation, which included many tribal members. Cassie stepped quietly to a seat in the back as the hymn continued.

After the service, the mourners milled around out in front of the mission, expressing their condolences to Ted Castillo's family in hushed tones.

Cassie stood politely just outside the circle of mourners. Shortly, Tony brought his wife and son to meet her.

"Marshal Del Rio, I'd like you to meet my wife, Gloria,

and our son, Tony junior."

"It's a pleasure to meet you, Mrs. Mirada." Cassie poured on her best dose of charm. "You have a lovely son."

"Tony told me you and he and had thing in college, but said it was ancient history," Gloria shot back. "It had better be, because he knows what I'd do to him if he ever cheated on me." She flashed a fake smile and abruptly turned away.

Tony hadn't noticed that Irene Magdalena had been watching and listening to this interaction from a nearby vantage point. Irene stepped forward, pretending she hadn't heard a thing.

"Tony, there you are," she said brightly. "Aren't you going to introduce me?"

"Oh, yes, of course. Irene Magdalena, I'd like to introduce Marshal Cassandra Del Rio. She's come down from Sacramento to-"

"Yes, yes, I know all that," Irene interrupted. "Welcome, my dear. I'd love to show you around our humble little reservation." Looking at Tony, she followed with, "That is, if you have time."

"You two go right ahead," Tony replied in relief. "I've got to see after Ted's family."

"Good. That's settled then. Cassie and I'll have a wonderful time, won't we, dear?" Irene winked at Cassie, causing Tony to cringe a little, knowing that a part of his past will now become common knowledge in the community.

Cassie caught on to both Tony's discomfort and Irene's

mischievous intent. She smiled, taking Irene's arm as they walked away together.

"This'll be great," Cassie commented. And then, over her shoulder to Tony she said, "I'll meet you at the bingo hall first thing tomorrow morning."

With that she turned her attention to Irene who whispered something into Cassie's ear that Tony couldn't hear.

Oh, the mischief those two could cause, Tony thought.

Early next morning, Tony arrived at the fire scene to find Cassie already on site wandering through the burnt ruins and examining the scene in search of clues.

"Up and at 'em early, I see," he remarked.

"I can't find any reference to the collection of evidence from the Sheriff's case folder. Did his men thoroughly check the area?"

"You'll have to ask him about that to find out for sure. They poked around for quite a while, said they didn't find anything."

Cassie continued looking around. "Irene and I got along great, by the way. She invited me to stay with her instead of the lovely Wine Country Inn. I'm going to take her up on it."

"That should prove very interesting—for both of you."

"Do you still have the bricks that were thrown through the windows the first time?" she asked, changing the subject. "I need to have them dusted for prints."

"I gave them to Sheriff McKenzie after the fire, but

they've been handled by a lot of people. No one expected anything else to happen."

"Well, we need to get them back. I'd like to have them tested anyway. We could get lucky."

"Okay, we'll go down to his office later today. What do you want to do right now?"

"Go eat breakfast in Springville," she answered, dusting off her hands.

"Really, why there?"

"Because it'll give me a chance to snoop around town, get the lay of the land, see what the locals are like."

"Okay, we can get coffee and a bite to eat at my favorite off-rez hangout, Happy Trails Café."

"How quaint," Cassie replied.

They got into Tony's pick-up and headed for town. On their ride into Springville, Cassie watched the valley scenery go by. It was a lovely place, she thought. In a few minutes, she broke the silence.

"Tony, my agency is a small, under-funded program, so I may need a few things to help me conduct this investigation."

"You don't have to explain," Tony replied immediately. "What do you need?"

"An office with a phone, a computer with e-mail and printer--oh and a fax machine."

"You got it. There's a spare room down the hall from me we can convert to an office."

"How soon can we get that started?"

"Is later this morning soon enough?"

Cassie smiled and gazed back out at the passing scenery.

Moments later, the truck arrived and parked in front of the Happy Trails Café. As they entered the weathered wooden structure, Cassie noticed a couple of cowboys eating in a back booth. Monica, the waitress, approached Tony and Cassie.

"Hey, Monica," Tony greeted her. "I want you to meet somebody. This is Cassie Del Rio, a special investigator here to–"

"I heard, Tony. She's staying with Irene. Pleased to meet you, Cassie. There's some bad shit going on here, excuse my French, and I hope you get to the bottom of it."

"Me, too," Cassie said.

Leaning closer to Cassie, Monica whispered, "On the surface, everybody's so friendly, and everything seems so peachy and sweet." She looked around to see if anyone was listening.

"But underneath, there's a seething cauldron of hypocrisy. Racism in this valley runs so deep you could drown in it. And they like to pretend it ain't even there."

From the kitchen, the sound of clanging pots, followed by a groan, could be heard.

"Oh, crap! Monica, I need you!" A man's voice boomed.

"That's my husband, Hector. He's the cook. He probably broke something again." Turning toward the kitchen, she shouted, "I'll be there in a minute. I've got customers."

Turning back to her guests, she suggested, "Why don't you

two sit down over there, and I'll bring you some coffee?"

The pair headed for a table.

"Is Jim around?" Tony asked. "I want to introduce him to Cassie."

"No, he'll be back soon," Monica replied as she made for the kitchen. "But I already told him about her. He's dying to meet your old flame."

Tony rolled his eyes as they sat down and picked up menus.

"I bet what Monica said about the racism is true," Cassie remarked, scanning the menu. "I've seen it in plenty of other places in this state, but it still amazes me how, in this day and age, people can get so angry they'd set fire to building. What do you suppose leads them to do it?"

"Fear," a voice sounded.

Tony and Cassie looked up to see Jim approaching their table.

"I think that's the bottom line. When you peel away the layers, it boils down to fear. Fear of change--fear of the loss of control."

"This is our local liberal cowboy philosopher, Jim Grover," Tony offered. "Jim, meet Cassie Del Rio."

"Monica wasn't kidding," Jim beamed. "She said you're as pretty as they come. Welcome to cowboy country, ma'am."

"Aw, shucks," Cassie kidded and batted her eye lashes for effect.

They shook hands.

"Join us," Tony requested.

"Don't mind if I do," Jim replied as he took a seat.

"Listen, I don't know if it's important, but right after the first news broke about your casino plans, the mayor and a bunch of irate locals were in here trying to figure out what they could do to stop it."

"That's interesting," Cassie said.

"What's even more interesting," Jim continued, "is how angry the Police Chief was about the whole thing. He hit the table with his fist and said it was time to take action. He told me I had to pick a side because when it comes to you Indians, there have always been sides."

"Doesn't sound like he'll be much help with this investigation," Cassie observed.

"Probably not," Tony confirmed. "He's a blow hard. I've known him since high school."

Just then, Monica returned, carrying two cups of coffee.

"I made a fresh pot," she announced. She set the coffee down as Hector came out of the kitchen.

"This is my husband, Hector, the cook. Jim here was good enough to give him a job when the dude ranch hired that new fancy cuisine chef from L.A. Hector used to cook for them."

"Howdy." Hector smiled a toothy grin.

The two cowboys from the back booth approached the cash register to pay.

"I'll be right back." Monica went to take care of the cowboys' bill.

"You guys want anything to eat?" Hector asked.

"How's the Cowboy Cobbler?" Cassie was getting hungry.

"My specialty," replied proudly. "Hot out of the oven just now."

"Sounds good." Cassie closed her menu.

"Make it two," Tony said.

"Make it three," Jim echoed.

"Comin' right up." Hector marched off toward the kitchen.

Ominously, one of the cowboys at the register took a lingering look at Tony and the group before heading out the door.

After Tony and Cassie had cleaned their plates and drained their coffee cups, Cassie got up the nerve to ask Jim a question she'd wanted to ask ever since she entered Happy Trails Café. "What's with the retro-cowboy theme, Jim?"

"The owner's idea," Jim answered easily. "Roy Evans. He says people long for simpler times, black and white issues, strong heroes who can save the day. That's what people want, and that's what he gives 'em."

"Never mind who gets left out or what gets swept under the rug along the way, right?" Tony asked rhetorically.

"Exactly," Jim responded enthusiastically. "Let's hear it for the bad old days."

Tony stood and laid a few dollar bills on the table. "Well,

we've got a few rounds to make this morning." He and Cassie started for the door.

"Cassie, don't let Tony here monopolize all your time," Jim called. "Come back and visit soon."

"Thanks, I may be back to pick your brain some more."

"Hear that, Tony? A woman who wants me for my mind and not just my body?" Jim laughed as Tony and Cassie stepped out the door.

Tony's cell-phone rang just as they reached his truck. "Hello, this is Tony," he answered, then listened. "Great. We'll be right there." Putting the phone away, he said, "That was the hospital. Don's awake and wants to talk."

That news got the investigative team revved up, so they hopped in the truck as fast as they could. Cassie got that rush she usually got when a new case kicked into gear.

"I'll have to come back to Springville real soon," she said.

"Oh yeah? To see Jim?"

"No, silly. To pay this Chief Dwight a courtesy visit – you know, from one peace officer to another--to see what kind of reaction I get from him."

Tony shook his head and smiled.

"Same old Cassie," he remarked. "Always stirring the pot."

"That's the only way you find out what's cooking," Cassie replied.

As they drove away down Main Street, the cowboy from the restaurant monitored their actions inconspicuously from across the street.

A few blocks away, at the Springville Community Center, Cathleen and J.J. passed out packets of papers to the dozen or so Springville residents seated in the room.

Cathleen was already into her spiel. "The top page has the names and addresses of the people you'll be writing to: county officials, newspaper editors, legislators, and even the tribal council members."

Folks in the room examined the material as she spoke.

"That's followed by sample letters," she continued. "Now you'll want to put these letters in your own words. Don't copy them word for word. We don't want them to all be exactly the same."

A few late arrivals got packets and took vacant seats. Cathleen moved to the front of the room.

"Once you've completed one set of letters under your own name, then start another set of letters under another name. We want this to appear to be a grass roots ground swell. We know there are plenty of other people out there who feel the same way we do, but they're just too lazy or intimidated to write their own letters. So we write for them. And it's important that we keep this going."

At their seats, people started writing. Cathleen and J.J. passed through the room like classroom monitors, observing their work.

Tony and Cassie arrived at the hospital and found Don's

room. As they entered, a nurse was checking his vital signs. Don was propped up in bed with bandages covering portions of his face and body.

"Nurse, can we have a few minutes with the patient?"

"Just a few," the nurse replied. "He needs his rest."

She stood aside as they approached Don.

"They told me about Ted," he muttered, in a depressed mood. "That old man never hurt a soul."

"I know," Tony agreed. "We're all upset about it. Listen, I want you to meet a good friend of mine. Cassie is here to help us find out who did this."

"Don, what can you tell us about the attackers?" Cassie asked.

"There was five of 'em," he started, interrupted by a cough. "They was running around squirting lighter fluid everywhere and throwing Molotov cocktails through the windows."

"Could you tell who they were?" Tony interjected.

"No, I couldn't see who they was. They wore ski masks, white ones."

Cassie had the next question.

"Did they say or do anything that might give us a clue about who they were?"

"One of 'em ran over to me when I was burning and tried to put the fire out. He saved my life. He was yelling: 'Nobody was supposed to get hurt.'"

A set of hardy coughs interrupted his description.

"I'm sorry, you're going to have to let him rest now," the nurse said, stepping forward.

"One last question, please."

The nurse nodded.

"Did you see what they were driving?"

"Yeah, it was a pick-up truck, but it was too dark to see what color. It might have been dark blue or black."

Tony patted Don on the shoulder gently.

"Thanks, Don. Now you get some rest."

Tony and Cassie headed for the door and opened it to leave.

"The medallion," Don asked weakly. "What happened to the medallion?"

Cassie stopped and turned. "What medallion?" She rushed back to him.

"The guy who tried to help me. He was wearing some kind of medallion on a chain. I grabbed it from his neck before one of the others dragged him off me."

Puzzled, she looked to Tony, who only shrugged his shoulders and shook his head.

"I don't know what happened to that medallion, Don, but we'll find it," she assured him. "It's good that you remembered it."

The nurse imposed herself between Cassie and Don, and the marshal joined Tony at the door.

With his remaining energy, Don called, "Find out who did this, okay? It's not right."

"Will do, buddy," Tony replied as they departed.

Cassie's mind was racing as she and Tony approached his truck.

"We've got to go back and find that medallion before something happens to it," she said. "If whoever did this knows it's missing, they may try to sneak back and get it."

Back at the fire scene, Sheriff McKenzie watched as one of his men strung yellow crime scene tape around the front of the building. Then Cassie and the Sheriff began surveying the area.

"Where exactly did you find Don?" she asked.

The Sheriff walked over to the spot.

"Right about here," he said, pointing to the ground. "But we didn't find anything."

Cassie joined him and began a meticulous search of the immediate area. She found nothing.

"I can have my CSI boys check it over thoroughly," McKenzie offered.

"It's too late," she said, standing and wiping her hands. "They've already been back to retrieve it, and we've lost a valuable piece of evidence." She was angry.

She stalked off toward the tribal office. Tony looked to the Sheriff.

"I'll look again, just in case," the sheriff said. Tony headed for his office to get some tribal work done, deciding that Cassie needed some time alone.

Down the hall from Tony's office, the former storage room

was in the process of being transformed into Cassie's office. One maintenance worker, an Indian man in his fifties, hauled boxes out while another younger man brought in a cabinet.

Cassie emerged from under the desk where she had plugged in the computer and a printer. She was in the process of testing them to see if they worked when Rose Marie stuck her head in the door.

"Tony asked me to see if there's anything else you need," she said brightly.

"Actually, there is. Can you print me out a list of names and phone numbers of all the tribal residents?"

"I'd better check with Tony to make sure it's okay," Rose Marie replied. "We keep that confidential."

"I need to find out if anyone on the reservation saw anything the night of the fire."

"Well, in that case I suppose it's all right," Rose Marie said tentatively. Stepping further into the room, she said quietly, "Tony's pretty great, isn't he?"

"Come again?" Cassie was puzzled.

"I heard you and he used to be together," Rose Marie confided.

"That was a long time ago," Cassie replied dismissively.

"I've worked here in the tribal office for quite a while, and I've seen tribal chairmen come and go. None of them were quite like Tony. Don't get me wrong, we've had some good leaders in this position." Then, almost swooning, she added, "but Tony is kind and generous and truly wants to help our people."

"Does he know you have a crush on him?"

Rose Marie snapped out of her daydream.

"Gosh, I hope not. That would be awkward, him being married and all. What happened with you two?"

"It was another time, another place. We were young, idealistic and trying to find our places in the world. I'm glad to hear that Tony has managed to keep some of his idealism alive."

"Me, too. I'll get that tribal list for you now."

Smiling, she exited the office as one of the maintenance workers returned with his dolly to remove more boxes and finish setting up Cassie's temporary office.

At day's end, Cassie followed Tony out to Irene's house.

The house was a frame structure set off by itself on a remote part of the reservation. Surrounded by flowers and greenery, the modest dwelling looked just like a thousand other HUD Indian homes built on reservations scattered across the country.

Tony saw that her front porch light was on as he pulled up in front and parked his truck. A few minutes later Cassie pulled in behind him in her OTJ car. Hearing the cars arrive, Irene came out on the porch.

"I was beginning to worry," she called to them as they got out of their cars and approached the house.

"Sorry, Irene," Tony answered. "I had to finish some work at the office before I could come show Cassie where you live. A tribal chairman's work is never done."

As Tony and Cassie reached the porch, Irene welcomed them.

"Come on in, both of you. Supper's ready."

"Oh, I can't stay," Tony protested. "I've got more work to do."

Irene accepted no excuses.

"A man's got to eat sometime," she replied flatly. "I made Indian tacos just the way you like them."

That was all it took.

"All right," Tony conceded, "but I can only stay for a little while."

Irene escorted Cassie to the door, allowing her to enter the house first. Irene turned back to Tony who was still on the porch.

"Where are your manners?" Irene asked in her Chamala language. "Go get her suitcases and bring them in."

"I offered," Tony replied in English, in a hushed tone. "She said she could bring them in herself."

"Haven't you learned anything about women?" Irene continued in the Indian tongue. "She only wants you to think she can do everything herself. Now you bring her luggage in."

Tony sighed and dutifully trudged out to Cassie's car as Irene followed Cassie inside.

Cassie was amazed by the interior of Irene's house, which resembled a tribal museum more than someone's home. The living room was filled with Native American ceremonial and cultural objects: drums, rattles, feathered staffs, blankets, paintings, etc. Cassie studied them as she strolled around the room.

"There is much power here," Irene said finally.

"I've been in Indian peoples' homes all over the state, but I've never seen anything like it, except maybe in a museum."

"These are mostly the gifts of grateful people who've come to me for help of one kind or another. Their love and gratitude lives in these objects and strengthens me."

Irene picked up a beaded leather pouch from a coffee table.

"They have spirit," she continued. "They are alive. Museum pieces are dead things." She carried the pouch to a corner of the room and placed it on an altar located on a table.

Cassie approached the altar. There were several pictures of Irene's family, small stones, two eagle feathers, a few pieces of medicinal root, and small containers of sweet-grass, cedar, sage and tobacco. In the center of the altar sat a large abalone half-shell and a small box of matches.

"Cassie, do you believe in Indian spirituality, in native medicine?" Irene asked.

"I don't know if I believe in it," Cassie replied honestly. "I respect it. I respect Indian people's right to practice it."

Just then Tony entered, carrying two suitcases.

"Where do you want these?" he asked, huffing and puffing a little.

"I told you I'd get those." Cassie was mildly annoyed.

"I'm just following orders. I always do what Irene tells me

even though I don't always understand why I'm doing it."

"Cassie's room is down the hall, first door on the right.

Tony headed down the hall carrying the luggage.

"It makes men feel useful when you give them some mundane task to take care of," Irene explained quietly.

Standing at her altar, Irene opened the leather pouch, removed a pinch of cedar and placed it in the abalone shell. She added a sprig of sage as Tony came back into the room.

"If you two will humor an old woman," Irene began, "I want to seek both a blessing and protection for the work you're going to be doing for our people."

"Okay," Cassie agreed. "I guess we could use all the help we can get."

"Please stand over here." Irene pointed. She lit a match and touched it to the cedar and sage in the shell. As the smoke began to rise, she picked up an eagle feather fan. Using the fan, she wafted the smoke over Tony and Cassie, front and back, top to bottom. As she moved, she repeated a prayer in the Chamala tongue.

Tony and Cassie stood silent and still as the smoke encircled them.

Satisfied with the ceremony, Irene ended with "A-ho" and put the shell and feather back on the altar.

"Now we can eat," she said with a smile, and led the way to the kitchen.

Irene's Indian tacos, served with rice and beans, were

every bit as good as Tony remembered, and the home-made berry pie was, well, icing on the cake.

During the meal, Irene kept the conversation light, but after dinner, she led their conversation in a new direction, the struggles faced by contemporary tribal communities.

"Indians seem to repeatedly suffer at the hands of powerful, ignorant outside politicians and decision-makers," Irene said, concluding her argument. "And the newspapers spread more lies and misinformation about us."

"Yeah, the negative press coverage on Indians is so unbelievable," Cassie added. "It seems they've all studied Indian issues from the same warped text book. Many tribes have had to wage public relations battles in their local communities just to try and overcome the prejudice."

"I don't think slugging it out in the newspaper is ever going to accomplish anything," Tony countered. "These people need a complete re-education about us."

Irene began clearing the dishes from the table.

"I mean," Tony continued, "They know nothing about the 200 hundred years of legal and political history that recognizes our tribes' government-to-government relationship with the United States. Nothing."

Cassie joined Irene in rounding up the dishes.

"Listen to you," she said to Tony mockingly. "All those fancy phrases: legal and political history, government-to-government relationship." Following Irene to the kitchen sink, she continued, "You should've heard him in college. I don't think he could even spell sovereignty in those days."

"I still can't spell it," Tony quipped. "Thank goodness for spell check." He checked his watch. "I've got to go," he said. "We've got a big tribal council meeting coming up that I've got to finish getting ready for. Thanks for the wonderful dinner, Irene," Tony said as he rose from the table. He headed for the door.

Cassie set her handful of dishes down and caught up to him at the front door. "Tony, hold up a minute." Tony did an about face, returning to the open door.

"Did Rose Marie tell you about the tribal list she gave me?" Cassie asked.

"Yeah. She said you need to interview tribal residents."

"I just want to cover the bases in case somebody saw something," she assured him.

"Why limit it to the reservation?"

"What do you mean?

"We can have the valley's local media, the radio station and newspaper, blast it all over. They both owe me, and somebody out there may know something."

"That's good." Cassie smiled. "Let's do it."

"I'll call an emergency tribal meeting and invite the media."

Their eyes locked momentarily, as an undeniable chemical spark flashed between them. Awkwardly, Tony said, "Well, I guess I'd better get going."

"Yeah, I guess you'd better," Cassie awkwardly returned.

Tony turned and glided toward his truck. Cassie watched him until he drove completely out of sight. There's something definitely still there, she thought.

After completing his work at the tribal office, Tony arrived at home rather late that evening. Entering his living room, he found Gloria lying in wait for him.

"Since your 'girlfriend' came to town, you sure have been putting in a lot of overtime," she said with a thick layer of sarcasm.

"I was working at the office," Tony replied in a neutral tone. "You know I've got an important council meeting to get ready for."

She almost pranced over to their answering machine, which was on a table in the corner of the living room.

"Whatever. There's a message for you," she said, pressing the play button.

"You Indians should be ashamed of yourselves, bringing gambling into this valley, endangering our families with who-knows-what kind of shady characters," the male voice on the machine complained. "Soon we'll be over-run with drugs and prostitution. Well, we're not going to stand for it."

The message ended, and Gloria turned the machine off. Then she picked up a stack of mail from a nearby counter.

"Your vice-chairman called, too. He got a similar message at his house." She thrust the mail at him. "And look at these! Hate mail from our neighbors! Is this what it's going to be like from now on?"

Tony took the stack of letters and examined them. There were four envelopes with Santa Juanita Valley return addresses. He took one of the letters out of an already-open envelope and read it.

"Dear Chairman Mirada," the letter began. "As a resident of the Santa Juanita Valley, I'm protesting your plans to open a casino here, especially without following the proper planning and approval procedures set out by the county that we all must abide by. The laws are meant for everyone!"

Tony dropped on the sofa as if he'd been punched in the chest. He put down the letters and rubbed his face.

"I can't even go to the hair-dresser any more," Gloria whined. "Women in there stare at me and talk in whispers when I come in."

Tony rose from the sofa and approached her.

"They're just using scare tactics," he said calmly. "We've got to stand up to them or they'll keep on bullying us like they've been doing for the past hundred years!"

He reached to touch her arm, but she pulled away.

"I don't want little Tony exposed to this garbage. So I'm taking him and going to my sister's in Sacramento while you figure out what to do about all this."

Tony returned to the sofa to pick up the mail.

"Maybe that's best. My plate's full right now, and I can't

afford to be distracted by your Native American princess bull-crap."

Now it was Gloria's turn to feel like she'd just been punched. She stormed out of the room.

"And while you're there, maybe you can get a make-over to have your head screwed on straight!" Tony yelled.

She marched down the hall, slamming the bedroom door. Tony prepared for a night on the couch, which was becoming a regular occurrence.

Soon enough it was time for the "get the message out" meeting that Tony had promised Cassie. Tony stood in front of the tightly packed tribal meeting room. Cassie sat near the front, while Ralph, the Radio DJ, the Sheriff, Irene, Monica and Hector were scattered among the crowd.

"Could I have your attention please?" Tony began. "I know it's crowded in here, but I've got an announcement to make, and then some serious business to discuss."

The crowd settled down and found their seats.

"First, the tribal council has voted unanimously to rebuild the casino as soon as possible," Tony reported. A rousing cheer arose from the crowd.

"I knew you'd be pleased," Tony continued. "Now, as most of you know, a criminal investigation into the fire-bombing of our casino and the death of Ted Castillo is being conducted by the federal Office of Tribal Justice. But your help is needed, as well. Cassie, would you stand up?"

She stood at her seat near the front of the room.

"If you haven't already met her, this is Marshal Del Rio, who's heading up the investigation. Cassie, please tell everyone what you need."

She stepped to the front and faced the crowd.

"Basically, what we need right now is information," she said in a somber tone. "If you, or anyone you know, saw anything the night of the fire or has information regarding this case, we want to hear about it as soon as possible."

She began passing out a stack of flyers.

"My temporary office, which is located in the back of the tribal headquarters building, is the operation center for this effort," she continued. "Please contact me with anything you think might be useful."

"And I want to call on our local newspaper editor, Ralph Bailey of the <u>Hitchin' Post</u>," Tony interjected. "Where are you?"

Ralph stood up at his seat a few rows back in the audience.

"And Gibb Wilson of KSJV Radio, the voice of the Santa Juanita Valley. Would you stand up?"

Likewise, Gibb stood at his seat.

"We particularly want to ask you two to help us pass the word along to the farthest reaches of the valley," Tony requested.

Each nodded his ascent.

"Somebody out there may know something about this man's death that we need to hear about." Cassie pleaded her case. "No matter what people in this valley think about the tribe or the casino, there can be no justification for this innocent elder's death. The guilty parties must be brought to justice, and I think you in the media can present this story in a sympathetic light."

This struck a chord with everyone in the room. No one moved or spoke. Cassie sat down as her words echoed in peoples' minds.

"I want to thank Cassie for the work she's doing," Tony said. "Let's all cooperate with her in every way possible. Cassie, why don't you get with Ralph and Gibb so they can get the wording you want for the announcement."

Cassie stood to look for Ralph. One by one, members of the audience began clapping for her, and in a few moments a healthy applause filled the room. Cassie smiled and blushed a little as she made her way to the back of the room to meet Ralph and Gibb.

"Now, let's move on to the other business on tonight's agenda," Tony said as the applause subsided.

Meanwhile, in the back of the room, as Cassie explained what information she wanted printed and broadcast, a set of wheels were put into motion. Listening to Cassie, Ralph rapidly jotted notes in his notepad. That evening back at the newspaper office, those notes were transformed into type being set for the next edition of the <u>Hitchin' Post</u>, and a front-page story took shape within his computer.

Later, over at KSJV radio station, Gibb Wilson converted his notes to script form and was ready to out on the airwaves with his announcement.

"This is KSJV radio, the voice of the Santa Juanita Valley," he said into the station's live microphone. "I have an important request that comes from the very heart of this valley, from the first people who lived here, the residents of the Chamala Indian Reservation."

Listening on his home radio, Tony turned up the volume.

"They are asking for your help, to bring justice for the murder of an innocent elder. And we at this radio station are joining them in this plea," the announcer continued. "We are urgently seeking information from anyone who may know something about the fire-bombing of the Chamala casino or the death of Chamala security guard and tribal elder Ted Castillo on March 21. If you have any information that might help with this investigation, please contact Cassandra Del Rio or Tony Mirada at the tribal office on the Chamala Reservation. If you've seen or heard anything that might shed light on this case, please call them."

The DJ gave the contact information and repeated the plea.

"We'll be repeating this announcement several times a day for the next several days," Wilson said.

At 3 a.m. the <u>Hitchin' Post</u>'s printing press rolled out fresh copies of the next day's news. The pressman grabbed a copy as it passed by him, and he scanned the front page. INVESTIGATOR

ISSUES PLEA FOR INFORMATION IN DEATH OF TRIBAL ELDER, the headline read. Under it were two photos, one showing Cassie making her presentation at the tribal meeting and the other, Don laying in the hospital.

Later that morning Cassie entered Don's hospital room and approached his bed. He lay there with his eyes closed.

"Don," she said quietly.

He opened his eyes and looked at her.

"Oh, hi," he said with a smile.

"How are you feeling," she asked.

"As well as can be expected, I guess. What's going on?"

"I brought a forensic sketch artist with me from the Sheriff's office. He's right outside in the hall. Do you feel up to working with him to describe that medallion so we can get a sketch to show around the valley?"

"Sure, sure. Anything to help find Ted's killers."

"Good," Cassie replied as she headed for the door. In a moment, she re-entered the room followed by an older Anglo man carrying an artist pad. He set up near Don's bed and began working as the recovering burn victim described what the medallion he's seen the night of the fire, and the artist began to rapidly sketch what he heard.

Cassie watched as an image took shape. The medallion was a round metallic piece with a horse's head in the middle of an interior circle. On the side of the horse's neck were the two letters "RR" that appeared to be a brand.

The artist showed the finished sketch to Don who enthusiastically approved of the image.

"Good work," Cassie told the artist. "I need several copies of this image to show around the valley, and can you get a copy to the newspaper for tomorrow's edition?"

"Sure thing," the man said. He collected his art supplies and headed out of the room.

Turning back to Don, Cassie said, "Thanks. I know this is going to help find whoever did this."

"I sure hope so," Don said. "Let me know if there's anything else I can do."

Cassie nodded and said, "What you can do is get well." She smiled as she turned to leave.

Meanwhile, on the other side of the valley, about fifty valley residents had gathered at the J.J. Cumming's Buckaroo Dude Ranch. Members of the media were present, as well. The focus of attention was several cases of Mission Wine stacked around. J.J. stepped forward, holding an open bottle of the wine.

"Today we begin our boycott of the products and services sold by Roy Evans," he announced, once he was assured that the cameras were rolling. "Our purpose is to make a point, and the point is this: we do not support his alliance with the Indians. We feel that the best way to make our point is by hitting him directly in the pocketbook. Mission Wine is one of several businesses owned and operated by Roy Evans."

He then ceremoniously poured the wine out of the bottle

onto the ground in front of him. Then others in the crowd proceeded to take previously opened bottles out of their cases and empty their contents on the ground.

"We ask all those who support us to do likewise with their stock of Mission Wine and not to purchase any more of this wine. And this boycott will extend to Evan's other businesses, the Valley Bed & Breakfast, the Mustang Saloon and the Happy Trails Café."

TV news cameramen and still photographers recorded the event while reporters hurriedly took their notes, anxious to feed the news beast's daily need for fodder.

Waiting for any response from their media plea for information, Tony and Cassie drove into Springville. Locals went about their business on this typical sunny day as the pair cruised down the main street in Tony's truck.

"You know I do come to the feed store to get supplies for my horses <u>by</u> <u>myself</u> all the time," Tony pointed out.

"I know, but this gives me a chance to snoop around Springville some more--see what the mood is," Cassie said.

"If I know you, you just want a chance to stir the pot some more."

Cassie smiled, but didn't reply.

Soon they arrived at Valley Feed Supply and parked in front.

Once inside, Tony headed for the feed counter, while Cassie took a look around. She wandered over to a section of western clothing and browsed through the racks.

She failed to notice that the store manager, who was reading a flyer lying near the edge of the check-out counter, recognized who she was. As Cassie held up a ladies western shirt, he took a second look to be sure. He was certain this was the investigator whose picture had appeared in the morning paper.

He pulled another employee aside and motioned towards Cassie.

"Go keep her busy," the manager said quietly, and the employee headed off toward Cassie. As he passed the counter, he knocked the flyer on the floor in front of the counter, but didn't notice.

Meanwhile the Manager grabbed the counter phone and ducked down behind the cashier's counter, out of sight, and dialed.

The employee approached Cassie as the manager crouched out of sight.

Whispering into the phone, he said, "That Indian investigator woman is here in the store. I thought you might like to deliver that personal message you were talking about."

He peeked over the counter and saw that Cassie indicated that she was only browsing and needed no assistance. The employee shrugged and wandered off toward the back of the store.

Quickly the Manager hanged up the phone and stood up just as Tony approached to check out with an armload of supplies.

"Uh, will this be cash or charge?" he asked.

"Cash," Tony replied, pulling out his wallet. Cassie

reached the counter.

"You know, I need fifty feet of quarter-inch diamond braid halter rope, but I didn't see any on the rack," Tony told the manager.

"There's some in back that ain't been put out yet. I'll get that for you."

After he shuffled off, Cassie noticed the flyer on the floor that the manager had been reading earlier. She tried to read it where it lay. Hearing the manager returning, she picked it up and quickly stuffed it in her pants pocket. Tony gave her a questioning look as the manager began ringing up the order.

Outside, Tony was putting the supplies he'd purchased in the bed of the truck when two police cars pulled up blocking them in. Chief Dwight stepped out of one car. Other cops stood by.

"Well, boys, look what we have here--an Indian with a badge and a gun," he said mockingly. Looking at Cassie, he said, "A little outside your jurisdiction aren't you, Marshal Del Rio?"

"Dwight, back off," Tony ordered. "We're just buying supplies."

One of Dwight's men stepped in front of Tony, blocking him.

"Stay out of this, Mirada," Chief Dwight said. "This is between me and the squaw. Oh, I forgot–that isn't a politically correct term these days, is it?"

Cassie's eyes flashed at the sound of the word "squaw."

"Squaw?! What friggin' century are you living in?"

"Easy, Del Rio," Dwight came back. "We heard about the little cry for help you sent out to the residents of our valley."

"I was just about to pay you a professional courtesy visit and ask for your cooperation in this matter," Cassie replied.

"Don't bother. I'm telling you right now--stay out of my town and out of my sight, because you definitely don't have any authority here."

"That's a violation of our civil rights," Tony protested.

"Open that casino and just see how many civil rights I violate!" He signaled his men that it was time to leave.

"Now, you two just get on back to your tipi and think about what I said."

The police chief and his men got back in their cars and pulled away. Cassie took a few steps towards them and yelled, "This harassment will be entered in my report to the Justice Department!"

As he drove away, Chief Dwight stuck his arm out of his police car and gave her the finger.

Tony got in his truck and started the engine as Cassie stood there dumb-founded.

"Get in," Tony said, but she didn't budge.

"I said get in," Tony repeated emphatically, and Cassie obeyed.

"Are you all right?" he asked, once she was seated in the truck cab.

"Hell, no, I'm not all right. I'm fighting mad. If that

redneck thinks he's going to get away with that, he'd better think again. What's up with that guy?"

Tony put the truck in gear and drove away.

"He only blames Indians for everything that's gone wrong in his life. In high school, I beat him out for the school's MVP football trophy, which he never forgot."

"That's it?"

"No, there's more. Years later his wife was killed by a drunk driver who happened to be a member of our tribe."

"So all Indians are to blame?"

"More or less," Tony replied. "He was just starting out as a local cop when it happened, and he came onto the reservation looking for the culprit. He started harassing any Indian he saw."

"Emotional rage," Cassie observed.

"He was brought up on charges of police brutality and operating outside his jurisdiction, but all he got was a slap on the wrist. To this day, he can't stand the thought that the county and the feds enforce the law on the rez, and he's powerless."

"Twenty years is a long time to hold a grudge," Cassie observed.

"That's nothing," Tony chuckled. "I've got tribal members who won't talk to each other because of what their grandparents did 50 years ago."

"You're right," she agreed calmly. "Indians have the longest memory of anyone on the planet."

At the tribal hall, Tony and Cassie got out of the truck and headed for the front door. Just then Cassie remembered the flyer she'd stuck in her pocket.

"I totally forgot about this."

She pulled it out and looked at it.

"What is it?"

"I found it on the floor in the feed store." She showed it to Tony.

The flyer was addressed to Sons of the Valley. "The Heathen are at the gate," the text read. "Our Children and our Way of Life are threatened. Meeting to be held at the old meeting hall. Wednesday April 21 at 8 pm. Signed: The Righteous Master."

"Who in hell are the Sons of the Valley?" Cassie asked.

"Watered down white-supremacists."

"Come again?" Cassie didn't think Tony said what she thought he'd just said.

"They're an old organization of European immigrant descendants who banded together for self-protection in the pioneer days," Tony explained, handing the paper back to Cassie. "You know, like the Daughters of the American Revolution. But I thought the Sons of the Valley was an extinct organization."

"I guess it's never too late for the South to rise again. What do you think the old meeting hall is?"

"I don't know. Some secret meeting place, I guess."

"If they're a secret organization, how come you know about them?" Cassie wondered.

"I made it a point to find out everything I could about the

people who settled in this valley, when, and why. They've even got a web site. You can look 'em up on the Internet now."

Moments later, Cassie and Tony entered the tribal office to find Rose Marie waiting for them with a funny look on her face.

"What's up?" Tony asked.

Rose Marie pointed with her lips across the room. Irene and Father McDougal were waiting in folding chairs outside Cassie's office.

"A more unlikely pair, I've never seen," Tony observed. "What are you doing here?"

"We want to help with the investigation," Irene asserted.

"Yes, Irene is very persuasive," Father McDougal admitted. "And there are others here, too." Standing up, he instructed, "Come with me."

The padre led them out of the tribal office building and into the Tribal Elders Center located across the way. There they found about two dozen people, Indian and non-Indian, chatting among themselves. About half of them were elderly and the other half teenagers.

"You asked for help," Irene reminded Tony. "A group of us from the Tribal Elder's Center decided to volunteer."

"And some of the students from our Sunday school suggested we get involved," the priest added. "You see I've been sharing with our high school students some of the tribe's version of mission history that Irene gave me."

"Yeah, it was good to find out the valley's true history, and we feel bad about what happened to the Chamala people in the past," one of the students offered. "We know it's not much, but this is, like you know, something positive we can do right now to help."

"Wow, this is unbelievable." Tony was almost in shock.

"So here we are," Irene stated. "Ready to go to work. What can we do?"

Cassie thought a moment. "Tony, you know that list of tribal residents we got from Rose Marie?"

"Yeah."

"Let's divide up the list, put an elder and a teenager together and send them out to get their statements. I can write up a list of questions for them to ask."

"It's worth a try," Tony said, relieved that someone had actually thought of something the group could do. "I'll get the list."

As he went to get the list, Cassie stepped to the front of the group.

"Now let's pair off--one elder and one student per team."

As they paired off, another idea struck Irene. A twinkle came to her eye and a grin formed on her lips. She approached Father McDougal and pulled him aside.

"Now if you really want to do something to honor the Chamala people and help repair some of the damage done in the past, I've got an idea."

Father McDougal indicated he was willing to listen. Irene

sat him down and began explaining her idea out of earshot of anyone else.

By late afternoon, the odd investigative pairs were on the job, scattered across the reservation conducting interviews. In each case, a tribal elder and a non-Indian student approached a reservation home. The student held a clipboard and a pen. The student knocked on the door.

An American Indian person--man, woman or child--came to the door, opened it and listened to what the elder had to say. Many residents indicated they'd heard something the night of the casino fire. Each student took notes on the clipboard, and then the pair moved on.

At the same time, Cassie began making the rounds with her sketch of the murderous group's medallion, showing area shop-owners the sketch artist's image. No one seemed to know the source of that unique piece of jewelry, or they weren't willing to share the information. Cassie wasn't sure which.

Over the next few days Tony focused on the reconstruction of the tribe's small casino, while Cassie spent some time back at the OTJ office in Sacramento catching up on other cases.

Tony watched with great hope and satisfaction as a new and more stylishly designed structure rose out of the ashes of the old one.

On one sunny Saturday, he met with the contractor on site late in the morning to go over a few changes in the blueprints. Around noon he finished up and headed off the reservation toward

Springville.

As he was nearing the entrance to the reservation he noticed some kind of commotion up ahead. As he got closer, what was happening became clear. Dozens of non-Indian people were staging a protest. Protesters carried signs that read NO CASINO and NO GAMBLING IN SJV and SAVE OUR VALLEY FROM THE INDIANS.

And there in front of the crowd was J.J. Cummings with a smartly dressed woman Tony had never seen before.

As he neared the crowd, Tony could hear J.J. bellowing through a megaphone, "JUST SAY NO! NO CA-SI-NO!" The crowd echoed his chant: "JUST SAY NO! NO CA-SI-NO!" This was repeated over and over again for the benefit of a remote TV news crew that was broadcasting the demonstration live.

Tony got out of his truck to watch the spectacle, and in just a few minutes, someone in the crowd spotted him leaning against the hood. Suddenly, the group rushed over to his vehicle and surrounded him, continuing their chant.

The reporter and camera rushed over, as well, trying to get Tony's reaction. But the crowd started to get unruly. They shouted angry taunts in Tony's face. The back of the group pushed to get closer, and the front of the crowd closed in on him. A shoving match ensued. Tony was engulfed by the mob.

Near the news truck, Cathleen Radcliff proudly watched as the results of her efforts unfolded. She looked to J.J. for approval, but found instead a severe look of disapproval. This is not the outcome he had in mind at all.

He quickly rushed to the unruly mob and tried to break them up. He wormed his way to the front and inserted himself between Tony and the front line. He created enough room for Tony to get back into his truck.

J.J. tried to apologize to Tony, but the chanting was too loud. Tony gunned his engine and tried to drive away, but the mob moved in front of his truck. Finally the exasperated mayor barked orders through the megaphone.

"Move away from the truck and let the man through," he commanded. "Blockading traffic is against the law and may result in your arrest."

The crowd pulled away, allowing the truck to pass. Tony gave the mayor a dirty look as he passed by. The mayor, for his part, was not pleased with how things had turned out.

That night, after another great dinner courtesy of her host, Cassie reviewed the casino fire case notes on Irene's kitchen table. She looked hard between the lines, trying to see what she might have missed. The phone rang.

"Can you get that for me, Cassie?" Irene called from the other room.

"Sure." Cassie answered the wall phone across the room.

"Hello, Irene Magdalena's residence."

"I've got information about the casino fire," the male caller said.

"Who is this?"

"Meet me in the Mission parking lot in one hour."

"How'd you get this number?"

The caller hung up, leaving the dial tone blaring in Cassie's ear. Puzzled, she hung up.

"Who was it?" Irene called out.

"Actually, it was for me." Cassie looked at her watch, then dialed the phone.

"Come on, Tony, pick up." All she got was Tony's voice-mail, so she left him a message.

"Tony, I just got an anonymous call from a man who says he's got information on the casino fire. He wants me to meet him at the Mission parking lot at nine. If you get this message in time, call me or just meet me at the Mission."

She hung up, pausing to think a moment, then grabbed her jacket and purse. She headed for the door.

"Irene, I'm going out for a while to check on something. See you later."

Irene came into the room. "What is it?" she asked.

"Maybe nothing."

"Be careful," the elder admonished.

Cassie nodded and pushed on through the door. Irene followed to the porch and watched her leave. She felt that something wasn't right but wasn't sure what it was.

Fifteen minutes later, Cassie's car pulled into the Mission parking lot. All was quiet.

She parked the car, got out, and scanned the grounds to see

if anyone was around. Finding no one, she returned to her car and checked her watch. It read 8:30.

"Nothing to do but wait," she said to herself as she leaned against her car.

Fifteen minutes went by, and then half an hour. Cassie was pacing around the parking lot, and by 9:15 decided to give up. Starting the engine, she turned on her headlights and drove out of the parking lot.

Driving down the empty rural road that led away from the Mission, she passed a car sitting on the side of the road with its lights off. Cassie didn't pay much attention to it. After she passed, the car pulled on to the road behind her without lights.

Cassie drove in silent thought. Suddenly bright headlights appeared in her rearview mirror, catching her attention just seconds before her car was rammed from behind.

She looked back in disbelief as she was rammed again. Disbelief was replaced by anger as she realized that the whole thing had been a set-up.

She increased her speed, but the mystery vehicle kept pace. Finally, the dark vehicle moved up beside her car on the driver's side. Cassie could now see that it was a dark pickup truck. It swerved and rammed into the side of her car.

The force knocked her car onto the gravel shoulder, but Cassie managed to steer back onto the road. She looked directly into the truck at her assailants and saw that there are four figures in white ski masks looking back at her.

The truck rammed the side of her car again, this time succeeding in forcing her off the road into a ditch. Cassie hit her head and felt herself go unconscious.

The pick-up stopped long enough for one of the masked figures to get out, light a Molotov cocktail and toss it at her car. The burning mass landed on the hood, exploding into flames.

Quickly, the masked bomber ran back to the truck and jumped in. The masked men sped away into the night as flames begin to spread over Cassie's car.

Moments later another pickup truck arrived on the scene. It pulled up behind the burning car and stopped. The driver ran to the burning car, pulling Cassie from the flames.

Cassie awoke moments later to find Tony hovering over her. She had a cut on her forehead.

"What happened?" Cassie was dizzy and light-headed.

"I was just about to ask you the same thing," Tony replied." He kneeled down to get a closer look at her wound.

"Four masked guys in a pickup truck forced me off the road and set the car on fire."

"That has a familiar ring to it."

Just then the flames surged, sending out a wave of heat. Tony helped Cassie to her feet, and they moved toward his truck. From this safer vantage point they watched as her car was engulfed in flames.

"Somebody around here definitely doesn't like you," Tony observed, helping her into his truck.

Opening the glove compartment, he retrieved a hand towel and handed it to Cassie. She applied pressure to her forehead and leaned over, resting on Tony's shoulder.

"I saw 'em, Tony. Four men in white ski masks. They were waiting for me."

"Don't talk now. Let's get you to a doctor."

She cuddled up closer to him. They drove toward the hospital leaving her car to burn.

The next morning, Cassie, head bandaged and spirits sagging, sat at Irene's kitchen table reading a newspaper and sipping coffee. Tony sat across from her feeling guilty. Irene, with her usual bright disposition, was at the stove cooking a hearty breakfast.

"I feel guilty as hell getting you involved in this," Tony admitted.

"Don't," Cassie assured him. "This is exactly the reason the Office of Tribal Justice exists, and exactly the kind of case I became a federal marshal to investigate. And besides, you know what they say: What doesn't kill you makes you stronger."

"I think what you need is a short break, a change of scenery," Tony replied. "There's a place I've been meaning to visit." He looked at Irene, then continued. "In a couple of days, when you're feeling better, you want to take a little ride with me up to Condor Mountain, to visit our ancestral springs?"

Irene set plates of food on the table.

"It's a very special place, Cassie," she added. "That's

where our people have gone for centuries to talk to the Creator and our ancestors, to get advice. I've been trying to get Tony up there for some time now."

Tony easily recognized the silent scolding Irene was giving him with her eyes.

"Well, seeing as how Irene thinks you should go. I don't mind keeping you company." She smiled as she shoveled a fork full of eggs into her mouth. And that was that.

It was a bright sunny morning when, two days later, Tony drove Cassie to the stable where he kept his horses. A large wooden frame archway announced that they were entering the Mountain View Equestrian Center. Tony parked his truck in the gravel lot and led Cassie to a brown barn shaded by a huge oak.

The large white bandage that two days earlier covered Cassie's forehead had now been replaced with a much smaller, more discreet beige-colored patch. She watched as Tony put an Indian blanket over the back of one of his horses.

"This is Sienna," Tony explained. "Why don't you come on over and get acquainted while I get her saddled up, since you'll be riding her."

Cassie approached the sandy brown mare and patted the white star on her forehead.

"It's been ages since I've been up on a horse. This one's not going to plow me into a low hanging branch trying to knock me off, is she?"

"She's as gentle as a lamb," Tony assured her. "I usually

let little Tony ride her. You'll be just fine."

After saddling up Sienna, Tony opened a neighboring stall and escorted out a remarkable Paint with a pattern on his right flank that strikingly resembled a human handprint.

"This magnificent animal is Sonny, named after my grandpa. Ain't he a beaut?" Tony stroked his neck fondly. "Nobody rides Sonny but me. Ain't that right, boy?" The proud owner beamed with pride and admiration.

"You two need a moment alone? I can step outside, if you like." Cassie's comic sarcasm was noticeable.

"All right, smart ass." Tony quietly turned his attention to saddling up his prized possession.

"Is the spring located on the reservation?" Cassie asked cheerfully.

"No, it's on National Forest Land now, but tribal members have permission to go up there whenever we like. The Forest Service recognizes the area as part of our traditional homeland and allows us to have access."

Tony threw his saddle on Sonny's back and cinched up the strap.

"Before this trouble with the casino even started, Irene told me I'd have an opportunity to visit the mountain. I didn't really believe her then."

"What about now?"

"I hate it when she's right, which is most of the time."

Hand extended, Cassie walked over and petted Sonny's

neck. "How long a ride is it?"

"We'll get there in time for that picnic lunch we packed," he said. "Ready?"

She nodded, and Tony helped her mount her horse before mounting his own. With Sonny in the lead, they rode out of the stable into the crisp morning air.

By mid-morning, the pair was already deep into National Forest land, riding leisurely through the rugged, scenic beauty. Cassie noticed that their journey was a fairly steady climb. She couldn't remember when she'd taken time out for such a luxury as a lazy ride into the wilderness. The day was clear and the landscape breathtaking.

By late morning they reached the edge of a ridge, which overlooked a herd of deer grazing in the valley below.

"What a view," Cassie observed. "It makes you wonder what it was really like for our ancestors."

"I'm sure life was hard," Tony replied. "But I also think it was very special. I'm still learning about our traditional ways myself, the philosophy of our people. It's something I missed growing up."

"I remember. You told me about how your family struggled just to make ends meet when you were little, how they focused on making sure you could function in the white man's world."

"You remember that, do you? Well, I remember how you used to think you were somehow superior to me even though you grew up in an urban community, just because your family did the powwow circuit."

"Did I act that way?"

"Yup, you did."

"I guess you're right," she said after a thoughtful pause. "I'm sorry. I don't know what made me think that."

"You're forgiven," Tony smiled. "Anyway, with the help of a few of our elders who managed to keep some of the traditions alive, I hope to someday integrate our culture into my daily life. They say it brings a feeling of wholeness."

Cassie nodded knowingly.

"We'd better move on," Tony urged and reigned Sonny toward the downward slope that led towards the river.

They continued their ride toward Condor Mountain, which loomed ever larger. They now moved alongside the clear Santa Juanita River as it flowed down from the mountain toward the valley.

In a short time, Cassie saw canyon walls ahead rising on either side of the river. Their trail along the narrowing stream took them straight into that canyon. Sienna gladly followed Sonny into the unfamiliar territory.

The wind whispered through the canyon, sounding every bit like the whispers of tribal ancestors. The hairs on the back of Cassie's neck stood up. She felt a presence. She had to look around to make sure there wasn't anyone there.

Tony broke the silence.

"It's been too long since I was up here."

"I definitely feel something here," Cassie admitted. "It's the same feeling I get in Irene's house, but stronger. It's hard to describe."

"A couple of times when I was a kid, the elders let us come here to swim in the warm spring water. It's supposed to be healing. A few of the older generation still come up here."

The trail narrowed. They dismounted and walked to the stream.

"This stream was the tribe's source of water for ten thousand years. Up here the water's still pure."

He dipped out a handful of river water and sipped it. Following Tony's lead, Cassie dismounted and scooped up a handful of the crystal clear water. It was warmer than she expected and tasted a little like fancy imported bottled water.

"Wow, what an interesting taste. What's the water like down where it passes through the reservation?" she asked.

"Unfit for human consumption, thanks to Springville's sewage run-off."

"That's ironic for a town named Springville."

"Tell me about it. We're trying to get the EPA to declare it a federal clean-up site." He looked upstream. "We're almost to the spring."

They remounted their horses and rode on. Shortly, the canyon walls suddenly opened up to reveal a hidden landscape, a secret world, at the base of the mountain. In the middle of this sacred space was a rock-lined pool of clear water. Hovering above the pool was a layer of steam.

To one side of the pool, a waterfall plummeted a hundred feet down a cliff face, splashing onto a jumbled pile of huge boulders. At that point the flow of water split in two, with half spilling into the pool and the other half descending into a channel that was the headwaters of the Santa Juanita River.

Upon closer inspection of the greenish rocks around the pool, Cassie saw that they were serpentine stone, a rather soft rock found all over the state and used by Indians in prehistoric time to carve pieces of jewelry. In the center of the pool, water bubbled to the surface indicating the source of the spring.

Tony climbed to a high rock outcropping that overlooked the pool.

"I'm speechless," Cassie muttered. "This is one of the most beautiful places I've ever seen. I can't imagine why you don't come up here every weekend just to clear your head."

"I guess I really don't have a good excuse, now that I think about it. You just get busy with daily life and--it just didn't seem all that relevant."

A silence hung between them for a moment. In the quiet, Tony looked at Cassie deeply and intently, realizing once again what a beautiful woman she was. Enjoying the moment, Cassie gazed into her former boyfriend's eyes with renewed appreciation.

"I'm hungry," Tony said, breaking off the spell of the moment. "Why don't we break out that picnic lunch we brought?"

"Yeah, sure, why not," Cassie replied almost reluctantly, and they spread their feast on a blanket in the sun. As they ate, Cassie was reminded of a secluded picnic she and Tony had shared many years ago.

After they'd eaten, Cassie took in the sights and sounds of the place: the sun, the bubbling water, the fresh smell of the mist gently floating in the air. Tony had climbed back up on the serpentine rocks above the pool, and Cassie watched him standing there lost in his thoughts, oblivious to the very scene that she was absorbed in. It wasn't long before he refocused and noticed Cassie watching him.

He stepped down from the rocks and approached her.

"What really happened to us, Cassie?" he asked. "I mean back in college."

"As I recall, we weren't sure of who we were or who we were supposed to become. We were changing, and what seemed like a perfect fit in the beginning got harder and harder to hold together."

Tony sat down on the blanket and poured two glasses of wine.

"We _were_ pretty mixed up," he admitted. "I can remember thinking you wanted to go too far too fast."

"All I really wanted was to have the freedom to find out what my potential was, without the limits my parents and my tribal culture were trying put on me as a female."

"I know it's way too late," Tony offered, "but… I'm sorry

I didn't understand that then."

"Thanks, that's sweet," she replied softly.

As tender feelings arose in her, she looked away. Gazing at the water, a big silly grin spread across her face.

"Want to relive some childhood memories?"

She had a mischievous twinkle in her eye. She jumped up and began stripping off her clothes. Tony was very surprised, to say the least.

"Last one in's a rotten egg," Cassie shouted as she ran toward the water, stripping as she went.

"My mother taught me you're not supposed to go in the water for an hour after you eat," he said with a smile.

Deciding to join her, he raced to catch up, stripping off his clothes as ran.

"That's an old wives tale," Cassie countered. "I've gone swimming right after I ate for years and never gotten a single cramp."

Reaching the water's edge, she stripped down to her underwear and slipped into the water. Tony stripped to his boxer shorts and followed her in.

Cassie swam toward the middle of the pool, with Tony not too far behind.

"Ooh," Cassie exclaimed. "The closer you get to the center, the warmer the water is."

"Don't go too far, you'll boil like a lobster."

Suddenly she turned to face Tony, and he almost collided

with her. She kissed him full on. Surprised at first, he finally gave into the kiss. Their kisses became more passionate as their bodies intertwined in the water. As they kissed, Tony moved them to shallower water, where their kissing became love-making, and their hearts once again became intertwined.

Later in the day, as the sun began to set and the horses were readied for the return trip, Cassie got up the courage to ask Tony a question that had been burning in her mind.

"What do we do now?"

"I don't know," he admitted. "I need time to think about it. It'll be getting dark soon, so we'd better get going." He patted his horse's neck. "These babies don't have headlights you know."

He kissed her as a means of reassuring her that their love-making had meant something to him, and then he helped her up on Sienna. Mounting Sonny, Tony led them down the mountain.

The following day, Rose Marie was, as usual, typing at her desk when the phone rang.

"Chamala tribal office," she answered, then listened for a moment. "Just a minute please," she told the caller, and punched buttons on the phone, connecting with Cassie.

"Cassie, there's a call for you on line one. A girl says she needs to talk to the 'woman investigator.'"

Cassie switched to the incoming call.

"This is Marshal Del Rio. How can I help you?" She listened intently to what the caller had to say.

"I know something about the fire at the tribe's casino," the caller said.

"What's your name?" Cassie asked.

"Julie," the girl replied.

"Can you come to my office, or can we meet somewhere?" Cassie asked. Julie gave her directions.

"Hang on, Julie, I'll come right over." Hanging up the phone, she headed for Tony's office.

Cassie stuck her head in his office door to find him reading.

"A very nervous girl just called and said she has information on who set the fire."

"Sure it's not another set-up?" Tony asked, rising from his chair.

"That's why you're coming along."

They headed for Tony's truck.

"Where does she live?" he asked.

"Outskirts of Springville, near the Valley Oaks Ranch. Know that area?"

"Yeah, I know it," Tony said with an edge to his voice.

They got in his truck. After starting the engine, Tony said, "When I was a kid, my father worked for Valley Oaks Ranch for a while. I helped him out there a couple of times."

The truck backed out, and sped away.

Driving down Valley Oaks Ranch Road, they came upon a nice ranch-style, two-story house situated next to an open green belt area. They parked on the street and approached.

As they walk up the driveway, Cassie noticed an old pick-up truck parked on the side of the house. She made a bee-line for it.

It was a dark blue Chevy truck, banged up across the front and on the right front fender. Cassie hurriedly jotted down the truck's license plate.

"That's the truck that ran me off the road," Cassie declared. "And I'd bet a million bucks it's the truck that Don saw the night of the fire."

Quickly mounting the stairs that led up to a wide porch, Cassie knocked on the front door. Tony surveyed their surroundings, and in a moment the door opened. A young woman in her early 20s came into view.

She stood there quietly for a moment looking at the two Indians standing on her porch, and then, without a word, pushed the screen door open. Tony and Cassie entered the house. A picture-perfect, upscale country-style living room greeted them.

"Are you here alone?" Cassie ventured.

"Yeah," Julie replied. "My parents are at work. I have something I think you're looking for."

"What's that?" Cassie asked.

"I'll show you."

Julie crossed to an end table and opened a drawer. She withdrew a small shiny object, clutching it tightly in her fist. Reluctantly at first, she stepped toward Cassie. Then, as determination set in, she stepped quickly to Cassie.

"This belongs to my boyfriend," Julie said, dropping the object into Cassie's hand.

What Cassie saw resting in her hand was the missing double horse medallion with its broken chain.

Cassie looked to Tony in disbelief, then to Julie who sat down in a nearby chair.

"I heard on the radio about the Indian elder who died. My boyfriend--"

Julie faltered and sighed heavily. She tried to continue.

"My boyfriend--."

Cassie pulled up a chair in front of her.

"It's all right, Julie," she said in a comforting voice. "Take your time. Start from the beginning."

Julie took a deep breath.

"My boyfriend, Jamie--that's his name. He's always been into calf roping and bull riding, the whole rodeo thing. Well, he was so jazzed when he became a member of the Ruff Ryders."

"The rodeo team?" Tony was surprised.

"Yeah," Julie answered. "So I had that medallion especially made for him from the Ruff Ryder emblem. And Jaime was so proud of that thing. He wore it everywhere. Only, he told me later, that he wasn't supposed to wear it when he went on 'missions' for them."

"Missions?" Cassie asked. "What kind of missions?"

"Secret stuff they did. Jaime didn't know anything about those things when he joined the team. He only found out later after

278

he was sworn to secrecy."

Tears began to quietly fall from Julie's eyes.

"It's all right," Cassie reassured her. "Everything's going to be all right."

Just then, the sound of a car door closing came from outside. Tony peeked through the curtains to see what was going on.

"A hot rod pickup with a flame design on the sides just parked out front," Tony reported.

"That's Jaime!" Julie exclaimed. "What's he doing here?"

Cassie drew her gun and moved toward the door. Julie panicked.

"What are you going to do?" she asked. "Don't hurt him. Jamie didn't want anyone to get hurt."

"Jamie's the one who tried to save Don when he was on fire?" Tony interjected.

"Yeah, he was against going to the reservation from the beginning, but he was out-voted."

Cassie replaced her weapon in its holster.

"All right," she said calmly. "I'll just go out and talk to him--see if he's willing to cooperate. Tony, you stay with Julie."

Tony nodded as he peeked out the window again. Cassie stepped out onto the porch and saw Jaime, a nice looking young Anglo man in his early twenties. When Jaime spotted Cassie, he froze.

"Jaime, I need to talk to you."

Jaime noticed her badge and gun, and took off running towards the nearby open field in a panic. The marshal sped after him, as a dumbfounded Tony watched through the front window. He ran out on the porch to get a better view of the action.

In an amazingly short number of strides, Cassie overtook the young man in the field next door and tackled him to the ground in spite of his larger size.

Tony arrived a moment later as Cassie was placing handcuffs on Jaime's wrists.

"That was amazing," Tony remarked, a little out of breath. "Where'd you learn to run like that?"

"In college," Cassie replied with a smile. "Don't you remember? You used to chase me around the campus trying to kiss me, just like a fifth grader."

"That's not the way I remember it," Tony replied.

Irene helped Jaime to his feet and escorted him back toward Julie's house. Tony followed, shaking his head in amazement. In her front yard, Julie ran to her handcuffed boyfriend.

"What have you done to me?" Jamie demanded bitterly. Julie was crying.

"I'm sorry, Jaime. I couldn't take it any more."

"Are we in the Springville city limits or in the county?" Cassie asked Tony.

"The county."

"Good. Why don't you call the Sheriff while I talk to

Jaime?"

"Sure thing," Tony said, and he pulled out his cellphone. He dialed and walked out a little way from the house to get a better signal.

"Jamie, is that your truck parked in Julie's driveway?" Cassie asked politely.

"No, that belongs to Travis." His tone softened. "He's the team leader."

"More like the gang leader, wouldn't you say?" Julie declared.

Jaime didn't respond.

"Here's the deal."

Cassie was all business now.

"Julie told us how you tried to help Don at the fire, so if you give us the names of the rest of your group, I'll make sure the judge goes easy on you."

She pulled out a pen and paper and handed them to Jaime. Awkwardly, he started writing with his handcuffed hands.

"I'll release one of the cuffs if you promise not to run," Cassie said calmly.

Jaime nodded, and she unlocked one cuff. He finished writing his list.

A short while later, they arrived at the Sheriff's office with the hand-cuffed Jaime who was immediately taken to the back for booking. Cassie handed the list Jaime made to Sheriff McKenzie.

"Here are the names Jaime gave me," Cassie explained.

"He said they were involved in the casino fire."

" It's essentially the membership list of the Ruff Ryders rodeo team," Tony added. "Jaime said from time to time the Ruff Ryders went on special missions for the Sons of the Valley to take care of business the Sons wanted done."

"Sons of the Valley?" Sheriff McKenzie responded as he examined the list. "I thought they disbanded years ago."

"So did I, but apparently they've only been laying low," Tony replied. "I guess they were waiting for just the right reason to rise up again."

"I guess the tribe's casino plans seemed to be the right reason," Cassie offered. "They're probably afraid that if Indians attain wealth and power, they might want to get even for past wrongs."

"Wow, this list contains the names of some of our most prominent Springville families," the sheriff said.

"I guess we'd better get the district judge to issue warrants so that the Springville police can pick them up," Cassie remarked.

"There's only one little problem," the sheriff pointed out.

"What's that?" Cassie asked.

The Sheriff showed Cassie the list. She saw the name Travis Whitfield at the top of the list.

"So?" Cassie replied. "I don't get it."

Tony grinned like a cat that had just caught a mouse.

"I forget that you're not from around here," he said. "Travis Whitfield is just the son of Springville's illustrious Chief of Police, affectionately known as Chief Dwight, but whose full name is Dwight Whitfield."

"Oh." Cassie replied thoughtfully. "No wonder Julie and Jaime were so nervous."

"So the Ruff Ryders are just the grunts in this little war," Sheriff McKenzie proclaimed. "We're going to have to find the generals, the sons-of-bitches that run the Sons of the Valley."

"It's not going to be all that hard," Tony assured them. "Awhile back I found an old membership list in the archives of the county library."

"You go to the library?" Cassie asked sarcastically.

"Guess whose name's at the top of that list," Tony said, ignoring her remark.

"A Whitfield?" Cassie asked rhetorically.

"Dwight's daddy, to be exact," Tony added with a smug grin. "Now maybe we'll finally be able to put an end to this valley's hundred and fifty year game of cowboys and Indians."

"Marshal Del Rio, this is your case, so who do you want me to call for prosecution?" Sheriff McKenzie asked.

"Technically, it's a federal case since the crime was committed on federal trust land," Cassie replied thoughtfully. "But since the perpetrators live outside the reservation, it could go federal or state. What would you like to do, Sheriff?"

"If it's up to me, I'd like to turn it over to the state courts. I've got a good relationship there, and I know they'd be delighted to follow through."

"All right then. Take it away," Cassie replied. "I'm up to my neck in cases."

"Thanks for your help on this," McKenzie said, shaking Cassie's hand. "Tony was right when he said he knew who to call."

"Now I'll make sure our prisoner is all snug and secure, and then I'll contact the State Attorney General." He headed for the jail.

Cassie looked to Tony, and their eyes met for a moment.

"Come outside," Tony said. "I need to talk to you."

They sat in Tony's truck as he tried to put something into words.

"Cassie, I--" he began, but faltered. Thinking she knew where this was going, Cassie helped him out.

"You don't have to say anything. I understand."

"No, I do have to say something," Tony objected. "It's just hard."

Cassie looked away.

"You made a mistake, right?" she said.

"Actually, no I didn't."

Surprised, Cassie looked back at him.

"You coming back into my life was the best thing for me right now. You reminded me of things I'd forgotten, things that are important."

Cassie was confused.

"What are you saying?" she asked.

"I'm saying that I need to properly end things with Gloria before I can think about a relationship with you or anyone. I'm saying that I need to follow Irene's advice and reconnect with my spiritual roots."

Taking her hand in his, he continued.

"I'm saying you mean a lot to me, and if you feel the same about me, I'd like to see more of you. I hope you can wait until I get my act together. It shouldn't be long."

As Tony talked, a tear formed in the corner of one of Cassie's eyes.

"I can wait," she said, trying to blink the tear away. "I'm in no rush."

He kissed her tenderly right there in front of the sheriff's office in broad daylight for anyone and everyone to see.

A few days later, a familiar cast of characters gathered in the courtyard of the Mission for a special event. It was a gloriously sunny day in the Santa Juanita Valley, and Tony felt a sense of new beginnings, represented by this day's unique proceedings.

He now stood with Irene and Father McDougal, neat rows of chairs set up before them. Seated in these rows of chairs was a collection of various friendly locals, both Indian and non-Indian. The chairs all faced a podium, which stood next to a large, mysteriously shrouded object.

On either side of the shroud stood two rows of children dressed in their finest attire: some of the tribal youth of the Chamala Reservation and the students of the Mission's Sunday school class.

Father McDougal stepped to the podium to address the crowd.

"Inspired by the ideas and efforts of our own children, the Church and the Chamala tribe have come together in this great collaboration. It gives me great pleasure today to announce the construction of a long-overdue memorial to the Chamala Indian people who, and I'll read the words that will be engraved on the dedication plaque. In the 1800s, built this mission, lived in this mission, died in this mission and are buried on these grounds. May we always remember their lives and their sacrifice."

He nodded to the children, and they pulled on the shroud. It fell away, revealing mock-up of a striking bronze statue of a traditionally-dressed Chamala family, father, mother and child, standing proudly together.

"When this sculpture is completed in about a year, it will stand near the entrance to the mission grounds," the padre added.

Overwhelmed with the emotion of the moment, the crowd stood and applauded vigorously. Many left the seating area to examine the artist's rendering more closely.

Later, at the reception following the unveiling, Tony stood talking with Jim, Roy, Irene and others. As Tony's eyes swept across the gathering, he was surprised to see J.J. Cummings approach from the back.

"Mayor Cummings, I'm surprised to see you here," he said politely. "Where's your sidekick from Speak Out, California?"

"I sent her packing," the Mayor replied.

"Really?"

"I didn't agree with her tactics – the same as I didn't agree with Whitfield's tactics. And so, while many of us are still opposed to your plans to build a casino out on the highway, we're going to run our opposition through official channels."

"Well, that's something," Tony replied, not sure what to make of this whole turn of events.

"Springville's name has really been tarnished by the criminal actions of some of its more radical citizens," Cummings said.

"Not to mention the bad publicity from that anti-casino rally that got out of hand," Jim added.

"That, too," the Mayor said, shaking his head. "What a terrible, shameful mess."

Turning to Tony, Cummings said what he came to say.

"Listen, Chairman Mirada, I took your advice and started studying up on federal Indian policy, tribal sovereignty and such."

"I'm glad to hear it," he said and meant it.

"What I'm hoping is that in the very near future, we'll be able to sit down at the table, air our differences and come to some kind of understanding."

"You can't ask for more than that." Tony was almost in shock, but he stepped forward, hand extended. Cummings did likewise, and they shook, another sign of new beginnings.

"By the way," the Mayor added, "Springville's got a job opening for a new Chief of Police. Let me know if there are any members of the tribe who'd like to apply for the job."

His message delivered, Cummings turned and left. Tony watched him depart in silence as Roy Evans stepped closer to Tony and spoke in a hushed tone.

"Once the casino land deal gets approval from the BIA, I'd like to discuss the possibility of jointly developing a theme park on another parcel of land I've got just down the road."

He made a sweeping arc gesture in front of Tony.

"Relive the thrilling days of yesteryear at the 'Cowboys & Indians' theme park in the beautiful Santa Juanita Valley." He held his hand up high as if you could see the neon sign against the sky. "What do you think?" he asked sincerely.

"Give it a rest, Roy," Tony said. "I'd like to give the whole cowboys and Indians theme a break."

He turned back to chat with Irene, leaving the former TV star in his own little fantasy world.

A few days later, Chamala elders sang an ancient tribal blessing song as they stood on the banks of Mount Condor's Indian Springs. The melodious chant blended beautifully with the sounds of the waterfall and the bubbling springs, creating a symphony of natural harmony.

Wielding an eagle feather, Irene wafted billows of sage and cedar smoke over and around Tony who stood on the rock outcropping above the springs. Dressed in traditional tribal regalia, he faced Mount Condor's peak as he received the elders' blessing in the old way and began his journey to becoming a true tribal leader.

He would take his contemporary Native nation with him as they began their own journey–a journey to recapture their language and culture, a journey to regain their very souls.

And this is the best journey of all.

THE AWAKENING

The autumn air hung crisp and cool over northeastern Washington's Pend Oreille River. Looking for breakfast, a great blue heron lightly skimmed across the face of the northward flowing waters that skirt the Kalispel Indian Reservation.

Finding nothing of interest, the bird altered its course and headed for the wooded land along the river where dozens of modest frame houses had been built decades ago for the native people who still called the reservation home.

Smoke gently rose from the chimneys of several of the homes whose inhabitants sought to fend off the chill of the Saturday morning air.

In one such home, fifteen-year-old Jason Black Bear settled into a worn, overstuffed chair juggling a bag of chips, a soda can, and a television remote control. Aiming the device at the aging television set across the living room, he flipped through several satellite-fed channels until he found the VH1 station he was looking for. The young man pumped the volume up several notches. His attire, fashioned after the hip-hop gangster musicians he admired, offered ample clues as to the style of music that blared from the TV.

The jarring noise Jason called music immediately found its way to the kitchen where his eighty-year-old, apron-adorned grandmother, Alice, chopped vegetables at the kitchen table. The lines in her ancient face spoke not of age, but of wisdom gained from a challenging, yet rewarding life.

Upon hearing the too-loud music, she paused midway into

the beheading of a carrot. With a deliberate whack, she finished the job and rose from her chair. Still wielding the chopping knife, the elder marched into the living room and took up a position between her grandson and the offending home entertainment apparatus.

"Grandma, I can't see the TV," Jason immediately protested.

"That's not all you can't see," Alice replied, using the point of her knife to turn the TV off. "Have you done your chores today?"

"No," the boy said, looking away.

"Have you done your homework," she asked, already knowing the answer.

"Grandma, it's Saturday," Jason replied in a whine-tinged voice. "I'll do it tomorrow night."

"You know my rules," the elder countered. "After the work is done, there's time for fun." The phrase came first in her native Salish tongue, followed by an English translation. "Why, when your grandfather was alive…"

"Spare me the old-time-Indian spiel," Jason complained, rising from his chair. "I'll take out the garbage." He trudged from the room.

Immensely resenting the whole process, the teenager extracted the overflowing garbage bag from beneath the kitchen sink and dragged it out the back door. Oblivious of the natural world around him, he thrust the bulging bag into the metal garbage can and slammed the lid back into place. His hated task completed, he trudged back into the house.

Later that afternoon, Jason listened to JZ's "American Gangster" album via iPod and headphones while half-heartedly attempting to do his homework. When a loud knock came at his bedroom door, he quickly hid the contraband equipment in his desk drawer. Alice stuck her head in the door, smiling.

"How's it coming," she asked cheerily.

"Slow," Jason said, less than enthusiastically.

"Want a break," his grandmother asked.

"Sure," he answered brightly, rising from his chair.

"Drive me up the hill and help me pick some bear root."

"Aw, Grandma," Jason said, the brightness gone from his face and voice. "Why don't you just go to the drug store like everybody else?"

"The forest is my drug store," the ancient woman answered, taking a step into the room. "Where do you think those white doctors got their medicines from in the first place?"

Opening the boy's top desk drawer, she removed the iPod.

"It would do you good to spend more time in the woods, out in nature. Its part of who you are."

"I'd rather do homework," Jason snapped. "Any way, I need to go over to Franklin's house today so we can get in some practice before next week's game."

"You know I haven't been able to drive since my stroke, and your aunt Katie's gone into Spokane for the day."

"Okay – I'll drive you up there and come back to get you in a couple of hours if I can go to Franklin's to shoot hoops."

"All right – deal," Alice said with a sigh. She put the iPod back on the desk.

That afternoon, Alice, toting a gunny sack, slowly made her way to her well-used Ford Focus wagon parked in the gravel driveway in front of her house. Jason zipped past her and slipped into the driver's seat. After starting the engine, he noticed that his grandmother needed assistance.

Jumping out of the car, the boy ran to the other side of the car and opened the passenger door for her. His impatience was apparent as he attempted to close the door before she was completely inside the car. With a rush, he shot back to the driver's seat and sped out of the driveway.

Roaring up the graveled mountain road like he was going to a fire, Jason drove Alice to her favorite root-gathering spot deeper within the forest. Reaching that location, he stopped at the side of the road allowing the engine to idle.

"Hand me that sack in the back seat, would you?" Alice asked.

Jason pivoted in the driver's seat and , locating the brown woven bag, gave it to his grandmother.

"Here you go," he said. "You sure you'll be all right out here?"

"Of course, I'll be fine," she said, getting out of the car. "I've only been coming up here all my life."

"Okay, I'll be back in a couple of hours."

"Now don't forget and leave me up here," she admonished

before closing the door.

As soon as the door slammed shut, the teenager sped away, kicking up a cloud of dust in the elder's face.

Fanning the air in front of her face, Alice watched the car disappear in the distance.

"Okay, here we go," she said as she slowly turned towards the woods. Reaching the forest's edge, she took in a deep breath of pine-scented air, and then started picking her way through the underbrush. An ancient Salish gathering song sprang from her lips as she moved between the silent pine giants that had awaited her arrival like old friends.

An hour later, Jason sweated exuberantly as the competition in his game of one-on-one with his Kalispel friend, Franklin, intensified. With sneakers squeaking on the homemade blacktop court and the other teenager guarding him closely, Jason drove in for a lay-up, but missed the shot.

"Foul!" Jason cried. "Two shots from the free-throw line for me!"

"I didn't touch you, man, and you know it," Franklin protested. Breaking from the game, he approached his friend.

"What's up with you, anyway? You've been missing easy shots all afternoon."

Realizing the accuracy of Franklin's observation, Jason exhaled heavily and said, "Let's take a break." He headed for the nearest sideline, plopped himself down next to his gym back and took out a bottle of Gatorade. After a few long gulps, he sighed.

"It's my grandma. I mean, ever since I started living with her, all she talks about is the old ways. I don't know how long I can take   it."

"Maybe she just doesn't want you to end up like your parents." Franklin blurted bluntly. This statement clearly took Jason by surprise.

"That didn't come out right," Franklin apologized, and tried again.

"Look, I know how you feel. My parents ride my about one damn thing or another all the time. I feel like my head's going to explode.

Jason just nodded.

"But my grandparents are gone," his friend continued. "My mom and dad know next to nothing about our culture or history, and I kind of wish they did. I don't know – I think being Indian is somehow kind of – special."

"Hah! Where have you been?" Jason retorted. "Being Indian is like going through life with a dead weight around your neck. Look around you, man. Everything about Indians is relevant to what's going on in the rest of the world. It just ain't cool!"

"That's a little extreme, isn't it?" Franklin replied, dumbfounded.

Checking his watch, Jason said, "Yeah, whatever. I've got to go. I'll see you at the game." He stood, picked up his gym bag and headed for his grandmother's car, leaving Franklin a little puzzled.

Meanwhile, having located one of the medicinal plants she'd

been looking for, Alice dug in the ground with a stick.

"There you are," she said to the root, almost melodically. "Come to Grandma." In a moment, she came up with a dirt-covered root, and treating it like it was a nugget of gold, held it between her fingers.

"You're getting harder and harder to find, and you're good for so many ailments." She placed her prized discovery in the gunny sack, and then, with difficulty, she stood, suddenly feeling dizzy. Managing to make it to a nearby stump, she collapsed. After a few minutes, her head cleared.

"What are we going to do, Old Man?" she said, looking up beyond the trees. "I don't think I have much longer here, and the young ones aren't learning our ancient ways."

She listened to a voice no one but her could hear.

"Hm-hm. I know you thought I was never going to learn anything when I was young. But at least I had respect for the ways - respect for my elders. But that's mostly gone now." A sadness settled onto her face. "Sometimes I feel like the last Indian left."

Filled with a sense of natural sacredness, Alice sat quietly for awhile, listening to her surroundings and soaking up the spirit of the place.

That evening, she and Jason ate dinner quietly together.

"There's a stick game at the community center tonight," Alice remarked.

"Are you going?" Jason asked.

"I was, but after my dizzy spell in the woods today, I don't think I should. I don't suppose you're interested in going."

"I'm going to the movies with some friends."

After taking a pause to build up some courage, she asked, "Jason, why have you turned your back on your people and your culture?"

"Why do <u>you</u> keep living in the past?"

"It only looks like the past to you, because you've put it behind you," she answered patiently. "These ways are as alive and real as they ever were. You just can't see it."

A car horn honked outside. "There's my ride," Jason said. He took his dinner plate to the kitchen counter and turned to leave. Pausing, he turned back to his grandmother.

"Need anything from town?"

"No, but thanks for asking. How late are you going to be?"

"Don't know – don't wait up."

Jason shot out the front door to join his friends, leaving Alice alone at the table. She waited until she heard the car leave with her grandson before getting up to clear the table. Shortly after beginning her dish-washing chore, fatigue overtook her, and she decided to get ready for bed. Leaving the dishes where they lay, the elder turned out the kitchen light and headed for her bedroom.

She sat on the edge of her bed in her flannel nightgown and picked up the framed photo on the nightstand. In the photo, a younger version of herself stood beside a much older Indian man in front of a weathered wooden shack. She wiped a little dust from the edge of the frame.

"Well, Old Man, the future of our people doesn't look so good," she said with a heavy heart. "These kids are lost. What the army, the missionaries, the government and the boarding schools couldn't do in four generations, the TV, the Internet and the iPod are doing in just one."

Resigned to defeat, Alice put the picture back on the nightstand.

"I'm all out of ideas, so if anything's going to get done, I guess it's up to you now."
With that, she turned out the lamp and crawled into bed for the night.

At around midnight, Jason returned from his outing. The teen-filled car screeched to a halt in front of Jason's house, and as he exited the automobile, one of the girls in the back seat let out a loud peel of drunken laughter.

"Not so loud!" Jason reprimanded. "You'll wake up my grandma."

"You'll wake up my grandma," the inebriated driver mocked. "Dude, how long are you going to live with that old lady?"

"Shut up and get out of here," Jason commanded, slamming the car door. More laughter erupted from the car's interior as it sped away into the night.

Stumbling and weaving ever so slightly, Jason slipped inside the unlocked front door trying not to disturb his grandmother. Then, tiptoeing down the hall, he peeked in her room to confirm that she was indeed asleep. The sound of restful snoring let him know that all was well, so he retired to his own room and fell into bed without changing clothes.

Within a few hours, the boy's fitful sleep delivered him into an unreal dreamscape. Jason found himself winding through a fog-enveloped space with no discernible boundaries. The low roar of a distant wind could be heard all around him, though the air seemed calm. Jason was trying to figure out where he was and what was happening when a tall dark figure emerged from the fog.

An elderly American Indian man with long braids and dressed in white buckskin coalesced before him. Upon closer examination, Jason found that the man looked familiar. It might be the same man in the picture next to his grandmother's bed, the one she called "Old Man."

"Who are you?" Old Man asked, speaking the Salish language.

"What did you say?" Jason responded.

"Who are you?" Old man repeated, again in Salish

"I don't understand what you're saying."

"I guess I'm going to have to do this in English," Old Man said, annoyed. "Who are you?" he asked in English.

"Oh, I'm Jason Black Bear."

"I don't want to know your name, boy. I want to know who you are inside."

"It's a trick question, right?" Jason said.

"In the sweat lodge, or on the hill where visions are sought, you receive your true identity - you find your place in the people's circle. So I ask again, who are you?"

"I don't know. I don't have an answer."

"That's too bad," Old Man replied.

"Where are we," Jason asked. "What is this place?"

"This is the entrance to your peoples' home in the spirit world, where generations of your ancestors have come when their lives on earth ended."

"Oh," was all Jason said.

"But only those who know who they are, those who have found their place in the sacred circle, may enter," Old Man said somberly. "Otherwise you may wonder the outer darkness among the shadow souls for a long time in search of your true self."

As Old Man finished speaking, the surrounding fog began to thicken and his body seemed to fade.

"But wait!" Jason cried. "How do I find out who I really am? Who can help me?"

"The answers you seek lay within your grasp," the disappearing spirit replied. "The one who can help you most has been placed within your reach, but you see it not."

The apparition's words became a receding echo as Jason struggled to understand what he was being told.

"Don't go - I don't understand what you mean," Jason pleaded.

"You must act before it's too late." Old Man's final words died in a reverberating echo.

The fog completely engulfed Jason as the spirit disappeared.

Jason began searching through the fog for a way out, a way back. As he swatted at the fog, Jason awoke in his own bed. Sitting up, he blinked and looked around. He listened intently, but all was quiet–too quiet.

"Grandma!" Jason called out. There was no reply.

He leapt from his bed and ran down the hall. Entering his grandmother's room, he called to her as he rushed to her side. She didn't move.

"Grandma," he whispered in her ear as panic seized the boy. He felt her hand and touched her face. Both are cool.

Realizing what he must do, Jason bolted from the room and made a bee-line for the phone. When the 911 operator answered, the frantic teenager shouted into the receiver.

"You've got to come quick! My grandma's not moving and I can't find a pulse."

"Calm down, young man," the dispatcher replied calmly. "It's hard to understand what you're saying when you shout."

Releasing a big breath, Jason tried again.

"My grandmother is not moving and I can't find a pulse."

"Okay, son. I've got to get some basic information. Who are you?

"Oh no, not again," Jason said, panic returning. "I went through this last night."

"It's not a trick question. Tell me your name and your location."

Jason calmed down enough to give her the necessary

information that would bring a emergency medical team to his grandmother's aid.

"An ambulance is on the way," the dispatcher assured him. Stay with your grandma until it arrives so you can report any changes to the EMTs."

"Okay," the boy said. "Please hurry."

He returned to his grandmother's bedside and knelt by the bed.

"Grandma, don't die. Not now. Something important happened to me last night. I need you to teach me. I'm ready to listen." Tearfully, he continued. "It can't be too late. He said it wasn't too late."

Sobbing uncontrollably, the boy fell to the floor.

In a few minutes, the wail of a siren pierced the morning stillness. With hopeful anticipation, Jason ran to the front door in time to see the ambulance back into the driveway. He ran to meet them just as two Anglo paramedics leapt from the vehicle.

"Are you Jason?" one of the men asked.

"Yeah, but hurry - this way," Jason commanded. "Before it's too late!" He led them to the back bedroom, where the lead EMT knelt beside Alice.

"Mrs. Black Bear, can you hear me?" he said loudly.

"Jason, has there been any change in her condition since you called us?" the second man asked.

"No, she's just been lying there not moving."

"Okay, let's turn her on her back – on the count of three."

Stepping up on the bed, the paramedics turned her as the bed springs creaked beneath their weight.

To his partner, the lead EMT said, "Unpack the defibrillator," and to Jason, he said, "it'll be better if you wait outside."

Jason, who stood by feeling helpless, asked, "What's wrong? Will she be all right?"

"We'll let you know as soon as we have anything," the man said as he escorted the boy beyond the bedroom door and closed it.

As he paced the hallway, Jason could here the sound of the men charging and discharging the defibrillator. Moving toward the kitchen, the sound of the tediously slow clock pounded in his ears. Stepping out on the front porch, the boy looked to the sky with a yearning to speak forming in his heart.

"You can come in now," the second paramedic said, breaking Jason's concentration. Jason studied the man's face as he peered at him through the open screen door, looking for a clue about his grandmother's condition, but found nothing.

Entering the bedroom, he found her propped up on a gurney – weak, but alive. Jason rushed to her side.

"Grandma, I thought I'd lost you," the boy sobbed joyfully.

"I was almost there," she said calmly, "I could see it, but he sent me back."

"He? Who are you talking about?"

"You know who I mean. He told me he saw you last night."

Her words shot through him as a clear realization seized his mind.

"You mean that wasn't just a dream?"

"Excuse me, ma'am," the lead EMT said. "We need to get you to the hospital so a doctor can thoroughly examine you."

"All right – if you have to. But I need my grandson to come with me."

"Okay." After a pause, he added, looking at Jason, "I hope you both know it's a miracle she's alive."

Jason nodded as they wheeled Alice down the hall.

The paramedics slid the gurney into the back of the ambulance, and Jason climbed aboard.

"You know, Jason, you can live in two worlds – learning about the old ways while enjoying your music and your friends."

"I suppose so," Jason agreed thoughtfully.

"We're almost ready to go," the lead paramedic said. "We just have to repack our equipment." He busied himself with the task.

"I think your friend Franklin was right," Alice said to Jason.

"Right about what?"

"Being Indian is kind of … special."

"Wait a minute – how did you know he said that?"

"You'd be surprised what I learned while I was visiting the spirit world. I think I can read minds and foretell the future now."

There was a gleeful twinkle in her eye.

"Great!" Jason said, jokingly. "My Grandma, the psychic medium. Maybe you can open one of those psychic hotlines. Or better yet, have your own TV show: Crossing Over with Grandma

Black Bear."

The pair shared a hearty laugh as the ambulance pulled out of the driveway, carrying them down the reservation road toward a life charged with new meaning and hope. Crossing the bridge that spanned the Pend Oreille River, the emergency vehicle passed under the wings of another great blue heron in search of a meal along the gold-tinged waters illuminated by the rays of a rising sun.

PERSONAL JUSTICE

Carson Ryder neatly folded the orange jump suit he'd worn daily for the last five years and laid it on his bunk. The letters "Property of State Penitentiary" stenciled on the back of the one-piece outfit were cracked and faded. Dressed in his only set of street clothes, the six-foot Blackfeet Indian stuffed the last of his few personal belongings into a green Army duffle.

As he took one last look around the dingy cell, his eyes found a small white object nestled on a corner shelf above the stainless-steel sink. Picking up the carved creation that had once been a bar of soap, he traced the creature's smooth outlines.

The miniature masterpiece, a stately white bison, represented many peaceful hours he'd spent thinking about his home on the reservation. He'd released the animal from its soapy prison using a contraband plastic spoon he'd modified to resemble a knife. Carving the piece had been a glacially slow process, but he'd been in no particular hurry.

"Time to go," said the surly guard outside Carson's cell. The man's gruff voice pierced the 40-year-old's thoughts and brought him back to reality.

Nodding to the overweight guard, the prisoner wrapped his prized buffalo in a clean rag and gently placed it into the duffle. Now ready to go, he presented himself at his cell door. Almost begrudgingly the guard unlocked it.

The Montana sky loomed large and blue above the walls of the state prison just outside of the town of Deer Lodge. Carson stood inside the main gate waiting for the grey-suited sentry to push the button that would lead to freedom.

The July morning air, already thick with humidity, felt good on the Indian's dark brown skin. In a few moments, he'd once again be able to breathe free air.

A loud buzzer rang out as the prison gates swung open.

"Try to stay out of trouble," the guard said as Carson hoisted the duffle's strap to his shoulder.

"Not my style," the now-free man replied as he quickly passed beyond the prison gate's grasp. With a mournful moan it slowly closed behind him.

He inhaled hungrily. Free air at last. The smell of it was crisp in his nostrils. The feel of it was fresh in his lungs. He savored the moment.

Then, scanning the graveled parking area across from the prison, Carson found what he was looking for: a familiar, aging red mustang that sported a double black racing stripe. As he approached, an attractive American Indian woman in her thirties emerged from behind the car's steering wheel. Carson's girlfriend, Hattie, was a welcome sight for the convict's deprived eyes.

Wordlessly, she popped the car's trunk, allowing him to dump the duffle inside. After a thorough examination of her topographic features, Carson pulled her towards him. Hattie resisted. He insisted. Eventually she relaxed into his embrace, and they kissed deeply for a long moment.

Having partly fulfilled his craving, Carson released her, and she, visibly affected by this sexually charged event, almost lost her balance.

"To be continued," Carson said, wiping lipstick from his mouth as he moved toward the passenger seat.

Pulling herself together, Hattie exhaled sharply before slipping back into the car. They headed for Helena.

Meanwhile, back on the Blackfeet Reservation, Robert Heavyrunner, the 40-year-old Blackfeet Indian police chief, grabbed a cup of coffee from the stained coffee-maker that had seen better days. After collecting a short stack of incoming messages from the department's dispatcher, he headed for his corner office. Although none of the offices in the tribal cop shop had windows, his at least boasted a mural. Briefly he glanced at the painted night scene featuring a circle of glowing tipis illuminated by internal fires.

Setting the coffee cup and messages on his desk, he took off his gun and holster. Along with his cop hat, he draped them over the hat rack in the corner and sat down at his desk. Like everything else in the aging tribal police station, the desk was scarred and worn.

He sipped the dark black liquid as he thumbed through the messages, all of them routine complaints from reservation residents. Then he glanced at the calendar resting on his desk.

In the square marking the day's date he found a note reminding himself that his old friend, Carson Rider, was getting out of prison. Gazing at his office mural as though it was a portal to the past, he thought of an experience he'd shared with Carson many long years ago during Operation Desert Storm on the southern fringe of Iraq.

The hot desert wind pelted my goggles with gritty sand. My mouth was dry, my eyes were red and my stomach was empty. Carson was over an hour late for their scheduled rendezvous. Where was he?

I gazed through the electronic binoculars one more time. Finally, I saw it. Small and almost imperceptible in the distance, a sand-colored Humvee sped toward me. But what were those puffs of sand and smoke all around it? I zoomed in.

They were mortar shells exploding very near the vehicle. The Humvee was weaving frantically back and forth to avoid them. Gradually the driver began outrunning the shells.

As he got closer, Carson started waving his hand out the window. It looked like he wanted me to move further away from his location. I was on a small hill so it was easy to jog down the slope behind me.

I waited. In a few minutes his Humvee came bounding over the hill. He stopped in a cloud of dust and sand.

"Jump in," he yelled breathlessly. Mortar fire was creeping closer. I jumped in.

"What's going on?" I asked once I was on board.

"Change of plans," he said as he put the pedal to the metal. "The recovery zone has been breached."

We roared away across the desert.

Lost in that memory, Robert didn't notice when the

department's plump, middle-aged dispatcher, Marlene, strode into his office.

"Trying to remember where you lost your youth?" she asked sarcastically.

"I gave up on that years ago," her boss replied as he turned toward her. "No, my old buddy, Carson, gets out of the joint today."

"Oh, yeah," Marlene replied, taking a seat in a Goodwill-reject chair across from Robert's desk. "I vaguely remember that you knew him in some long-forgotten past."

"We served in Marines together—I guess it's been twenty years ago or so." His gaze returned to the tipis. "Funny how peoples' lives can take such different directions."

Halfway across the state and a couple of hours later, Carson rose from the motel bed he'd just shared with Hattie.

Filling a glass half full of water from the bathroom sink he asked, "Did you bring it?" He drained the glass in one long gulp.

The nude native woman rose from the bed and slipped on Carson's shirt, which hung from the headboard of the bed. She retrieved a small paper sack from her oversized purse and pitched it to him. He opened it to find the stack of cash he was hoping for. There was also a small key in the sack.

After a quick count, he asked, "Did you have any trouble getting it?" and tossed a small portion of the bills back to her. He put the key in his pocket. She put the cash in her purse.

"No. I found it in the deposit box just like you said," she

replied.

"This is the last time we can do this," she added after a pause. Carson just looked at her.

"I have a new boyfriend," she explained and waited.

"So this was a farewell fuck, for old time's sake?" he asked.

She merely nodded.

"Who is it?"

"You don't know him," she answered. "He's not from the Rez. And he's not involved in criminal activities." She picked up her watch from the nightstand and looked at it.

"We'd better go," she said, picking up her clothes and heading for the bathroom. "I'll be late for work."

Fifteen minutes later they arrived curbside in front of a Helena pawnshop with a window displaying American Indian blankets, artwork and jewelry, mixed with the usual pawnshop wares. Reaching across and opening the glove box, Hattie pushed a button that popped the trunk so he could retrieve the duffle.

"Do you have some sort of plan?" she asked, resting her hand on his knee.

"Yeah, I do," was his only reply as he gave her a parting kiss on the mouth. Taking one last look at her, he said, "See you around, I guess."

With that he retrieved his duffle and headed toward the pawnshop without looking back. What's gone is gone, he thought. He had no use for regrets.

Inside the overstocked, run-down shop, Carson approached the front counter clerk, an older American Indian man. He seemed to be admiring Hattie through the window as she drove away.

"I'm looking for Bowman," Carson said.

With a nod of his head and the point of his lips, the clerk motioned toward the back of the shop.

Carson found the old white man hunched over a workbench polishing a piece of sterling silver jewelry that featured a large chunk of turquoise in the center.

"Creating another piece of authentic Indian jewelry, I see," Carson commented. Bowman looked up, saw who it was, and removed the magnifying glasses from his face. "Has it been five years already?" he asked. "Man, that was fast."

"Not really," Carson returned. "Felt like fifty. But that's ancient history. I need to retrieve that item you've been holding for me. Didn't sell it, did you?"

"Thought about it," Bowman said as he shuffled over to a large cabinet filled with American Indian shawls and blankets. He opened a false bottom in the cabinet, pulled out an ornately carved wooden box and handed it to Carson.

Opening the box, Carson removed the Colt .45 stored inside. He took a moment to admire the pistol that had once belonged to his father. The raised features of a horse were still visible in the worn ivory handle. His father's initials, RR, were right where they'd always been, stamped on the butt of the handle.

Carson flipped open the cylinder and checked it. Then he held the gun up toward the light and examined the inside of the barrel.

"Needs cleaning," he said as he closed the cylinder. "And what about the ammo?"

Bowman pulled a box of .45 shells out of the same hiding place and handed them over. After stuffing the gun and the ammo in his duffle, Carson looked around.

"You wouldn't have an old police band radio for sale, would you?"

Bowman led him back towards the front of the shop to the electronics section. After a quick survey of the inventory, the old man opened a glass case and placed a dash-mountable police radio on the glass counter.

"Comes complete with installation instructions," Bowman offered.

Carson examined the dusty piece of equipment, turning over in his hands.

"I'll take it," he said. "How much?"

Bowman did some quick figuring in his head.

"A hundred will cover it."

Carson peeled a hundred-dollar bill from his stack and handed it to him, took the radio with the instructions and stuffed them in the now bulging duffle.

He nodded and said, "Thanks." Bowman returned the nod.

"No need to tell anybody I have this forty-five," Carson said before leaving Bowman.

"No need," Bowman agreed.

Exiting the pawnshop, Carson headed down the block, coming

to a nearby grocery store parking lot. After checking to make sure no one was watching, he began peering into cars parked in the lot. None had the keys anywhere within sight. It was times like this he wished he'd learned how to hotwire a car.

In an aging pick-up with a rodeo decal on the window, he found a set of keys dangling from the ignition. Without hesitation, he jumped in, started her up and checked the gas gauge. Half a tank—enough for the trip he needed to take.

"Sorry, Pardner," Carson said as if he was speaking personally to the truck's absent owner.

With one final scan of the area, he made for the Interstate headed northward.

In Great Falls, he stopped the truck in a curbside parking space about a block from Montana Motors. This used car lot featured, in Carson's opinion, the worst cars at the highest prices in the state.

Leaving the keys in the borrowed truck's ignition, Carson grabbed his duffle and walked onto the lot. The lot owner, a white man named Dwight who wore a faded double-breasted navy-blue suit, recognized him immediately.

"You old degenerate redskin!" Dwight exclaimed. "When did they let you out?"

"They didn't," Carson replied with a deadpan tone. "I escaped."

Dwight was taken aback for a moment. Then Carson smiled, and the car peddler realized the joke. Laughing a big laugh of relief, he grabbed Carson's hand and shook it vigorously.

After a quick reunion in Dwight's less-than-luxurious office, Carson was ready to get down to business.

"Where is it?" he asked. "Did you keep it up like I asked you to?"

"Sure thing, my friend - just like I promised. It's in the back garage."

Dwight led the way out the back of the building toward a separate garage. Inserting a key in a large padlock, he unlocked the wide garage door. The dented door swung open to reveal a well-kept, bright orange 1969 Chevy Camaro.

Dwight handed Carson a set of keys, and the ex-con slipped in behind the wheel. A click of the ignition immediately brought the engine to life. Carson smiled and gunned the motor a couple of times. Opening the glove box, he examined the insurance papers. Seeing that they were current, he shoved them back in the box, killed the engine and climbed out of the car.

"The car looks great," Carson admitted. "Thanks for looking after her. But I've had a change in plans." He threw the keys back to Dwight.

"I need to sell it. Want to buy it?"

"Are you sure, man? This car was your pride and joy."

"Yeah, I'm sure. Got something more important to take care of. If you don't want it, maybe you can sell it for me."

"No, no, I'll buy it off you. What are you going to drive?"

"What I need right now is an old beater from your lot—a Rez

car. Something unnoticeable."

Dwight couldn't figure out what was going on in Carson's mind, but the car salesman was sure Carson would regret selling it sooner or later.

"I think we can find something," Dwight said. "Follow me." He led Carson back to the lot and made a beeline for a rusty old tan Oldsmobile station wagon.

"If it runs, it'll be perfect," Carson said.

Dwight stuck the key in the car's ignition, turned it and the engine sputtered and groaned a couple of times. After two more cranks, it sprang to life.

"It'll do," was all Carson had to say.

They drew up sales papers, and Dwight paid Carson the difference in cash. Driving away in the old bomb, the ex-con left the car salesman to admire his newly acquired muscle car.

Carson steered the rusty wagon North on I-15 to Shelby and then westward down old Highway 2 that led to Cut Bank, a reservation border-town of a mere 3,000 souls. The town was the county seat of Glacier County and would play a major role in the plan that was developing in Carson's mind.

Not yet ready to alert anyone in Cut Bank to his return, Carson slowed to the speed limit as he cruised through town. The town of Cut Bank sat on the east side of Cut Bank Creek, a waterway marking the eastern border of the Blackfeet Reservation.

Carson always chuckled when he thought of Cut Bank history. The good white folks originally created the town on the west side of the creek as the railroad was being built in that area. It was later determined that the town actually sat on Indian land within the Blackfeet Reservation boundary so they had to relocate the entire town eastward across the creek.

From Cut Bank, Highway 2 continued westward across the rolling grassy hills through the town of Browning, Montana, the heart of Blackfeet country. The one-and-a-half-million acre reservation was home to some ten thousand people, but was only a small part of the original homeland of this once great tribe.

The Blackfeet lands had been created by Old Man in the beginning of time. The Backbone of the World, the Rocky Mountains, ran down the western edge of the reservation along its shared border with Glacier National Park.

The sun was just setting beyond the Backbone as Carson pulled into the Towne Pump with its rows of gas pumps and well-stocked mini-mart. A marquee above the store entrance declared: The Best Chilli-Cheeze Fries on the Rez! No matter what the sign proclaimed, the place showed obvious signs of age and neglect.

Inside, Carson approached the clerk, a native man with a look similar to his own. Their eyes met, and the clerk nodded ever so slightly. Carson shook his head ever so slightly in return, indicating that he didn't want to be visibly acknowledged. He nodded toward the surveillance camera in the corner.

After picking up a few snacks and a soda, Carson placed the items on the counter and spoke quietly.

"Can you meet me at the Heart Butte cutoff in a little while?"

"In about half an hour when I get off work," the clerk replied in a whisper.

"Give me forty's worth on pump five," Carson said in a louder voice. He plopped down a fifty-dollar bill, then exited the mini-mart to pump the gas.

As he began fueling his car, Robert Heavyrunner pulled into the station to fuel up his BIA police cruiser. He saw Carson and went over to talk.

"Hu-rah," Robert said, extending his hand. Carson reached out to shake it, and Robert unexpectedly pulled his old friend close in a bro-hug.

"You don't look any worse for wear," the tribal cop said, releasing Carson from the hug. "How ya doin?"

"Not bad considering," Carson replied, genuinely happy to see Robert. "Looking forward to enjoying the wide-open spaces again. Spend some time with Gramps. What have you been up to?"

"Same old same old. You know, cop stuff. We've got North American Indian Days this weekend. But me—I'm thinking about changing professions."

"Doing what?"

"I don't know," Robert replied, looking out into the darkening landscape. "Maybe I'll become a park ranger over at the Glacier. Anything that gets me out from behind that desk and back into the wilderness."

"Back to the roots, huh? Sounds good," Carson said, thoughtfully. "Life's short. If I was you, I'd go for it."

"The more I talk about it the better it sounds," Robert said, heading toward the mini-mart. "If you get a chance, stop in the cop shop for a visit," he added.

"I'll do that. We can talk about the bad old days," Carson said, "Semper Fi, and all that shit."

He watched as his old friend entered the mini-mart, probably to load up on the best chilli-cheeze fries on the rez. He didn't think he'd have time to stop at the cop shop to talk about old times, though. He had other more pressing matters to tend to.

Carson waited in the dark at the rendezvous point on the side of the highway. Soon a pair of headlights approached. Moments later a muddy grey Ford pick-up pulled up next to Carson's parked heap-of-a-car. The mini-mart clerk stepped out of the Ford carrying a brown paper bag.

Carson got out of his wagon, lit a cigarette and leaned on the hood of his car. The clerk, Carson's cousin Eddie, joined him. Carson acknowledged him with a nod and the simple greeting, "Cuz."

"You got out," Eddie said in the way of his own greeting.

"I did," Carson replied without looking at him. "What's in the bag?"

Eddie looked down at the bag as though he'd forgotten he had it.

"Oh—its a welcome home drink," he said, pulling out a bottle of Jack Daniels. He opened the bottle and handed it over to Carson who tipped it slightly, allowing a few drops of the amber liquid to spill on the ground.

"To the spirits," he said, holding the bottle skyward. He then took a long swig of the juice, his first taste in five years.

"Are you going through with it?" Eddie asked as his cousin passed the bottle back.

"Yep."

It was Eddie's turn to take a draw from the bottle.

"Are you in?" Carson asked as Eddied finished his swallow.

After a pause and a deep sigh, Eddie replied, "Things change, man. I can't."

He put the lid back on the bottle.

"There's a lot of that going around," Carson said. "Hattie's got a new boyfriend."

"I heard," Eddie replied. He put the whiskey back in the brown paper sack.

Carson snuffed out his cigarette on the ground.

"No big deal," the ex-con said. "I'll go it alone. No sense in there being more than one criminal in the family."

"Best of luck, man," Eddie offered as he handed the sack to Carson. "Sorry I can't help."

"Don't sweat it," Carson replied, taking the whiskey and shaking Eddie's hand. "It's really my thing any way."

Eddie was feeling guilty for letting his cousin down as he ambled back to his truck. He knew Carson had always helped his side of the family out when needed. Eddie watched as Carson jumped back into his wagon and drove off into the night.

The station wagon's faded headlights probed the darkness as Carson drove down recently paved reservation back roads.

After awhile he came to an isolated old house with peeling paint that stood at the end of one of those roads. He parked the car along side the sagging structure, picked up the duffle and entered the unlocked front door, which hung loosely on its hinges.

Inside he found an elderly Indian man asleep in a tattered armchair that sat not far from an ancient TV set. Carson was startled by how much the man had aged since he'd seen him last. His grandfather shouldn't be living out here alone in the ramshackle old place, he thought.

A "Mork & Mindy" re-run was barely visible through the snowy TV image. When Carson turned the TV off, the old man woke up.

"I didn't mean to wake you, Gramps," he apologized.

It took awhile for his grandfather to fully awaken and realize who it was standing in his living room. A smile emerged on the elder's face.

"Carson! You came home." With a good deal of effort, he got out of his chair and attempted to walk to Carson. "I was afraid I'd give up the ghost before I saw you again."

Carson quickly moved to support the beloved old man. "I told you I'd be out before you knew it," Carson replied as they both sat down on a dilapidated couch.

Suddenly a sad memory clouded Gramps' happy mood.

"I still miss Charlie, though," he said. "He never did nothin' to nobody, and he ain't ever comin' back. Creator knows how much I miss him."

"I do too, Gramps. I do too."

Suddenly Gramps was racked with deep guttural coughs.

"Let's get you to bed. We can talk tomorrow."

The old man allowed Carson to lead him toward the bedroom and put him in bed. Carson wandered down the hall to the bathroom. Finding the light switch, he stepped into the tiny room only to discover a fist-size hole in the floor between the toilet and the tub.

"Damn," Carson said out loud, shaking his head. His grandfather's house had turned into an absolute shit hole. And Carson had no one to blame but himself.

He made his way to the back bedroom and fell on to the worn mattress of an old bed. Sleep overtook him as he thought of what needed to be done on the coming second day of freedom.

First thing the following morning, Carson checked Gramps' refrigerator. Its meager contents consisted of a half-dozen eggs, a half gallon of milk, two sticks of butter, a jar of peanut butter and a few slices of white bread. All of the items displayed the federal government's generic commodity foods logo.

He checked Gramps' bedroom, but the old man wasn't there. He called for him all over the house. No answer.

His search took Carson to the barn behind the house. As he neared the leaning wood structure, the sounds of a familiar Blackfeet song floated in the air. Rounding the corner, Carson found his grandfather standing in the middle of a medicine wheel made of stones. Holding a small clump of tobacco between his thumb and forefinger up over his head, Gramps was praying to the four directions.

Not wanting to disturb the old man, Carson backed away and retreated to the house. Though he'd never participated much in such tribal rituals, Carson respected the rights of others who wished to do so.

Later, after breakfast, Carson borrowed his grandfather's dirty brown pick-up truck to drive to a cemetery located not far from the elder's house. He parked the truck outside the low, rusted chain link fence that enclosed the graveyard. Picking up the small paper sack that sat on the front seat next to him, he got out and went to the cemetery entrance.

Seeing that the gate was padlocked, he jumped the three-foot high fence and walked purposefully toward a cluster of simple headstones. Buried there were Carson's grandmother, his parents, and his brother, Charlie.

He paused at his parents' double tombstone and read the familiar words etched on its surface: Geraldine and Redmond Rider, together in life, together in death. Remembering the tragic and fatal car accident that occurred when a drunk driver plowed into them head-on, he allowed the memory to linger.

It had been one of those rare times when his mom and dad took time for themselves. Carson, then fifteen, had stayed home with Gramps while they'd gone on sort of a date to North

American Indian Days. The tribe had splurged on bringing in a big-name country star to perform that night.

Once the memory had run its course, Carson moved on to Charlie's grave. There he knelt and spoke.

"I just wanted to let you know I'm out of prison, Charlie, and I'm gonna try to make things right." Suddenly he felt a little awkward and looked around to make sure nobody was watching. Seeing that he was alone, he continued.

"Gramps is right. You never did nothin' to nobody, and you certainly didn't deserve to die the way you did. If things don't go like they should, I may be joining you sooner than you think."

He then reached into the paper bag and withdrew the special gift he'd brought with him. He gently placed the miniature soap buffalo on top of Charlie's gravestone. "Take care, little bro." Taking one last look at the grave, Carson walked back to the truck and climbed in.

Now it was time to get down to business.

Carson drove the few miles across low rolling hills to the house of his uncle Clifford. As the ex-con arrived in front of the old wood-sided house, Clifford was leading a horse up into a dented, rusting trailer attached to the back of his much newer, nicer pick-up. Clifford, a dark-skinned Blackfeet in his 50s was clad in jeans, t-shirt and cowboy boots. He saw Carson approaching. The large-boned man finished securing the horse in the trailer.

"Hello, nephew," Clifford said. "Done your time, huh?"

"Yeah, that's all behind me now."

"I'm glad. That was some sorry business you got mixed up into, and look where it got you." He closed up the trailer and checked the hitch to make sure it was tight. Carson waited quietly.

"If you ask him," Clifford continued, "I'm sure the Lord'll forgive you, but I'm not sure I can."

"I'm not asking for anybody's forgiveness," Carson replied matter-of-factly. "All I want are my horses. Are they out back?"

Clifford nodded his head towards a nearby pasture. "They're all yours. I took care of 'em as best I could."

"Thanks for that," Carson said as he headed for the pasture.

"I've got to get over to the relay grounds to make a few practice-runs for this weekend," Clifford added as he got into his truck. "Try to stay out of trouble now," he advised as he drove away.

"If you only knew what was coming next," Carson quietly said to himself as he climbed up on the pasture fence. There he sat for a few minutes just looking at the two horses he'd severely missed while serving as a guest at the state's Deer Lodge accommodations.

One dark brown, the other a dappled Appaloosa, both were products of the Blackfeet Buffalo Horse Coalition – sturdy stock descended from Spanish Mustangs used by his tribesmen in the 1800s to hunt buffalo on the plains. The Appaloosa was a male Carson had named Pono. The Brown was a female he'd named Kamita. The two names combined, Ponokamita, was the Blackfeet word for horse, literally meaning "elk dog."

The pair fed peacefully on the pasture's summer grass. Carson made a clicking sound with his mouth, and they became aware of him for the first time. After a moment, a hint of recognition flickered in the animals' eyes, and they ambled over to him. Pono, the larger, more dominant horse, came right up to his old friend, allowing the human to caress him. Stepping down from the fence, Carson stroked the magnificent beast's neck and sides.

This prompted Kamita to jealously nudge Carson's arm, asking to share in some of the affection being dispersed. Carson stroked both animals simultaneously, acknowledging the equal feelings he had for both.

"Hey, you big dogs," he said in a gentle voice. "How's it going? Sorry I had to leave you so long. I'm hoping you guys'll forgive me, even if Uncle Clifford won't."

He led his equine companions into the nearby barn where he retrieved two saddles that had been resting there, straddled over the walls of two stalls.

Moments later he was driving slowly back towards Gramps' place with the horses tied to the truck's back bumper. They plodded along behind the truck, looking every bit like an entry in the Blackfeet annual parade.

Gramps sat on his front porch drinking lemonade as Carson and the horses approached. The old man seemed very lucid today, and Carson wondered if these days were growing fewer as time progressed.

"Are you riding in the parade tomorrow?" Gramps asked.

"I can't, Gramps. I got other plans."

"That's too bad. You know we're descended from that famous Blackfeet horse breeder, Many Horses."

"I know, Grandpa. You told me about a hundred times."

"Oh, yeah. I remember."

Carson led the animals to the corral behind the barn and gave them food and water. Then he joined his grandfather on the porch.

"I've seen the way you are with horses. You have the horse medicine powers that my own grandfather had."

"That's good," Carson replied absently, staring out at nothing in particular. "I'm probably going to need those powers in the next few days."

"What are you talking about, boy?"

Carson snapped back to the present.

"Nothing, Gramps. Just ignore me. I'm still getting used to being out." Standing up, he asked, "Can I get you some more lemonade?"

They spent the rest of the day and evening just being grandfather and grandson, talking about the weather, tribal politics, the pretty woman who lived down the road and the glory days of the Blackfeet people.

Early the following morning, Carson headed for his grandfather's barn. He opened the creaky door and peered inside. Going in, he located a shovel, sledgehammer and a few other tools. He loaded the shovel in the back of the station wagon and placed the sledgehammer in the pick-up bed right next to the crow bar already there.

Then, with Gramps looking on with less awareness than he had yesterday, Carson installed the police radio he'd bought in the pawnshop under the wagon's dash. Afterwards he checked and cleaned his pistol, loaded it and stuffed it into the wagon's glove box.

Borrowing his grandfather's pick-up once again, Carson drove into the town of Cut Bank, just beyond the reservation borders, and visited the hardware store there. The clerk, a tall 50-ish year old white man, recognized Carson as he entered, but tried not to show it. Carson intentionally picked this store for his shopping needs because this man had served on the jury that had sent him away for five years, a jury assembled precisely because its members were known to be friends of the county sheriff.

The clerk busied himself at the counter while Carson went to buy a few hardware odds and ends. On his shopping list was a battery-powered drill with bits, one hundred feet of rope, three rolls of duct tape and a large knife. He took everything to the counter.

"I don't want no trouble," the counter man said nervously.

"Don't know what you're talking about," Carson replied. "I'm just picking up a few items I'll need when I pay a visit to an old friend. We got some unfinished business to take care of."

"Oh, I see," the counter man said, thinking he knew what that unfinished business could be.

Seeing a refrigerated snack display close to the checkout

counter, Carson picked up a couple of packaged sandwiches, drinks and chips, and added them to his pile. Noticing that the counter man seemed a little nervous, Carson decided to have a little fun with him.

Smiling a big smile, Carson said, "Need to keep up my strength up while I'm taking care of my unfinished business, don't you think?"

"Yeah, sure, whatever you say."

Carson dropped the smile and gave the man a hard look.

"Don't you just hate it when trusted officers of the law turn out to be dangerous, corrupt criminals themselves?"

"I'm sure I don't know what you're talking about, Mister," the counter man responded.

"And then the very judicial system that's supposed to treat you like your innocent until proven guilty turns out to be corrupt, as well?"

"I still don't know what you're talking about."

"I hate when that happens," Carson continued. Looking at the clerk, he added, "I guess we're lucky to be living in a country where you or I can run those bums out of office."

"Yeah, lucky, huh," the clerk replied, laughing nervously.

The smile returned to Carson's face as he paid his bill and left the store.

Through the front store window, Carson saw the man pick up the phone and nervously dial. He excitedly described the pick-up truck Carson was driving as it drove away, and Carson had a pretty good idea who the clerk was talking to.

Carson's next stop was a warehouse located in an industrial district at the edge of town not far from the railroad tracks. It was a place he was quite familiar with. Parking in the alley, he grabbed the crow bar and sledgehammer from the back of the pick-up. He walked straight passed a row of warehouse doors until he reached the one he was looking for. Using the tools at hand, he forced open the padlock and entered.

There were rows of palettes stacked with appliances, flat screen TVs, computers and other electronics. With the sledgehammer, Carson began smashing as many boxes and their contents as he could, except for one, a big flat-screen TV that he spared. Carrying it out of the warehouse, he put it in the bed of the truck and drove away.

Carson arrived back at Gramps' house with the new TV and set it up for his grandfather in the living room. He left his grandfather happily watching a "Wheel of Fortune" re-run on the big, bright screen while he parked the pick-up inside the barn, out of sight.

Late that afternoon, Carson donned a pair of dark sunglasses and an old cowboy hat. Then he drove the old station wagon back to Cut Bank and found a secluded spot that had a view of the Glacier County Sheriff's office. He parked and turned on the police scanner, listening to snippets of law enforcement chatter on different channels until he found what he was looking for. The dispatcher for the Glacier County Sheriff was sending one of the deputies out on a call. Carson opened a packaged sandwich and began his stake-out.

It wasn't long before he heard the call he'd been waiting for. One of the sheriff's deputies had been patrolling the warehouse district and came across the broken lock. He called in to ask the sheriff to come out and take a look.

In a matter of minutes, Carson saw the sheriff's car pull out from behind the building and head down the street. Inside that car was Carson's target, Sheriff William T. Ollinger, an overweight redneck in his 50s. Carson followed him at a safe distance.

A few minutes later the sheriff pulled up to the warehouse and parked next to the deputy's car already on site. Ollinger got out of his car, slamming the door. As the sheriff checked out the warehouse, Carson parked discreetly down the block.

Soon Ollinger emerged from the warehouse, his beet red face signaling the anger that was coursing through his veins.

"That son-of-a-bitch prairie nigger," he said as he kicked a nearby dumpster. "We're gonna nail his ass good this time. We shoulda whacked him when we whacked his brother."

He rushed to his patrol car and made a call over the police radio, which Carson picked up on his scanner.

"All units, be on the look-out for a late model brown Ford pick-up with Montana plates being driven by one Carson Rider. He's probably armed and dangerous."

After making the call, the sheriff scanned the area around the warehouse and saw only a beat up old station wagon parked in the next block. In the growing darkness, it was hard to see if anyone was in it, but since it didn't fit the description he'd just put out, he ignored it.

The sheriff drove away, and again Carson followed at a safe distance. Minutes later the sheriff arrived at Big Sky Bar & Grill, a local watering hole. Parking in the back alley, Ollinger entered the crumbling brick building through the rear door.

Carson parked his car nearby, positioned for a fast getaway. Concealing his movements from possible witnesses, he sneaked over to some bushes near the sheriff's car to wait him out.

In about an hour, Ollinger emerged from the bar, slightly inebriated. The man wobbled as he walked toward his car, just as Carson had hoped. Quickly and quietly the convict approached the sheriff from behind. A swift blow to the head brought the sheriff down with a thud.

With some difficulty, Carson dragged the overweight man to the station wagon. With even more difficulty, he stuffed the heavy man into the back. After taping up the sheriff's mouth and tying his hands and feet, Carson jumped into the car and sped away.

Had anyone seen him kidnap the lawman? Carson didn't think so, but it was too late to turn back now. The opportunity he'd been hoping for every day during the past five years had finally arrived. Now to carry out the rest of the plan.

Driving back to his grandfather's house, Carson backed the car up to the barn. Dragging the sheriff's unconscious body out of the car was easier than putting him in. He rolled out of the back and landed on the ground with a thump.

Locking the barn doors from the inside, Carson propped Sheriff Ollinger up in a corner and threw a bucket of water in his face. Once the sheriff was good and awake, the interrogation began.

"Where's the loot, Bill?" Carson demanded, "The loot you framed me for stealing? The loot you killed my little brother for?"

Ollinger was defiant. Wide-eyed and shouting through the tape, he indicated he was not going to tell Carson anything.

"You didn't know I was a P.O.W., did you," Carson asked the sheriff, not expecting an answer. "As a captured Army Ranger, I learned first hand some very effective methods of extracting information. They say confession is good for the soul, so what I'm going to do is supply you with some incentive to talk, and when you're good and ready to spill the beans, I'll remove the duct tape and hear your confession."

Ollinger attempted to speak at that point, so Carson removed the tape to hear what he was trying to say.

"Eat shit and go to hell," is what came out of the sheriff's mouth, and the tape was immediately replaced. So, Carson began a methodical campaign of torture designed to inflict the maximum amount of pain while encouraging his captive to share the required information. He started with repeated blows the sheriff's bloated mid-section.

"You had the perfect system going, didn't you?" Carson said. He was calm as he spoke, taking on an almost joking tone.

Ollinger's head and face were Carson's next targets. Blow after blow took their toll. The interrogator spoke between blows.

"Robbing cargo trucks as they passed through the area–you knew when and where to strike."

Blood oozed from the man's wounds. His hair dripped with sweat.

"I joined your secret little ring of thieves at a very low point in my life," the Indian confessed. "I should've realized that you'd never let me un-join your club when I was ready to get out."

Carson paused to take a long, slow drink of water from one of the bottles he'd purchased at the hardware store in Cut Bank. He took another bottle and poured over the sheriff's face, washing some of the blood out of his eyes. However, the duct tape over his mouth prevented any of the liquid from quenching his considerable thirst.

Carson sat on the tailgate of the station wagon to rest for a moment.

"You decided I was a liability to the operation," he continued calmly, "and so you planted evidence at the site of the last robbery. That was smart. You pulled all the strings, arresting me after a heist you supervised."

Pulling the sledgehammer out of the wagon, he stood up.

"What really put your plan over the top was your idea to frame my younger brother as the driver of the getaway car," he said. "That was the icing on the cake."

Suddenly, the calmness in his voice disappeared. The rage that had lurked beneath the surface now flooded onto Carson's face.

"And so you hunted him down and killed him for no other reason than to punish and enrage me!" he shouted as he slammed the sledgehammer into Ollinger's right foot, shattering the bones. The sheriff's cry of pain escaped through the duct tape, tapering to a whimper.

"Feel more like talking now?" Carson asked.

The sheriff nodded his head rapidly and grunted his agreement through the tape. Before peeling back the gray adhesive, Carson turned on a miniature tape recorder that he'd hidden earlier to capture the sheriff's words.

The almost repentant peace officer admitted to running a long-standing theft ring in the region, planting evidence against Carson at a crime scene, and having Carson's brother framed and then killed in a faked get-away attempt. And it was all recorded.

Then Carson stopped the recorder, because the last bit of information he would squeeze out of the crooked lawman was meant for his ears only.

"You've been so cooperative, Bill," the Indian said with a false air of sweetness. "I want to thank you for coming forward with that confession."

Blood and sweat ran down the sheriff's face. His eyes were closed and his breathing was labored.

"We're almost done," Carson continued. "There's just one last little piece of information I need. Then I'll let you go."

The sheriff opened his eyes.

"I need a doctor," he gasped. "You've got to get me to a doctor."

"Where have you been hiding the funds you received from the most recent sale of the stolen goods?" Carson asked, ignoring Ollinger's request.

The sheriff went silent. He closed his eyes and held his breath. Not the money, he thought. That was his retirement fund.

"Final question," Carson prodded. "Answer this and we're all done. You'll be free to go. Where's the money?"

Carson raised the sledgehammer for one more blow.

"All right, all right, all right," Ollinger cried in desperation. "I'll tell you. It's in an empty explosives crate just inside the abandoned copper mine. You know, out past the old boarding school."

Carson pictured it in his mind. He remembered that school, used by the U.S. government to rob generations of Blackfeet kids of their culture, language and family ties.

"How fitting," the Indian said, then knocked the lawman unconscious.

Loading the cut, bruised and broken body of the still-breathing sheriff back into the station wagon, Carson drove out to the hiding place revealed in the sheriff's confession. The mine had been one of the tribe's earlier attempts at profiting from the mineral resources on their rez. It had been a resounding failure.

Leaving the sheriff in the station wagon for the time being, Carson crawled through a hole in an aging chain-link fence and entered the mine. After a brief search, he found the stash of cash just where the sheriff said it would be. After dragging the explosives crate back to his car, he pulled the bound-and-gagged out of the station wagon.

Finally, Carson dragged him to the mine and propped him up near the entrance. Before leaving the scene, he stuffed the tape recorder, sealed inside a plastic bag, in the sheriff's pocket. Tired but elated, Carson drove away.

The following day, Carson distributed some of the sheriff's cash to a few of the poorer reservation families, made an anonymous donation to the tribe's home for military veterans, and stashed several bundles in various out-of-the-way places in Gramps' house. He kept a few thousand for himself.

The day after that, Robert Heavyrunner showed up at Gramps' house looking for Carson. Using his lips, Gramps points toward the barn. There Robert found Carson tending to his horses. There was no sign of the previous day's torture session.

"We've got some pretty happy tribal members," Robert said. "They reportedly received cash donations from you. Where'd the money come from?"

"Didn't you hear?" Carson replied without interrupting his work. "I spent five years in prison for grand theft. I just thought I'd spread the wealth around."

"And I suppose you wouldn't know anything about why Sheriff Ollinger is missing, would you?"

"I'm sure he'll turn up somewhere. You know he's notorious

for disappearing for a few days at a time. I wonder if anyone will ever find out what he was up to all those years."

"Well, I hope I don't have to come back out here and haul you in for doing something stupid."

Carson stopped brushing the Appaloosa and looked straight at Robert.

"You know if I were you, I'd seriously consider starting that new profession you've been thinking about," he said.

After a pause, he resumed the brushing. Not quite sure what to make of Carson's comment, the tribal police chief turned and left.

The following day some rez kids were playing near the abandoned mine and found the sheriff's mangled body. They reported their find to their parents who in turn called the tribal police.

Robert and a couple of tribal cops drove out to the location and discovered a very dead Sheriff Ollinger. Inside his pocket was the tape recorder. As Ollinger's body was loaded on to a stretcher and carried to the county coroner's van, Robert played the tape and heard the sheriff's story.

Robert and three of his men drove to Gramps' house, finding him once again sipping lemonade on the front porch.

"Carson said you might be showing up," Gramps said between sips. "He's gone. He packed up some food and supplies and left last night on horseback. Said to tell you he was… what was it? Oh, yeah - going to get back in touch with his native roots."

Robert and a couple of his men rounded up their own horses,

loaded them into trailers and drove to a campground on the western edge of the reservation.

"Where do you think he went?" one of the rez cops asked Robert.

"He's headed for the Backbone," Robert replied, indicating the mountain ridge west of the reservation. "This is where we used to come and ride when we were young. Let's mount up. We've got a lot of ground to cover if we're going to catch up with him."

The men mounted their horses and split up to head out in three different directions. Each was equipped with a satellite phone to keep in contact with the others. Robert headed out on a trail he thought Carson most likely took, a trail that passed by the tribe's abandoned "survival camp" where years ago city Indians did indeed come to get back "in touch with their native roots."

As Robert moved along the trail, he discovered signs that Carson had passed that way. Once he'd traveled a little deeper into the wilderness, the lawman came to a fork in the trail. He dismounted to check for tracks. He took a few steps on the path that seemed to lead toward Carson, and he unwittingly stepped into a trap. A large hidden cargo net swooped Robert up, and he found himself suspended from a tree.

In a little while Carson came back down the trail to find Robert still hanging from the net. Robert tried to pull his gun from its holster, but due his awkward position, the weapon dropped to the ground. Carson, who had drawn his own gun, merely laughed.

Resigned to his fate, Robert spoke.

"We heard the tape you made of Ollinger's confession," he said. "Too bad you had to kill him to get it."

"I didn't kill him," Carson protested. "I only wounded him severely. He was quite alive when I left him."

"Sorry, my friend," Robert replied. "His heart burst from the trauma, and he died before we found him. I'm afraid you are now wanted for murder."

"That was never part of the plan," Carson said. "I only wanted him to suffer for what he did to me and my brother."

Carson let Robert down from the net and, keeping the gun trained on the cop, instructed him to handcuff himself. They headed for a more secluded area, off the beaten path, where Carson had set up camp.

Although Robert remained cuffed, the two old friends sat on a log talking about the bad old times as they'd agreed to do a few days earlier. Their conversation covered time spent in the military, the lack of jobs on the rez, and how sad it was that Carson's brother had been murdered by the sheriff.

After a pause in the conversation, Carson looked northward thoughtfully.

"You know we Montana Blackfeet have tribal cousins in Canada, just across the border. I've always wanted to go up there and meet them." He turned toward Robert.

"Are you thirsty?" he asked, offering his cop friend a canteen. Robert nodded, taking the canteen and enjoying a long drink.

Soon Robert began to feel groggy, and he realized too late that

Carson had put something in the water.

"Clever," Robert said as he made himself a little more comfortable. "Blackfeet sleepy time tea."

Within a few minutes, the cop was asleep, sitting on the ground leaning back on the log.

Hours later he awoke to find himself alone. He also found that his handcuffs had been loosened, and that Carson had left him a note.

"You won't find me," the note read. "Don't waste your time looking. Check on Gramps for me when you can."

That's about the time the other cops showed up, telling Robert they came in search of him when he hadn't checked in at the appointed time. They had found Robert's radio off on another trail, which had sent them off on a wild goose chase.

After hearing a slightly altered version of Robert's recent ordeal, a version that left out a few details, the officers were ready to continue the search.

"Carson is gone," Robert said, shaking his head. "The trail is cold. There's no use in searching any longer."

He mounted his horse as his subordinates scratched their heads, puzzled as to why their leader was giving up. He pointed to a sign that stood not too far away in the direction Carson had headed. The sign read: You are Now Leaving the Blackfeet Reservation and Entering Glacier National Park.

"He's out of our jurisdiction now," he added. "Let the feds look for him."

With that, Robert started east back down the trail. In his mind, he saw Carson riding on Pono, the Appaloosa, and leading Kamita, the pack horse, up a narrow, winding mountain trail that stretched along the Backbone of the World into Canada.

And he knew without a doubt that it was time to change professions.

UNCHARTED

Joshua Breedlove strained every muscle in his body as he scaled the almost sheer face of a marbled granite cliff. A cloudless, blue sky hovered overhead, but his attention was focused tightly on each point of contact with the mountain. His sweaty palms grasped for any nook or cranny to hold on to. His feet fought for purchase on any solid protrusion. Every inch of progress, he was all too aware, was fraught with danger.

Then, from out of nowhere, a majestic female golden eagle swooped down out of the sky toward the climber, screeching her displeasure at his presence. With a flurry of feathers, her brown and white speckled wings beat the air near his face. Startled, Josh lost his grip and tumbled downward toward the jagged rocks below. For what seemed like an eternity, he plummeted earthward. The sound of the eagle's repetitive screech echoed in his ear.

As he neared the ground, though, the screeching strangely transformed into ringing, and just before the moment of impact, the man awoke with a jolt to find himself in his own bed. With adrenalin still pumping, he quickly sat up to get his bearings, realizing the mountain climbing episode was just a dream.

Still groggy, Josh looked around his sparsely furnished bedroom, searching for the source of the ringing. It was, of course, the phone on his nightstand next to the bed.

Quickly he reached to answer it.

"This is Josh," he said, wiping the sleep from his eyes.

"What are you doing, boss?"

It was his lab assistant, Bob Thornton, calling from the

research lab where Josh worked.

"Our demo starts in half an hour," Bob said.

"Say what?"

Josh looked at his clock in disbelief. It said 8:30. He was wide awake now.

"That's today!?" Josh exclaimed. "I thought they were coming <u>next</u> week."

"Didn't you read the memo?" Bob asked.

"You know I don't read memos."

"Well, they're here, and Carmichael's pissed that you're not."

"All right," Josh replied as he tried to think of a decent excuse. "Tell him—tell him I had to pick up a replacement part for today's demo, and I'll be there as quick as I can."

Josh slammed down the phone, and, wearing only satin boxer shorts adorned with atomic particles, he jumped out of bed and raced to the bathroom.

In a faded color photo next to the phone on the nightstand, a smiling ten-year-old Josh stood with his older brother and their parents. The photo was his constant reminder of the family he no longer had.

Forty-five minutes later, the research scientist pulled his muddy Jeep Cherokee into his parking space in front of the New Wave Technologies research lab. The facility was located in Palo Alto, California—part of the world-renown Silicon Valley.

It was raining lightly, so Josh jumped out of the SUV and

raced for the doors of the sleek, high-tech structure. He was shaking the rainwater off himself as he reached the front receptionist's desk.

"You're late, Dr. Breedlove," Jenna said with a smile. The young, red-haired receptionist always had a smile for the best-looking geek in the company. "Carmichael's about to blow a gasket."

"Is that vein in his neck bulging?" Josh asked as he stopped to button his top shirt button and straighten his tie.

"Looks like it could rupture any time now," she replied.

"Good," Josh said with a smile of his own. "I love when it does that. How do I look?"

Jenna motioned that his tie was a still little crooked, and he straightened it before hurrying off.

Rounding the corner of the building's east wing, the young scientist found Winston Carmichael, head of New Wave Technologies, down the hall addressing a half dozen men and women. The CEO was a sharply dressed businessman in his late forties.

"This puts New Wave Technologies well ahead of schedule on most of our government and military research contracts," Carmichael was saying as Josh approached. Seeing Josh, Carmichael paused. "Ah, Dr. Breedlove, how good of you to join us."

"Good morning, Winston," Josh said brightly. "Ladies and gentlemen, sorry I'm late."

"You're just in time to give our guests from the National Science Foundation an update on your research project, unless of course, you're not ready. Your assistant said something about a replacement part."

"Oh right—the replacement part," Josh replied as he fished around in his briefcase. He held up a small computer circuit board and smiled. Then, affecting a British accent, he continued, "If you'll kindly step into my laboratory."

A sign on the wall next to the door identified the space within as The Mind-Sync Lab. Carmichael pulled Josh aside as the others stepped inside.

"I really stuck my neck out for you on this one, Breedlove," the CEO said in a peeved tone. "These people are looking for results that will translate into industrial and military applications. Otherwise, the funding for your project could be shaky."

Josh shook off Carmichael's hold.

"And, as I've said before, <u>Mr.</u> Carmichael, you know just where you can stick your industrial and military applications. This research is being conducted to help people, not promote—"

Just then Bob Thornton, a chubby cherub of a man in a rumpled lab coat, stepped out of the lab and interrupted their heated conversation.

"The system's ready, boss," the lab assistant said. "Should I fire it up?"

"You'll need this." Josh waved the circuit board and smiled.

"Oh right," Bob replied, taking the board from him.

"Go ahead and get it started. I'll be right in."

Bob retreated into the lab, closing the door behind him.

Josh's smile immediately faded.

"We'll have to continue this conversation later, Winston," he said, following Bob into the lab.

Moments later, Josh stepped into the Mind-Sync Lab's control room to find his guests already examining the array of electronic devices installed there. The EEG monitors, video screens, temperature gauges, and other digital equipment gave the room the appearance of a small NASA space command center. Bob cleared his throat and addressed the group.

"Based on research begun by Dr. Breedlove's father, we're investigating the positive impact that certain sound and light wave frequencies can have on improved brain functioning, when both halves of the brain are brought into what we call 'synchronized thinking.'"

Josh picked up the story.

"So far, our research has shown that the brain can be led from one frequency to another, leading the mind from the waking state to a slower frequency. This change produces a variety of results including accelerated healing in the body among other things. From this control room, we monitor the body's vital functions while recording changes in brain-wave activity during sessions."

After a moment's pause, Bob led the group out of the

control room. In the center of the main lab area sat a device that resembled an iron lung from the 1950s.

Bob resumed his role as tour guide.

"This is the heart of the project, the SIC—sound isolation chamber. Here, sound and light wave patterns are fed via the ears and eyes into the test subject's mind."

After Bob opened the chamber's round hatch, Josh climbed inside. Lying down in the twelve-foot long cylinder, Josh demonstrated what Bob was explaining.

"A special headset is used to feed tones and light patterns to the subject. The headset contains both visual and aural components. After a brief relaxation period, the subject is fed the mind-sync tones and gently led into a meditative, sleep-like state."

"Is this a joke, Breedlove?" one of the guests, a Mr. Foster, asked. "You *are* going to show us the real project, aren't you? Or are you so obsessed with your late father's work that you've traded science for science fiction?"

Standing at the edge of the crowd, Carmichael smiled. Josh came flying out of the chamber, ready for battle.

"This is the <u>best</u> kind of science, Mr. Foster, the kind that improves peoples' lives."

"Where's the data that supports your premise?" Mr. Foster asked curtly.

"It's being analyzed now," Bob replied politely. "Our initial report will be ready by the end of the month, right on schedule."

"The Foundation is going through a financial transition right now, Dr. Breedlove," Foster said. He removed his glasses and rubbed his eyes. "Projects like yours are being called into question and their value re-assessed. I hope, for your sake, that the Mind-Sync process has marketable applications."

Somehow Foster knew how to push Josh's buttons.

"Marketable applications? Why that's the most—"

Carmichael stepped forward and made the very noticeable gesture of looking at his watch.

"I'm sorry, Dr. Breedlove, but we're all out of time. Our guests have a busy day ahead of them, and *must* move along if they're going to see every project."

He turned to face the gathered guests.

"Now if you'll follow me, we've prepared quite a sumptuous meal for you in the corporate commissary."

Carmichael and the guests exited the lab as Josh and Bob started walking rather slowly towards the control room.

"Has Carmichael always hated you, or did you do something recently to give him a reason to start?" Bob asked with a slight smirk.

"He's jealous."

"Why, what would he ever have to be jealous of?" Bob asked, feigning total ignorance on the matter.

"Maybe because I'm receiving the Scientific Achievement award tonight, and he's not?"

"I always knew his ego was bigger than his IQ," Bob noted

with a chuckle.

Just as they arrived at the control room door, Laura, an attractive lab technician in her late 20s, approached with a clipboard. Her crush on Josh was quite apparent.

"Dr. Breedlove, here's the sound wave sequences that are programmed for this afternoon's session, just like you asked for."

"Thanks, Laura." Josh took the clipboard from her, and she turned to leave. His eyes followed her as she slowly made her way across the lab. She turned and gave her boss a coy smile before exiting the room.

"Is the gear ready?" he asked Bob, who noticed his boss watching Laura.

"Yeah. Oh, and I installed the remote-control unit you asked for so you can run a session by yourself from inside the chamber."

Bob proceeded to demonstrate how the remote-control worked.

An interesting assortment of people from the local scientific community had gathered for the evening's award ceremony and a catered meal. Bob and a few other New Wave Technologies employees sat at a table near the front of the room. Carmichael was conspicuously absent.

On stage at the head table, Josh was seated amongst a group of rather eccentric-looking, scholarly older people. His energy and youthfulness stood out in stark contrast to most of the others on the podium.

The evening's MC, a mild-mannered, bespectacled man in his mid-thirties, stepped to the podium. He tapped a fork on his glass to get everyone's attention.

"If I could have your attention please," he said to almost no affect.

"Yoo-hoo," he crooned.

The chattering continued unabated.

"Quiet!" he finally demanded in a surprisingly assertive voice.

The chatter in the room subsided.

"Thank you."

He straightened his bow tie for affect.

"As you know, each year the American Scientific Association honors someone who they believe has made significant contributions to the field of scientific research in our community."

He looked towards Josh briefly and smiled.

"Tonight's honoree is a man whose work has been called 'radical' by his critics and 'revolutionary' by his admirers. And, as those who know him can testify, once he decides to tackle a scientific problem, he allows nothing to deter him from solving it."

Bob smiled in recognition of the description of his friend and co-worker.

"And he's got science in his blood, so to speak. His father was a pioneering research scientist on the verge of new discoveries in the fields of neurology and brain functioning when he met his untimely death."

Josh listened appreciatively, glad for the mention of his father.

"And so tonight I am proud to present the Golden Eagle Achievement Award to Dr. Joshua Breedlove of New Wave Technologies. Josh, would you come up and say a few words?"

A loud and hearty applause welcomed Josh as he stepped to the podium.

"Thanks, Nigel, for those kind words. I love your pocket protector. Don't change. Really."

The MC smiled awkwardly as he took his seat.

"Thank you all," Josh continued, "and thanks to the American Scientific Association for this recognition of my work."

He removed a handkerchief from his pocket and wiped his eyes and his forehead.

"As many of you know, I lost my parents in a car wreck twenty-five years ago on a rainy night much like this one. My brother went into a coma, from which he never regained consciousness. Six months later they unplugged his life support systems. This tragedy has shaped my life and my work."

Every eye in the room was focused on Josh. In rapt attention, people hardly breathed.

"I do what I do because of this event. I carry on my father's work because he can't. I try to unlock the brain's secrets so that others who may suffer serious head trauma, like my brother did, might regain consciousness and one day live normal lives again."

He paused to take a drink of water from a glass that stood at the edge of the podium.

"I accept this honor tonight in their names and will place it next to their memory in my heart and beside their picture in my room. Thank you, again."

As he sat down, members of the teary-eyed crowd jumped to their feet cheering this courageous man. Josh was overcome with emotion but smiled at his colleagues. The rousing applause continued for what Josh thought was an uncomfortably long time.

Later that evening, Josh, Bob and a couple of other New Wave Technologies employees enjoyed a laugh over a drink or two, or three at a nearby trendy bar. Josh, not participating too much in the frivolity, studied his award, which sat on the table in front of him.

"Quite a speech you gave tonight, Josh," Bob remarked. "Not a dry eye in the house."

"Do you believe in God, Bob?" Josh asked, not hearing what his friend has said.

"What?"

"Do you believe in God… or the soul?"

"Yeah, sort of, I guess. Why?"

"I've looked, but I haven't been able to find signs of either one—only brain cells and bio-chemicals and random activity. That's all. And when those cells or those chemicals quit working, the mind appears to evaporate. Lights out."

"I think you've been spending too much time in the experimental sound chamber, Dr. Breedlove," one of the lab techs offered.

Everyone at the table, but Josh, chuckled.

"Sorry. I—"

"What the hell," Bob said. "Let's have a toast."

He raised his glass and the others at the table did likewise.

"To Dr. Joshua Breedlove, for his brilliant brain cells, all his hard work... and for putting up with Winston Carmichael all these years!"

"Here, here!" someone said as they clinked their glasses and downed another drink.

"Hey, look at the time," Josh said, glancing at his watch. "I'm going home. We <u>do</u> have work tomorrow, gentlemen, so don't stay out too long."

Josh made his way through the drizzling rain to his Jeep, award in hand. Slightly inebriated, he fumbled with his keys until he found the right one. A flash of distant lightning ripped across the sky as he flung himself into the driver's seat.

Before long, he was on the winding road that led down the hill from the banquet hall back towards his own part of town. The Jeep's windshield wipers were barely able to keep up with the ever-increasing rate of rainfall, and he struggled to see where the edge of the road was.

Suddenly, a bright flash engulfed the car as lightning struck the vehicle's antenna. This was immediately followed by a loud, sharp crack of thunder. The high voltage charge quickly killed the Jeep's electrical system, which, in turn, froze the car's power brakes and steering. The car veered off the road and crashed headlong into a tree.

The driver of another car coming down the same hill behind Josh had witnessed the whole bizarre episode. He immediately came to a screeching halt close to Josh's Jeep. The good Samaritan, an insurance salesman on his way home, ran to peek into Josh's window, finding him slumped over the steering wheel. Blood dripped from above Josh's eyebrows.

"Oh my god!" the driver exclaimed, pulling out his cellphone. "Hang in there, buddy," he said to the unconscious Josh. "I'll get help."

Somewhere deep in Josh's mind, a twenty-five-year old memory was triggered and came to life. It was a rainy night, just like now, in front of a modest home somewhere on a college campus. A ten-year-old Josh, his mother, father and brother ran to their station wagon and got in. His father started the car and took off.

The Breedlove family's station wagon moved through the rain on a poorly lit college campus road, unaware that a rusty VW van chugged through the same rainy night a few streets away. The van's driver and his passenger, both rather carefree college students, passed a joint between them as they rode. A fogged windshield and smoky interior made it next to impossible for the stoned pair to see the signal light they were approaching.

Nearing the same signal from a right angle, Josh's father saw that he had a green light and proceeded through the intersection only to discover too late that the VW van was headed right at him without stopping or slowing.

Suddenly, Josh's mother screamed loudly as she saw the van just a split second before it plowed into them. The van struck the station wagon's front driver's side fender, spinning the car like a top on the wet pavement. In those days before strict seat belt laws, everyone in the Breedlove's car was tossed like rag dolls around the interior of the car.

Within seconds, the sounds of crunching metal, screeching tires, and screaming people ceased. An eerie quiet came over the scene. The hissing from steam escaping the Breedlove's radiator was the only sound, the only movement.

A long minute later, the van's side door slid open. The vehicle's young driver, blood dripping down the side of his face, stumbled out. In a drug-induced haze, he staggered over to the Breedlove's car and peered inside.

There was blood everywhere. The car's occupants appeared dead.

Feeling something oozing down his own cheeks, the stoned driver reached up and touched the wound on his head. He winced in pain.

"Bummer, man," was all he said before his eyes rolled back in his head and he passed out, falling to the street motionless.

Paramedics wheeled the adult Josh into the ER at a nearby hospital. A team of doctors and nurses took over from the EMTs to rush the injured man into a vacant operating room. They hooked him up to the familiar array of medical monitoring equipment, and the attending nurse reported what she saw.

"His pulse is weak, doctor, and the heart rate is slowing," she announced.

"Start an IV drip," the doctor ordered, and followed the order with several additional, specific instructions. "Lightning does strange things when it courses through the human body," the doctor added, more to himself than anyone else.

Just then, Josh flat-lined.

"We're losing him, people!" the doctor shouted. "Set up the de-fib paddles, and be quick about it!"

Surrounding Josh's lifeless body, the medical team quickly began the emergency medical procedures they'd practiced hundreds of times. The doctor took hold of the paddles, and when the device was fully charged, yelled, "Clear!"

The doctor applied the paddles to Josh's chest as other members of the team took a step back. The electric current lifted Josh's body, then dropped it back on the bed. No response.

The team prepared to repeat the action.

"Get the heart needle ready, nurse," the doctor commanded as he waited for the defibrillator to recharge.

Although Josh was, of course, totally unaware of this activity, he somehow seemed to be slowly regaining consciousness. At first, he became aware of the bright lights in the operating room. Then he began to hear what the members of the medical team were saying to one another. Finally, his sight returned. But what he was seeing was impossible.

The doctors and nurses were gathered around someone's body lying on a hospital bed. Josh realized he was viewing the scene from above, from what must have been the ceiling of the room. What the hell?

Below him, the medical team stepped back from the body, preparing for a second zap from the defib paddles. That's when Josh saw just who it was lying on that bed. It was himself! Impossible, he thought.

That's when things began to shift. The sounds of the room faded and were replaced with a soothing hum. The sights of the room faded as well, and were replaced with a soothing white light. But the new sight and sound didn't seem to come from outside him. Instead, they seemed to permeate his being.

In a few moments, Josh found himself standing in a white space. It felt like a room, but it didn't have visible physical walls. There were, however, three arched windows, which provided a view of a beautiful park-like setting outside. Josh could feel the peacefulness of that park, and that feeling absorbed him for a moment.

Then he became aware of a presence inside the room. He turned to find his parents standing nearby smiling at him. They appeared as they did some twenty-five years ago. But they weren't alone. Standing next to them was a tall bald man wearing white. The man, possibly eight feet tall, glowed from within.

The tall man's glowing whiteness was almost more than Josh could bear. Sensing this reaction, the man's intensity decreased.

Both puzzled and delighted, Josh said, "Mom? Dad? You're alive!"

"Well, yes and no," his father said. "The universe is even more vast than we scientists ever understood. But you're soon going to discover that with the help of a couple of old friends."

"Did I die?" Josh asked.

"No, you're going to be all right, Josh," his mother said. "We're here just to show you that we've been safe and well all these years."

"Who's he?" he asked, indicating the man in white.

"One of the old friends I mentioned," Josh's father answered. "He says you have to go back to finish your work."

"What's happening right now?" Josh asked, feeling confused and disoriented.

"In terms you'd understand, we're at the meeting place between two dimensions, son," he father. "We've been allowed a momentary interaction."

"Everything's going to be just fine, sweetheart," his mother said. "We're going back where we belong while you return to help people, lots of people."

As she finished speaking, she and Josh's father began to

fade from view.

"We love you," his mother said even though she was only half visible.

"Keep up the good work," his father said just before vanishing.

Josh stood alone with the Glowing Man.

"You don't remember me, do you, Josh?" he said. "We've met before."

Josh shook his head.

"You've been here before, too, when you were ten, after the car wreck."

Josh stared blankly. He had no memory of such an event.

"That's okay," the man said. "We'll meet again soon. But right now, I want to show you something."

The Glowing Man turned and gestured with one hand. One of Josh's experimental sound chambers from the lab materialized before him. Simultaneously, Josh transformed back into his adult self.

"There are a few adjustments you can make to improve the effectiveness of your experiments," the Glowing Man said. "Here, this should explain."

He closed his eyes and nodded his head towards Josh. A translucent ball of soft, liquid-like energy was tossed from the man's head to Josh. It hit Josh in the chest and was absorbed into his being.

"You can review this information later," the mystery man

said. "For now, you must go back. I think your body is calling you."

Josh heard the sound of roaring wind as the Glowing Man disappeared. Momentarily, the scientist stood alone in the white room. Then he felt a sort of sucking sensation as he was pulled away.

The Glowing Man's voice say, "Goodbye, for now" just before Josh was jolted awake back in the hospital operating room.

The sound of a regular heartbeat issued from the monitoring equipment, and the members of Josh's medical team were undeniably relieved and delighted that their patient had responded to their resuscitation efforts.

Josh's eyes blinked at the harsh lights in the OR. Closing them, he immediately remembered the experience he'd just had. What was that? A delusion caused by diminished brain activity? An hallucination created by a mix of medications?

Or was it something else?

Two days later, a recovering Josh was propped up in his hospital bed with a bandage wrapped around his head. An IV tube fed him nutrients even as the patient forced down mysterious substances the hospital had assured him was food. And, simultaneously, a nurse checked his vital signs when a scholarly looking man in his late forties entered.

"So, it takes an act of God to get you to call me," Doctor Andrew Wahlinski said, approaching Josh's bed.

"Doctor Wahlinski!" Josh said brightly. "Man, am I glad to see you."

"From what I hear, you should be glad to be seeing <u>anybody</u> these days." Speaking to the nurse, Andy added, "Could you excuse us for a moment please? I'm the patient's psychiatrist."

The nurse exited as Andy stepped closer to Josh's bed.

"Really, thanks for coming," Josh said. "I need somebody to talk to."

"Josh, after your parents died, I raised you as if you were my own son, but now that you're a grown man, you can call me Andy."

"I respected you so much, and for some reason, calling you Doctor Wahlinski always reminded me of when my parents were still alive."

"Well, whatever you're comfortable with, but speaking as your psychiatrist, I recommend getting out of here for a little while. Let's go get a cup of coffee."

"Gladly," Josh replied.

He threw back the covers and ripped the IV from his arm. Andy helped him out of bed and into a robe.

A few minutes later, the pair was in the hospital cafeteria drinking coffee. Grabbing a napkin from the dispenser on the table and a pen from Andy's pocket, Josh began drawing a diagram. After finishing the sketch, he slid the napkin across the table.

"And this is what he showed me," Josh said.

As Andy studied the image, Josh added, "These are precise

detailed adjustments that are supposed to improve the efficiency of my sound wave chamber.

Andy continued to examine the drawing.

"So what do you think?" Josh prompted. "This whole vision with my parents and the glowing man was an hallucination, wasn't it? I'm cracking up, right.?"

"It may or may not have been an hallucination," the psychiatrist said finally. "And you may or may not be cracking up. I can't say."

"You're a lot of help," Josh quipped.

"But many otherwise sane and rational people have reported near death experiences like yours, and have been transformed by them," Andy said flatly.

Josh merely rolled his eyes.

"You're are a man of science, so I suggest you put your empirical skills to work," Andy continued. "Make the changes described by your glowing man."

He handed the napkin back to Josh.

"Make notes of your adjustments and, if they prove beneficial in later experiments, use them and be thankful," Andy concluded.

"Thankful?"

"Great people from Einstein to Mozart attributed some of their best work to inexplicable visions and episodes of revelation," Josh's friend answered. Looking at his watch, he added, "I'm sorry, Josh, I've got to go."

He stood to leave.

"That's it, huh?" Josh said. "No psychiatric pronouncement? No mumbo-jumbo?"

"There _is_ one more thing," Andy said before taking his leave. "You should talk to someone more experienced in mysticism, psychic phenomenon—that sort of thing—to give you deeper insights into your NDE."

"You mean some kind of kook?!"

"I mean Marlena," Andy said and turned to leave, knowing that suggestion would give Josh plenty to think about.

A few days later, Josh was ready to return to his lab. Laura was especially glad to see her boss, and communicated her concern about the small bandage on his head.

"We really missed you around here," she said with a smile. "I really missed you, Josh."

"I missed you guys, too," he replied, trying to politely ignore her unwanted advances.

He quickly made a bee-line for Bob who was working on the sound chamber and asked, "How are the equipment changes coming?"

"Welcome back, boss," Bob said. "I'm just starting the last one. I'll be done by the end of the day. You know these settings are—"

"I know—they're weird," Josh said before his assistant could finish his thought. "Multiple harmonic frequency patterns.

But I've got to give it a try, anyway."

"Okay, you're the genius," Bob replied as turned back to the task at hand. "Oh, I heard Carmichael's looking for you.

"What could he want?"

"Probably wants to see if you brought back any secrets from the dead he can sell to the army," Bob answered with a chuckle.

Josh laughed as he stepped into the control room to check out the equipment and recent experiment results. He spent the remainder of the day at those tasks.

That evening, after everyone but Bob had left the lab, Josh looked up from his work. He yawned and stretched as his assistant stuck his head into the control room.

"I'm done," Bob said. "All you have to do is switch the system to auto-pilot in here, and you can run the experiment from inside the chamber."

"Thanks, Bob. Leave everything on. I'm going to try it out tonight."

"Suit yourself. See you tomorrow."

After Bob left, Josh put his paperwork aside. switched the system to the auto-pilot mode, and made a few adjustments to the controls. Then, stepping out of the control room, he headed for the sound chamber. There, after checking the settings on a control panel on the outside of the chamber, the scientist climbed in.

Once inside, he put on the head piece with its built-in headphones and electronic goggles. Using the remote-control unit

Bob built, Josh switched the system on. He was pleased to hear the familiar sound of pulsating tones through the headphones. This was soon followed by the expected pulsating flashes of light emitted by the electronic goggles.

Finally, he looked towards the tiny video camera mounted inside the chamber and gave the "thumbs up" sign.

"All right, Andy. Here goes nothin'."

Fully reclining inside the chamber, he closed his eyes and began to relax. The pulsating flashes and tones continued at the same frequency for a few minutes, allowing Josh's brain to synchronize itself to that frequency.

Soon, the tones and flashes began to gradually slow down in pace, while simultaneously, a second, higher frequency pattern begins. Everything in Josh's field of experience began to pulsate in rhythm with the pulsating sights and sounds.

Soon, another shift took place. The slower frequency resembled a deep, pounding heartbeat while the higher frequency increased in rate and pitch.

In response, Josh began squirming where he lay in the chamber. Suddenly, the pulsing tones peaked and shifted into a multi-layered, harmonic humming. Josh's body went completely limp. Within seconds, a ring of energy sparks shot out from Josh's body in all directions.

Josh continued to lay motionless within the chamber, eyes closed. However, within his mind, his environment became visible to him. The sleep chamber appeared to be somewhat transparent, and the ring of pulsating energy extended away from his body several feet out into the lab.

The unexpected experience caused Josh to panic. He opened his physical eyes, ripped the headpiece off and jumped out of the chamber. Standing beside the unit for a long moment, he looked around the room expecting to maybe see the ring of sparks. But the room was still and silent. Everything looked normal.

"What the hell was that?" Josh asked himself, the room and anything else that might've been listening.

He rushed to the control room and played back the digital recording of the session. The video screen displayed an image of Josh laying in the chamber. Superimposed over the image was a record of the frequencies that had been generated along with his vital signs--heart rate, body temperature and EEG.

He fast forwarded the playback to the point just before the sound waves shifted and then hit the play button. When the recording reached the point of the sound-wave shift, every part of the digital read out changed.

On the video monitor, his body went limp. His heart rate dropped dramatically, as did his EEG. However, his body temperature rose, and there was no sign of the ring of sparks, which he could only interpret as some sort of energy field.

"Amazing," Josh said. "Okay, Breedlove, let's put those scientific skills that you're so famous for to work. Just like Andy said."

He reset the controls in the control room and once again

headed for the sound chamber. Again, he climbed into the chamber and put on the headpiece. Again, he gave the thumbs up sign to the video camera, this time without the smile. No longer was Josh going through the motions to humor Andy. After what he'd just experienced, this whole thing was too weird to dismiss as a delusion.

The pulsating light and sound frequencies began again. The process repeated itself until the system peaked and the harmonic humming returned. Again, the energy field radiated out from Josh's body. Although his body had gone limp, his mind was active.

"Stay calm, Breedlove," he told himself. "Nothing to panic about. Just go with the flow. You're a scientist. This is an experiment."

Then he noticed a fly buzzing around inside the sound chamber.

"How did that get in here," he asked himself.

Without thinking, Josh reached up with his hand to swat it. But his hand passed through both the fly and the glass on the sound chamber! He examines this hand more closely. He could see right through it!

Quickly, he sat up in the chamber and looked back down to find that his physical body was still lying limp and asleep on the bed of the chamber!

"Ahhh!" he yelled mentally. "I'm coming apart at the seams!"

The force of his mental yell separated his translucent body

from his physical body with the ripping sound of Velcro and propelled him upward through the sound chamber.

Stunned and confused, Josh floated above the sound chamber in his transparent body, looking down at his physical laying below.

But the shock of the sight sucked him back into his physical body. Now back inside his physical body, Josh sat up, this time hitting his head on the inside of the sound chamber. He responded with a very loud "Ow!"

He removed the headpiece, unplugged the electrodes from his body and climbed out. Stunned, he stood beside the sound chamber as the reality of what just happened began to sink in.

"There's a logical explanation for this," Josh said out loud. "I just can't think of what it is right now."

Josh paced back and forth beside the sound chamber.

"I can't tell anyone about this," he said out loud. "They'll think I'm nuts."

He stopped pacing and ran his hand through his hair.

"I'm talking to myself. *I* think I'm nuts."

He paced again.

"But I've got to tell someone."

An idea hit him, and he rushed to the control room. After removing a little black phone book from his briefcase, he flipped through the pages. Finding the section marked "S," he ran his finger down the listings until he found the words "MARLENA SUNRIDER."

His finger moved across the page, coming to rest at a

couple of phone numbers that had been crossed through. A third number had been squeezed in the remaining space along the margin.

He bit his lower lip and took a deep breath. As he released the breath, his determination faded and he decided not to make the call. After returning the book to his briefcase, he removed a journal notebook from the case. He sat down at the control console, opened it and began writing.

"Private Journal Entry 1.1. Tonight, I crossed a threshold. What awaits me on the other side, I'm not sure. But I know I must pursue it with every ounce of scientific vigor within me."

He continued to write and describe the details of his experience on into the night.

Morning found Josh asleep on a cot in the corner of the control room with notes, sketches and diagrams scattered about. An intercom on the control room console buzzed loudly, rousing Josh from sleep. He rushed to silence the annoying sound, pushing the speak button.

"Yeah, I'm here," he said groggily.

Winston Carmichael's voice came through the tinny speaker.

"Dr. Breedlove, what a pleasant surprise. Worked all night, did we?"

"Yeah, Winston, I was just catching up on my research notes."

"Well, isn't that nice," the man replied in a condescending

tone. "Listen, I need to see you. Would you come to my office?"

"Sure. I'll freshen up and be right there."

Josh collected and stacked his journal and notes, placing them in his briefcase.

Minutes later, Josh, looking fresher and less crumpled than before, entered Carmichael's office. The man, wearing an expensive suit and tie, sat at his desk writing.

"You wanted to see me?" Josh said.

"Why don't you have a seat?" Carmichael replied, motioning for Josh to sit in the only other chair in the room.

"What's on your mind?" The scientist asked as he sat down.

"I'm afraid I have some rather bad news, Josh."

"Oh, really."

"The National Science Foundation is cutting your funding."

"What?"

"You have thirty days to close out the project and submit your final report."

Josh jumped to his feet.

"This is an outrage!" he shouted. "They can't do this!"

"On the contrary," Carmichael said calmly. "They can terminate a research project any time they feel like it. It's in the contract."

He produced the contract and dangled in front of Josh. Grabbing it, Josh quickly read the paragraph that his boss had highlighted in yellow marker.

"You really should pay more attention to paperwork, Dr. Breedlove. You can get screwed, if you're not careful."

Josh collapsed back into the chair.

"I'll just take the project somewhere else," he said in defeat.

Carmichael pulled out another copy of the document.

"Afraid not," he said, almost joyfully. "Page four, paragraph three of your contract with New Wave Technologies specifically states that all equipment, findings or discoveries remain with the company."

Josh quickly flips through the pages looking for that wording.

"I expect you out of the lab by the end of the month," Carmichael continued. "You're finished in the research business!"

Josh parked his muddy Jeep in a lot at the edge of the University of California-Berkeley campus and placed the paper parking permit on the dash. Walking briskly across campus, he entered Barrows Hall and headed for the Native American Studies office.

The departmental secretary said he could find what he was looking for in a classroom down the hall. Approaching that room, he found the door to be open as the voice of a female lecturer spilled out into the hallway.

"The gold rush gave Anglo immigrants the excuse they were looking for to virtually wipe out northern California tribes," the confident voice was saying.

Just as Josh arrived at the door, the bell rang, ending the class. Josh peaked in. Students were gathering up their books. Shifting his angle, Josh spied the lecturer, Marlena Sunrider, closing up her notes and stuffing them into a briefcase. She was a strikingly beautiful American Indian woman in her mid-thirties. He was suddenly reminded of why he fell in love with her all those years ago.

"Tomorrow we begin the unit on native spirituality," Marlena announced to her students. "Be sure to read chapter three in the Burgess book."

Students streamed out of the classroom passed Josh as he worked his way into the classroom.

Marlena, engaged in answering a student's question and gathering up her teaching materials, didn't notice Josh's entrance. He hovered near the door until the student had gotten the answer to his question and left the lecturer alone.

"Hello, Professor Sunrider," he said in a quiet voice.

"Actually, I'm only an associate professor," she answered before looking up to see her former boyfriend coming toward her. At the sight of Josh, her face barely revealed the long-hidden emotions of both love and pain before she regained her composure.

"J-Josh," she said with a slight stutter. "What a surprise."

"Hello, Marlena," he said, moving closer as her hands momentarily lost their coordination. Several pages of neatly stacked paper fell from her fingers and spread across the podium in front of her.

"What are you <u>doing</u> here?" she asked as she gathered the papers again.

"Come to see you... about a professional matter."

"All business, as usual," she said with an edge.

"I need your help," he replied. "Can we go somewhere and get some coffee?

"Sure," she said and snapped her briefcase closed.

"Congratulations on the professor job," Josh said as they walked across campus to an outdoor cafe. "You always were a good teacher."

"That's one of the nicest things you've ever said to me."

The scientist smiled awkwardly.

"So, are there any little Marlenas running around somewhere?" he asked, if only to change the subject.

"You know me," she answered. "Too independent. Too head strong. I ran off every man who ever got close. Not much in that department has changed."

They reached the cafe and sat down at one of the tables. A waiter quickly approached with set-ups and glasses of water.

Coffee and food was ordered, but the former couple had some difficulty finding a rhythm for their conversation. When their order arrived, Josh moved on to explain his reason for seeking out Marlena. Talking about his own research work was easy for him, and he became especially energized as he described his recent experiences both in the hospital and his lab.

"This whole thing is definitely way outside my area," he admitted after finishing his explanation. "When we were together, I remember you were always talking about far-out fringe topics like this."

Marlena remained quiet for a long moment before responding.

"You don't even realize what you've done, do you?" she said finally. "This is clearly one of the most important breakthroughs in human history. Why, you should be shouting this from the rooftops."

"I can't tell anybody about this."

Moving closer to him, Marlena said, "Medicine men and tribal healers have been astral traveling for thousands of years. Today, people call it out-of-body experiences, OOBEs."

"That's just what I mean," Josh said. "I'd be laughed out of every scientific research facility and publication in the country if I started talking about astral projection or my OOBEs."

"That doesn't matter," she responded excitedly. "What you've done is punch a hole in the wall separating science and religion. And now you've got to keep working at it until the wall comes completely down."

"But in thirty days I'll be locked out of my own lab."

"A lot can happen in thirty days," Marlena replied assuredly. "We'll find a way."

This took Josh completely by surprise.

"We?" he asked.

"We," she confirmed.

That evening, when Marlena finished teaching her final class, Josh took her to the Mind-Sync lab. As she sat at the control console, he explained how the system worked and gave here step-by-step instructions for conducting a session.

"Are you sure you're ready for this?" he asked after completing his instructions.

"I've been ready for this all my life," she said. "The question is, are you sure you're ready?"

"Ready as I'll ever be."

He left the control room and headed for the sound chamber. After climbing in and slipping on the headpiece, he said, "Remember the goal is verifiability. I've got to be able to prove this is real before it'll make a difference to the scientific world."

He laid back and got comfortable inside the unit. Marlena watched on her monitor screen as he gave the thumbs up.

Marlena flipped the switch Josh has shown her and observed as the frequency generator begin its sequence. She heard the pulsating tones through a pair of headphones as the familiar pattern began.

Everything appeared normal, but when the tones reached the harmonic humming stage, Josh's bodily functions dropped noticeably in rate. At first Marlena felt panicked, but then she remembered that Josh said this was also part of the sequence.

Back inside the chamber, Josh lifted himself out of his physical body. His transparent, "other" body floated up and out of the chamber. In a few moments, he floated up to the ceiling and hovered there.

"Freaky" was the only word his scientifically trained mind could come up with.

Then, moving like a weightless astronaut, he maneuvered himself down the wall of the lab toward the control room. Marlena continued to watch the monitors attentively. Josh's physical body, visible on the video monitor, remained limp and still in the sound chamber.

Meanwhile, what Josh could only think of as his energy body floated into the control room and moved toward Marlena. In another few moments he hovered above her.
Awkwardly, Josh pushed off the control room ceiling, propelling himself down towards the control console.

He overshot his target and bumped into the console. He thought it odd that he had moved through the solid surface of the sound chamber, but the room's ceiling and now the console seemed impenetrable. That's something he'd have to record later in his notes.

For now, he tried to think of some way to get Marlena's attention. First, he tried to pick up a pencil on the console with no luck. Then he tried to hug Marlena with his transparent arms, but only succeeded in passing through her.

At that same moment, Marlena felt chilled. She reached for her sweater draped over the back of the chair and draped it over her shoulders. Josh smiled and looked at the clock, noting the time.

Just then, a loud clunk came from somewhere above the lab. Both Marlena and Josh heard it. The interruption caused Josh to be sucked back toward the sound chamber where his physical body lay.

Immediately he woke up in his physical body. Ripping the headphones off, he jumped out of the chamber.

"We did it, Mar!" he shouted as he ran toward the control room. "We proved that I was out of my body."

"How'd we do that?" she asked, not feeling Josh's level of excitement. "I didn't see anything."

"You put on your sweater when I tried to touch you," he replied with a smile.

"That chill I felt was you?"

"It may not seem like much, but it's a start."

Thinking ahead to future experiments, he paced the small room.

"And we can devise other specific observable events that I could only report on if I was present in the room to see them."

"But what was that noise I heard?" Marlena asked.

"I don't know. Nothing to worry about, I'm sure. Something in storage upstairs probably fell. But I'm so excited, I could kiss you."

Impetuously, he did. She kissed him back. Then they broke it off, each looking at the other intensely for a moment before turning away awkwardly.

"We've got to talk," Marlena said. "Can we go get some

food?"

Josh welcomed the suggestion, and they left the lab.

It wasn't too long before they were sitting at a corner table in a local diner. Sipping coffee, they both felt a romantic tension hanging in the air. A waitress approached carrying two plates, which she placed before them. An omelet for Marlena, burger and fries for Josh.

"Still eating breakfast in the middle of the night I see," Josh commented as he squirted ketchup on his pile of fries.

"Yeah, but no one has ever made me omelets like you used to."

She started to take a bite, then paused.

"Why did you leave me, Josh? You never really said."

Josh choked a little on the bite he was chewing.

"I thought it was obvious," he said after swallowing. "As I remember, we argued all the time."

The both took time to take bites of food and chew.

"Is that what it was to you--arguing?" she said, after wiping her mouth. "I thought it was more like sharing feelings, sorting out differences."

"Whatever you call it, I found it very unpleasant. It seemed like you always had something to prove, and you always had to win. I just couldn't go on like that."

"Sounds about right, but I've learned a lot since then, Josh. Like how sometimes winning is really losing, especially if it destroys a relationship. "

He looked into her eyes.

"I've learned a lot, too," he replied in a quiet voice. "Like how to say I'm sorry."

Stretching across the table, Josh moved in for a kiss. Noticing that he had a bit of food in the corner of his mouth, Mar moved away and motioned for him to wipe his mouth.

"Josh, let's take this real slow, okay?"

"Okay," he replied, wiping his mouth. "If that's what you want."

She nodded and then quickly kissed him. Smiling, she dug into her plate of food. Not quite sure what was going on, Josh smiled and focused on his food, as well.

Next morning, Josh strolled into the New Wave Technologies offices with a rather large grin on his face. Jenna noticed.

"My, but we're chipper this morning," she commented. "What's the cause?"

Josh stopped long enough to pluck a flower from an arrangement on the receptionist's desk.

"My project's been cancelled and I have less than thirty days to clear out of the building," he replied still with the grin in place.

"Oh, that makes perfect sense," she said, almost as a question.

He stuck the flower in his lapel and moved on, leaving

Jenna perplexed.

Next the scientist strolled into his lab, finding Bob busy with equipment maintenance chores.

"Ain't life grand, Bob?"

"What have <u>you</u> been smoking?" Bob asked, halting his work.

"A pipe filled with hope," his boss replied.

"What?"

"Never mind," Josh said. "I've got something to show you."

They headed for the control room. Once inside, the lead researcher excitedly explained and demonstrated to Bob what had been happening with his experiments, using video playback, EEG read-outs, hand gestures and elaborate body movements.

"And you expect people to believe this cockamamie story?" Bob asked, shaking his head. "They'll take your science award back."

"I know it sounds totally kooky."

The lab phone rang, and Bob answered. The call was for Josh.

"Yes, this is Breedlove."

"Josh, there's someone following me," Marlena in a panicked tone.

"Marlena, what are you talking about? Where are you?"

"In my car on campus," she said, scanning the faculty parking lot. "I have to tell you I felt something weird last night when we were in the lab—like someone was watching us.

"Is this another one of your paranoid government conspiracy theories? I thought you were over that stuff."

"Let's hope that's all it is," she replied as she continued to check her rearview mirror. "But that noise we heard last night activated my internal sensors. And today I spotted an unmarked black car on my tail."

"It's probably nothing, Mar," he assured her. "You always had an over-active imagination."

"Maybe, but we've got to be careful. I remember in the seventies the military conducted secret research into the use of ESP and Remote Viewing to see if they those techniques would work for spying."

"Okay, but what does that have to do with us now?"

"You're still as naïve as ever," she said. "But what you've stumbled onto could be the most powerful and effective espionage weapon ever discovered.

This thought hit Josh over the head like a sledge hammer, but he found it too outlandish to really consider.

"It's too outrageous, Mar," he said. "I can't believe someone would do that, even if we could convince anybody that I really can leave my body and come back again."

"It's not too outrageous at all. Look, I'm getting off the phone now, because someone could be listening in. You think about what I said. I'll talk to you later."

Marlena ended the call and got out of her parked car. As

she closed the car door, she spotted the black car in the distance. The silhouette of a man was visible in the front seat. She quickly put on her sunglasses and hurried toward her classroom.

Back in the lab, Josh hung up the landline phone. He looked at Bob and shook his head.

"What a wild imagination that woman has," he said.

What neither he nor Bob knew was that at that very moment a miniature microphone, attached to the underside of the control console, was capturing their every word.

Above the Mind-Sync Lab, Winston Carmichael and a security guard stood before a bank of closed-circuit television monitors. The monitors displayed views from several different labs and offices in the New Wave Technologies building. The two men watched the events in Josh's lab and eavesdropped on his conversation.

"Some people are just suspicious by nature, I guess.," Bob said.

"Well, keep all this under your hat, just to be safe," Josh instructed. "We wouldn't want Carmichael finding out about it, now would we?"

Unseen by Josh and Bob, Carmichael smiled a big, knowing smile.

"Too late," Carmichael told the security guard.

The following day, Josh and Mar decided to get away for the day. They hiked up a steep trail that wound its way up the side of a mountain. The setting bore an eerie resemblance to Josh's mountain-climbing dream.

This similarity was not lost on Josh. Standing on a ledge just above his climbing companion, he reached down to give her a hand up. Marlena ignored his offer, preferring to make her own way.

Soon they reached a resting spot near the top of their climb to share a sip of water. A golden eagle swooped down to check them out, then rose to settle into her nest higher up the mountain.

"Wow, I dreamed about all this just the other night," Josh remarked in astonishment. "It's the first time that's ever happened. "It was a prophetic dream," Marlena said matter-of-factly.

"Except in the dream, the eagle made me fall to my death, and that's not what's happening now."

"That's not how prophetic dreams work. You have already died, in more ways than one."

"Please explain, professor."

"First, you experienced a physical death in the car wreck when you were struck by lightning."

"Okay," Josh said.

"And now you are experiencing shamanic death as you are being forced to give up your old vision of reality as well as your old self. A new, more open, self is being born, a self literally capable of flying."

Using a hand gesture and a verbal "swoosh," Josh indicated that Marlena's comment went over his head.

"What about the dream?" he asked. "What did it signify?"

"The dream was a signal that life-changing events were about to come. In Native American cultures, the eagle is often the spirit messenger."

"I think I get it."

He put the water bottle away and looked at his watch.

"We'd better get moving if we're going to make it back down before dark," he said.

He took a step, but Marlena stopped him.

"What you've been through is very significant," she counseled. "In some tribal cultures, people who are struck by lightning are admitted to sacred or secret societies, because it is understood that you have been born again, so to speak."

Josh pulled her closer to him.

"Next you'll be telling me I'm going find religion."

"I wouldn't be surprised."

She kissed him and just as he started to get into it good, she broke it off. Smiling an impish smile, she headed down the hill.

Josh drove back toward the city while Mar scanned the horizon in search of government spies. Seeing none, she relaxed and moves closer to him.

"What's on your mind?" she asked.

"Something that's been bugging me since my last out of body trip."

"Oh, that," she responded.

"If I can pass through the walls of the sound chamber, how

come I can't pass through the ceiling. It felt hard when I pushed against it."

She tapped on the side of his head and said, "That's something for that little scientific mind of yours to find out, isn't it? I'm going to rest my eyes."

Mar reclined her seat and got comfortable as Josh drove. Then, a momentary reflection of light in the rearview mirror caught his attention. He checked the mirror.

There was black car that Marlena had complained about. It was a few car links back.

Josh adjusted the mirror to get a better look, then looked worriedly at Mar. Not wanting to alarm her, he remained silent, but increased his speed.

They got back to the lab without incident and began another out-of-body experiment. Again, Mar monitored the session from the control room. Again, separated from his physical body and floated up toward the ceiling of the lab.

After gently bumping into the ceiling, he pushed against it to see if he could penetrate it but was gently propelled away from it instead. He glided over to a wall in the lab. Using his, feet he pushed away from the wall like a swimmer under water.

To his surprise, his small effort shot him across the room at an exhilarating speed!

Josh put out his hands to break his impact against the far wall of the lab, but discovered that just his <u>intent</u> to stop was all that was required for him to stop.

Just then, a thump was heard from above the lab's ceiling. Josh looked up.

"Josh, I don't know if you can hear me, but there's that noise again," Mar said into the control room intercom. "Please find out what it is."

Thinking about an earlier conversation she'd had with him, she added, "If you're having trouble breaking through the ceiling, try pretending it isn't a hard surface, that it's more like water."

Brilliant idea, Josh thought, so he decided to follow her suggestion. After moving himself up to the ceiling again, he spent a moment in concentration. Then he easily stuck his hand through the ceiling. With his arm embedded in the ceiling up to his elbow, he smiled.

Way to go, Mar, he thought. Next, he poked his entire upper body through the ceiling, and what he saw in the space above the lab startled him. There were Winston Carmichael and a middle-aged man in an army colonel's uniform watching a set of closed-circuit television monitors.

Josh concentrated on not reacting strongly to this surprise so he wouldn't be sucked back into his physical body. Instead, he allowed himself to completely float through the floor and into the room where the two men stood.

"If what you say is true, Mr. Carmichael, then this could seriously compromise my agency's project, and I just can't let that happen," the military man said.

"I've already taken care of it, colonel," Carmichael replied.

"He thinks the project's being shut down because of a funding shortage."

"I don't think you quite get the picture," the colonel said angrily. "Dr. Breedlove and anyone else he's talked to about his discovery, may have to be silenced—permanently."

As the shock of this revelation passed through Josh, he was sucked immediately back to his physical body. Waking up in the sound chamber, he tried to remain calm and appear to still be unaware of his eavesdroppers. He stepped out of the chamber and calmy walked to the control room.

"Well, what happened?" Mar asked. "Did you get through?"

Trying to think of an answer, Josh paused.

"Actually, no," he finally said. "I didn't even reach the delta phase. There must be something wrong with the equipment."

"Oh, that's disappointing."

Josh put his index finger to his lips, giving the universal "shhh" sign.

"Oh, gee, look at the time," Josh said without looking at his watch. "I just remembered someplace else I'm supposed to be right now. We have to go."

He quickly shut down the system and signaled to Mar that they needed to leave immediately. Once they reached Josh's Jeep, she finally spoke.

"You want to tell me what the hell is going on?"

Josh started the engine and said, "I'll explain on the way."

He pulled out of the parking space and sped away.

"Where are we going?" Mar asked, totally in the dark about what was happening.

"My hideout," Josh answered.

As they left the parking lot, the black car that had been following them pulled out of a space a short distance behind. Seeing the tail, Josh darted and wove in and out of traffic trying to lose it. The follow car began having trouble keeping the Jeep in sight.

After several blocks, Josh quickly pulled his Jeep into a corner used car lot and parked in an empty space. He turned off his lights and killed the engine, making the Jeep look like another car for sale on the lot. He and Mar duck down just before the black car rounded the corner. The two men in the black car, looking every bit like the legendary Men in Black, scanned the area. Seeing nothing of interest, they sped away.

Josh and Mar sat up, and seeing that the coast was clear, Josh started the Jeep.

"I don't think that was Will Smith and Tommie Lee Jones, do you?"

"So, what is this hideout?" Mar asked as they drove.

"It's my family's old cabin. I go there sometimes to get away and clear my head," Josh said. It's my cave."

After driving out of town for about forty-five minutes, they came to a wooded, hilly area and turned off the main road. Another few minutes brought them to the cabin. Josh parked the Jeep next to a white cargo van sitting in front.

"You're just full of surprises," Marlena commented as she got out of the Jeep.

Josh unlocked the front door, entered and turned on the lights. Mar stepped in the front room to find a compact replica of one of Josh's experimental sound chambers. She opened her mouth to ask a question.

"It's my back-up unit in case something ever happened to the gear in the lab," Josh said. "You know, a fire, an earthquake, a spy take-over. The usual."

She walked around the chamber, continuing in her surprise and delight. Josh headed for the corner of the room where he turned on another light, revealing a smaller version of the console in the control room of the lab.

"Like I said, you're just full of surprises."

"After losing important research data in the last big quake, I vowed never again."

He turned the system on.

"We can download all the data from the lab and then wipe the system clean."

"Then what?" Marlena asked.

"I don't know, but I can't stand by and let Carmichael and that colonel get their hands on this."

Josh turned his attention to the console, typed a few strokes on the computer keyboard and waited for a response. Mar headed for the cabin's kitchen.

"You got coffee stashed away somewhere in here?"

"In the cabinet above the sink," Josh replied, still focused on the computer. "The coffee pot's next to the fridge."

Meanwhile, Josh smiled as he watched the screen fill with rapidly scrolling lines of data.

"Take that, Carmichael," he said as all his lab's digital information transferred to his back-up unit.

Later, Mar brought two cups of coffee into the front room where Josh was writing in his project notebook. She put Josh's coffee cup down, picked up the journal and read aloud from it.

"Controlling your movement may be purely a function of thought," she read. "Simply thinking of your destination, picturing it in your mind, takes you there. From what I've experienced so far--"

She looked up from the page and directly at Josh.

"What <u>have</u> you experienced so far, Josh?"

"That I've possibly put you in grave physical danger," he said with genuine concern. "And I'm sorry. Also, that I'm angry and frightened, and I don't know what we're going to do."

She sat down comfortingly in his lap.

"Experience has taught me that when someone tries to shut the door, that's when the revolution begins," Mar replied. "I know that sounds sort of hokey."

She took a sip of coffee.

"I don't know what this colonel is trying to hide, or what financial reward your boss expects to gain, but you started something important and <u>we're</u> going to finish it!

"That's my Mar," Josh said with a smile. "Thanks."

He gave her a kiss, then stood up, still holding her. Putting her down, he headed for the computer console.

"The first thing we've got do is find out what the bad guys are up to," he said.

"And how are you planning to do that?

Josh turned on the mind-sync system. The familiar sound pattern could be heard.

"With the most powerful espionage tool known to modern man," he replied with an almost sinister-sounding voice.

"And then what?"

"And then we find someplace else to lay low to continue our experiments," he replied, putting on the headpiece. "It's only a matter of time before they find us here."

He climbed into the chamber. As the sound wave pattern reached the moment of separation and Josh's energy body pulled away from the physical, the cabin and the rest of normal reality dissolved into a dimly lit grayness. Simultaneously, Josh becomes aware of the annoying sound of hundreds of people whispering.

Josh reached out in the gray space to discover that he was enclosed on all sides by a smooth, round, seamless surface. Finding no opening, he tried shouldering his way through the spherical barrier. He slammed into it several times as his sense of panic intensified. He screamed in frustration and fear.

Then suddenly someone slammed into the barrier from the

outside, startling Josh. Then another "someone" slammed into the sphere from another direction. Then another, and another. Each one mirrored the panic that Josh was experiencing. Each one screamed in fear.

Soon Josh was surrounded by a horrifying sea of trapped and panicked souls who were pounding, clawing and screaming to get out. Seeing the futility of trying to escape, Josh closed himself into a ball on the floor. Then, in his relaxed state, he remembered and repeated his own words.

"Controlling your movement may be purely a function of thought. Simply thinking of your destination and picturing it in your mind, takes you there."

As he closed the eyes of his energy body, bright white light engulfed the space.

When Josh opened his eyes, the found himself inside some sort of large glass structure. Through the glass he could see billions of stars suspended in a black velvet sky. The structure's interior was filled with an odd assortment of holographic images and objects, like a museum.

The glass structure itself exhibited an unusual architectural style, almost as if its creator had taken elements from many earthly cultures and blended them into an ethereal building that barely even existed.

In the back of the building was a rough granite wall that echoed the surface of Josh's mountain-climbing dream. In the center of the room there was a seating area with a floor that looked like grass and a circle of moss-covered tree stumps and boulders.

As Josh began exploring the space, a gentle breeze blew refreshingly through his being. And, upon closer inspection, he discovered that all the images and objects in the building were from his own life. There were a few toys from his childhood; his first science experiment kit; his recent scientific achievement award; huge blow-up photos of his family; the car wreck that killed his family; his college graduation.

Then a soft white light appeared from outside the glass structure and above Josh. He watched as a large sphere of white light descended into the center of the space. As it descended, its intensity decreased, revealing that it was the tall glowing man from Josh's near death experience.

As the man floated to the floor of the structure, his appearance began morphing from one human identity to another. There were a dozen people of widely differing racial and ethnic back-grounds in the mix: An American Indian Man, an Asian Woman, an African Elder, a Rabbi, a nurse, a Middle Eastern bedouin, a British Lord and others.

The Glowing Man identity was the root of all of them and, momentarily, the identities stopped shifting from one to another.

Sounding like multiple synchronized voices speaking at once, he said, "Welcome, Joshua. I've been expecting you."

"Did I really die this time?" Josh asked.

The Glowing Man chuckled in a dozen or so simultaneous voices.

"No," he replied. "Your body is still very much alive, but you've traveled far beyond your familiar physical domain. I can tell you have many questions."

"Yes. For starters, who are you?"

"I am what some in religious circles have called an over-soul," he said. "That's many personalities in one, reflecting multiple experiences in the human form. I retain the individuality of each while also being able to use our combined focused energy."

"I don't think I understand."

The Glowing Man's appearance began shifting again. In a few seconds, his identity took the form of an American Indian.

"Let's just say that I, or rather _we_, are your friends, here to help you and guide you in your quest," the Native man said.

"Okay, let's for a moment pretend that I accept that. Next question: where am I? What is this place?"

"This is your space, your base camp in the non-physical realm, so to speak," the Native man answered. "You'll be able to begin all your explorations from here."

"Again, let's pretend I accept that answer. How did I get here?"

The Glowing Man's identity and appearance shifted as he transformed into a rabbi.

"We brought you here," the rabbi said. "It's time for you to step fully into your destiny."

"These answers are really only prompting me to ask more

questions. For example, that space I was in before, where I was trapped," Josh said. "How did I get there?"

The rabbi transformed into an eighteenth century British lord.

"Your own emotions sent you there," he said. "You were feeling angry and scared just before you left your body. As you already discovered, thoughts are things here. Feelings have substance. It takes some getting used to, and you will."

"Why is all this happening to me?" Josh asked.

The British lord morphed into a desert Bedouin before saying, "Because you chose it to happen."

"I chose it?" Josh asked. "I don't remember doing that."

The British lord dissolved and the Asian woman answered Josh's question.

"It's complicated, but you are on a path that a part of you chose a long time ago, and we encourage you to continue on this path no matter what happens. There *is* danger for both you and your companion, so you must be careful.

"What sort of danger?"

The Asian woman became a male African tribal elder and said, "Danger is relative. Everything in your world is relative. Einstein brought that theory into man's world and made it known."

Josh's own coloring shifted and he began to fade a little.

"I'm beginning to feel a little weak," he said, rubbing his forehead.

The African elder dissolved into the Glowing Man who

said, "I think it's time for you to go back now. Your physical body may need some attention."

The Glowing Man began to move away.

"But wait," Josh called out. "I want to know what your name is. What do I call you? You're not God, but you seem to be some sort of quasi-spiritual guide."

"My name you can't pronounce," he replied as he continued to recede in the distance. "You can call me whatever you're comfortable with. We all have names which have meaning beyond the physical plane."

"When will I see you again?"

"Soon enough," the Glowing Man said. "Until then, remember that you've stepped through a very real doorway that will allow you to explore the multi-dimensional planes of life. Humankind has been trying to get peek beyond that door for centuries. Now they may have that chance thanks to you."

The Glowing Man transformed back into the glowing ball of light, moving further up and away as the whole scene dissolved like liquid.

Moments later, Josh woke up back in his physical body. He ripped the headphone off and sat up. In a state of wide wonder, he stepped out the front door of the cabin and gazed up at the night sky, as if searching for a view of his new glass home-away-from home. Mar followed him out of the cabin.

"What's wrong, Josh?" she asked as she took him by the hand.

Turning to her, he said, "Nothing--you were right, Mar. This _is_ mankind's greatest discovery, and we do have to see it through, no matter what." After a pause, he added, "But we'll have to find a safer place to carry out these experiments."

Marlena thought for a moment.

"I know where we can go," she said finally. No one will think to look for us there."

"Oh yeah, where?"

"My tribe's reservation. My grandfather still lives there, and it's only about a three-hour drive east of here."

"All right then," Josh said. "We'll load the equipment in the van and leave before dawn."

He looked skyward again.

"There's a bigger universe out there than anyone ever imagined," he said. "We're going to explore it, and report our discoveries to anyone who'll listen."

"Weren't you the one who was worried about being laughed out of the country or the science boy's club something?

"Yes I was, but that's not important any more. Humanity deserves to know the truth, whether they're ready for it or not."

In the distance, the howl of a coyote echoed across the woods as a shooting star raced across the night sky.

Josh's lab assistant Bob Thornton was bleeding from several cuts on his head and face. The skin around his right eye was puffy and red. He had been tied to a chair while Carmichael supervised the dismantling of the Mind-Sync Lab. Army Colonel Dan Mitchell stood over Bob menacingly.

"It's too bad you didn't choose the easy way to do this, Bob," Mitchell said. "It would've been so much less painful."

He hit Bob across the face yet again.

"I told you already I don't know what happened to the data in the system," Bob said weakly, spitting blood from his mouth. "It was there the last time I looked."

"Bob, Bob, Bob" Carmichael said in a syrupy sweet tone as he walked toward the lab assistant. "Loyalty is a wonderful virtue, but in this case, it's misplaced. As an employee of this facility, you owe your allegiance to Uncle Sam, not a traitor like Breedlove."

Reaching Bob, Carmichael's tone became threatening.

"Now, for your sake and the sake of your country, tell the colonel everything—where Dr. Breedlove is, where the data is and how this Mind-Sync chamber works."

"Even if I knew the answers to any of those questions, I wouldn't tell you," Bob replied defiantly. "Or him," he added, nodding toward Mitchell.

"What you people see in Breedlove, I'll never understand," he said and walked away, indicating that Mitchell could do whatever needed to be done with Bob.

Mitchell turned to one of his men.

"Get the scopolamine," the colonel commanded. "This guy will have to tell the truth."

Meanwhile, Josh's van sped eastward along a winding and

scenic mountain road in California's Sierra Nevada Mountains. They were headed for the Tuolumne River Indian Reservation. Josh, who was driving, grabbed a few corn chips from a bag on the console between the seats and tossed a few in his mouth. Mar, in the passenger seat, gazed out the window.

"So you grew up out here," Josh asked between chews. "What was it like?"

"How come you never asked me that when we were together before?"

"I'm sorry. It didn't seem important then. I'm asking now."

Mar took a deep breath.

"It was the best of times," she said. "It was the worst of times. But I guess the good outweighed the bad."

"What was so bad?"

"Unemployment, despair, a rampant sense of low self-worth," she replied, then looked at Josh. "Indians are the forgotten founders of this land, and the price of Manifest Destiny has been high for our people."

"That was a long time ago," Josh said.

"When your sense of time flows with the earth's rhythms and patterns, it seems like only yesterday."

"Okay. What were the good things?"

"Summer ceremonials, for one," she said, thinking back. "Relatives and friends from all parts of the country come back to sing and dance for four days and try to remember when it felt good to be Native."

"Oh," Josh replied, afraid to reveal his blatant ignorance of all things Indian.

"And my grandmother—she was one of the really good things. She mostly took care of me after my parents left. And then she passed away while I was off busy being an activist. I never got to say goodbye... or thank you."

Silence hung in the air for a couple of beats as both of them returned their attention to the scenery. It wasn't long before the couple arrived at her grandfather's house.

It was an aging frame home with a sagging covered porch. Hearing the van's arrival, Marlena's grandfather, Woodrow, came out on the porch to greet them. He was a portly Native man with short white hair. He wore a faded flannel shirt and pants held up with a pair of suspenders.

"Grandpa!" Marlena shouted with delight as she scampered up to greet him. He gave her a big hug that Josh could see made her feel very good and safe.

"Granddaughter," the old man said. "It's been much too long."

"I know," she replied, pulling away after the hug. "Are you sure it's all right for us to stay here for a while?"

"Have you been gone so long that you've forgotten who you are and where you belong? Of course, it's more than all right."

Josh climbed the steps and approached Woodrow.

"Is this the scientist fella you told me about?" the elder asked.

"Yes, Grandpa, this is Dr. Joshua Breedlove," she said, taking Josh's hand. "His discovery has stirred up quite a bit of trouble, which is why we're here."

Woodrow gave Josh's hand one good shake, the Native way.

"Welcome to the social fringe, doctor," Woodrow said with a smile. "We Indians have been living out here for a long time, forgotten and ignored. It's the perfect place for you to hide out."

"Thanks for your help," Josh said warmly.

"Come inside and have something to eat," Woodrow said to Josh. Then, addressing Marlena, he added, "Your Uncle Wallace and some others are here to see you. You can tell us all about whatever it is you're up to."

The three headed in the front door.

Soon, a number of additional reservation residents joined them for a potluck dinner. Mar, Woodrow and a half dozen Native people sat around a large dinner table eating, talking and laughing. Josh, who was returning from a visit to the bathroom leaned against the dining room door frame watching them.

Mar's Uncle Wallace, an elderly man with long grey braids, began to reminisce.
His chiseled face and the twinkle in his eye made his story all the more magical.

"I'll never forget the time during one of our summer pow wows," he began. "I think Marlena was about fourteen. She thought her and her boyfriend were all alone. We'd just finished dancing at the pow wow, and we were tired so we walked quietly back into camp.

"Uncle Wallace!" Mar said loudly. "Don't you dare tell that story."

He was not about to be deterred.

"You should've seen the look on her face when she realized that all of us were standing there watching the two of them making out. It was a real hoot!"

Marlene turned bright red as everyone else at the table had a good laugh. Josh continued observing Mar's family from the doorway, only half listening. Woodrow noticed that Josh wasn't fully present and got up from the table. He motioned for Josh to follow him out the back door. Woodrow's unfenced yard was dotted with trees. An old barn sat at the back of the property.

"Your mind is far from here," Woodrow observed.

"Yes, it is," Josh admitted.

"You're worried about the army finding you."

"Among other things," Josh replied.

"What can you do?" the elder asked.

"I need a place where Marlena and I can continue our experiments. Someplace private."

"I'm just an old herb doctor," Woodrow said. "My brother, Wallace, is the expert in spirit travel and such. He thinks you're messing around with something that's over your head."

"He's probably right," Josh said. "But I've sort of been given an assignment to carry out, and I need to try and follow through."

"Assignment?"

"I know it sounds weird, but there's this kind of guide I met when I was out of my body. And he told me that it's sort of my destiny to do this."

"That's not weird," Woodrow admonished. "That's inspirational. Indian people go on vision quests and hold Sun Dances seeking such guidance for their lives all the time."

"He said it could be dangerous and that I and Marlena have to watch our backs.

"Well, son, now you've got more than that," Woodrow assured him, placing a hand on the younger man's shoulder. "We'll all be here to watch your back from now on."

Looking toward the barn, he added, "Follow me."

Woodrow headed for the barn and Josh followed. The old door into the barn complained loudly as Woodrow opened it. Woodrow stepped and turned on a light, illuminating a single bare bulb hanging from the ceiling. Josh looked around the large area. The space was part tool shed, part barn, part resting place for rusted truck parts.

"We can haul most of this stuff out of here, clean it up a little," Marlena's grandfather said. "You can park the van in here to keep it out of sight and set up your equipment. What do you think?"

"What about power?" Josh asked, looking at the bare bulb. "The gear pulls a lot of amps."

Woodrow turned and headed for the barn's large back door. Opening it, he took a few steps and arrived at a power pole with multiple plug-in boxes.

"This ought to handle the load just fine," Woodrow said. He flipped the switch on the master box and a red light on top of the box came on.

"What's this set-up for?"

"RV hook-ups. When we have our annual pow wow, my field here becomes a camp ground."

He indicated the large field spread before him. A powwow arena with its circular brush arbor was visible about a hundred yards away. Josh stepped to the power box and flipped open the cover, revealing multiple circuit breakers.

"We'll get you fixed up, plugged in, turned on and you'll be flying around in no time," Woodrow said.

Within a couple of hours, the barn had been cleaned out and orange extension cords run from the power box into the barn. In another hour, Josh had set up the portable sound chamber and the remote-control panel.

"All right, turn it on," he told Marlena, who flipped a switch. The system came to life, emitting a low frequency hum. Josh checked all the monitors and readouts to make sure everything was working properly.

"It's alive!" he exclaimed, affecting a ghoulish accent.

"Good work, Dr. Frankenstein," Mar offered sarcastically.

Josh grabbed the headset from atop the sound chamber and

began to put it on.

"Time to test it out," he said.

Mar touched his arm to stop him.

"I think it's my turn," she said. "I believed in this long before you did, remember?"

"Something could go wrong, and I don't want to be responsible for anything bad happening to you."

"I'm a big girl," she replied. "I can take care of myself. You don't even know if this frequency works on anybody else. Sooner or later you've got to try it out on other people."

"All right," he said, handing her the headset. She climbed into the chamber, lay down and plugged the headset into the control panel.

"If you are successful in separating, don't go too far," Josh suggested. "Let's take it one step at a time."

He kissed her and Mar put the headset on. Josh sat down at the console and started the system. The familiar pulsating frequency began. From Marlena's point of view, everything in her field of vision began to vibrate, then separate into multiple, slightly out of phase images as the tonal rate increased. Josh checked the monitoring equipment for the status of Mar's vital signs. The read-outs indicated that she had reached the ideal separation condition.

Mar watched as her non-physical body shifted slightly out of phase with her physical body. She became aware of two distinct bodies, a physical one and an energy body. She tried to sit up in the chamber and succeeded in fully separating the two different bodies. They seemed to vibrate at two different frequencies. Her translucent body sat up, leaving her physical body lying in the chamber.

She looked around the barn, noticing that physical reality had taken on a kind of drab appearance with dull colors. Suddenly, there was a distortion of some kind in the back wall of the barn—a warping.

A moment later an animal came through this distortion. It was a beautiful, yet ethereal, white wolf. Its radiance shone brightly in stark contrast to the drab surroundings. The animal calmly approached the sound chamber.

Meanwhile, Josh sat calmly watching the read-outs. Nothing unusual was visible to him.

However, in Marlena's view, the wolf spoke to her with a low howl, then turned to leave. Mar glided out of the chamber to follow, leaving her physical body behind. Soon, the barn scene dissolved away into nothing and was replaced with a beautiful natural landscape that included a circle of tipis that stood near a river.

Suddenly, cavalry soldiers in nineteenth century uniforms, came riding on horseback toward the lodges. The peaceful silence of the scene was shattered by the soldiers' gunfire and blood-curdling war cries. American Indians in buckskin, mostly women, children and the elderly, exited the tipis in terror. They ran for their lives, but most were killed by sword or by bullet within a few steps.

Surprisingly, it was Colonel Dan Mitchell, dressed in a nineteenth century officer's uniform, leading the cavalry charge. Marlena watched in horror as this gruesome scene unfolded, but she was unaware of Mitchell's identity. In a few minutes, little American Indian girl came out of a nearby tipi and looked towards Marlena.

This girl looked like Marlena might have looked at that age. Her piercing eyes met Marlena's, and then the girl ran away towards the river, escaping from the carnage.

Back in the barn, Mar's vital signs and EEG had begun moving out of the normal range and were fluctuating abnormally. Seeing the read-outs, Josh punches a couple of buttons and the audible sound frequency slowed down. He rushed to the sound chamber.

For Marlena, the white wolf and the horrible massacre scene were fading away. Before long, all she saw was the barn. Josh helped Mar, now back in her physical body, sit up in the chamber.

"Are you all right?" he asked. "The read-outs went nuts."

He helped her climb out of the chamber.

"My medicine animal came to me," she said, still in a daze. "The white wolf. He took me into the past where I saw a whole camp of Indians being slaughtered by the cavalry. It was horrible!"

"I don't understand how that is possible, Josh said with a perplexed look.

Mar began pacing.

"In my tribe, we believe that the past is still alive

somewhere, and so is the future," she said. "Time is not linear like in western culture, but circular, even simultaneous."

"But what about this animal?"

"I've seen that white wolf off and on since I was a little girl. It comes to help me sometimes."

Josh's face says this is all nuts.

"Spirit animals often help humans, but you've got to be open to the idea to be aware of their presence," Marlena offered.

"At this point, I'm open to anything," Josh admits.

"So, I traveled through time instead of through space. Didn't Einstein prove that time and space are opposite ends of the same phenomenon?"

"Something like that."

"Maybe I'll get the space travel part later."

"Later?" Josh asked. "What do you mean by that?"

"Later, as in when you've built a second chamber so we can begin traveling out-of-body together."

"Hold on just a minute," Josh protests. "We've got a few other problems to worry about first. Like what to do about the ESP military squad that's on our tail."

Mar shot Josh a serious look of disappointment. Josh pulled her to him.

"Let's find out more about this colonel who's after us and what he knows," he said in a consoling voice. "Then we can talk about traveling together. Okay?"

Mar took a deep breath.

"Okay for now."

As a matter of fact, right now I want to find out what's going on back at New Wave," Josh said as he reset the system. "Maybe we can also figure out what that colonel is up to."

"All right, Josh, but be careful," Mar reminded him. "There is more to this than just flitting around without your body."

Josh nodded his agreement as he climbed into the chamber. Mar started the separation sequence, and soon Josh was headed west toward his old lab. Flying over the nighttime landscapes, he saw the city lights up ahead. Although he was intently focused on the task at hand, in the back of his mind he thought he could get easily used to this.

Moments later, he entered the Mind-Sync Lab through a side wall. A body lay on the floor with two men in army fatigues huddled over him. Two other men argued in a corner of the room. Not understanding what he was seeing, Josh moved in closer. The two arguing men turned out to be Carmichael and Colonel Mitchell.

"This has gone too far," Carmichael said. "No one was supposed to die!"

Mitchell, not wanting their argument to be overheard by the men, moved in close to Carmichael.

"That's where you're wrong," the military man explained. "We're all expendable, even you. I'm going to find Breedlove, his equipment and his research data, no matter what. You can either cooperate or wind up in a body bag like Breedlove's lab assistant

416

over there. It doesn't matter to me."

Mitchell walked away as the body was being zipped up inside a body bag. Before the bag closed completely, Josh got a glimpse of the face. It was Bob Thornton.

Josh rapidly moved up and away from the corpse. As he drifted upward, another translucent non-physical human came into view. Again, it was Bob Thornton. Josh did a double-take. In the scene unfolding below him, Bob's body was being carried out of the building in a body bag. Yet, here was Bob also floating near the ceiling of the lab.

"Bob, is that you?"

Bob just looked at Josh in confusion. Josh moved closer.

"It's me, Josh," he told his lab assistant. "What happened?"

"I'm not sure," Bob said. "They were beating on me, trying to get me to tell them about the Mind-Sync project and how to find you. But I didn't really know anything to tell them."

Unnoticed by either Bob, the Glowing Man descended into the scene behind him. Josh saw him, but continued to focus on Bob.

"Then I felt a sharp pain in my back and I blacked out," Bob continued. "When I woke up I felt so strange, so light. I tried to talk to them, but they ignored me. I sort of floated up here, and then you showed up. Josh, what's going on?"

"Joshua, it's time for your next lesson," the Glowing Man said. "Your friend needs help moving on. His life on earth is over. You don't want him stuck down here haunting this lab for a couple of centuries, do you?"

"What do I need to do?" Josh asked.

A wide stream of bright light appeared just above and behind Bob near the ceiling.

"Just encourage him to float up into the light. Someone will be there on the other side to help him."

Still floating, Josh moved toward his lab assistant.

"Bob, I want to thank you for all your help, but your work here is done," Josh said. "It's time for you to go. Come on, I'll help you."

Josh reached out and took Bob's hand.

"Where are we going?" Bob asked, still in a daze.

"Someplace where you'll be taken care of. People are waiting there for you, and hopefully I'll see you again soon."

Josh escorted Bob closer to the beam of light. As they moved closer to the light, Bob was pulled toward it without any further assistance from his boss.

"Okay, I'll go," Bob said. "It looks nice."

Josh stopped moving and let Bob proceed on his own. Just before moving into the light beam, Bob said, "I didn't tell them anything, Dr. Breedlove. Honest."

"I know. You did good, Bob. Farewell, my friend."

Bob entered the light beam and then disappeared, along with the light.

"You did good, too, Joshua," the Glowing Man said. "You've performed your first rescue."

"Rescue?"

"Yes. Sometimes people get stuck hanging around the places they lived or worked while they were in their earthly bodies, because they're so focused on the physical plane."

"You mean like ghosts?"

"That's the human name for them, and one of the things that keeps us busy on the other side is rescuing souls who are stuck and have to be rescued. But it's actually easier for someone like you, who still has a physical body, to relate to them. Your vibrational energy is closer to theirs, and they can perceive you better."

At that moment a swirl of reddish-orange energy passed through Josh's translucent body. He looked off into the distance as if hearing his name called.

"I feel a signal from my physical body," he reported. "I need to go see what it is."

He started to move away, then stopped.

"Oh, I decided what to call you," he said to the Glowing Man.

"Ah, a name," the entity said. "What shall it be?"

"Copernicus. I've decided to call you Copernicus after the sixteenth century astronomer who forever changed the way people looked at the universe. For me, that's what you're doing, but at a whole new level."

The Glowing Man seemed pleased with his new moniker.

"Then Copernicus it shall be," he said. "Go now and check

on that body of yours. I will see you again soon enough."

Josh turned, thrust himself away and exited the lab.

As Josh departed the lab grounds, the dark translucent figure of a man began tailing him, flying at a distance. Josh, sensing this presence, stopped and looked back to see who was there. All he saw was a dark figure, a shadow really, that darted into the shadows to hide.

Certain this wasn't a trick of his mind, Josh raced away and the dark figure followed. Not sure what he could do to lose the tail, Josh began twisting and turning, trying to take evasive maneuvers. However, the dark one seemed to be more adept at these maneuvers and kept on following.

Suddenly another being, a lighter being, intervened, coming between Josh and the dark one. Focusing on the newcomer, Josh saw that it was Mar's Uncle Wallace.

"I'll handle this," he said.

Wallace circled around the dark spirit, chanting a Native American prayer. He produced what looked like a large bubble and thrust toward the dark spirit. The bubble trapped the dark one inside.

With a loud cry the chant ended. Wallace then cast the bubble away and it flew out of sight, taking the dark one with it. Wallace turned to Josh.

"Let's go home," the elder said, and away they went.

Later, Mar, Woodrow and Wallace sat around a camp fire in back of Woodrow's house. Josh was quite justifiably agitated. He paced near the fire.

"They killed him!" he announced for the umpteenth time. "This research is supposed to help people, not get them killed."

"It can only mean one of two things," Marlena offered. "They either desperately want this discovery for themselves and no one else, or they already know how to do this and they don't want anyone else to have it."

"They must already know something about how this works, or have someone working for them who does," Josh reasoned. "Who else could that dark figure have been?"

"He represents one of the dangers we warned you about," Woodrow said. "He's probably a captive spirit held by some wizard or dark magician bent on doing evil to others, usually for money or personal gain."

"But those who misuse these powers, especially the power of spirit travel, eventually get into serious trouble," Wallace added.

"What kind of trouble?" Josh asked

"If he is still a living human being with a physical body, then he may become trapped outside his body," Wallace replied. "One way or another, he'll be drawn into and trapped by the lower, denser layers of the spirit world, unable to rise into the higher dimensions. Like attracts like on the other side."

"Who or whatever it is, you're messing with something you know very little about," Woodrow said. "It could be too dangerous to continue."

"They killed my friend, and they're trying to steal my work.

I'm not about to stop now."

"Then at least let me help you," Wallace suggested. "You need spiritual protection, both on this side and the other."

Josh looked doubtful.

"Wallace is right," Marlena said. "You've seen what he can do to help. Let him do his thing."

"All right," Josh said finally. "How will this take?

"A couple of days," Wallace answered. "Now I must go and prepare. There is much to do."

He rose from the tree stump he sat on.

"In the meantime, niece, see to it that he keeps both feet on the ground," he added with a smile and a wink.

The following morning, Josh, Mar and Woodrow watch the morning news while sipping coffee. A news anchorman was reporting the day's news when a photo of Bob Thornton appeared in the upper right corner of the screen.

"Research lab assistant Bob Thornton was found beaten to death at his Silicon Valley home late last night," the newsman said.

The photo of Thornton was replaced by a photo of the New Wave Technologies building. The reporter continued.

"Thornton, an employee of New Wave Technologies research labs, had been working on a top-secret project at the time of his death. We go to reporter Tom Richards who files this report from the lab."

A reporter stood with Winston Carmichael in front of the New Wave Technologies building.

"I'm with the director of New Wave Technologies, Mr. Winston Carmichael," the field reporter said. "And he says he knows who is responsible for Bob Thornton's death."

The reporter tilted the microphone towards Carmichael.

"Dr. Joshua Breedlove is obviously the one who killed Bob," the CEO said. "Breedlove stole valuable research data intended for U.S. military applications and then disappeared."

"Any ideas where Breedlove might be?" the reporter asked.

"No, and that's probably why he killed Bob. To keep him from talking. I'm appalled at Breedlove's actions. I've always held him in the highest regard, until now. Now if you'll excuse me, I've got to get back to work."

"We'll keep you updated as new developments come in on this tragic story. Back to you, Kevin, in the studio."

Stunned, Josh turned the television off and looked at Marlena.

"Now we have every law enforcement agency in the country looking for us," Marlena said. "What are we going to do?"

"I don't know," Josh said. "I need to think. Maybe Copernicus can help us."

Josh headed for the barn.

"Wait!" Mar called after him. "Uncle Wallace may not be finished with the protection ceremony yet. It might not be safe."

"Safe or not, I have to go. What good are these spirit guides if they can't help us when we need it?"

As they neared the barn, the sound of a Native American

prayer chant is heard coming from inside. Josh opened the door and smoke billowed out.

Ceremonial smoke filled the interior, making it hard to see. Josh and Mar moved through the smoke toward the source of the chanting sound. Finally, they saw Wallace near the control console. He held an eagle feather in one hand and an abalone shell in the other. A bundle of sage in the shell generated the smoke, which he fanned with the feather. He spread the smoke over the console, finished the prayer and turned to them.

"It is finished," Wallace said. "You can come and go as you please. Those dark spirits shouldn't give you any more trouble."

"Thanks, Uncle Wallace," Mar said.

Wallace spoke to his niece in their tribal language.

"White men always think they need fancy equipment to do things. I hope one day your friend discovers that he can do spirit travel without all this."

"But he believes in it, and that's part of what makes it work for him," she replied, also in their Native tongue.

Wallace nodded and turned to leave. Josh shook his hand, thanked him again, and then Wallace exited the barn.

"What did he say?"

"Only that you should let me use the chamber more since the gift of spirit travel is supposed to run in the family," Mar replied.

"Yeah, I'm sure that's what he said."

"No, really," she said with feigned innocence.

They prepped the equipment for Josh's next journey.

The process of firing up the equipment, getting in the chamber, running through the frequency patterns and separating from the physical had become quick and routine for Josh. After running through all the steps, the scientist soon arrived at his home-away-from-home to find Copernicus and his multiple personalities waiting.

"Ah, Joshua, we sensed that you were coming," Copernicus said. He spoke of himself and his multiple identities in the plural. His voice sounded like a chorus of individuals speaking in unison.

"Yeah, I need divine guidance or spiritual wisdom or something."

"You've come for another lesson?"

"No, actually, in case you haven't noticed, there are some pretty serious things going on back on earth," Josh said with a sarcastic edge. "Can't you help a little?"

"We do what we can, but since we are not operating on your plane, the physical plane, it isn't that easy. And sometimes difficult things happen for a reason, as are part of your learning experience."

"So, you aren't a god or a group of gods," Josh said. "You can't snap your fingers and change things on earth?"

"No, we aren't gods, or angels, for that matter, though we have been mistaken for both. We, and others like us, do have our influence on human experience, but if we snapped our fingers every time things got tough, it would diminish the educational value of earthbound experiences. Remember, man does have free will."

"What if someone chooses to do bad things, you know, takes a negative path?"

"If someone chooses a negative path, they must discover or experience the results of that choice. There will be consequences, eventually. Take your former employer for instance. Winston Carmichael made certain choices. Would you like to see the consequences of those choices?

"Maybe later. I really don't have time for this now."

"Trust me," Copernicus said. "You won't be disappointed."

"Okay," Josh replied, letting out a sigh of frustration.

"Focus on Winston Carmichael and stay close to me," the glowing man said.

Copernicus lifted off and Josh followed. The pair seemed to be transported almost immediately to a neighborhood of mansions. They stopped moving and hovered above one particular house.

"Who's house is this?" Josh asked. "Carmichael's?"

"That's who you were focused on, right?

Josh nodded.

"Then he must be here."

With Copernicus in the lead, they drifted across the rooftop and then hovered above a backyard swimming pool. Carmichael was tied up at the edge of the pool, his mouth taped shut. Mitchell and two of his men stood over him.

"It's too bad it has to end like this, Winston," Mitchell said. "You've unfortunately become too much of a liability to me. Your little appearance on the news was not authorized. When they find your body, they'll think you drown in your own pool."

Panicked, Carmichael struggled against his bonds. He tried to scream to no avail. Mitchell gave a signal, and his men rolled Carmichael into the pool. Carmichael splashed into the water and sank. Struggling mightily, eyes wide in terror, all he managed to do was use up his oxygen more quickly.

Josh drifted down for a closer view. Carmichael's frantic splashing was the only sound to be heard.

"Carmichael, you greedy bastard," he said, which Carmichael, of course, couldn't hear. "You got Bob killed, and now you're getting just what you deserve."

Josh propelled himself downward until he was underwater near his former boss.

The sound of multiple whispering voices replaced the sound of the splashing.

A large group of what appeared to be desperate ghost-like entities materialized around Carmichael as the whispering got louder. To Josh, they looked like translucent beggars wearing tattered clothes. They seemed to be attracted to Carmichael's energy, and were feeding on it.

Josh drifted upward and out of the water, continuing to watch the scene unfold. Soon, Carmichael's physical body went limp and, a few moments later, his translucent energy body rose up and out of it. The greedy ones moved in on that energy form. He let out a scream of horror as the whole writhing mass rises and faded away.

"Who or what were they?" Josh asked as he returned to Copernicus' side.

"Greedy materialists, like Carmichael," the glowing guide replied. "They are aware of nothing but their own hunger for money or power. That hunger had consumed them while they were alive, and it will continue to consume them until each of them becomes ready to give it up."

"Can't they be rescued, like Bob?"

"You can give it a try sometime if you'd like, but it's usually a waste of energy. They aren't like Bob. Until they change their own minds, they'll be engaged in this low-level feeding frenzy."

Carmichael's physical body now floated on the surface of the pool. Using the pool's cleaning net with its long handle, one of Mitchell's men dragged the lifeless form to the pool's edge. He quickly cut away Carmichael's bonds and removed the tape from his mouth. Both men gave the body a shove, moving him toward the middle of the pool.

As the three men set about the task of straightening up and removing evidence of their presence, Mitchell's two-way radio crackled to life.

"Colonel Mitchell, come in, sir," a voice called out from the radio.

"Mitchell grabbed the radio from his belt.

"Mitchell here. Go ahead."

"We think we know where they are, sir."

"Oh yeah, where's that?" Mitchell asked.

"The woman grew up on an Indian reservation about a three hour drive east of San Francisco. Her grandfather still lives there."

"Good work, corporal. Get the unit ready. We'll head out first thing in the morning. Out."

The colonel turned off the radio and placed it back on his belt.

"And by god, we'd better get to them before anyone else does," he said more to himself than anyone else.

Hearing that the colonel knew where he and Mar were hiding caused Josh to suddenly rejoin his physical body.

Josh's physical body awoke, and he jumped out of the chamber in a panic. Mar rushed to him.

"What's wrong?" Mar asked.

"They know we're here," Josh said. "We've got to pack up and leave."

"Where to?"

"I'm not sure, but they know about your grandfather."

The couple began shutting down the equipment as Woodrow entered the barn with an announcement.

"Corn soup and frybread'll be ready in—what's going on?"

"That colonel knows we're here," Mar answered. "We've

got to clear out."

"They'll be here in the morning," Josh added.

"Then you'll have to head for the hills deeper on the reservation," Woodrow said. "I know just the place."

Mar stopped what she was doing and approached her grandfather.

"You and Uncle Wallace should leave too. These are dangerous men."

"No way," the elder replied. "I'm not gonna let 'em scare me off my ancestral land. I'm gonna stay and make a stand. If it's the last thing I do!"

"Woodrow's last stand," he said with a grin as he folded his arms defiantly. "I'm calling an emergency clan meeting so we can have a show of force!"

Marlena was familiar with her grandfather's tendency for drama when it came to standing up for Native rights, so she didn't try to talk him out of whatever he was planning. She turned her attention back to helping Josh dismantle the Mind-Sync system.

A couple of hours later, as the couple finished loading the last of the equipment in the van, a large group of American Indian people gathered in the barn. Woodrow had sent out a call for help, and many Native neighbors heeded the call.

Josh and Mar were ready to go, and Woodrow approached Josh. The elder handed the younger man a hand-drawn map of the reservation.

"The camp is about 30 miles up in the hills," Woodrow

said, indicating a spot on the map. The map will help if you get lost." Turning to Mar, he added, "It's not too far from Medicine Lake where we used to pick sage when you were little."

"I'm sure we'll find it, Grandpa," she said, giving him a hug.

"Thanks, Woodrow," Josh said with a hand shake. "Are you sure you'll be all right?"

Gesturing to those around him, the old man said, "We'll be just fine. There are still a few old Indian tricks we know to keep the cavalry off your trail for a while. Now you two get going. Those fellows up at the camp are expecting you."

Mar climbed into the driver's seat as the Indians in the barn said their goodbyes. Josh manned the map and took charge of the navigation for their short trip.

At an abandoned industrial property near San Francisco bay, a Jaguar pulled into loading dock area and parked. A dark, rugged man in his mid-fifties, stepped out of the car. He was dressed casually, obviously unhappy about being interrupted in the middle of something or other he was doing.

Another man stood in the shadow of the building. He'd been forced to wait longer than he wanted to and was already irritated.

"It's dangerous for us to meet like this," the man said as he slammed the Jaguar's door. "What if we're seen together?"

The man in the shadow stepped into the light. It was Colonel Mitchell.

Ignoring the man's concerns, Mitchell said, "You disappoint me, Yuri. What happened out there?

"Those Indians have been doing this for a long time," Yuri replied. "They put up a protective psychic barrier my operatives can't get through."

"But you're supposed to be this master of the black arts. You came highly recommended by the former head of the Russian National Security."

"Don't worry, Colonel. I'm ready with another technique. We should be able to get through this time."

"There's no need," Mitchell said. "We've already found them."

"Breedlove's technology will be mine soon, and I'll have no further use for your second rate, hit-or-miss magic tricks."

The military man pulled out a pistol and aimed it at Yuri's head. Nervously, the Russian took a step back.

"That's where you're wrong, Colonel. Before I defected, I supervised the Soviet's military psychic research for twenty years. No one knows more about these matters than I do."

He backed up another step.

"And no one is better qualified to run the American military's out-of-body intelligence unit," he added.

"That's where you're wrong, Yuri."

Yuri turned and began to run. Mitchell fired once, and Yuri fell to the ground. Mitchell walked over to the fallen body and looked down at it.

"There's not going to be an American out-of-body intelligence unit," he told the dead man.

He fired a second shot into the back Yuri's head, just for good measure. Then, checking to see if anyone had been watching, he walked away.

The headlights of Josh's van momentarily illumined a sign that read NATIVE CULTURE SURVIVAL CAMP - ESTABLISHED 1971.

"What did Woodrow say this place is?" Josh asked as Mar continued driving.

"It's a place where urban Indians get re-introduced to their cultural roots."

"Re-introduced?" Josh asked.

"Yeah. A few of generations of concerted effort by the army, missionaries, boarding schools and government programs brought us to the brink of extinction, genetically and culturally."

In a few more minutes, the van's headlights swept across a cluster of A-frames.

"Camps like this one sprang up in the early seventies and helped us begin to capture what a few of our elders had managed to preserve and pass it on to a young, hungry generation."

A half dozen American Indian men, carrying weapons, came into view.

"Who's this?" Josh asked.

"The welcoming committee," Mar replied.

Josh eyed the armed men suspiciously.

"Why all the guns?"

"Some of these guys are fugitives from one federal law enforcement agency or another, just like us. Others are just cautious."

As the van came to a stop in the parking lot, the man in charge approached the driver's side window. Mar rolled the window down and the man peered into the van. After a tense moment, he said something to her in their tribal language, and she replied in the same language. Another tense moment passed before the man broke into a big grin. Mar did the same.

"This is my cousin, Roman," she told Josh. "He runs this place now."

"That's a relief," he said. "You had me going there for a minute."

"Come in and meet the guys," Roman said. "Tomorrow morning I'll show you where you can set up your experiment or equipment or whatever it is. Nobody will never find you here."

Josh and Mar exited the van. Roman gave his cousin a big hug, and then they all headed inside the center.

Next morning, as expected, a convoy of military vehicles rolled down the same road that Josh and Mar had driven on. The vehicles pulled up around Woodrow's house, surrounding it. Mitchell exited the lead vehicle and signaled for his men to surround the house. Woodrow came out on the front porch.

"What the hell's going on?" he yelled at Mitchell. "You

can't just come in here like you're invading some third world country. This is Native American land."

"Are you Woodrow Sunrider?" Mitchell asked the elder.

"Who wants to know?" the elder asked although he knew perfectly well who the intruder was.

"I'm Colonel Daniel Mitchell, United States Army. Where is your granddaughter, Marlena Sunrider?"

As if on cue, several American Indians of different ages and sizes stepped into Mitchell's peripheral view. Acting like curious, naive Natives, they began inspecting the military vehicles, the soldiers and their weapons.

"I haven't seen her, but she called and said she was on her way out here to see me. What's wrong? Is she in some kind of trouble?

Mitchell eyed the curious Indians.

"If we could step inside, I can explain the situation in private."

"I was in the Army, served in Nam, and I know you don't have any jurisdiction here on American soil or on this reservation," Woodrow said. "But sure you can come inside and we can talk."

The two men entered Woodrow's house as the rest of Mitchell's men continued to stand guard around the house. The Natives continued to appear curious, closely examining the men, their weapons and their vehicles.

At the survival camp, Mar drove the van inside a large, mostly-empty building that Roman had allowed them to use. Josh closed the large garage door behind her. Together, they surveyed the area, judging its suitability to their needs.

Roman entered a side door carrying two mugs.

"Thought you might like fresh coffee," he said, handing over the mugs. "There's breakfast in the mess hall, if you're interested."

"Thanks," Josh said after taking a sip. "I really appreciate what you're doing for us."

"Well, I don't know what you're up to, but if Marlena believes in it, then it has to be okay. And if the army is after you, then you must be doing something important. Stay as long as you need to. I've got to get back to my crew."

Roman left the pair to their work. Mar sipped her coffee as she looked over all the electronic equipment they'd been carting around with them.

"We've got to do something to cut back on the amount of equipment we're lugging around," she said. "We may have to cut and run at a moment's notice. What can we get rid of?"

"A lot of this gear is monitoring and measuring apparatus," Josh replied. "Stuff you'd need to collect and record data in order to publish a scientific report on the findings."

"This is no longer an experiment to be reported in some science journal," Mar observed. "This is a matter of life or death in the real world."

"When you're right, you're right."

"So, let's strip it down to the bare essentials."

They got to work.

While the colonel and Woodrow were having their talk inside Woodrow's house, Mitchell's men were combing the barn and surrounding grounds for clues. A soldier came out of the barn holding something in his hand. He pulled the two-way radio off his belt and spoke into it.

"Colonel Mitchell, sir. Do you copy?"

Mitchell's voice came back through the radio.

Mitchell here. Go ahead."

"Sir, I found something I think you should take a look at."

"What is it, soldier?"

The man held up a crumpled card closer to his face in order to read from it. It was the business card of Dr. Joshua Breedlove, New Wave Technologies.

"I think they've already been here, sir, the soldier said. "I think they've already come and gone."

Back at the survival camp, two cots had been set up head-to-head with a small table between them. A small electronic device, a portable version of the Mind-Sync system, sat on the table. Two pairs of the Mind-Sync headpieces attached to the device rested on the cots.

Josh and Mar each sat down on one of the cots and picked up their headgear.

"Do you think I'll meet your Glowing Man?" Mar asked. "What do you call him--Galileo?"

"Copernicus," Josh corrected her. "I don't even know if you

and I will end up in the same place. A thought in the back of your mind might send you off somewhere else."

They lay down head-to-head on the two cots. Josh pushed the start button on the device and a pre-programmed tonal sequence began. As the vibrational sound pattern accelerated, Josh and Mar simultaneously reached the peak point and the familiar ring of sparks appeared around them.

They separated from their physical bodies, and their translucent doubles rose into the space above the cots. Drifting upward together, they floated through the ceiling. Once they were above the building, Josh took Mars hand in his, and they shot upward away from the ground.

Momentarily, the couple zoomed through a familiar transitional space together.

Soon, Josh's glass building became visible ahead. As Josh prepared to descend into the space, he discovered that Mar was no longer at his side. He look around frantically for her, but couldn't find her.

"Marlena?! Marlena!"

Copernicus materialized nearby.

"What happened to her?" Josh asked the guide.

"She's all right," Copernicus said. "She had some important business of her own to attend to."

Copernicus somehow provided Josh with a view of Mar's location. A clear stream ran through a green valley on what appeared to be a sunny day on earth. Mar dropped down into the scene and was in awe of the place. She walked along the stream and a log cabin materialized up ahead.

Mar headed for the cabin as her white wolf friend emerged from the woods behind the cabin and approached. She knelt down to embrace the animal as the front door of the cabin opened. An elderly American Indian woman emerged. A look of perplexed recognition registered on Mar's face.

"Grandma--is that you?"

"Yes, dear, it's me," the woman replied with a smile.

Marlena ran toward her.

"Am I dreaming?" Mar asked. "After you died, I dreamt of you often."

"I know. You came to see me often in your sleep. This time you're awake."

The two women hugged.

"Oh, Grandma, I've missed you so much."

"I'm never really far from you," the elder said. "From time to time I drop in to see what you're up to. I'm very proud of what you're doing with your life."

They walked toward the log cabin together.

"You've been watching me?"

"Not really watching," Grandma replied. "Just paying attention. It's one of the perks you get over here."

Grandma opened the cabin door, they entered and began a joyful reunion.

Back in Josh's glass building, he and Copernicus were

engaged in conversation. They were focused on a holographic image that floated between them. The 3-D image of the earth was surrounded by seven layers of energy. The densest layers were closest to earth, graduating to less dense layers farthest from earth.

"So, the earth is surrounded by multiple dimensions?" Josh said.

"Yes," Copernicus replied. "There are seven invisible planes of non-physical reality--zones of energy really, each vibrating at a different rate, each containing other sub-zones within."

"Then the densest layers are closest to earth," Josh said. "That's where the human energy forms can get trapped after depth?"

"You get the idea. But theses souls—and it's okay to use that term or not—are only trapped because of their own consciousness, not because a judgmental supreme being is punishing them. Fear of the unknown has prompted humanity to create some powerful myths, and religious figures throughout history who've caught a glimpse of these very real realms have contributed heavily to those myths."

Copernicus defocused from their conversation and seemed to be seeing or listening to something Josh wasn't aware of.

"That's all we have time for now," the guide said. "There's something back on earth that requires your immediate attention. I'll make sure Marlena gets back safely."

Without another word, Josh's awareness began to transition

from the glass building back to Woodrow's house.

Josh soon found himself hovering over Woodrow's barn and immediately became alarmed at the sight of the military vehicles and soldiers. Peeking into the barn, he saw a small group of soldiers hunting for clues. He pushed himself toward Woodrow's house and through the roof.

There he found Woodrow tied up in a chair with Mitchell standing over him.

"I know they've been here, old man, so there's no use in denying it," Mitchell yelled. "The sooner you tell me where they are, the sooner this'll all be over with."

"Since when does the U.S. Army terrorize American citizens?" Woodrow yells back.

"Oh, this isn't official Army business. We live in a competitive global economy, and Breedlove's little discovery is going to be auctioned to the highest bidder on the worldwide espionage market."

Both Woodrow and Josh were stunned by this revelation.

"So, for the last time, where's Breedlove?"

"Go to hell!" Woodrow yelled at the colonel.

Mitchell struck the elder across the face. Woodrow winced in pain.

Panic seized Josh and he was pulled away.

Josh and Mar woke up in their cots simultaneously. Mar had a blissful look on her face, having just come from the reunion with her grandmother. Josh, on the other hand, was frantic.

"He's got your grandfather, and he's trying to make him tell where we are," Josh told her. "And there's one other thing. This isn't even official Army business. Mitchell's doing this so he can sell this discovery to the highest bidder on the spy market. We've got to do something fast."

"Roman's probably got everything you'd need to start a small war right here."

"We're going to need more help than just Roman and the guys. We've got to call in some outside help. But who?"

"The outside world still thinks we're murderers and traitors," Marlena said.

An idea hits her.

"The rez cops! They're not much, but they're all we've got. And there's some kind of satellite phone hook-up out here Roman told me about."

"What are we waiting for?" Josh said, and the pair went to find Roman.

After hearing the gist of Marlena's explanation, Roman and his rag-tag collection Native guys sprang into action. Using the mess hall as a staging area, the team collected all their weapons and began loading them. One of the guys handed Josh a rifle and showed him how to load it.

Mar came in from the kitchen carrying a box filled with bananas, sacks of sugar, jars of molasses and other odds and ends. She set it down on the table, and Josh picked through the box, examining the strange assortment items.

"What's all this?" he asked.

"The weapons of grass-roots sabotage," Roman replied.

"Uh?"

Josh didn't get it.

"You'll see," Roman assured him.

Roman waited until dark to initiate his plan. He and his men, dressed in black, quietly made their way to the wooded area near Woodrow's house and did a little reconnaissance of the situation. They found Mitchell's men in a relaxed mode as they continued their watch in front of Woodrow's house. Seeing no imminent danger, most had let down their guards, put down their weapons or fallen asleep.

One soldier, sitting on the edge of Woodrow's front porch had put his weapon down beside him. As he nodded off to sleep, Roman crept in close to the man and quietly confiscated the gun.

One of Roman's guys crept up to one of the Jeep's parked in front of the house. Quietly removing the vehicle's gas cap, the Indian poured sugar into the tank.

Hiding in the shadow of the porch, Roman poured molasses into the firing mechanism of the rifle he'd seized.

A third Native sneaked up behind another military vehicle and stuffed a banana up the tail pipe.

Who has wandered away from the house near a line of trees. The suspicious sound of a bird call is heard O.S. The soldier goes to investigate.

Trying to stay awake, one of Mitchell's men was walking

sentry near the edge of the nearby woods. A suspicious-sounding bird call came from within the woods, so he decided to check it out. As he stepped into the tree line, something yanked him forward.

A hard blow to the back of the head laid the soldier out cold. One Native man took the reclining man's rifle while two others tied and gagged him.

A few moments later, Roman and his men rendezvoused behind a cluster of trees. Satisfied with their work, they silently slipped away.

Not long afterward, a convoy of tribal police cars approached the house, sirens blaring. Mitchell's men jumped to their feet and grabbed their weapons.

The soldier on the porch looked down incredulously at his hands and his weapon, which are both covered in molasses. Another jumped into a Jeep and tried to start the engine. It only produced a grinding noise, but wouldn't start. A third man had his rifle come apart in his hands. Disgusted, he threw the pieces on the ground, and began to run. He was blocked by a tribal policeman.

"Hands on your head!" the cop commanded.

Woodrow's front door sprang open, and Mitchell ran out on to the porch.

"What the hell is going on out here?"

Seeing that his men were being rounded up, he made a dash for his Jeep. Jumping into the vehicle, he tried to start it. The starter cranked and cranked, but the engine wouldn't cooperate.

Roman waltzed up to the driver's door holding a banana like it was a pistol. Angrily, Mitchell jumped out of the Jeep and was about to pull his own pistol when he heard the sound of automatic weapons being cocked. It was then he noticed he was surrounded by tribal cops, each with his pistol pointed at him. The Tribal Police Chief stepped forward.

"Officer, arrest this man," he commanded of one of his men.

Mitchell realized he and his men had been outmaneuvered and allowed himself to be handcuffed. The cop was about to lead the colonel away when Josh stepped up.

"Wait a minute," he said.

Josh approached Mitchell, followed by Marlena. The cops held Mitchell where he was. Mar, who was seeing Mitchell's face for the first time, was visibly shaken.

"I've got something to say to this man," Josh said as he stood in front of the colonel.

"I saw what you did to Bob Thornton, and I watched you kill Winston Carmichael," the scientist said, just inches from Mitchell's face. "It's ironic. I may have created the best spy weapon ever discovered, but I'll never allow it to fall into the hands of men like you. This is going to be used to free men's minds all over the world."

"You can't be everywhere, Breedlove," Mitchell said defiantly. "Somebody's going to get a hold of it some day. Maybe it won't be me, but some secret army in some country is going to get a hold of it, and when they do—"

"You thought we were just a bunch of dumb Indians," a voice rang out from the front porch. It was Woodrow, his head bandaged, as he was escorted by a tribal cop. The elder was unsteady and weak, but walked up to Mitchell on his own.

"Well, you were wrong, mister," the elder said when he was face-to-face with the colonel. "We are proud and determined people. We don't roll over and play dead for anyone."

He turned to the tribal cop and said, "Get him off this reservation. He doesn't deserve to stand on native soil."

Mitchell was led away. Woodrow began to feel weak and sat down on the fender of a nearby Jeep.

"We got him, didn't we?" Woodrow said to Marlena who was standing nearby.

Marlena, who was standing nearby, didn't respond.

"What's the matter?" Josh asked. "You look like you saw a ghost."

"He was in my out-of-body vision," Mar replied. "He was leading the cavalry as they slaughtered everyone in a Native camp."

"How can that be?" Josh asked as they watched Mitchell being driven away in a tribal cop car.

"I'm not sure, but something tells me that he's had it coming for a long time."

A few days later, TV news vans and reporters poured into the parking lot in front of the Survival Camp headquarters. They were all headed to a news conference that was about to begin. Above the door a new sign announced THE COPERNICUS INSTITUTE.

Inside a conference room, reporters, scientists and other guests were already seated in rows of folding chairs that faced a podium at the front of the room. A bandaged Woodrow was seated in the front row, along with Roman and Nigel, the nerdy MC from the science award banquet.

On a screen behind the podium was projected an image containing the words COPERNICUS INSTITUTE along with a logo depicting a translucent human body leaving the earth's atmosphere.

Josh and Mar stepped up to the podium together.

"Thank you all for coming today," Marlena said. "We have several important announcements to make, and so we'll just get started."

"First, we want to thank Roman Cutnose for allowing us to transform the Cultural Survival Camp into the Copernicus Institute, dedicated to scientific research for the benefit of humanity."

A smattering of polite applause came from the audience as Roman stood up from his folding chair, waved and smiled.

"The Institute's first and foremost endeavor will be the Explorer Project. I'll let the project's co-director, Marlena Sunrider, tell you all about it."

Josh took a couple of steps backward as Mar began.

"First, let me assure you that what I'm about to describe is science, not science fiction or spiritual fantasy. But we do stand on the verge of a new era, an era where scientific investigation and spiritual insight will converge, and it is an exciting time to be alive."

As Marlena continues with her scripted presentation, Josh controlled the images displayed on the large screen. It was a graphic simulation of a recent out-of-body journey he and Mar had taken a few nights before.

On the screen, he and Mar arrived at Josh's home-away-from-home on the other side where Copernicus had been waiting for them.

"In the middle ages," Marlena continued. "Europeans believed that dragons and sea monsters inhabited the outer oceans and that you'd fall off the edge of the flat earth if you sailed too far."

On the screen, Copernicus took both their hands, and all three began to glow brightly.

"But, at much risk to themselves," Mar said, "Independent minded explorers and scientists were able to break free from superstition and dogma to investigate new realities, make new discovers and bring back information that forever changed the way people viewed the world."

Next, Copernicus led Josh and Mar up and out of the glass structure. They were surrounded by blackness, seemingly pierced by pinpoints of starlight.

"And so," Mar continued to her earthbound audience, "We'll be using techniques and technologies discovered by Dr. Breedlove during his own near-death and out-of-body experiences that will allow volunteer explorers to voyage into the uncharted territories that lay beyond the borders of normal human awareness."

In the accompanying visuals, the threesome flew over a fantastic "heavenly" city laid out neatly and symmetrically below them, illuminated by twinkling points of light. Other beings, appearing as points of lights and wispy spheres of energy, flit about.

"Ultimately, this project will take mankind beyond the final frontier, death itself, to bring back the knowledge that banishes fear and the truth that casts out superstition. And we will come to know the meaning of life as never before."

Finally, Josh, Mar and Copernicus descended into the beautiful city, becoming moving points of light themselves and disappearing among the others. The on-screen images faded as Marlena said, "That concludes our presentation."

The audience sat in stunned silence a long moment. Suddenly, dozens of people jumped to their feet all at once, firing off questions at a hundred miles-a-minute.

Josh took Mars hand in his as they relished the moment.

"This is only the beginning," he whispered in her ear as they turned to greet the frenzy of faces clamoring to find answers to humanity's oldest questions.

About the Author

Gary Robinson is an award-winning writer and filmmaker of Choctaw and Cherokee descent who has been creating Native American content in print and video since the 1980s. Born and raised in Dallas, Texas, his first job in Indian Country was with the Communication Department of the Muscogee (Creek) Nation in eastern Oklahoma. While there, he began producing educational, informational and documentary films on Native American historical, cultural and contemporary topics.

Since then, much of his work has been for and/or about Native American people, companies, tribes and organizations as an independent writer/producer.

His first book, <u>From Warriors to Soldiers</u> published in 2008, examines the history of American Indian service in the U.S. military from the Revolutionary War to modern times. That was the beginning of a productive career as the author of twenty fiction and non-fiction books about Native American characters and situations.

You can find out more information at his website www.tribaleyeproductions.com or on his Lands of our Ancestors website www.LandsOfOurAncestors.com.